On the Edge
(The Grange Complex Book 1)

by

Joanna Mazurkiewicz

One

Dexter

"Babe, your tits feel fucking amazing," I growled into Penny's ear, moulding her hard nipples with my thumb. We were on the top floor, standing in the hallway outside my apartment, and my back was pressed against the doors of the lift. I was planning to move this party into my place in a minute or so. I didn't want to cross the line with my precious neighbours, otherwise I had to forget about late-night parties.

Penny was going to make me lose my mind in a second, grabbing my cock so eagerly and playing with it, like it was a fucking toy.

"Your apartment, Dex. Let's just go in already," she moaned when I shoved my fingers into her knickers, touching that delicious spot between her legs. I was hungry for her soaking pussy, and she responded to my touch eagerly.

Penny arched her head back gasping for breath, while my fingers worked her sweet spot thoroughly. She was so wet for me, and I was planning to fuck her all afternoon, until she couldn't move. It was one of those days. My mind was racing like fuck and I had to get distracted. Sex was the only cure.

"Do you like it when I stroke you so fast?" I asked her, knowing that she was going to come for me at any moment if I continued. Women loved it when I took care of them. I knew their bodies, their most sensitive parts.

She gripped my cock harder and slid her fingers around my balls. I was in heaven, my pants ready to burst into flames.

"I love it, Dex," she moaned. With my other hand, I held her face in place and devoured her mouth. I didn't do slow and gentle. I liked to be in control at all times. Even the kiss had to be the way I wanted it, deep and rough. "Just don't stop... please... I'm so close."

I laughed and bit her lower lip, ignoring the vibration of the lift behind my back. I knew it would stop long before it got to this floor. No one used the elevator to come up here; I was the only occupant of this floor.

"Don't fucking come yet," I warned her, slowing down the movement of my fingers. I wanted to torture her a little bit, spice things up.

All of a sudden I felt something behind me—the lift stopped and the doors opened. I was too busy concentrating on Penny's pussy to care, but then someone or something pushed me forward.

I lost my bearings, Penny yelped, and I flew to the floor, losing my balance. Something hard hit me. I felt a sharp pain on the back of my head and heard a loud, "Motherfucking boxes! What the hell is wrong with the lift?"

Penny lay on the floor next to me, giggling. I glanced up and saw shit everywhere. Books, DVDs, magazines, and clothes were scattered around the floor. My head was banging and I was more than pissed. My johnson went flat like a tire, and that never happened to me before. What the fuck?

"Oh my God, I'm so sorry. I didn't see you there."

The voice came from a blond girl who picked herself up off the floor, blushing red in an instant. She wasn't Scottish. English, maybe; she didn't have that thick accent that I was used to.

I narrowed my eyes and glanced at Penny. One of her tits was hanging out and her trousers were unzipped. She was pulling herself together, but it was obvious that we had been busy with each other only a minute ago. I glanced back at the girl. Her mouth hung wide open as her eyes moved from Penny to me.

She was fit. Not slim, but she had nice curves in just the right places. Suddenly I had an urge to check out her ass.

"You just cost Penny an orgasm, Barbie," I snapped and pushed myself off the floor, ignoring the girl that I was just about to fuck. I was raging with fury.

What the fuck is she doing on my floor?

"Excuse me?" the girl asked. My eyes scanned downwards involuntarily, checking her out. My breath caught in my throat when I stopped at her breasts. She had a great large rack, probably D cup, and I felt myself going hard again. Penny complained and wanted me to help her, but I wasn't listening. She was still on the floor, pathetic.

Barbie had platinum-blond hair, the most stunning green eyes, and she was taller than most women. Only a few inches shorter than me. Whoever she was, she wasn't my type at all, but my dick was telling me a different fucking story.

"Penny was just about to come," I said and took a step towards her in order to intimidate her. Her eyes widened as she processed what I said, and she sucked on her bottom lip. "This is my floor. No one apart from me is allowed in here, unless I make an exception and you're here for my cock."

She laughed nervously, placing her hands on her hips. My fucking intimidation game wasn't working.

"I'm not here to *fuck* or explain myself to you. I'm sorry that I bumped into you and your friend here," she said while rolling her eyes, which meant that she wasn't sorry at all. "But if you hadn't been banging her by the lift, this wouldn't have happened."

She was worked up and this was turning me on. Fuck, it was like my dick had a mind of its own. She was wearing jeans and a tight red top that exposed her tits amazingly well. I wanted to motorboat these bad boys right now. Besides, no one had ever questioned me and I wasn't planning to go easy on this smartass chick at all.

"Penny, get inside the apartment, and put some porn on for entertainment while I deal with Barbie here," I said with a stern voice. Penny was mumbling something, but she obeyed me and that was the main thing. The girl inhaled, going red again, and glaring at me like she wanted to stick a fork between my eyes.

"Don't call me that, you arrogant prick," she hissed and looked around. Yeah, there was shit everywhere. She ignored me and started picking up her stuff off the floor. I cocked my head to the side, watching as she bent down, showing me her sexy round ass while picking up her books, paperwork and some items of clothing.

"You didn't answer my question, Barbie," I said, watching the way she moved. No other woman had ever ignored me while I was giving her my full attention. Anger rushed through me. She kept ignoring me and I was getting agitated. What the hell was wrong with her?

I looked down and saw a slutty pink thong lying by my feet. My cock twitched when I lifted it up. It wasn't the kind of underwear that women wore to work, but wore to fuck. And she wore a size twelve.

"I'm not obligated to give you an explanation, fuckface, but fine. If you must know, I'm moving in next door. I inherited apartment twenty-one," she finally said, and then she noticed what I was holding. She got up and launched forward wanting to snatch her knickers from my hand, but I didn't let her, stepping away and catching a wave of her perfume. Orchid and blackberry. I had an instant sense of deja vu, as if I recognised the scent.

"No so fast, Barbie. You have to earn the privilege to have these back." I smirked.

Her face grew harder. Her nipples were erect and I was so fucking turned on just by looking at her that it was unbelievable. She couldn't have inherited the apartment from Joey. He had no family, no friends, or anyone that I knew was even interested in burying him. The solicitors were dealing with what he left. The bitch had to be here for my cock; she was probably playing me.

"Tell me why you're here and I might consider giving you these back."

"Be careful, your fuck buddy might be getting off right now without the help of your precious dick. I told you, I'm not here to waste my time with douchebags like you. I'm busy," she snapped, staring at me like she was ready to kill me.

It was kind of hot, so I continued to goad her. "Be careful how you speak to me, Barbie; otherwise you might not be here for long," I said and brought her knickers to my nose, inhaling the vibrant scent of pussy, watching her face the whole time. My mind swirled and I imagined having her sitting on my face. Hell, she was just some stupid chick, but it looked like she was also my new neighbour.

Her eyes grew wider and her skin paled with shock. Yeah, I was pushing her, playing a twat, but I liked that game. She was working her jaw, probably thinking up about a thousand ways to hurt me. After a few seconds, she turned around, picked up something from a box, and threw it at me.

A tennis ball hit my head and then bounced off the wall. I hissed, reaching for my forehead. I didn't see that coming.

"Keep them, asshole," she snapped with a delicious smile, picking up her boxes and marching away. I stood there like a fucking moron, watching as she swayed her delectable hips towards the next-door apartment. That ass, so firm, round and just bloody perfect. I wanted to devour it with my hard-as-rock cock. "I'm filing a complaint," she said, "and you may keep the knickers for a souvenir, a memory of what you will never have."

Then she just slammed the door, disappearing inside. My forehead was throbbing with pain, but I didn't care. I clenched my fists and strolled back to my own apartment, ready to deal with her later. First I had to get her out of my head.

I found Penny in the bedroom. She was switching the channels on the TV. Her hand was in her knickers and she was playing with herself. Just in time.

"Ready to be fucked?" I asked her, closing the door, furious with the fact that some random chick had beaten me at my own game.

Sasha

My breathing was coming in short, ragged pants. What an absolute asshole! I couldn't believe that he dared to speak to me like he owned the whole floor—and my body for that matter. He had no right to ask questions or demand answers. I detested men like him. This was just my luck to get a neighbour from hell.

When my mother asked me to take care of the inheritance in Gorgemouth, I thought that I had struck gold. Couple of weeks ago, Mum received a phone call from a solicitor claiming that she had inherited a penthouse twenty miles away from Edinburgh. Apparently Mum's distant stepbrother, who I didn't even know about, had just passed away and we were his only living relatives. The penthouse was just about to be taken by the government, but her uncle's solicitor had discovered Mum's name in some old documents from years ago.

The complex consisted of over three hundred apartments that were situated right on the coast, with the rocky beach a minute's walk away. It was a perfect place to take a break from life and get away from the noise of the busy city.

Grange Complex had been bought by a private developer and turned into luxury apartments. I read that the building had served as a hospital almost fifty years ago.

My own family was from Exeter, but we had lived in Glasgow since I was twelve years old. Although I didn't have the accent and I was born in England, I felt like Scotland was my real home.

When Mum received this unexpected message I was in London, trying to patch my miserable life back together. After my breakup and various other traumas, I was sick of Scotland. I was done with relationships and love. My move to London was only supposed to be temporary, but I ended up staying for nine months.

Mum worked her ass off as a paediatric nurse just to keep the house going in Glasgow, while Dad was driving trucks to earn a decent wage. She called me in the late evening almost three weeks ago, sounding really upset. Apparently she had a stepbrother that she hadn't spoken to for years. His name was Joey. Mum normally didn't talk a lot anyway if she didn't have to, so I wasn't too surprised when she didn't go into much detail, but I knew that he was my uncle. She didn't want to deal with the property left to her, so I offered to take care of it. At the time Dad was somewhere in Germany and he wasn't going to be back until the next month. Mum couldn't take time off work. My parents hadn't had any holidays for as long as they could remember and they were planning to go away as soon as Dad was back.

I thought that this kind of surprise couldn't have come at a better time. I hadn't had a permanent job since last year. The nursing agency that I worked for was willing to transfer me to care homes or hospitals around Edinburgh, and I had a car, so it would be easy to commute. Mum wanted me to stay in the apartment for a bit, sort the paperwork, and sell the place. I guessed that she didn't want to talk about Uncle Joey at all.

The pictures of the apartment looked amazing and I was excited to have a well-deserved break. I needed to forget about the past, recoup my energy, and move on with my life. My move to London changed me. Every day I was merely existing rather than living, hoping to move on and forget about the past. I had nothing that kept me in the capital: no friends, no boyfriends, no family, just an alcoholic roommate. I had to figure out where to go from there.

When I arrived at the Grange complex I wanted to jump for joy, I was so excited. The modern building looked better than in the pictures. I didn't want to waste any time, so I headed straight to the concierge. There I was given the key to Apartment 21. After going over a number of rules, a nice young ginger Scot showed me around the building. The complex had a fully equipped gym and pool, a conference room, and it was surrounded by hundred acres of landscaped gardens. It was like a dream come true. My heart kept racing until I walked into that asshole who was fingering the girl just by my door.

I didn't even have time to take a good look at him. I was so angry that he called me Barbie and talked to me like I was a child. The girl disappeared behind the doors. All my stuff was scattered all over the floor, while that cocky bastard picked up my favourite pink thong.

He was definitely Scottish. He had a very thick local accent and dirty-blond hair. It was just my luck to get the place opposite the biggest player in the building, a guy who had no manners and behaved like a prick. I didn't even know his name yet, but I already hated him with a vengeance.

Two

Sasha

Once I was calm enough, I looked around the apartment. It was bigger than I expected; at least five times the size of our living room back in Glasgow. When I finally noticed the view, my breath caught in my throat. I was looking straight at the wild sea that stretched over the horizon. On my way here I was expecting the apartment to be more traditional with a lot of clutter and old-school furniture, but this was far from it. The walls were painted in magnolia. Hardwood floors. A kitchen with shiny black countertops and filled with modern appliances.

My anger was slowly replaced by never-ending joy. I was going to have the best time in my life here, away from my shitty room in London.

My mouth was hanging open as I walked around, hardly believing that Mum owned this place. She didn't want to keep it, but I had to bring her here at least once and show her what she was missing. I walked onto the terrace and slid the door open. When I thought it couldn't get any better, it truly did. The terrace was almost of the size of the living room, stretching over the entire floor with the most stunning views of the sea and grounds. Shaking with excitement, I walked up the balustrade and looked around. It was summer and the sun was blazing hot. Joey had sunbeds and I was already imagining myself lying here sipping a cocktail. I was just about to walk away to check the bedroom when I heard someone's screams. The noises were coming from the other side of the apartment.

"Yeah, babe! You like it hard, don't you?"

I knew that voice. My Scottish neighbour from earlier on. The arrogant prick was banging that girl. Of course, my apartment was next to his and I could hear him quite clearly. For a split second I had an urge to run next door and pound on his door to tell him to keep it down, but somehow I restrained myself. I didn't want to give him the satisfaction. Tomorrow morning I was planning to file a formal complaint about his behaviour with the management.

I strolled back inside and checked out the two bedrooms. The master bedroom had a walk-in closet and it looked like I was able to get to the terrace from any room. This was awesome.

In the living room there were several framed photographs. I didn't recognise anyone in them, but I assumed that the older guy in most of the pictures was Joey Mitchell. He died of a heart attack three months ago. All his personal effects were still here in the apartment. My first job would be to pack everything, sell it, or give it away to charity. The furniture was modern and in excellent condition, so I could make a deal with whoever was going to buy this place.

It looked like uncle Joey had liked travelling. He was sixty-six when he died. He reminded me a bit of my grandfather: short and stocky with that big nose. Tears welled in my eyes as the memories from nine months ago clouded my mind.

I shook my head; it was time to forget about the past and start over. My first shift at the hospital was starting in a couple of hours. The agency was happy with giving me two or three shifts a week. I liked having my own money, and for now I didn't have any bills. The solicitor told me that Joey had been very good with his finances. He'd paid all the utilities and everything off for the next year, so I was lucky.

I went back to the hallway and picked up the boxes with my belongings. Most of my suitcases were in Glasgow. I took what I could from my room in London and shoved it into boxes. That hot Scot from the opposite apartment had my favourite thong. God, I hated him.

I chose the bigger bedroom for my room. I was planning to empty the cupboards tomorrow. I had a twelve-hour shift ahead of me tonight, so I needed to relax before the clock struck seven.

Dexter

Penny knew that I wasn't myself when I was fucking her. She came a few times, screamed that my cock felt amazing, but I was already slipping back into the oblivious mood after we were done. My head had been racing since my encounter with Barbie outside, and that wasn't good.

"Make sure you close the door behind you," I said afterward as we were lying on the bed panting. I took the condom off and threw it into the trash. Leaning on her elbows, she looked at me like I was talking in fucking Chinese.

"What? Do you want me to go? I thought I was staying for the night."

"I hate repeating myself. You aren't staying. I've got shit to do," I barked, staring at the ceiling. I heard someone next door, opening and closing the drawers. Fuck, it'd been months since Joey passed away. It was unnerving to hear someone on the other side of the wall once again. I couldn't quite believe that he wasn't around anymore. His death only added more confusion to my life.

I felt Penny's hands on my chest. She was moving them down to my dick, slowly teasing me, when I wanted her to leave. I was growing hard again thinking about this Barbie next door. It was time to call Ronny to find out who she was and what the hell she was doing in Joey's apartment.

I caught Penny's hand when she was just about to grab my balls. Her dark hair was loose and streaming down to her bare tits. I hated myself right now, the pressure mounting in my shoulders. Fuck, I didn't need to feel like shit right now.

"I'm going to count to five and I want you out of here," I said, narrowing my eyes at her, but she giggled as she caressed my ball sack, obviously not taking me seriously.

"Dex, don't be so mean. I want to suck you off," she muttered.

"One."

"Oh, come on, we're having fun. I always stay for the night. It's our routine."

"Two."

She was annoyed now and I felt the rage pushing through me faster than ever. I struggled to push away this heavy shitty mood that was embracing me.

"Three."

"Dex, I'm still horny."

"Four," I counted.

"Lick me, Dex."

"Five!" I roared and jumped out of bed, not thinking straight at all. I put my boxers back on, grabbed Penny and started dragging her across my apartment, not caring for the world if I was hurting her or not. She was still naked, but at that point I didn't fucking care. I was slowly losing my shit. She was screaming, calling me all sorts of names. I threw her outside into the empty corridor and shut the door behind me. I started picking up some of her clothes, my pulse racing away. I needed to get high fast; otherwise someone was going to either die or get hurt. I opened the door and threw the clothes at her.

"Dex, you're horrible. I don't even have a ride," Penny screamed and started putting her dress back on. Yeah, I wouldn't think that she wanted to parade naked around the complex. The next door opened up and Barbie peered out, looking at me and then at Penny. I had to pretend that I didn't care that she stood there watching the scene unfold.

"Penny, I made you come five times today. Stop whining. I'll see you in a week."

"Fuck you."

"I already did." I chuckled and pinned my eyes on Barbie, who was still standing there, looking concerned, probably for Penny's sake. I narrowed my eyes and then slammed the door behind me, grabbing my head and tangling my hair. She wasn't Joey; she was some fucking ordinary girl that I didn't need to know about.

For about a minute I couldn't gather my thoughts. My head felt like it was just about to blow up. I knew what was coming and I had to simmer down, before I did something I would regret later. Calling Jack wasn't an option. He had shit of his own that he had to deal with.

Then I heard Penny shouting.

"And I won't be coming back ever again, you self-centred asshole!"

She was going to be back; she loved my dick.

I reached the kitchen counter and started shaking out the pills I needed to take. Some of them were good. My supplier knew how to get certain things that helped with whatever was going on inside me. Today I was angry, livid, and my pulse was racing like a car on the motorway. Yesterday I felt great. I finished up tons of projects and went shopping. Despite that, I had no idea what tomorrow would bring. My mood swung whichever way the wind blew.

I swallowed a few pills and went back to the sofa. I picked up the rest of the weed that I had and started making a rollie. The dark waters were suffocating, covering me, and I couldn't breathe. My anger was mounting and I had to calm the fuck down.

I lay back and lit my joint, thinking about my poor Pap. I hadn't visited his grave in a while. My stomach revolted, so I took a few deep puffs. Pills, weed and sex... all this stuff helped, but it was never enough. Mum was worried about me, all these late phone calls. She didn't know that she was the one that killed Dad. He had no choice and hung himself. His love for her killed him, but he was a weak man.

I wasn't like him. Or at least I slept around, fucked whoever I could, and never got involved emotionally. Love was for losers.

The pressure in my head eased off as the meds started to kick in. I was numb again for a while, not feeling trapped anymore. It was going to be a long evening. Joey used to come over to keep me company when I didn't have a woman in here. He was a good man, always listening to my meaningless problems. He had no idea that he helped. Doctors couldn't help me; no one could. Every day I needed a different distraction in order to keep going.

After my father killed himself, I graduated and got a business degree, got angry, smashed a few jaws, drank way too much, and finally after a few nights in jail I decided to sort myself out. I invested some money in properties. I started with small projects—flats, apartments—and then I moved to houses. Soon I had profits in my pocket. It took me eight years to get where I was now. I bought Grange complex for peanuts, spent shitloads of money and turned this wreck into luxury apartments. I had more debts than I could think of, but I had enough years ahead of me to pay them off.

Every year I tried to invest in something new. After Dad's death I felt isolated, lost. He was the person that I was aspiring to be like—until he decided to hang himself.

Women were attracted to successful guys like me. All of a sudden I had plenty of money. I thought that a lot of dosh could make me happy, but life didn't work like that. I still felt down all the time, so I fucked as many women as I could to deal with whatever the hell I was going through. I didn't want to be a slave of fucking love, so I replaced women that didn't understand what I was looking for as soon as I had a chance.

Finally after an hour, I felt numb enough not to feel like shit anymore. I put the joint in the ashtray and walked to the kitchen to get myself a whiskey. There was only half a bottle left, but that was enough to put me back to sleep, to get rid of the mounting grief that kept bothering me for days.

Three

Sasha

I couldn't believe what I was seeing when I opened the door. That asshole next door threw a naked woman out of his apartment and then he disappeared inside. A moment later he opened the door just to throw her clothes at her. Then he stood there with his magnificent chest, scowling at me. Dex... I think that was what this woman, Penny, had called him. Maybe it was short for Dexter. Either way, I had no idea.

For about ten seconds we just stared at each other, and my eyes moved down to his perfectly ripped stomach and muscular arms. Along with a dirty beard that looked sexy as hell, the bastard was really good-looking, and he knew it. His boxers hung low on his hips, exposing the bits of dark hair that were hidden underneath the waistband hem. My mouth went dry and I was ready to say something back to him when he slammed the door, going inside.

"Penny, right?" I asked the woman, trying to act like I gave a damn. She was very pretty, with dark long hair, brown eyes and a slim body. For a second I thought that she must have been a model.

"Don't worry, I'm going already," she said, putting her underwear and dress back on. I looked away for a second, allowing her some privacy.

Then she yelled, "And I won't be coming back ever again, you self-centred twat!"

Wow, I had to give it to her; she had balls. She picked up her bag and strolled to the stairs, blatantly ignoring me.

I closed the door and went back to my tasks. I would definitely be going through with the complaint in the morning. Someone had to teach that douchebag a lesson. Obviously he didn't know how to treat women with respect. Just like Kirk.

No, I couldn't compare him to my ex-boyfriend. Kirk was trash, not worth thinking about at all.

After doing some research online, I knew that I had one of the desirable apartments with the sea view. Before I left for work I made a mental note to speak to the estate agent tomorrow and start the ball rolling.

***

It was a long night and by the time I drove back to the complex it was six a.m. After I graduated high school, Mum convinced me to do nursing in uni. She told me that this was the easiest way to find a job and the money was decent. I chose the same specialisation she had, working on the paediatric ward, dealing with all the sick children. I should have switched to something else when I had a chance. Every time I had to walk into the hospital, memories flooded back to me and I felt like I was experiencing the same sorrow from three years ago all over again.

I fell asleep pretty much straight away. When I woke up, the clock on the wall was showing four in the afternoon. The sheets smelled great and I didn't want to move, but it was Monday and I had many things that I needed to sort out.

When I got my breakfast and shower out of the way, I started going through the wardrobes in the apartment. It looked like uncle Joey had worn a lot of stylish and expensive clothes. I packed a few bits away and put out them in the living room. The fridge was empty, so I knew I needed to do some grocery shopping, particularly if I wanted to eat today. I had to file that complaint first, so the douche next door wouldn't think that I was bluffing. I had no idea who I needed to speak to about the asshole from my floor; maybe I'd try the young lad that spoke to me yesterday. He seemed pleasant enough.

I checked my reflection before I left, examining myself from head to toe. My blond hair was naturally light. I was curvy but a slender size twelve and I'd always hated my oversized boobs. My body had bothered me at times, especially when all my friends were super skinny. Of course, every guy I'd dated had always liked my curves. I'd tried fad diets and I did lose a couple of pounds, but my weight always came back to the usual after a few months.

I put on a cute comfy outfit, made some phone calls, and managed to arrange a meeting with Mum's solicitor. Some of the apartments had been on the market for months, so I wasn't so sure that it was possible to make a quick sale. I had to do more research about the prices in this area.

I loved the grand, opulent feel of this complex; even the lifts were done up to the highest standard. The complex was actually two buildings joined together by a long, wide, glass-fronted corridor with meeting rooms and offices off it and a central atrium where the concierge was based. There were also small bungalows scattered around the grounds. As I walked to the concierge desk via the corridor, I felt good in my own skin for the first time in months. Mum was glad that I was helping her with this project and it was good to start over away from London.

"Hi, we met yesterday. I'm in apartment twenty-one, and I already had a small clash with one of the residents. I was wondering if I could speak to someone about it," I said, diving straight to the point.

The same young guy smiled, eyeing my boobs. He couldn't be any more than eighteen. I wanted to sort this out as soon as I could, so I pretended that I didn't notice.

"You have to see Mr. Tyndall about any complaints. He's the owner of the complex and I believe he might be in his office right now," shot out the ginger boy, keeping his eyes on my rack. I sighed, knowing that it was pointless talking to anyone else. I might as well go directly to the top. Normally I didn't pick on people or complain for no reason, but the guy upstairs crossed the line and he took my favourite thong. He could go to hell for all I cared.

"All right, where is his office?" I asked.

"Carry on straight through. It's on your right, office number eleven," he pointed out with a smile, finally meeting my eyes.

I smoothed my hair, took a deep breath, and walked further down the corridor. This was going to be a bit embarrassing. I hadn't even moved in yet and I was already complaining. This guy, Mr. Tyndall, whoever he was, would probably think I was pathetic.

Tingles passed through me, but I didn't hesitate. I simply knocked three times, then walked in, stopping abruptly in the doorway.

Dexter

I lifted my head from the paperwork that I was dealing with to see who was interrupting me. Barbie was standing in my doorway, looking numb with shock, staring straight at me. I darted my eyes up and down her body, imagining tying her up to the chair and telling her how badly I wanted her mouth on my cock.

She was rooted to the spot, her eyes darkening with twisting excitement and mixed astonishment. I'd had a shitty night's sleep, but surprisingly, this morning I woke up feeling all right. Cranky, but better than most days.

My dick twitched again. She was wearing a low-cut top and jeans. Why the fuck did she have to tease men like that? Those large tits were practically popping out of the thin material of her top, looking so inviting. I had her knickers in my pocket. I liked keeping a souvenir, especially of a sexy bitch that I was planning to screw shortly.

"Barbie, what can I help you with?" I asked politely. She parted her lips, staring at me like she was chewing a cable. I bet she wasn't expecting me when she walked in here a moment ago. What can I say? I have this kind of effect on women.

"You're Mr. Tyndall? The landowner of this place?" she asked with obvious disbelief in her voice.

I got up, fastened my suit jacket and walked over to her. I was right: she was only a few inches shorter than me. I wanted to play with her, so I came closer, leaning over and around her to shut the door, recognising the same perfume that she wore yesterday. She didn't move and I was enjoying making her uneasy.

"I don't see any other fucking Dexter Tyndall here," I pointed out, watching as she fought with her urge to slap me. Barbie was pretty. It was a shame that I normally didn't fuck blondes, but for this blonde I was willing to make an exception to that rule.

"All right, whatever. I'm here to make an official complaint about you," she hissed, moving around me. She flopped her sexy ass on the chair that was opposite my desk and dropped her eyes to her nails.

"I didn't ask you to take a seat," I said to her. She rolled her eyes and I was instantly hard. Fuck, what was it with this woman?

"As if I was going to ask for your permission. The chair was empty and I sat. Now let's get to the point. I'm on a schedule, asshole," she said. I walked back towards her, sat on the edge of the desk, and leaned over so I was close enough to smell her perfume. *Tick, tock*, the clock was counting slowly and my cock was hard from the moment she burst into my office.

"That's not very ladylike, calling someone that you don't know an asshole."

"Okay, well, I can call you a douche instead, or a knob or a jerk. Which one of those do you prefer?"

Funny mouth she has there.

"Why are you in Joey's apartment?" I demanded, ignoring her insults. She was one of my residents and I had to try to act professional, but she was so infuriating, plus I wanted to fuck her badly. English or not, she was going to ride my cock tonight.

"I'm not obligated to tell you anything, Mr. Tyndall. I'm here to file a complaint, so let's get to it."

21

I had to step up my game.

"What's your name, Barbie?" I challenged, imagining her naked. It wasn't easy to keep my dick in my pants, especially when I was this close to her. One downward glance and she would notice my strained erection.

"I guess that as a knob, you're also incapable of listening. My name is Sasha, not Barbie," she snapped.

Sasha, hmm. I once knew a stripper with that name. I liked it.

"For me you're still a Barbie. Now as I recall, yesterday you said that Joey left you his apartment. He didn't have any family. If you're family, how is it possible that I have never seen you here before?"

She sucked in a breath, glaring at me. Joey was a Scottish man, and this girl sounded English. They couldn't be related.

"You're supposed to be the landowner, so you should know these things," she stated, dismissing my questions.

I was getting tired of this. For some unknown reason she wasn't planning to make this easy for me to deal with and I hated wasting time pissing about with this kind of nonsense. I moved even closer, meeting her eyes. She froze. My dick was rubbing over the seam of my zipper. Fuck, I wanted to bend her over my desk and bang her fast and hard. She would love every second of it, but she was a resident and I didn't get involved with women that lived in the complex.

"The longer you take to answer me, the longer you have to stay here, Barbie, but I'm a busy man. My six o'clock fuck is going to be here soon, unless you're volunteering to satisfy me instead?" I said, watching as she struggled to breathe being so close to me.

The tension was palpable and I was holding my breath waiting.

She finally snapped. "For Christ's sake, fine. You want to know why I'm here? Gee, let's see. A couple of weeks ago my mother got a phone call from a solicitor. Apparently we were the only living relatives of Uncle Joey. I never knew that he even existed. He and my mother hadn't spoken for years and she wasn't prepared to deal with this place, so I offered to help her. I needed a break, so I signed the paperwork and here I am."

That was a lot of unnecessary words, but I liked my women feisty. I bet she was good in bed. "See, that wasn't too difficult. I ask questions and you answer them."

"Give me the damn paperwork for the complaint. I don't need to waste anymore time with you. I've got stuff to do," she said. My dick stiffened as she bit on her lip.

"Well, before I let you go I would like to say that I'm sorry about yesterday. I get a bit stressed when I don't get pussy."

"Apology not accepted. Paperwork, now."

"You're stressing me out, Barbie, and you know what that means, right?"

Four

Sasha

Dexter was a good-looking man, but not just jaw-dropping good-looking. He was a knickers-drenching, fist-clenching, heart-pounding, fever-inducing, sizzling hot man. Some men were born with a great voice, charisma and looks, but obviously Dexter thought that he was blessed with all of these things. He apparently had this irresistible talent for melting women's knickers off just with one look. How did I know it?

Because right then I was one of those women.

His eyes were sending scorching heat through me into my bones, melting me like boiling lava. I was so lost when I stared back at his strong jaw, untidily trimmed beard and fit body. He either didn't like to shave or he preferred looking scruffy. Okay, I had to calm down, because right then I was dribbling over his level of hotness. This was pathetic and wrong on so many levels. I had to fill out the damn paperwork and get the hell out of his office before I lost all my self-respect and became one of those women he played with. His eyes scanned my chest every five seconds and he knew that I noticed.

"Is that your pick-up line? Is this supposed to work for the ladies?" I laughed, trying to mask the nervousness in my voice. Nine months ago, I had sworn off men, promising the universe that love wasn't for me. Now, I was getting wet because of some hot asshole. I couldn't let him spoil my stay here just because he was horny. The problem with guys like him was not only the fact that he thought he was God, but also the fact that he had so much money he didn't know what to do with it, and it gave him a superiority complex.

I shifted my body on the chair, mildly aware of my increasing lust; he was seducing me slowly and painfully. "I'm not one of those girls, so give me the damn paperwork," I quipped, failing to hide my uneasiness.

His eyes roved over my chest, flickering with something—hunger, desire; whatever it was, it made me feel even more lost to him.

Dexter opened the drawer and threw a paper towards me, smirking. I detested the fact that he was the exact type that I would go for: rough, toned and confident. It was a shame that I had to stay away. Guys like him would eat women like me for supper. Besides, I assumed that he had some sort of dark, twisted, secret side to him. All men have one.

It took me a minute to write down everything that went on in the corridor. After I signed my name on the bottom, I stood up ready to leave. I wished I'd decided to wear something much more elegant. I looked completely out of place in my old jeans.

"There, deal with it, Mr. Tyndall," I said firmly. "It's a good thing that I won't be here for long."

"I assume that you want to sell the apartment?" he asked in much gentler tone, like he was indeed curious.

"My mother wants me to put it on the market as soon as possible."

"That's a shame; if you had been nicer to me, maybe I could have helped you with finding a buyer," he stated and then he stood up suddenly. My skin prickled with a wave of lust that dove down to my core. His eyes were stripping me of my clothes as he lowered his gaze for the hundredth time to my boobs.

"I don't need your help. I'm putting the place on the market today. It's a desirable apartment. I'll have a secure deal by the end of the week, I'm sure."

"That depends." He chuckled, stalking closer.

I had to freaking move, but I couldn't. My legs weren't working. I felt like I was the prey to his hunter. "That depends?"

"Depends on if you have a buyer."

"I'll have one by the end of the week," I assured him.

"If you say so, Barbie," he purred, moving even closer. I backed away until I hit the wall. My knees were shaking. He stood inches away from me, and I could smell his earthy aftershave. My heart was racing, his eyes drilling me back to the wall. Why did he have to be so good-looking? I really didn't need this right now.

"The apartment is going on the market tomorrow," I said quietly, almost whispering, backing as far away as I could, but I had nowhere to run. His lips turned up at the corners and he moved an inch closer. I felt his magnificent erection pressed against my groin, rubbing gently against my sex.

"I don't know what is it about you, but you make me instantly hard. I don't fuck blondes, but I want you," he whispered into my ear. My head swam, and desire overtook my usual thought processes. I wanted him and I hated myself for it. "I'm already imagining you in my bed, with me devouring your tight, wet pussy, hearing you scream for me. You could have an offer on this place in an hour. I'm that good."

There was no way that I was sleeping with him for the sake of a sale. Who the hell did he think he was? I wanted to come up with something, anything, but no sound came out. Desire consumed my mind and I just stood there waiting for him to kiss me. *How lame.* His eyes searched my face, watching and expecting me to lose this battle. My hormones were screaming with need. I hadn't had sex for months; well, nine months to be exact. The throbbing between my legs wasn't helping.

Dexter Tyndall didn't give me much time to think about my answer. His lips crushed mine and he tasted divine. I couldn't remember when I had ever been kissed this way. He devoured me. His hands were on my body under my top, running over the naked flesh on my stomach. He pressed me harder against the wall, drenching me as his lips moved against mine.

His self-assurance made me soaking wet for him. He kissed like he had been starving for me since the moment he laid his eyes on me. I caressed his lips with my tongue, wanting and expecting more. A moan escaped my mouth, and that must have given him confidence, because he began tracing his smooth fingers down between my legs. He unbuttoned my jeans and slipped his hand into my knickers. I shut my eyes, completely overwhelmed by his touch.

"Your pussy is so wet for me, Barbie," he growled, touching and circling his thumb around my swollen clit. Heat sizzled through me, sliding down under my skin, and I couldn't help but anticipate more. I almost wanted to beg him not to stop. His cock was pressed against my pelvis and I imagined how would it be if I had him inside me now. Dexter's fingers melted my flesh, teasing and exploring as my breathing grew laboured.

Then the images slipped away, pulling me away from the bliss, and I realised that I couldn't let him play me like this. Men were deceitful.

I opened my eyes and shoved him away from me, breathing like I needed an inhaler. Without even thinking about it, I slapped him.

My palm burned and his hand shot out of my pants. My body cried over that lost intensity. He'd bewitched me and I lost my concentration for a moment.

Dexter

Fucking bitch slapped me. In one moment, I was almost fingering her and in the next I felt a sharp sting on my face. Okay, I didn't anticipate her being violent. I couldn't even think straight when I pushed her against the wall, wanting to consume her slick sex. My cock was so rock hard. Her smooth orchid perfume was driving me crazy.

"Stay away from me and never touch me again," she hissed like an angry cat.

I clenched my fists, knowing that my dick was popping out of my trousers. I smiled wolfishly. Hell, I wanted her, needed to have her wrapped around my cock. This time it wasn't just about the fact that I had to stop thinking about the demons or

27

my fucked-up past—I had this sudden craving for her. The blond Barbie girl with an amazing ass and tits.

"You're so wet for me."

She started walking away, so I took that opportunity to stare at her ass.

"I'm not your fuck buddy. I'll be out of here before you know it."

I wanted to listen to her pant for me again. "I told you, I can get you a buyer, but I don't want to let you go yet, not until you've ridden my cock."

I was perfectly serious. From then on I knew that I had to jeopardise whatever her plan was. There was something about this girl. She wasn't like the others, needy for my attention. She actually detested me. Her steaming anger was an even bigger turn-on that I imagined.

"Dream on, Mr. Tyndall, because you will never see it, never taste it. I'm putting the apartment on the market today whether you like it or not," she said, sounding furious and glaring at me.

"Challenge accepted, Barbie girl. You don't know it yet, but your pussy already belongs to me."

Then she shut the door behind her. I pressed my cock down, trying somehow to cover my erection, and followed her. In the corridor I instantly spotted Mrs. Jenkins with her shopping bags, so I ran out to her like a gentleman. Around women that wanted me I behaved like I didn't give a fuck, but around the residents and my associates I was that perfectly well-mannered guy.

Sasha was standing not far from me, as if she was waiting for something.

"Dear Mrs. Jenkins, let me help you with your shopping bags," I offered, eagerly taking bags off her hands. She beamed at me like it was fucking Christmas morning. "Groceries for the week, I presume?"

"Yes, dear. I wanted to get it out of the way. Thank you, Dexter; you're always so helpful," she said, patting me on my back. I started to imagine an old guy naked. That sort of made my johnson go flat. I couldn't walk around the complex with a hard-on. I had a certain reputation to uphold.

"I had a very important conversation with the new resident," I answered and glanced back at Sasha. She wasn't moving, still watching me. She was pissed. I brought my fingers to my nose and inhaled the scent of her sweet juices.

"Dex, don't work too hard. You need a nice young woman to look after you," the old lady added.

"I think I have my eye on one, Mrs. Jenkins, but she isn't as beautiful as you."

Mrs. Jenkins started laughing, slapping me and calling me a charmer. I winked at Sasha, who dropped her arms, turned around, and continued walking away.

Her ass, that's all I kept thinking about when I was walking back to Mrs. Jenkins's apartment. Most of the elderly ladies loved me. I had almost an entire floor to myself, so there was never a problem with the possibility of them witnessing the noise or my female visitors coming and going. Now I had to worry about Barbie. For some reason I needed to break her, devour her, ease the curiosity that she seeded in me.

On the way to my car, I thought about all the things I could do to her.

I had one more meeting in Edinburgh this evening and then the dinner with Julianna, one of my associates. I could start working on my new pet project of getting Sasha into my bed tomorrow.

I had plenty of useful contacts among the estate agents. She was pretty sure that she would have a quick sale, but she didn't know who she was dealing with yet. She'd find out soon enough.

The game had begun. I took my iPhone out of my pocket and dialled Ronny's number.

"I have a task for you, an important fucking task, so listen to me very carefully."

Five

Sasha

I didn't have a very good day yesterday. It was late when I finally got into the city and the estate agent that my solicitor had recommended was already closed. The adrenaline was coursing through me and I was so pissed off that I wasted so much time in Dexter's office. This wasn't the only thing that I was angry about. I let him touch me and I liked it when I wasn't supposed to.

Kirk was the reason that I couldn't gain control of my emotions. For nine months I had been avoiding men, slowly picking up the pieces of my broken self. Now I was falling under the spell of a man that only wanted to use me for sex, and that was a huge mistake. Kirk had violated me: he had been sleeping with my best friend the entire time we had been in a relationship. When I found out, he turned into a violent and sadistic man. I didn't want to remember the pain, the trauma and sleepless nights. It was all in the past, it had to be forgotten.

I knew that Dexter was going to be a problem. He wanted to play with me, knowing that I was attracted to him. Well, he'd have to show me that I was more than just a quick, easy lay. I wasn't ready for a full-blown relationship, but I didn't need Dexter Tyndall to bang me just so he could get me out of his head.

It had been months since I'd last been in Edinburgh. Even when I visited my parents in Glasgow, I never used to go out anywhere. I was too scared of bumping into someone that I knew. Kirk was a very outgoing guy and we had shared the same friends. When I left the hospital I didn't know that he had set them against me. A few weeks after our breakup, everyone that meant something in my life turned their backs on me. At that point I was too traumatised to deal with it, so I moved away.

The loud horn brought me back to reality and I looked around, realising that I'd wandered off further away than I anticipated. I spotted a fitness centre in the next building. There was no point hiding anymore and I was out of my grief, done with playing the victim. I walked towards it, wanting to see what kind of classes the centre had to offer. My stomach made a funny jolt when I saw pole-dancing lessons on the poster. Fate slapped me on the wrist. It'd been nine months since I last practised. I checked the time and realised that the class was starting in about five minutes. I was so out of shape, but I loved pole dancing and I wanted to prove to myself that I could still do it.My friend Donna had convinced me to try it when I was only twenty-two. She dropped out after a few sessions, telling me that it wasn't for her. I stayed, learning from an award-winning pole dancer. She taught me all the basic moves before I started creating my own routines. A few months after meeting Kirk, I started lying to him, saying that I was going to yoga twice a week. I didn't know why, but I felt embarrassed. Turned out he had too much time on his hands, so he started shagging my best friend when I didn't give him the attention he wanted.

During the class I had felt sexy, invincible and on the top of the world. It was hard work, but the satisfaction that I got out of it kept me going. My problems and worries didn't matter.

"The hell with it," I said aloud and opened the door to the studio. I needed to feel it again, the thrill of excitement deep in my stomach, the joy after the class. I could sort the stuff with the sale of the apartment tomorrow; tonight I wanted to dance again.

I climbed the stairs, knocked on a white door, and walked inside. My heart accelerated when I saw a large open classroom with mirrors on the wall and three stations with poles. There were only a few women there, stretching and talking amongst themselves.

"Are you here for a lesson?" asked a very pretty woman with curly red hair.

"Yes. I just saw your poster and I was wondering if I could join in?"

"The beginner class is tomorrow at the same time."

"No, sorry, I'm not a beginner. I've been dancing for a years, but I don't have the proper clothes," I told her, massaging the nape of my neck, feeling like an idiot. Who comes into the gym without the proper gear?

"Great, please join us. I should have spare shorts in my bag if you're okay with that. The fee is six pounds," she said smiling, not looking fazed at all by my awkwardness. Two other women looked pleased to have more company. I dug money out of my bag and handed it to her.

"It's been nine months since I last danced and I'm not in shape, but I know quite a few good routines."

"That's superb. I haven't been teaching that long anyway, but I'm sure we can learn something from each other. My name is Gina, by the way."

"I'm Sasha." Gina handed me her black shorts and showed me to the dressing room. Several minutes later I was out, standing by the pole.

After a quick stretch, Gina asked me to pair with her and two other women. They were already moving around the pole, trying a few simple spins. I knew that I was going to be sore tomorrow, but I felt good. When Gina showed us some of her moves, I knew that I made the right decision.

It didn't take me long to remember what I needed to do. For some time I only watched Gina as she moved her body around the pole with finesse and elegance. My own self-confidence was buried deep inside me, but I knew the lessons would remind me that I was no longer that broken woman, but a damn good dancer.

"Now, your turn. Show us what you can do," she said, jumping off the pole and wiping the sweat off her forehead.

I nodded and started walking around the pole with my inside arm holding onto it. I used my outside leg to gain momentum, swinging and hooking it around the front of the pole. As my inside leg left the floor, I brought my arm to the pole. I crossed my legs at the ankles and then I slid down the pole. I did a few more circles to get ready for a fireman spin. Nine months was a really long time, but it seemed as if my muscles remembered the moves.

The girls looked like they were expecting more, so I lay on my back next to the pole, then I reached out and gripped it strongly. I used my upper body to roll myself to the other side of the pole, keeping my lower body flat like a plank at the same time.

From then I went back and repeated the fireman spin. My upper body had lost its strength and I knew that I had to practise a lot harder in order to get to the same form that I'd had nine months ago. Soon my muscles were burning and my breathing was shallow, but I was ready for more.

Gina and the girls looked impressed when I did hollywood, martini and stag spins, one after another. These were still basics, but I felt like I executed them well. I was high from the adrenaline.

The girls started clapping once I successfully showed them the basic inversion, breathing hard. My heart pounded against my ribs as I slid down trying to catch my breath. The skin on my arms tingled with excitement.

"Good job. You obviously had great training. I think you should start coming at least twice a week," Gina said, beaming. I was exhausted but satisfied. It seemed like I was getting back on the right track. I didn't understand why I stopped dancing. I always loved it so much. When Gina started showing the other girls more advanced moves, I joined a short red-haired girl who looked like she needed a partner. I showed her the fireman spin again and we practised that a few more times.

"Thank you so much. I love these classes; they're a great reliever," Marianna said, bending down and stretching her legs when I moved around the pole.

"Yes," I agreed. "I can't believe that I stopped training. It's good to be back."

We talked a bit more until Gina decided to mix us up a bit. Everyone was working with each other well and in the end we all stood in a circle panting. I knew that I was going to be back tomorrow. London had left me bitter and I knew that I was done with my miserable life in the capital. Edinburgh was a good city to start again. New city and a new adventure. It was the new beginning that I needed.

I took Gina's number and promised her that I would show up tomorrow. I was done with playing a victim—from now on I planned to turn everything around.

Dexter

"Fancy riding my cock tonight?" I asked Laura, holding my phone between my neck and my shoulder whilst trying to roll a spliff at the same time. My head was pounding and I was in one of those shitty moods. I lost money on one of the properties that I'd made a bid on a few weeks ago and on top of that, my mother wanted to see me on Sunday for dinner. I hated going home and listening to my younger brother Connor whine about how unfair his life was. At least Jack seemed happy.

"I'm busy today. Maybe tomorrow," Laura replied, sounding bored. What the fuck? She could at least have made an effort, pretending that she gave a fuck, while I was on the phone with her.

"Tomorrow afternoon. I want you standing outside my apartment ready for a big O," I said remembering that she liked when I made her come with my tongue. "I'm going to fuck you hard and by the time I'm finished you won't remember your name."

"Oh, Dex, chill. I'll be there."

"Two o'clock sharp, Laura, and try not to be late; otherwise, I will punish you," I said and then hung up.

My cock strained in my trousers when I heard the door. Sasha was going somewhere. It'd been a few days since our talk in my office and, still, I couldn't get her out my fucking mind. The estate agent put her property on the market yesterday. She wasn't bluffing when she said that she wanted to sell it. My contact couldn't delay the issue with paperwork any longer.

I'd fucked two girls since Monday and every time I closed my eyes I imagined it was Sasha naked rather than the random shag under me.

A few hours ago I had a phone call from Darren, my contact in the estate agent's office. He informed me that Sasha had managed to secure a first viewing. The apartment was desirable and people were prepared to pay a lot of money for it, but I didn't want her to leave yet, not before I got her out of my system and fucked her in every possible position. It was a shame that she was out. I had an urge to knock at her door and talk to her about tomorrow. I wanted to know where she was going and if she had any other guy in her life.

I shook my head, telling myself that it was bullshit. I didn't need to know if she was fucking someone else. All I wanted was to have sex with her. These thoughts about Sasha were making me nervous. I didn't fucking want to go there.

My limbs felt heavy and my head kept banging, even after I smoked a full joint. I took some more painkillers and decided to stay on the sofa until the drugs kicked in. I hated that part of the day when I was alone in my apartment. Normally I made sure that I had a girl, but today, for the first time in a while, I wasn't in the mood.

A couple of months ago I was still looking forward to my deep conversations with Joey. Since he died I'd been drowning, pulling myself into a hole of self-destruction. I felt like I had no one in this world that understood me. Sometimes when I was talking to myself, I pretended that there were other people in my apartment, standing and watching whilst I wasted away on the sofa, lying there like a sick, lazy fuck.

It took me hours to feel numb again. My gut twisted and I locked my eyes shut, knowing that in a few seconds I was going to drift away from this world.

Six

Dexter

I woke up at four a.m. feeling worse than yesterday evening, but at least the few hours' kip had got rid of my banging headache. There was a vile taste in my mouth, probably because I drank too much whiskey last night. It was still dark outside, so I tossed and turned before I decided to get up. I hadn't been sleeping well since Joey died. A few weeks ago I tried a few different pills to get me through the night, but in the end I had problems with breathing, so I stopped taking them.

Thank fuck it was finally Saturday. But I couldn't stay in bed and just lie there for no reason, so I went to the office in my apartment and started drafting emails to potential clients, checking properties, doing anything to keep me busy. I thought I could get through millions of tasks before lunchtime.

After two hours I noticed that my hands were shaking like fuck, so I went to the kitchen, took orange juice from the fridge and drank it all. Six o'clock was my workout time. The gym downstairs was small, but fully equipped. For as long as I could remember I've kept fit and looking buff. Women loved running their smooth fingers over my six-pack and I had to keep my stamina up for all that pussy I had on tap.

I made a coffee and decided to go out on the terrace to watch the sunrise.

Despite the early morning, it was relatively warm. The temperatures were going to shoot up to around thirty degrees Celsius later on. The boys from the office wanted to drive to the beach on the weekend, but I wasn't up for it.

I slid the door wide open, welcoming the crisp, fresh air. The sun was rising slowly above the horizon, the red sky reminding me of the day I found my father in the attic. He hadn't been a very good sleeper either. By the time the medic got to our house, the morning sky burned with pigments of red, pink and gold, but Dad was already cold and free of his misery.

For a split second I thought that I was having hallucinations. Sasha was standing by the balustrade leaning over it, looking at something below. She wore a silky red nightgown which was short, exposing her perfect, firm ass.

A couple of months ago, I came back to the apartment drunk and smashed the fence that separated my side of the apartment terrace from Joey's. We got on quite well and I think it was because he reminded me a lot of my own father, although Joey wasn't shut down emotionally like him. Sometimes in the evenings we met on the terrace and talked for hours. Since that drunken episode I never bothered to put the fence back up, and it seemed that Joey didn't mind.

Right then I knew it was the best decision I had ever made.

I had an amazing view of Sasha's ass, giving me an instant hard-on. Glimpses of a pink thong were showing, similar to the one that I had stolen from her. Seeing her so exposed, unaware that I was watching, made me so bloody crazy.

I didn't care what she was looking at. All I wanted was to part that sweet pussy and to bury myself inside her where she would take every inch of me, screaming, growling and waking up all the neighbours with her sensual, loud moans.

"Beautiful view; so inviting," I said loudly. She flinched and turned abruptly, finally noticing me. There was no way she'd just woken up. She still had her makeup on. Maybe she worked during the night. Whatever; she could wake me up like that every day and I would love it.

Slowly her eyes took me in and a cute flush crept over her face. I knew that she couldn't help herself glancing down at my bare chest. The image of her exposed bum cheeks danced in front of my eyes. I didn't need to hide my erection that was popping out of my boxers.

"Like what you see?" I asked, cocking my head to the side, smiling and winking at her. She swallowed hard, looking like she couldn't make her lips work.

"How long have you been standing here?" she barked, her voice vibrating in my head, sending a shudder of heat to my groin. She was so hot when she was angry. The hell, I couldn't stop thinking about what I could do to her.

"Long enough to admire your sexy backside," I smirked.

She parted her lips with shock, looking around. "Why are these terraces joined together? Wasn't there supposed to be a dividing fence somewhere in the middle?" she asked, narrowing her eyes at me. True, I was standing on her side, but Joey's paperwork didn't say anything about the fact that we never put the fence back up.

"Not relevant," I said, closing the gap between us. She shivered and small goosebumps broke out across her shoulders. My fingers itched to grab her hair and pull her head down to my cock. I noticed that she had stopped breathing altogether, and suddenly my internal sound system began to play Marvin Gaye's "Let's Get It On." Her eyes had already checked me out and now that I was so close I had a chance to see her impressive cleavage. Her big juicy tits were in need of my touch. "My proposition stands. I want to watch as your pussy grows moist with excitement and then I'm going to thrust my cock deep inside you."

She inhaled and I saw the heat igniting in her green eyes. Then she leaned over and for a split second I thought she was going kiss me.

"I would rather eat dirt than go into bed with you."

She could say whatever she liked, but I knew she wanted me. Her erect nipples were popping out of the thin material, making my cock twitch. Her breathing changed, growing harder and laboured. She smelled delicious and I was ready to push away whatever restraints were holding me back and just take her, here and now.

"Liar. I bet your pussy is already wet for me." I moved closer. The tip of my dick brushed her thigh and she inhaled sharply. "Come inside and I'll fuck you so hard that you'll beg for more."

I had her then, seeing how she trembled under my touch. Flaming desire was fucking with my head.

"No chance, fuckface. I'm selling the apartment today and then I'll be out of here. You keep dreaming about my pussy— the only pussy that you will never have."

Then she was back inside her apartment. I stood there not believing that she fucking left me high and dry. She closed her curtains and I swore loudly. For that split second I thought that she would give in, but I was wrong. I loved that she wouldn't back down from me, but kept fighting. I also loved the fact that she was more stubborn than was good for her. The chase kept this pussy hunt fun.

I didn't stay to watch the sunrise; instead I went back inside riddled with sexual frustration. She had no idea what I was planning, but she would know in exactly eight hours. The fun had only just begun.

Sasha

Why did he have to be so good-looking? And that deliciously defined torso. Hell, I didn't even know how to pull myself together after our naughty encounter. We were sharing the terrace, of course; how could I miss that? I had to investigate this because the solicitor's paperwork clearly stated that the terraces were separated.

I had just finished my shift, changed into something more comfortable and gone outside to admire the view. How was I supposed to know that he was such an early bird?

Who on the earth got up at six o'clock on Saturday morning?

My heart was racing away when his body moved so close to mine. It'd been so long since I had sex and now my hormones were driving me absolutely berserk because I had the Scottish sex god next door.

I stripped, switched off my lights, and went back to bed. The apartment was finally on the market and I had my first viewing later on. I had to get some sleep. There had been some issues with the paperwork and the estate agent took ages to sort it out. On Thursday morning I kept going up and down to the city to make sure they had everything they needed.

Dexter and his super-hot body kept playing tricks in my mind. I couldn't believe that there were so many women that only wanted to sleep with him—well, I could but he paraded them like an event at Crufts. The ache between my legs didn't just disappear while I tried to get to sleep. His bedroom was next door to mine. I could hear him through the walls and it was infuriating.

He wanted to sleep with me. But why? I wasn't like the girls that visited him. They were mostly brunettes with small boobs and perfectly formed, slim bodies. Kirk had been great in bed, tender and gentle. I didn't want to think about him at all. He had hurt me, ruined my life, and it took me months to lift myself up. Sleep came after some time when Dexter finally settled in his own apartment.

The sound of my annoying alarm woke me up several hours later. I dragged myself out of bed and headed to the shower. When the water traced my skin I stroked myself, moaning and imagining how it would be to be one of those girls in Dexter Tyndall's bed.

Several minutes later I came out not feeling better at all, only more frustrated. I needed to get out with the girls from pole-dancing class. I didn't need a man.

I dressed in a smooth black dress that hung below the knee, styled my hair, and did some last-minute sprucing of the apartment, getting it ready for the viewing. I put some bags in the cupboards. In Joey's old bedroom, I'd found pictures of him and Dexter on a yacht. I didn't want to believe that they were friends, but the pictures suggested otherwise.

At five to two I had a call from the concierge, and the couple that had arranged a viewing arrived five minutes later with the estate agent. I opened the door for them, smiling politely. They were loaded, I could tell straight away. The woman was petite with wavy black hair, wearing designer clothes. The guy had a watch that cost more than my car.

I let them in and showed them around. The apartment and the complex were a style-conscious couple's wet dream. Everyone was in love with this stylish, modern building with top-notch appliances in the kitchen. The en-suite bathrooms were classically styled yet with modern accents, and the two bedrooms were spacious. I didn't know what to make of this couple. The man seemed quiet, not that impressed, but the woman, Sally, kept saying that she wanted to get it off the market today.

She loved everything about it and was already planning what she could do to one of the rooms. At some point I left them to it, smiling to myself, knowing that they were going to put in an offer today. Dexter could go to hell for all I cared. I had at least six weeks left here and I was planning to use this time to enjoy myself. After that I'd rent a small apartment somewhere in Edinburgh.

"Beautiful, and the views are mesmerising," Sally said, coming back to the living room with her husband and the estate agent. "How long have you been here?"

"Only a couple of days actually; my parents recently inherited this apartment from a relative and my mother wants to sell it," I explained.

"Well, you must enjoy it. I would love to get it today, but Mike wants to look over the paperwork with Pat here," she added. The husband gave me a silent nod to confirm what she said.

When we were just about to go out, she leaned over and whispered, "We will call you today. I want to buy this place."

I wanted to jump up and down. This couldn't get any better. We went outside while the men talked about the service charges and ground rent.

"Oh, Dex... harder, please... fuck me harder. You're so good at this."

We all stopped, turning towards the other terrace door. There was Dexter, still dressed in his suit, banging yet another brunette right out in open view of us all. The colour drained from my face and I stood horrified, watching as he moved inside her, as if completely unaware that he had an audience.

"You like that, yeah? I can keep fucking you all day long, baby," he rasped.

I looked at the potential buyers, who were standing bewildered, their faces twisted in distaste. Pat mumbled something about going to the lift.

Dex knew that we were there. He glanced at me briefly and flashed me one of his best smiles. I was ready to strangle him.

"This is outrageous," Sally muttered and started moving towards the lift. Finally Dexter's brunette noticed us and started hitting him.

"Dex, let's get inside. There are people here."

"Hold on, I'm close... God you're tight."

The wait for the lift was the longest few minutes in my life. I was mortified and wanted to disappear. The wife kept glancing back and then at me, like it was all my fault. That prick. I thought that he wasn't at home.

"I'm so sorry about this. I'll be having a word with the owner about such behaviour," I mumbled, trying to rescue the situation when the lift finally arrived.

"We will be in touch, Miss Scott. Goodbye," said the husband before Sally could add anything else.

That was it then. The elevator door closed and I stood there trying to breathe as the anger clouded my mind. They weren't going to make an offer. Dexter and his dick ruined this sale for me, probably intentionally. I was so livid that I could barely stand still.

After a few deep breaths I marched to his door and started banging at it, ready for a full-blown argument.

Seven

Sasha

I was caught completely off guard when he opened the door and was suddenly standing there shirtless, wearing only boxers. Every time I was in front of him, I was unable to form a coherent sentence. This was getting out of control. I had to get laid, sleep with someone, anyone, so I could push this asshole out of my head.

His eyes took me in, stopping as usual on my cleavage.

"You have picked the wrong person to play your stupid power games with. I know exactly what you are doing, Dexter," I roared in frustration, at the same time trying to dismiss his gorgeous brown eyes that were trailing down my body.

"It's Mr. Tyndall to you, Barbie, and I have no idea what you're talking about," he snarled, coming closer. He was barefoot and the heat from his body was like a new drug that I couldn't live without: addictive, but deadly. Why the hell did he have this kind of effect on me? We didn't even like each other.

"You won't win, fuckface, and you'll regret starting this, because I promise you that I'll make your life living hell," I shouted, poking my finger into that wide chest, losing my control. I wanted to punch him and I hated myself for feeling that irresistible pull of attraction to him. He was arrogant, intense, completely selfish and had no idea how to talk to people. So far I wasn't seeing any redeeming qualities in him, so what was the point of this?

"I want you in my bed, Barbie. Just one night. You really turn me on when you're angry," he growled, leaning over and bringing his face inches away from my lips. He smelled so masculine.

"I don't sleep with losers," I said, then turned around and marched back to my own apartment, slamming the door behind me.

Dexter

"I can't believe that you used me like that."

I turned around noticing Laura by the kitchen with her arms folded over her chest. She was one of the women that didn't take my nonsense until I made her come at least three times. Hard work, but a great fuck.

"Used you? I fucked you hard and you loved it."

"God, Dex, you're such a fucking asshole sometimes," she hissed.

"Maybe, but you like me anyway."

She shook her head and disappeared into the bedroom. I didn't fucking know what her problem was. Besides, she was putting her nose where she shouldn't have, trying to dig information out of me. I sat on the sofa and started switching channels on the TV. Laura appeared from the bedroom completely dressed.

"Where the fuck are you going?" I asked her, watching her put on her shoes by the front door.

"Home, you wanker! I want nothing to do with you anymore. I can't believe that you would stoop so low. The girl next door was having a viewing!" she said, raising her voice.

"Go to hell," I muttered.

"Gladly," she shouted and slammed the door behind her.

I ran my hand through my hair wondering what the hell was wrong with women these days. She had no idea what was going on between me and Sasha and it was none of her business. Besides, it wasn't like I wanted to fuck her again. The only person that I really had any desire for had compared shagging me less favourably to eating dirt.

I had to find out what Sasha's problem was. Okay, so maybe in the beginning I wasn't very nice to her, but all the women loved my bad-boy attitude and snappy tongue. She was different, and the fact that I didn't know anything about her was slowly driving me up the wall. I didn't do well in normal conversation. Yeah, I could simply go over there, apologise and try to woo her over, but that fucking well wasn't me.

I had sex when I needed it to tame the inner darkness, to ease the gloom that kept following me every day. She was so stubborn and my gut feeling told me that she just wasn't going to let me fuck her easily.

***

The next couple of weeks passed quickly and I wasn't getting anywhere near Sasha's bed. We hadn't had a chance to meet out in the corridor again, but I knew that she had more viewings. I paid someone at the estate agency to let me know of her progress with the sale. I wasn't comfortable with digging too much into her past so I didn't have her full history investigated. Everyone had their skeletons and all I wanted was to bang her, not marry the bitch.

I was surprised when I found out that she was a nurse. My contact told me that her parents were living in Glasgow and she'd moved out a few years ago. She had been working for the same agency for about ten months, doing a few shifts a week. Before she moved to Joey's apartment, she had lived in London.

Potential buyers kept coming and I was doing everything I could to turn them away. I knew that I wasn't doing myself any favours with winning her over, but I wasn't prepared to face a new resident in the apartment next door just yet.

Since that day on the terrace I couldn't think straight and my mood swings were more pronounced than normal. The guy in the estate agency that she dealt with was a greedy bastard. I knew his father and he kept filling me in with her upcoming appointments. A week from her first viewing, I borrowed three cats from my brother and let them run around the corridor when some older chick arrived for her viewing. At first I thought that it was an awesome idea, but when the cats started pissing everywhere I fucking lost it. The smell was horrendous and I had to pay a fortune to clean their stink out. But I achieved what I wanted: the woman didn't come back for a second viewing.

I paid Darren a fortune to put off some of the interested parties, but I didn't want Sasha to suspect anything, so I told him to keep at least one viewing a week.

For three straight weeks I was sabotaging Sasha's appointments. I played loud music, told one of the pensioners that the landlord didn't want any resident over sixty, and pretended that I was having a loud party when a family with two kids showed up.

Sasha didn't react and that worried me the most. She hadn't said anything to me while this whole thing was going on, but I knew that she was aware of what I was doing. It had been three weeks and I was getting tired of her indifference.

It was Thursday night and I was waiting for Courtney to come over. When I checked the time I realised that she was an hour late. We met through a mutual friend and she became my regular Thursday fuck.

In the past week, my messed-up mind kept waking me up at three in the morning every day. The weed didn't seem to be doing anything. I needed sex or more pills.

Three hours later there was still no sign of Courtney. My dick was hard and I was bouncing off the walls. Sasha's beautiful ass kept me high and dry. I grabbed my phone and dialled Courtney's number.

"Hello."

"Where the fuck are you? You should be here riding my cock," I shouted into the phone.

"Dex? Is that you?"

"No, it's Father Christmas. What the fuck?"

"I thought that you weren't in. The girl outside the complex said that you had some emergency."

"A girl? What the fuck are you talking about, Courtney?"

"The girl came out and said that she had a message from you. She said that you weren't in. Blond hair and terrible fashion sense."

"Fucking Sasha," I growled at the phone and hung up. I was up on my feet before I knew it. Bitch! How did she know that Courtney was coming over? Rage rippled through me as I slid the door to the terrace open and headed around to her apartment. When I reached her door, there was a piece of paper attached with a message on it.

Don't mess with me, fuckface. This is just the beginning.

Sasha

My pole-dancing training was going well. I made great progress in the first three weeks, slowly getting back to the shape I was in nine months ago. Everything in my life besides my apartment was falling into place, although today I was a little unfocused. My mind kept wandering off to Dexter.

It was easy to figure out the schedule he followed with the ladies and I couldn't help but mess with his sex life a little. Tonight, when I was leaving for my pole dancing classes, I spotted one of the brunettes outside in the car park, all groomed up and ready to see him. I made up a story about Dexter having an emergency and that stupid cow bought it all. I couldn't believe how easy it was. I decided to leave him a little message on my balcony door. My revenge was finally coming together.

He kept messing up my viewings, turning potential buyers away. I wasn't stupid—loud music, cats peeing in the corridor, and moans in the late hours of the morning. Well, he didn't know, but it was the beginning of a war.

I didn't like confrontation, but I grew up in a council estate in the rough part of Glasgow and I had to fight my own battles there. Life was hard and sometimes people took advantage of others, just because they could.

Dexter Tyndall was the landowner of the complex, but he didn't know that in the short period of time that I lived next to him, I found out a few very interesting things. He never went out during the week. He had his groceries delivered and he took short naps at four each afternoon. Yes, I was creepy enough to watch him from the terrace.

Turning women away was just the beginning of my plan. I wanted him to suffer, badly. He was probably going berserk without his favourite brunette.

Within two weeks, Gina asked me to work on my own routine. She showed me a few more advanced moves on the pole, then said that I was capable of training on my own. At first I struggled, but after doing exercises at home I was back on track. I normally worked out. I was slowly coming out of that vacant and dormant phase of my life. It was great to have people around me again.

I was exhausted by the time I drove back to the complex. Dexter was probably in his apartment. My phone rang when I was getting out of the car.

"How are you, darling? I haven't heard from you since you moved to that isolated place and I was a bit worried," Mum said. Yes, I meant to call her so many times and we kept missing each other. We'd had a little chat when I moved in, but we hadn't spoken since then.

"Yes, sorry, Mum. I meant to call, but I have been so busy with everything."

"I know, darling; don't worry about it. You sound much happier though."

"Yes, I am. It's great here."

"See, I told you. The timing was good. You weren't yourself in London," she said. My mother and I used to have a great relationship, but after my trauma with Kirk, I began distancing myself from her. Now I wanted to fix it by helping her with the inheritance, hoping that things could go back to the way they were.

"You were right. It's amazing here, but the guy next door is so annoying. He sleeps around with tons of women and he scared all the potential buyers away. I don't know how long it will take before we get an offer on this place," I explained to keep her in the loop. I didn't want to tell Mum that I was attracted to Dexter and that I kept dreaming about his amazing ripped body. It was embarrassing enough.

"Do you like him?" Mum asked.

Shit, I couldn't hide anything from her. She always knew that tone of voice. "No, I don't, Mum. He's arrogant, selfish, and he owns the whole complex. I can't stand him," I grumbled, closing my eyes and forgetting about how good it felt to be pinned down by him in his little office.

"Sasha, bunny, you haven't spoken about anyone else for almost a year. This man, your neighbour. I think maybe you should let yourself to get to know him."

"But, Mum, he's infuriating. Every day there is a different girl at his door and he's playing a game with me. He has plenty of money and even more connections. We are constantly fighting," I said, biting my lip and swallowing the gulp that suddenly appeared in my throat. Dexter Tyndall was stubborn, but I wasn't going to let him win.

"There is no rush with the apartment, darling. I'm happy that finally after months I'm talking to my Sasha again, my short-tempered, cranky and stubborn girl. I think you're finally passing through your grief. It'll never go away completely; you just learn to live with it. So go ahead and get to know this boy. I know you like him—I can tell—but you won't admit to it. Listen to what your heart wants, not your head."

I swallowed my tears, pushing away toxic memories. Mum was right. I had been hiding, pretending that my past hadn't crushed me. She knew me so well.

"He's not a boy, but a hot bastard that is not interested in relationships," I muttered.

"You can change him."

"I don't think so," I replied, hearing a beeping noise on the other side of the line. Mum was getting another phone call.

"Sorry, bunny, I have to go. I think your father is calling me."

"All right, Mum, talk to you later," I said and hung up.

Deep down I wanted to get to know Dexter, but I wasn't going to reach out to him. He had to stop sabotaging my viewings and apologise for the way he treated me.

When I walked up to my apartment, the corridor was empty. Dexter was either sleeping or he was out. There was a white envelope sitting on my doorstep. My stomach made a funny jolt. For some reason I had a feeling that somehow this was his revenge for turning his fuck buddy away.

I walked inside, locked the door and looked at it. On the top of the envelope there was a message.

To the Owner of Apartment 21

An Invitation for a Private Party in Apartment 30

Eight

Dexter

Mixer parties. I loved them and it had been a while since Harry had organised one. It wasn't one of those parties where people had sex with other people and by the end of the night everyone joined together in one big orgy. I wasn't into shit like that, and I didn't like myself in social situations. The aim of the mixer party was to bring together men and women who were single, but were only looking for no-strings-attached sex.

It was the best place to pick up the right women. I was done with Internet dating sites. I met women online that lied about everything: their age, height, their relationship status, the colour of their hair and their whole life in general. Sometimes I managed to find a few that only wanted sex, but most of them expected more from me. Always fucking more.

Harry was a banking investor. He bought a penthouse from me on the other wing last year. We got on pretty well and when I told him about the mixer party that I went to couple of years ago, he seemed intrigued. I didn't have many friends at the time, but Harry became one of them. He was single, affluent, and he didn't have to worry about his reputation amongst the other residents, so he decided to organise a similar thing.

A month later I received an invitation for a "Private Party" as he called it. He brought together over thirty single men and women and provided the food and entertainment, but that was just the beginning. The rules were simple. No couples were allowed and only certain select people were chosen. I had to make sure that no other resident in the building knew about what I was involved in.

Harry used his contacts to attract men and women from the local area who enjoyed uninhibited sex. Laura and Penny had come from the "Private Party." They knew exactly what I was looking for. Women filled my evenings and I had a gift for attracting them naturally.

Sasha's note on her balcony door made me furious. For a moment I was ready to smash her windows, but I thought better of it. I went back inside, thinking about ways of getting back at her. It was clear that she wasn't planning to sleep with me, so I had to change my game. She was ready to go to war with me over her stupid apartment.

I didn't think that she was a prude and I knew for a fact that she didn't have a boyfriend. The solution was simple: the mixer party. I asked Harry to send her an invitation. We both avoided attracting the attention of the residents, although at this point I was willing to risk anything to have Sasha in my bed.

Harry agreed and the invitation was left outside her door on Thursday evening. When I left for a meeting on Friday morning, the envelope was gone, so I knew that she must have read it. I smiled to myself and left to make another costly investment with one of my clients.

I drank half a bottle of whiskey last night, but the alcohol wasn't making much difference in my sleeping pattern. I still woke up at four this morning. My thoughts were racing and I was certain that Sasha had something to do with it. I couldn't fucking stop thinking about her.

I felt like I was walking in a thick, never-ending mist. The heaviness on my chest hadn't gone away. Each fucking day was a struggle. Thoughts about Pap kept invading my mind.

Maybe Mum was right; maybe it was time to see the doctor. I didn't know what was wrong with me. I was fit, ate well, but I felt empty. I was never tired. For some reason I always wanted to do stuff—and have sex. Yeah, the sex was never boring.

On Saturday at six a.m. I went to the gym and worked out for an hour. On the way to my apartment I caught the lift. The doors were just about to close. When I slid inside I couldn't fucking believe it. Barbie was there, scrolling through her phone. She hadn't noticed me yet.

She must have just finished her shift, because she was still in her sexy nurse's uniform. Her blond hair was tied up in a messy knot. Fuck me, she was so cute I was already imagining her playing naughty nurse with me.

"You know, I did enjoy your little note," I said, startling her. She lifted her eyes at me and inhaled sharply.

"What, are you stalking me now?" she asked.

"I'm in the fucking lift, Barbie. Don't be stupid."

"Ha, funny. I told you, stop messing with me. You don't want me as your enemy," she snapped and went back to looking at her phone, ignoring me. She was more stubborn than me and for some reason I liked that about her. When the lift stopped on our floor, I wasn't done with her yet. I had to know if she was going to show up at the mixer party tonight.

When she stepped forward I blocked the door.

"I jerked off last night thinking about your wet pussy," I said. Okay, sometimes I talked like a fucking horny teenager, but right now was all about pressing her angry hot buttons. This party would give me a chance to show her what she was missing out on.

"Get out of my way, fuckface. I'm tired," she said, looking more pissed than usual.

"Private Party, you got an invite, right? You have been selected, Barbie," I threw it out there watching to see how she would react.

"I don't do swing parties, asshole. I can meet people in a civilised way. Now get out of my way."

"You're afraid of what might happen when you get cornered by me at the party," I teased her, knowing that she liked being challenged. She bit her lip and my cock twitched. Fuck, I was getting hard again imagining what those lips wrapped around my throbbing dick would feel like.

"You will see exactly what happens tonight when I have other men around me. Apparently I can pick up men up there for sex. Well, you can watch me around others, knowing that you will never have me," she said, then pushed me aside and strutted out of the lift.

Sasha

I hurried away before I dropped myself into more crap. Why did I have to say that I was going? I wasn't even thinking about it when I got the invitation. There was no return address or the name of who sent it. The instructions simply stated that I had to be outside Apartment 30 at eight o'clock sharp.

It was the perfect opportunity to show Dexter that I could do better than him. I needed to have sex and he had challenged me yet again. These days nothing scared me. Yes, for nine months I allowed myself to be a prisoner of my past, but I was done with hiding. Dexter was going to be there and I wanted to piss him off by talking and flirting with other men.

Today's shift was exhausting and I had to get some sleep, at least until late afternoon. The invitation stated that I needed to wear something sexy. The food and drinks were provided.

I had a gut feeling that I was making a big mistake, but I couldn't let him beat me with whatever game he was playing. Half an hour later, I was stripped to my pyjamas and cuddled in my comfortable sheets.

All Joey's stuff was packed away in boxes. I'd emptied out the other bedroom. He owned a lot of expensive electronics. Mum wanted to get rid of this place, but this whole thing was going to take time. I had to either sleep with Dexter or ask him for help, and that wasn't going to happen.

I fell asleep pretty much straight away. Several hours later, when the clock showed four in the afternoon, I felt rested. Last night I was running up and down around the ward. A lot of children couldn't settle into sleep, so I spent all night watching them.

After a quick shower I threw some clothes on and opened the balcony doors to let some fresh air through. The terrace was empty and I exhaled with relief that Dexter wasn't there to annoy me. He'd surprised me again, being up at six on Saturday morning. He looked so good in a T-shirt and sweatpants.

After I puttered around the house, I made a quick, late lunch and ate it on the terrace. I had no idea if he was inside or not; his balcony doors were shut. The sea was calm today, so after I polished off my meal, I went down and walked around on the coast, trying to prepare myself mentally for tonight's party.

Two hours later, I was back in my bedroom, picking out an outfit. Sexy? God yes, I needed to get laid, but the only person that I wanted was Dexter and he was off limits.

I went for a body-hugging, silky black dress that showed off my body and emphasised my boobs and my long legs. After almost three and a half weeks in pole-dancing training, my body was firm and nicely toned. I felt good in my skin. I decided to curl my blond hair, then added heavy eyeliner to my eyes and put on red lipstick.

When I looked at my reflection in the mirror I felt sexy as hell. It had been a while since I went out anywhere looking like this. The questions in my head remained. Was I willing to push my boundaries enough to have sex with a complete stranger? In the past few weeks Alistair, one of the male nurses that I worked with, kept asking me out on a date. He was cute, but I promised myself I didn't need another man in my life. Dating and relationships terrified me. Alistair was pretty funny; not quite physically the type that I would go for, but he actually made me laugh. So far I kept turning him down.

I didn't sleep around, but I also wasn't the same weak woman I was.

I sprayed on my favourite Dior perfume and took a few deep breaths, feeling ready for the party. I had no idea where Apartment 30 was, so I went to the concierge for directions.

My stomach was churning when I knocked. A handsome man who appeared to be in his late twenties opened the door. He was wearing an expensive-looking suit and had a glass of champagne in his hand. His piercing blue eyes seemed to acknowledge me instantly. Maybe Dexter already told him that I would show up.

"I see that you got the invitation," he said and stepped away to let me through. My legs were like jelly, but the sound of his voice was comforting. Soft music played in the background; men and women gathered around in a stylish living room talking. In the middle of the room by the terrace, there was a pole. My heart hitched in my throat. Of course, the pole fit perfectly into the sexy, slightly deviant atmosphere.

"Yes, I did. I'm not sure why," I mumbled, suddenly feeling like I didn't belong here.

"I'm Harry, the host," he introduced himself.

Then he began going over the rules, which were pretty straightforward. Everyone here was single and available for sex. Harry mentioned that people used this party to get to know each other and exchange contacts, not to have sex straight away.

"You seem nervous. Come on, let me get you a drink, Sasha," he said and pressed his palm over my lower back as he led me towards the kitchen. My stomach was in knots.

This wasn't at all how it was supposed to turn out when I inherited Uncle Joey's apartment.

Harry broke my train of uncomfortable thoughts and handed me a glass of champagne. He was very confident, but he didn't make me feel uncomfortable.

"Thank you, I think I need that," I said.

"Okay, let me introduce you to a few people."

"No need, Harry. She knows me and I'm the only person that she is going to fuck tonight," said the familiar sexy voice behind me that sent a shiver through me.

Dexter. He was already there.

Nine

Dexter

Sasha looked amazing with that short black dress that barely covered her ass. She didn't notice me standing on the other side of the room when she walked through the door. Hell, I had to take control of my fucking dick, because I was already rock hard for her.

She had the perfect body, curves in the right places and fantastic breasts. Wow, I was going to come in my pants just looking at her. I wasn't the only one that noticed how beautiful she looked tonight. All the other sad fuckers in the room had been following her every move since she walked in. This wasn't going to be easy. I wanted to grab her and claim her as mine, but I knew that this wasn't the way to do it. She hated my guts, so I had to play it carefully.

"I'm not your property, Dexter. I'm here, which means that I can choose whoever I please," she replied, lifting her glass to sip some of her champagne. I glanced at Harry, who was watching us silently. He looked amused. He knew that I was interested in her. A wave of jealous rage was slowly filling me and I needed to calm the fuck down. I wanted to spread her legs and slide my cock between these gorgeous thighs and claim her right there.

"I'm the one for you, Barbie," I said.

"Harry, would you please introduce me around? I'd rather jump out of the window than stay here and listen to this asshole."

"Your wish is my command. Safe hunting, Dexter," Harry said, winking at me. Bastard, he was mocking me, but it was just a warm-up. Sasha was going to be mine by the end of the night.

I watched as he started introducing her to a few guys that I knew from the previous parties. Gavin, Rich and the new guy with a black beard. A lot of times Harry invited the same men and women, but tonight there were only a few faces that I recognised. I needed to get laid, and Sasha wasn't buying my cocky attitude, but ever since I met her I couldn't think about anyone else but her.

I hated crowds and being around people in general. Normally I felt shut in, trapped, almost claustrophobic. It was easier to overcome these fears in my day-to-day job, but I struggled during parties and functions.

"Hey, handsome, how are you?"

A short brunette in a long red dress touched my shoulder. She was new and she was exactly the type that I was used to. Small, perky tits with a slim, almost waif-like stature and dark hair. That was before I met Sasha.

"Let's get straight to the point, darling. We're both here because we like to fuck," I said, finishing my whisky. This was my second glass, but the alcohol was helping me with the mounting darkness that was slowly creeping through.

She looked shocked that I was so blunt. The problem was that I wasn't interested in any other pussy tonight except Sasha's.

"Well, I'm sure that we can come to some sort of agreement," she purred with a smile.

"Whatever, lady. Go and find something to do. I'll find you when I'm ready," I snapped at her.

"Show some respect. I'm not going to be treated like some cheap whore." She scowled at me.

"If you're not a cheap whore, then what the hell are you doing here?" I asked her. She called me an asshole and walked away. Good. I wasn't in the mood anyway. This was going to be long night and I had to get myself drunk enough to numb the asshole me and switch to a nicer Dexter. Screw it, I didn't do nice, but Sasha hated the real me and I was desperate for her to come back home with me.

For the next couple of hours I stood alone in the corner watching her talk to other men. She looked uncomfortable, but she was doing everything in her power to hide it. Women came and went away after trying to talk to me, but I wasn't making an effort. The food was brought around on little trays, and I shoved some canapés into my mouth so at least I had something to do rather than just feeling like shit. My head was screwed and I had no idea why I wanted Sasha so much. She glanced at me from time to time from under her lashes, with that cute flush on her cheeks. When Gavin wrapped his arm around her waist, I thought I was going to smash his jaw.

I should have known this was going to happen when I challenged her to show up here tonight. It was a fucking swing party, for Christ's sake, but Sasha wasn't like the others. She didn't have that predatory hunger in her eyes. She needed the closeness the intimacy of a lover. Why was I thinking this? I was turning into a total fucking pussy.

"How long are you going to stand here and pretend that you don't give a fuck?" Harry asked, approaching me. He had changed the music into something more sensuous: Massive Attack's "Angel," I think. The waitresses that carried the canapés were dressed in Playboy bunny costumes. Only Harry could pull off something like that.

"I don't. Pussies come and go. There's plenty here, but I'm not in the mood tonight."

"Are you ever *not* in the mood? You turned down Dorothy and she models for top fashion houses," Harry said, sipping his drink. Fucking model, it was probably the one that looked like a skeleton. She was just skin and bones, nothing to grab on to, no curves, no luscious flesh to press into. She was usually my type, but I just wasn't interested tonight.

"There will be more," I muttered. Harry turned to face me, but I ignored him.

"You like the blondie, don't you? You've been watching her like a hawk all evening," he observed.

"I want to fuck her and she wants it, too, but she's pretending that she isn't into me," I growled, trying to hide my annoyance, but Harry picked up on it. He just knew me too well, like Joey used to.

"There's more to it. Why she is here anyway? She doesn't strike me as a type that would sleep with anyone that freely."

I fucking know it. You don't need to tell me that.

He was screwing with me, clever bastard. I knew that as soon as I fucked Sasha I could move on to someone else and get back to my usual routine of daily random fucks.

"Tell Gavin to keep his dick in his pants. Blondie is mine," I said, seeing how that asshole was touching her all over while she was trying to push him off. Harry laughed and was just about to say something else, but the sound of his phone distracted him. He picked the call up, walking away.

My hands were itching and I was battling with myself about whether or not to go and talk to her. I wasn't scared of anything, but I was anxious about playing the nice guy. Women expected me to behave a certain way.

Sasha managed to pull away from Gavin and his company and she was heading to the kitchen. I was just about to follow her, when someone grabbed me from behind.

"Hello, stranger, long time no see. My pussy has missed you."

Victoria, of course. How could I not suspect that she would be here, fishing for my cock yet again?

Sasha

"What do you mean you can't dance?"

I was eavesdropping on Harry's conversation while helping myself to some food. Was this about the pole dancer?

That guy Gavin kept running his fingers over my spine, asking me if I was interested in him. He seemed nice but a bit over the top, and I wanted to slap his hand that traced my naked flesh. Dexter was watching me the whole time, I'd noticed. I could see that women were approaching him, but he didn't react, as if he wanted to send them away.

"Jackie, I don't have a replacement, and my guests are waiting. What am I supposed to do now?"

I almost dropped my plate. Harry's dancer had stood him up. I glanced at the pole and imagined myself up there as everyone's eyes were on me. In the past few weeks I had been working very hard on my own routine. Hell, I was confident enough to perform the dance here. Dexter wanted to use me, but there was no one else at this party that I wanted.

"Crap, she was a waste of my valuable time," Harry muttered, standing behind me.

I bit my lip. If I wanted to do this, I had to say something now. "What's the matter?" I asked him.

"My pole dancer cancelled on me. Apparently she twisted her ankle, but I bet she had another performance somewhere else that was much more important to her. Why do I never learn? This isn't the first time."

"I can replace her," I said quietly looking at him.

"Replace her? What do you mean?" he asked furrowing his brow.

"I've been doing pole dancing for years. I can perform for your guests," I said, feeling embarrassed all of a sudden because he was staring at me as if I had lost my mind. I shouldn't have said anything.

"You can dance on the pole? Seriously?" he asked.

"Oh, forget that I said anything," I snapped and turned away, but he grabbed my elbow.

"Seriously, Sasha, I'm not joking right now. If you're good, then you'd be doing me a great favour," he argued.

I glanced at Dexter, who was kissing some black-haired supermodel. Great, so he already had moved on to someone else. "I think that I'm good enough."

"Sorted then. What do you need to get ready?"

Gee, I hadn't thought about what I could wear. This party needed a stripper, so I had to scream of sex and pull out the most erotic routine I could think of. I couldn't dance in my current outfit.

"I have to pop into my apartment for a minute and then we can start."

"Excellent. You're a life-saver, darling, and by the way, Dexter may be unstable, but he's a decent guy when he wants to be."

I smiled and left Harry's apartment as soon as possible. Dexter and the girl had vanished and I wondered if he was having sex with her in one of Harry's rooms.

When I got to my bedroom, I started searching through my clothes. After throwing more than half of my wardrobe on the floor, I slowly realised that I didn't own anything sexy enough.

I was looking through my underwear drawer when I noticed a small bag in the bottom, hidden between my other clothes. When I looked inside, my heart kicked in my chest.

Remembering my shopping trip from a year ago, I pulled out a skintight, red-hot, strapless sequin romper with a pitchfork and devil horns. Could this be it? I bought this costume over a bet and never got to wear it. I hadn't intended to bring it with me to Scotland, but somehow I must have packed it with other stuff.

I didn't have much time to think about this. Harry was waiting. I stripped and put the costume on. It was tight, almost too tight and I felt self-conscious staring at myself in the mirror. The top curved in a sweetheart neckline over my boobs, clinging to them so that you could see the exact shape and size of them including my nipples. The suit moulded itself to my body and was cut like a pair of boy shorts so that my arse cheeks were more than half visible. Dear God, could I actually do this? I put the horns on, and my red heels. For at least an hour I could transform myself into someone else. This outfit exposed everything I was trying to hide—my ass and huge thighs—but I knew that Dexter wouldn't be able to take his eyes off me.

I ran back to Apartment 30, using the stairs this time, thinking that I couldn't back out now. I had thrown a black silk robe over me, so as not to upset the neighbours. When I slipped back into Harry's apartment, everyone was still there talking and laughing. A few couples were scattered around in the corners. There was no sign of Dexter, thank God. He was probably still screwing the brunette in the back bedroom.

Harry dragged me to the hallway and made me take my robe off. As his eyes took me in, he stopped breathing altogether.

"Sasha, oh dear lord, you look sexy," he whispered.

"Oh shut up, I didn't have anything else."

"If you won't pick up that idiot, Dexter, I would be honoured to ask you out," he said with a serious expression. I giggled nervously. Harry seemed nice, not like any other men out there.

"I thought you don't date?"

He grinned. "For a girl like you I would change into a monogamist."

"Stop embarrassing me. You don't even know me."

"You don't even know how sexy you look right now. Bloody gorgeous," he said. "Anyway, I'll catch you after. I need to let everyone know that you're going to perform. Are you ready?"

"Yes," I said confidently.

He gave me a warm smile and walked back to the living room. All of a sudden I was terrified. The lights went off, leaving only the area around the pole lit.

"Ladies and gentlemen, it's time for the best part of this evening. Sasha has agreed to perform for us. Please welcome her warmly."

Someone whistled and I heard a few claps. It was time to lock up my pride and do what I could do best—dance on the pole.

Ten

Dexter

"How many times do I have to tell you, Victoria? I don't fucking want your needy pussy," I shouted, trying to concentrate while these assholes in the living room were whistling and clapping. Harry mentioned something about the pole dancer, but I didn't give a damn.

"We had a great time together, Dex," she purred, spreading herself on the bed and showing me her tits. Her eyes glittered as she started licking off her finger. She was poisonous, draining me of my precious energy.

"Stay the fuck away from me, or I'll ruin you," I snapped and left the room ready to smash something. She was unbelievable. We fucked a few times and then she started talking some shit about being in a relationship, following me around and spreading some silly rumours.

I ran my hand through my hair, cursing her off in my head. All the lights in the living room were off and everyone looked mesmerised by the girl that was performing. I lifted my gaze to check what all the fuss was about, and my heart fucking stopped. For about thirty seconds I tried to figure out if I was having problems with my eyes. This wasn't possible. There was no way that she was doing this shit.

Sasha was on the pole, wearing a strapless sequin romper and red devil horns attached to her head, exposing her magnificent body, bending and spinning around the metal bar.

How could I have fucking missed that?

My Barbie was like a fantasy come true swirling itself around me, thickening my desire for her as my heart pounded away. I couldn't breathe. Surging heat shot down to my groin, hardening my cock in an instant. I watched as Sasha smiled and grabbed the pole. She kept her outside leg straight as she swung it out to the side and stepped all the way around the pole, pivoting on her inside foot at the same time.

The shit she was doing with her legs was unreal and I was so fucking turned on that I thought I was going to lose my mind. This was better than a strip club. She finished whatever she was doing by arching her body backwards, lowering her hand to allow for a deeper arch.

I stood there watching her as she was doing all sort of spins, looking comfortable and shooting her audience sexy glances. I wanted to devour her lips, biting her softly, teasing her tongue with mine. I felt like I was in a fucking lustful trance the whole time I had my eyes on her. I could feel my blood heating every second she bent her body on the pole, exposing her glorious ass to all these men in the room.

The next thing I knew she was lying on her elbow, extending her legs straight up towards the ceiling and pointing her toes. Then she bent one leg at a time and rotated clockwise.

If Harry switched on all the lights now everyone would be fucking aware of my stiff cock. Blood pounded in my ears, and it looked like she was only just starting this show.

She was dancing and crawling up the pole. This shit was unbelievably erotic. I imagined bending her over my bed and pounding my cock into her, replacing that metal bar. She used her hand to hold herself and lifted her lower body up, over her head. Then she wrapped her legs around the pole, crossing them at the ankles and gripping the pole tightly between her legs. She had a devil-may-care attitude about some things and I loved that naughty sparkle in her eyes when she was mischievous like that.

Her every move was provoking, pulling me in deeper, and this whole thing was happening right in front of my eyes. I pictured my head between those strong thighs, licking her swollen clit. Sasha was one hundred percent woman. She was perfect, sensual, beautiful and all I wanted was to have her in my bed.

She loosened her grip to slide down the pole, tucking her head in. My cock kept throbbing painfully and sweat broke out on the sides of my neck. Sexy, rough music was blasting. Every time she bent over or gripped the pole with her legs I almost came in my pants. This wasn't fucking normal. It was a torture.

Several minutes later, she was done, and men around me were whistling, women were clapping. My head was clouded with lust. The lights came on and she bowed, smiling. I licked my lips waiting for her to look at me, but after a second she disappeared, not paying much attention to anyone.

I pressed my dick down with my palm, breathing like I'd just run a mile, and strolled after her. Harry stepped in, blocking my way.

"Get away. I need to see her," I said, ready to force my way past him.

"Come on, man, give her some space. She's changing," he said, looking at me with irritation. What the fuck did I do now? "Dex, you really need to be careful with this girl."

"Why? What did she say to you?"

"She didn't need to say anything, but she isn't like the ones in here that you can use and then toss away."

"What the fuck happened to you? Did those blond curls fuck with your mind too?" I challenged him, trying to figure out if he wanted Sasha now. This was getting out of control. I was ready to beat on my friend over a blonde.

"I mean it. Just don't screw with her, and we shouldn't have a problem. She's in my bedroom," he added and then stepped away. Shit, maybe he was right. I couldn't just barge inside and continue behaving like an asshole. This wasn't getting me anywhere.

I knew Harry's apartment like the back of my hand. I didn't want to knock. I just had to see her again in that hot outfit. I pressed on the door, aware that I had to step out of my comfort zone to make her mine.

Sasha

I was aching all over and my breathing was irregular, but I felt amazing. The performance went better than I expected. I glanced at the mirror and saw that my face was red. Then I noticed that I wasn't alone anymore. Dexter was standing in the room, not moving.

"What the hell do you want?" I asked, glaring at him. He didn't even knock, just barged in here like he owned the place.

"That was fucking hot, Sasha, and I would like a private dance... please," he said, losing his usual superior and demanding tone. That was a first, but I couldn't just forget his pranks.

"I don't give private dances, so you can leave now."

"What if I won't?"

I rolled my eyes and kept trying to sort out my messy hair in the mirror. He was still standing there, his eyes hovering over my backside.

"What do you want from me, Dexter? I mean apart from sex?"

He shoved his hands deep into his pockets and looked away. Wow, for the first time since we'd met he had nothing to say, no witty remarks or insulting ways of saying that he wanted to stick his cock inside me. I couldn't believe it. Maybe Dexter Tyndall wasn't so mouthy after all when it came to normal conversation.

"I'm not the nice guy you need, but there is something about you, Barbie, that makes me want you."

"If you want to sleep with me, then you need to learn how to treat me with respect. I'm a person, not a thing that you can play with," I said and picked up my horns that I had taken off earlier on. When I looked up, he was just behind me. His eyes changed, bringing warmth and heat, silencing my internal battle with what was wrong and right.

"I admit, we got off on the wrong foot and I'm sorry about the way I've acted around you. The truth is that I'm fed up with running after you," he whispered, leaning over and pressing his hard chest over my back. Lust curled up my toes, taking away that reasonable side of me and replacing it with the old me. I was amazed with the fact that he was trying to sound genuine. Maybe he did care?

I took a deep breath and turned around to face him.

"What if I tell you that I want to hang out, get to know you, before I drop my knickers for you?" I said very quietly. I could see my own flustered reflection in his deep brown eyes. The kiss... *oh my*, I wanted him to sink his mouth into mine, so I could taste his soft lips.

"I'm incapable of being in a relationship, and in my opinion, love is for losers. All I know, all I've ever known is sex and only sex. I can assure you that you will be screaming with pleasure when I feast on your sweet pussy."

There was a lump in my throat and I couldn't swallow it. His eyes were stinging my skin with lust, heat paralysed my joints. My knickers were wet and he hadn't even touched me yet.

"I'm not looking for a relationship, Dexter, but at the same time I expect you to treat me with respect. I know that you're no Prince Charming, but make the effort at least once in a while. Get to know me and then we will see," I said, pushing this whole thing where it shouldn't be going. He fucked his way through life. He was right. I didn't know the real him. Maybe he wasn't capable of behaving any other way.

Okay, so what? I wanted him to devour me hard and fast. This was bad and all, but I couldn't help myself. It'd been almost a year since I looked at another man the way I used to look at Kirk.

Staring into Dexter's rich brown eyes, I saw his despair, hollowness and pain. He was hiding behind his arrogance, acting to cover his real self.

Then his mouth was on mine. His kiss was forceful, primal, claiming my mouth but sensual at the same time. I thought that my knees were going to give out at any moment when he brought me closer to his chest. The kiss was more than just him running his mouth over mine; it seemed like he was consuming every inch of me, until I couldn't draw any more oxygen into my lungs. My heart pounded between my ribs as his tongue slid into my mouth.

I moaned, losing whatever resistance I had. The muscles around my abdomen tightened. I felt his hard cock pressed over my thigh, slowly teasing the entrance to my core. When he pulled away, I wanted to cry out for the lost touch. I was turned on, so wet for him when I shouldn't have been. My body craved more, expecting it, demanding it. When I looked at his eyes there was pure lust there and he was smirking at me.

"I told ya that you would want me, Barbie. Don't worry, we will get to know each other better tomorrow. I can't promise I'll change, but I'll make an effort for you, with the dating and all that. Now you need to let me leave or I swear to God I'll bend you over the bed and fuck you in that sexy little costume of yours. Stay away from guys in the other room and remember your pussy belongs to me."

My lips didn't seem to be working again. He left the bedroom before I had a chance to ask him if he was still messing with me or was he serious? I turned into mush around him. I glanced at my own reflection in the mirror, asking myself the same thing. Was I crazy?

Yet again I let him play me, but that kiss—I felt it in every inch of my body. The throbbing between my legs was like hot lava, drenching me with need.

I was just about to pack my stuff and leave when I spotted a white, crumpled paper lying on the carpet. I turned around and picked it up and started unfolding it slowly. It was some sort of message. I was sure that something had fallen out of Dexter's pocket when he was leaving. Or did it fall out of my bag? The writing was small and very uneven. It took me a moment to grasp that it was personal letter to Dexter from Uncle Joey. I didn't waste much time thinking about the content and started reading it straight away.

Dex!

I know that you don't want to hear me rambling about the other evening, but I'm a stubborn old man and I needed to tell you how much I appreciate what you have done for me.

Yes, I have a laptop, but I have been writing to people all my life and I'm not planning to stop for the sake of technology. Besides, letters are personal and more meaningful. You should try replying to one, out of courtesy.

Right now I'm enjoying myself in sunny Marbella, drinking Pina Coladas with fifty-year- old Priscilla. She is a stunner and if you could see her right now you'd agree. We are planning to sail to Portugal in a week or so.

I'm going to give you the same advice as always.

Stop locking yourself in your apartment and start to socialise, explore Edinburgh, and start a new hobby. Grow some balls.

I don't get it—why do you want to spend all your evenings with an old grump like me? You probably think that I don't know what I'm talking about, but in the past two years I got to know you pretty well. Your problems won't magically disappear if you stay locked away in an empty room.

I haven't had any seizures for years. My epilepsy is mild and it had always been controlled by medications. That evening when you found me, I was under a lot of pressure. Some unexpected news had reached me and I was stressed, worried about someone that used to be very close to me. I guess it was my lucky day that you decided to visit me just after the attack started. I can't thank you enough. You reacted quickly and efficiently, placing that cushion under my head, moving me away from any danger, and I'm still thankful you stayed with me until the ambulance arrived. After I stopped convulsing I was amazed that you didn't simply panic, like other people would.

I know what you're probably thinking: that I'm too old to look after myself and I need someone to check up on me once in a while. Dexter, you couldn't be more wrong. I'll be fine, so don't plan to hire anyone for me.

I also want you to start considering your own future. Yes, you do have a business and your family, but you have to start thinking about settling down. You need a loving and beautiful woman in your life. Trust the old man on this. Too much fun is never good for you.

Our friendship means a lot to me. I appreciate our evenings together, and our golf tours on the weekends. I even started watching some shows on that Netflix thing you showed me a few weeks ago. You were right—I do like those Sopranos. *Why is Tony always eating though? Now I don't think I'll ever be bored.*

I'm proud of you, proud that you didn't lose control that evening.

Go out, meet new people while I'm enjoying my time in Spain. Don't sit around and wait for me. You have a couple of weeks to practise golf, because I'm planning to beat you as soon as I get back.

Joey

I re-read the letter a few times, digesting the words, the message and that strong unique voice that belonged to a man I had never met. Dexter and Joey were friends. I didn't want to believe it, but the proof was right in front of me. My dead uncle was an epileptic, liked gangster movies and golf. And apparently Dexter had found him when he was going through a seizure. From this letter I found out more about Joey than I ever had.

It looked like Dexter had looked after my uncle and spent a lot of time with him when he was living next door.

Was it possible that there was more to Dexter beneath the nasty, obnoxious behaviour he'd shown me since I got here? Harry said that very thing to me only a few moments ago.

I knotted the paper back into a ball and hid it in my cleavage. Dexter must have dropped it accidentally when he was here in the room. There wasn't any other explanation.

I took my time changing, convincing myself that I was a challenge to Dexter, that he wasn't actually planning to date me.

I was afraid to come out, to face him again. I didn't believe that he simply had left. After fixing up my makeup and exercising my breathing for about a minute, I stepped back into the living room wearing my black dress. My eyes searched for Dexter, but he wasn't around. There was a possibility that he had picked up a woman and taken her to his apartment. What did I expect anyway? That he could change for me? Why should I believe that one statement he made about making an effort for me? I couldn't be that stupid. Maybe his friendship with Joey meant that he was someone else, but what if he wasn't ready to show me that part of himself?

"Sasha, that was superb and so sexy," Harry said, embracing me in a hug. "And Dexter, I have never seen him so mesmerised by anyone. Don't tell him that I told you that."

"Where is he?" I asked.

"He left a few minutes ago. I have no idea what you said to him, but this is the first time that he ever left alone."

Okay, that didn't mean anything. Besides, I shouldn't care. I didn't want to admit it, but I was relieved. I couldn't help thinking that maybe he would see more in me than just a quick fuck. After all, I was Joey's niece and he had respected the man.

When I glanced at the clock I realised that it was after eleven. I was bullshitting myself, thinking that I could do this, pick up some random guy for sex. The truth was that Dexter had been rocking my boat since I moved in here. Now I had a clear indication that I needed to get to know him.

"Thank you, Harry, for giving me a shot. I'm going to go as well. To be honest with you, this party isn't really for me."

Wow, Sasha, you just admitted to this hot guy that you don't sleep around. Pathetic.

"I know, darling. Go on, run to him. I bet he's waiting for you, and thank you for rescuing me tonight."

"Anytime. It was nice to meet you. Don't be a stranger. I'm in twenty-one, so pop in and see me before I disappear. And Dexter isn't my Prince Charming; he is just some guy that wants to get into my pants."

"Aren't we all?" he asked, grinning.

I shook my head and left. Gavin and all the guys that had talked to me were already busy with other women. I rolled my eyes and walked back to my own apartment, knowing that I wasn't like them. I wanted more, so why would I get hooked on a man like Dexter, thinking that he could fulfill this stupid need?

Dexter's placed seemed quiet. I was tempted to knock at his door, but I quickly went inside and locked the door, knowing that this would be a mistake. Tonight, he'd showed me a different side of him. It was just words and I had no idea if he was going to remember any of it tomorrow. There was definitely more to Dexter than his rude remarks and fiery attitude. He had a filthy mouth and I liked it, but I was ready to die rather than admit to him that he was turning me on.

Eleven

Dexter

Sasha had led me into one of my oblivious dark moods, pushing my self-control, so I left, locking myself in my apartment. I was inches away from taking her on that bed and fucking her until she couldn't take it anymore. I was so lost seeing her bending and crawling around that pole.

On top of that, Victoria crashed the party, screwing with my already fucked-up thoughts.

I wanted Sasha. She was the sexiest woman that I have ever met and her movements on the pole drove my lust for her even more. Whenever I closed my eyes I had her round ass in my face.

I didn't want to sink in deep, but as soon as my head hit the pillow I was out. My limbs felt like they weighed a ton. I'd left the party because I couldn't deal with the emotional garbage. Joey was gone, and there was no one that could listen to my raging rambles and make sense of them. I was on my own. This time I didn't get up at four in the morning, but I slept right through.

Whenever I hit one of these moods, I didn't need alcohol or drugs to get me to sleep, but then the morning was the worst, because I had no energy to get up. My cock was rock hard, and the world around me spun. For the first time in a while I had no motivation to do anything, but I promised Sasha that I would be nicer than normal.

I had to drag my body out of bed. When I put my clothes on, I was fighting against the hollowness that settled deep in my limbs. It took me an hour to convince my shitty self that she was just another task. Once I'd shagged her, I wouldn't have to worry about anything else.

I found the nearest Starbucks a few miles from the complex, bought two lattes and drove home thinking about what I was going to say to her. Back in my apartment, I went around my terrace.

I had no clue if Sasha was still sleeping or not, but I needed to see her. When I pressed my head to the glass, she wasn't in the living room, so I fiddled with the key for a minute and then slid the door open to get inside. Anyone else would probably call the police and they would charge me with breaking and entering, but Sasha loved my attention.

Most of Joey's stuff was missing, and I noticed a lot of boxes by the door. I was curious to know what Sasha was like, so I started nosing around. On the cabinet there were pictures of her smiling with a man and a woman, probably her parents. She looked happy.

I had to get a fucking grip. Fine; she wanted me to get to know her? All right. I could play nice for a day or two, but that was it. I wasn't planning to stay in her life for long. Besides, Joey's apartment was still on the market.

"What are you doing here?"

Fuck, how did I not hear her coming out of her bedroom? I turned around quickly and put my usual, arrogant smirk on my face. Some things weren't easy to change.

"I brought you coffee, Barbie," I said slowly, realising what she was wearing. White, very tight shorts and a loose top. She wasn't wearing a bra and her nipples were poking through the thin material of her top. Shit, this was going to end badly.

She took the coffee, glaring at me with suspicion. My dick started twitching as my eyes couldn't help but wander to her hard nipples.

"Stop staring at my boobs and you'd better tell me—how did you get inside my property? The balcony door was locked."

"Joey gave me a key. We were kind of close," I explained, not prepared to say anymore.

She looked a little surprised, but there was some sort of acknowledgement in her eyes. "So this whole persona? The bad Dexter? It's just an act, right?"

"I don't act, Barbie. This is who I am; you either like it or not," I said, lowering my eyes to her tits again. Hell, I was ready to shove my face between those knockers. That was my idea of heaven. She didn't need to know me. We were only going to fuck, that was all.

She rolled her eyes at me and sipped her coffee.

"Is there anything else you want?" she asked. She was throwing me out and I'd just bought her a coffee. She had cheek. I wasn't ready to leave her yet.

"We are having dinner at my place tonight, and then you're going to dance for me," I informed her.

She raised her left eyebrow. "You don't really know how to talk to a woman, do you?"

"Of course I do," I said. "Now, don't tell me that you changed your mind about dancing for me?"

"What? When did I ever… oh, never mind. Fine, I'll have dinner with you, but we'll have to see about that dance. You need to behave first."

I could see a small smile appearing on her sweet lips and I knew that I was already winning her over. A dinner, maybe a dance. This would be a night that she'd never forget.

"Be at my place at six, Barbie."

"You better stop calling me that if you really want me to dance for you," she called as I was just about to disappear.

"Don't talk rubbish. I know you love it, Barbie."

Sasha

78

When I saw Dexter standing in my apartment in his white T-shirt, with his trousers hanging low on his hips and staring at my photograph, he looked almost approachable. When I woke up, I knew that I needed to brush off our first meeting and just have a normal conversation with him. I had a feeling that it was too early to ask him about my uncle.

Dexter brought coffee and that was sweet of him. Maybe for a brief moment I lost my mind, agreeing to have dinner with him.

The key... I had to make sure that I got it back.

The apartment was still for sale. I was convinced that now, after we had made peace, I wouldn't have a problem with finding a buyer.

I was also convinced that this bad boy image, the machismo, was just an act that he put on. For some reason he wanted to keep people away. Anyway, I didn't want to get emotionally involved. It was all about sex and maybe a possible friendship. He was a dangerous man to be close to and I didn't expect much.

My body was aching a little from yesterday's performance, but I was glad that I did it.

Several hours later, after doing some intensive shopping in the city, I was back in my apartment, thinking about this evening. I'd broken my own rules. I was having a date with a guy that didn't actually believe in relationships, with a man that I used to hate. This wasn't normal, but maybe good sex would allow me to forget about that bastard Kirk.

At exactly six o'clock I stood outside Dexter's apartment wearing a V-neck cream dress that showed off a little cleavage. I didn't want to overdress, pretending that it was just a casual dinner. I knocked and waited. My stomach churned when I heard the steps.

A moment later Dexter opened the door, eyeing me up like he was a big bad wolf and I was a lost lamb in the forest. I wasn't scared of him, but rather apprehensive about what was going to happen.

"Barbie, you look fucking delicious," he said with a big smile on his face. I didn't wait for his invitation but walked right in, inhaling his cologne as I passed him at the door.

His apartment was a bit bigger than mine. The dining room table was set and there was a lot of activity going on in the kitchen.

"Here, have some champagne. That should loosen you up a little," he said, moving his arm around me to hand me a glass. I felt his body close to mine, and a surge of heat instantly passed through my core, reminding me to be careful. I took the champagne and walked to the table to get away from him.

"I'm fine, Dexter," I said a bit too sharply and sat down on the chair. He was still smirking, watching me. "So if you're capable of having a normal conversation with me, then tell me, what is it that you do?"

"I invest money into properties, renovate them and then sell them for profit. I choose my own hours and I don't answer to anyone," he explained and moved to the kitchen to check on whatever he was cooking. Only then did I notice that he was barefoot, wearing a blue jumper and dark jeans. A nervous tremor passed through me when I watched how he stirred something in the pan.

Holy hell, was it hot in his apartment or it was me? Feeling the sexual tension, I started pressing my thighs together. "You probably already know that I'm a nurse."

"Your sexy uniform gave you away the other day. I was ready to rip it all off you and take you in the lift," he said, turning around.

I felt a flush creeping over my cheeks. I had to stop getting turned on just by him talking about sex. This was my evening and my rules. "I don't have sex in public places."

"Of course. You're such a good girl." He chuckled.

"I might be, but not when I'm on the pole," I added huskily. He dropped the spoon and shot me a very heated look. I wanted to laugh.

"Stop teasing me, Barbie; otherwise I might forget about our discussion from yesterday, lift you up and take you to my bedroom where I will proceed to rip your good-girl dress apart. You will be at my mercy and I won't be nice," he said pressing his palms on the table and leaning over to me. He had beautiful eyes.

I was too bloody turned on to come up with something witty. Dexter had that effect on me, making me forget what I was going to say.

He licked his lips and went back to take care of our food. I began asking him boring questions about his work and the complex. It was supposed to be a good distraction, but it didn't work.

Half an hour later he served dinner: salmon en croute with new potatoes and salad, accompanied by white wine. I didn't want to say it, but it looked like Dexter was a great cook.

"Tell me about your family. Are they from around here?" I asked, chewing the delicious food.

"Yep. Mum lives in Edinburgh. Dad killed himself several years ago. Jack, my brother, moved to England; he's in the army."

I stopped eating then. His father had killed himself, but Dexter was talking about it like this didn't affect him at all.

"Dex... I'm so—"

"No, Sasha, spare me your pity. I'm over this shit. He was a weak man," he cut me off and shoved some food into his mouth. "Better tell me about your pole-dancing training. How did you get into that?"

"No one knows that I dance. I started when I was twenty-two. My friend wanted to try it, but she dropped out after the first class. I stayed and trained for years, and then I had a break when I moved away to London."

"How come no one knows? What, are you embarrassed about it? It's the sexiest thing that I've ever seen, and trust me, that's a compliment. I don't give them very often."

I laughed, breaking up the tension.

"I don't know. I just never had a chance to tell them," I said, looking down at my food. I was lying to myself. All of my old friends thought that I was a bore; I had no voice and no confidence. Kirk used to be the life and soul of the party and everyone loved him. When we broke up, I lost everyone. "I guess it was my secret for years until I stopped."

"Why did you stop?"

My stomach churned and when I looked back at him I sensed that he wouldn't be satisfied with a light answer. Dexter was the kind of guy that would dig deep.

I crossed the knife and fork on my plate and got up. I was planning to distract him. Like him, I wasn't ready to talk about my personal stuff, like my breakup with Kirk, so I started to dance.

Twelve

Dexter

We were trying to pull skeletons out of each other's closets. I sensed hesitation and possibly fear in Barbie's eyes, but I was fucking curious to know who the fuck made her stop training. This was why I never did dinner, diving straight to sex. This way I could avoid all the awkward moments. No one fucking knew that my father was weak and he took his own life. Those deep emotions killed him, and that's why I was doing everything I could to avoid them.

I liked the way she was going all shy on me when I talked about what I could do to her. Maybe I was turning into a total pussy, but I wanted an answer. Before I had a chance to press her further, she got up and walked away. She wasn't wearing any shoes and I nearly fell off the chair when she bent down and presented her fucking ass to me with glimpses of a red thong. I lost my shit then and in an instant I forgot what we were talking about.

"Barbie, what the fuck are you doing?" I asked her with a raspy voice, my cock straining already, pressing against my jeans.

She shot me one of her sultry looks, biting her lip. "Dancing for you, Dexter."

My mind emptied when she spread her legs and touched the floor. I wanted to grip her firm ass and sink myself deep inside those incredibly firm bum cheeks.

Whatever the fuck she was doing to me, it was a dream come true. Next thing I knew, she was walking away swaying her hips, lifting her leg up. I'd asked for a dance and now I was getting it, my own private performance, and we weren't even done with dinner yet. She reached the pillar that supported the ceiling. She walked over to it and started rubbing herself around it, up and down. My dick throbbed, begging to be buried inside her tight wetness.

Within a few seconds of her doing shit to the pillar I realised that nice Dexter wasn't in the room anymore. She was pushing my limits and right now I wasn't fucking thinking straight. She screamed of sex, drowning me in it like an animal in heat. I was uncomfortable knowing that I hadn't banged her yet. She was teasing me with her flexible body, inviting me over to fuck her senseless.

When she bent down and showed me her red slutty thong, it was over for me. I couldn't just sit there and pretend that I was patient enough to wait until the end. No, I needed to have her right then. I shot to my feet and was beside her before she even noticed me.

Sasha smelled like an erotic and wild adventure.

"Dexter, what are you–"

I didn't let her finish. I picked her up and threw her across my shoulder. Her ass was in my face and it was bliss knowing that she was at my mercy. She was shouting at me to put her down, but I was only thinking about entering her soft flesh with my rock-hard cock.

"We are going to fuck right now. We both know that you're drenched with need to have me inside you," I said, putting her down on my bed. And with inhuman speed I started taking my shirt off. She could say whatever, but I knew she wanted it from the moment she showed up in my apartment.

"I didn't say you could sleep with me now, did I?"

She was flustered as hell, and she had that hunger and need in her eyes.

"The only thing that your pussy needs right now is my tongue, so don't bullshit me, Barbie. I own it and I'm going to devour it," I said and tossed my shirt away, pulling my trousers down. She opened her mouth, dropping her sexy eyes to my hard cock. I didn't give her any time to think about this. I cradled her in my arms and began kissing her flesh. She responded, rubbing herself against my enlarged dick. When she moaned into my mouth, I thought it was the sexiest sound that I have ever heard.

She let me forget about the inner darkness, the crawling hollowness when my mouth was on hers, tracing my tongue down her neck. It was time to take what belonged to me.

"Stand up straight," I ordered her, pulling away.

"What? Why?" she whimpered.

"Because I fucking said so," I growled, deepening the kiss again, forcing my way into her mouth. She finally obeyed me. I was so hard for her that it was unbelievable, stretching the muscles around my abdomen until they were burning.

When she straightened her body, I started moving down, nipping and barely touching her skin. I used my other hand to unzip her dress and at the same time my tongue traced the lines of her collarbone. When the zipper came all the way down, I pulled her dress off abruptly.

"You're so sexy, Barbie, and your pussy is going to beg to be fucked over and over. I want you to scream for me when you come," I murmured, meeting her eyes. She wanted it. Her pupils were dilated and she was trying to cover the anticipation, but I knew that she was wet. Her breathing was even faster than mine.

I finally had her in my bedroom, standing in her red bra and thong, helpless and uncertain. For a moment I wanted to just admire her body, but my cock was throbbing painfully. I gripped her hand and unhooked her bra. It fell on the floor, giving me access to her amazing tits. She was still obeying me well, standing straight, so I connected our mouths, moulding her huge breasts. Her nipples hardened instantly.

Once her lips were swollen and she was panting, I started sucking on her nipples, taking one at a time, swirling my tongue around them. She moaned again and urged me to move faster, but I wanted to take my time. An alarm had gone off in my head. I fucking didn't do slow, but Sasha was like a delicate flower that bloomed with care and attention.

I needed to have all of her, taste every inch of her sexy body. I went down to my knees and stuck my face in her sweet pussy. She smelled like the musky scent of sex, her tight wetness begging me to lick her faster and to ravage her.

"Oh, Dex," she moaned and I hadn't even done anything yet. "Please, I need to feel you inside me."

I laughed, running my fingers over her folds. I was going to make her lose her mind. She closed her eyes and then I inched her thong down. I had no idea what was wrong with me. I fucked fast and hard, never slow and tender. With Sasha it was all about knowing that I owned her.

"Spread your amazing legs," I demanded. This time she didn't hesitate and just did what I asked.

I started licking her folds while my other hand was on her ass, holding her in place. She was so wet for me, begging me not to stop whatever the hell I was doing. I continued to move my tongue in her flesh, slowly, eagerly, to the point when I felt her hips trembling, pressing herself into my mouth. I wanted to hear her come for me, breaking apart with waves of pleasure. Fuck, she had the sweetest pussy that I'd ever tasted and I didn't want to let go of her ever.

Sasha

Fireworks exploded in my head. His lips were licking me and I couldn't take it anymore. I shut my eyes, trembling and wanting to get comfortable to enjoy his torturous moves, but his grip on my ass was like steel. Bastard, he knew that I was struggling to stay standing up while his tongue explored me deeper and further. My pussy throbbed with the need to release, tightening as I panted. I was so close, ready to explode. At any moment my knees were ready to give out.

My insides clenched and I thought he sensed that he'd pushed me to the edge, so he released his grip. I was on the bed before I had a chance to take some air. He moved so fast, spreading my legs wide apart and diving his head between them, nuzzling my clit with his tongue. I cried out when he slid two fingers inside me and started fucking my pussy with his hand.

"Barbie, you're unbelievable. Are you ready to come for me?"

His question didn't make sense; besides, my mouth wasn't working. Sweat broke out over my body as he continued thrusting his fingers in and out. I gasped for air as I exploded, coming apart as smaller orgasms rippled through me. His eyes were watching me intently, hungrily. My body trembled and I didn't want to move, but he wasn't done with me yet.

Dexter ripped the condom packet open with his mouth and rolled it onto his massive cock. I lost the sense of what he just did to me. My heart jackhammered in my chest.

With not much warning, he was between my legs and then he was inside me. His lips were on mine, kissing, pulling and sucking, as his body stilled.

"Barbie, your pussy is so tight, so fucking perfect. I won't go easy on you. Fuck, tell me if you want me to go easy on you," he urged.

Hell, I couldn't catch my breath, much less talk. "No, oh, fuck me," I pleaded as my pussy clenched around his cock. He pounded into me, losing control of himself.

"Shit, this is unbelievable," he shouted. His thrusts felt so damn good and I wanted more, needed to feel him deeper. He started nibbling on my breast while shoving his dick up and down inside me. I was losing control, shouting his name.

He made me come again and again. Then he went back down on me, licking and breaking me apart. It was a sweet and delicious torture, because I couldn't take it, my hips were numb, my core drenched.

I was trying to push him away, but he only laughed until I exploded again. I had no idea how much time had passed.

By the time he was done with me I was lifeless, so fucked that I couldn't move my limbs. I must have drifted to sleep when he wrapped his arms around me, but it was bliss.

***

I was watching him sleep. My body was pleasantly numb and I was sore. No other man had ever made me sore. I couldn't believe that I'd slept with him. Everything had happened so fast yesterday—the conversation, his hungry eyes, and my seductive dance.

I was expecting him to throw me back to my apartment after we were done, but he let me sleep. Dexter was intense, overwhelming, and he wasn't lying when he said that he could fuck.

I slid out of bed carefully, making sure that I didn't wake him. It was ten o'clock on Monday morning and I had no idea if he had to go to work or not, but he looked too peaceful to be disturbed.

I walked around his living room trying to picture myself in his life. Things were complicated with me, but Dexter helped me to ease the tension, to remember that there was more to life than work and worries about tomorrow. I contemplated going back to his bed. I could wait for him to wake up, but what for? This whole thing was awkward enough. There was no point staying and pretending that I wasn't like his other women. One sinful night was enough.

I was headed to the door when I heard the familiar voice.

"Where the hell are you going?"

Crap, he caught me sneaking out. I had no idea what to say or do. I turned around slowly. He stood in the hallway watching me, naked and absolutely beautiful. Heat rushed over my skin, curling up my toes.

"Home. I need to drive to the city and take care of a few things."

I needed to see Mum's solicitor for some paperwork that I missed, so this wasn't a total lie. He knew that I was running away. I was giving him an opportunity to move on, acknowledging that there wasn't going to be any repeat of last night, that I wasn't expecting more.

Wrong. I couldn't deny that I wasn't done with wanting him.

Dexter looked annoyed. His eyes wandered down to my boobs and a wide smile spread over his gorgeous face. "I thought that we could hump some more this morning," he said with a slight tension in his voice. I didn't get it. Was he angry that I was trying to sneak out?

"Or maybe we can talk instead?"

"Talk? About what?" he asked.

"Tell me about your relationship with my uncle. Were you two close?" I asked, not quite sure where this was coming from. I went straight to it, without preparation, without any small talk. This kind of conversation before coffee was too heavy, but I was lost; embarrassed with myself that I enjoyed rough, no-strings-attached sex.

He walked up to the kitchen and began setting up his espresso, like all of a sudden I didn't exist. Maybe he dropped that letter purposely for me to find it. I couldn't ignore it, but I had to know if what Joey had written about him was real.

What the hell was wrong with me?

"I don't want to discuss him right now, Barbie. You can leave if you want. I won't be crying after you."

Breathe... I needed to remember how to breathe. I stood by the door watching him for a bit, but he continued to ignore me. It was a clear indication that I shouldn't have asked about Joey.

I wanted to say that we didn't have to talk, but no sound came out. I turned around and left, telling myself that I shouldn't have expected anything else. Dexter wouldn't magically open up and explain why he behaved the way he did.

I went back to my apartment and changed, congratulating myself for being so pathetic. One night of crazy good sex and the mere beginnings of honest conversation didn't give me a right to think that we could be in a relationship. We both enjoyed the game of hide-and-seek, but enough was enough.

An hour later I was walking towards my car thinking about what I could do tonight when I received a text message.

Hey Beautiful,

I can be quite persistent and I won't stop trying. There is this new restaurant in the centre and my friend works there as a chef. I managed to score a reservation and complementary dinner.
I will be pretty disappointed if you say no to me again.

Alistair.

I sighed and bit my lip. This was the perfect opportunity for distraction. My Monday shift was cancelled and I didn't want to be stuck in the apartment. I was certain that Dexter was already planning to invite another girl to his bed this evening.
What the hell!

I guessed that one innocent date wouldn't matter. Sex with Dexter only proved that I was ready for anything. Healed enough to grab life by the balls and enjoy myself like I used to.

I texted back asking him to pick me up at seven.

Dexter

Stupid fuck. Why did I have to behave like I didn't care? Like she was just like the others?

What pissed me off the most was that she tried to sneak out while I was sleeping. Last night with her was different; she was so responsive and made me work harder than normal. Each time I collapsed on the bed panting, I was ready for more.

I was caught off guard when I woke up and she was gone. She had balls and I wasn't expecting her to leave first, but she

90

did, or at least she tried to. One night, that's all I ever promised her. Sometimes I wondered why I wouldn't just shut my stupid mouth. Sasha had crawled under my skin, wrecked my routine and seeded an unsatisfied desire for more.

I fucking decided to set her straight, to ignore her. She woke me up with questions about Joey. I hadn't even had a coffee yet and she was already digging. Where the hell did that even come from?

For a moment she just stood there, watching me, probably expecting me to say more. I didn't. It was none of her business if we were friends or not. As usual, I didn't think and told her that this conversation was off limits. And when she turned and left, I was too stubborn and stupid to go after her. She went back to her place and I spent the day wondering what was happening to me.

The sex was fucking unbelievable, and I was ready for another round. I liked her strong personality, her sharp tongue and the fact that she wouldn't back down from me. All of a sudden I didn't need coffee. I wanted to screw her again, to hold her again but this time never let go.

It was time to get busy, so I took a shower, dressed in a suit and went to work. This way I didn't have to think about her or dwell on the incredible night we had spent together.

In the office, things didn't go well. Barbie occupied my fucking mind like a shadow. I remembered her smooth skin, her loud breathing and her moans.

When it was time to go on a conference call with other clients, I could barely focus.

After I told everyone that I wasn't feeling well, I locked myself in my office. My phone was silent. At least I could have taken her number, but what was I supposed to talk to her about?

We had dinner, talked and then fucked. That was it. So why the fuck couldn't I simply forget about her? There were plenty of other women out there.

I left the office at six and headed back to the complex. Most of the time Jennifer was up for a good session of screwing, and she was just a phone call away. In the end I didn't call her. Within half an hour I was back in the building, ready to have an honest conversation with Barbie. While waiting for the lift, I made an instant decision to stop fucking around and tell her that I was ready for more.

A few moments later the lift opened up and I strolled up the corridor, walking straight to Barbie's door. Some unfamiliar, bulky-looking guy was standing there.

Sasha looked delicious in a black and navy short dress and navy heels. I didn't know what the occasion was, but she gave me an instant raging hard-on.

"We need to talk," I snapped, getting straight to the point. Barbie paled and glanced nervously at the guy next to her.

Who the fuck was he?

"We'll talk another time. I'm kind of busy right now," she explained, almost stuttering. I had to get a grip. There was no point beating around the bush. I wanted her and that was it.

"Sasha, I need to talk to you right now, so tell whoever the fuck this is to get lost and come back later."

"Dexter, please—"

"Mate, she's with me and there is a cab waiting for us downstairs. She said she's busy," said the guy, slipping his palm around Sasha's waist. Then, this whole thing finally clicked. Barbie was going out on a fucking date. She'd been with me this morning, we had epic sex at least ten hours ago and now she was with someone else, some asshole who wanted what belonged to me.

In that moment I knew that she had power over me, and she was going to make me lose my fucking mind.

Thirteen

Sasha

"You're fucking unbelievable Barbie! You fucked me last night and you're already going out with some loser?" Dexter shouted, not caring for the world that Alistair was standing right next to me. This was the last thing that I was expecting tonight. Alistair wanted to see the apartment, so I invited him upstairs. That was a big big mistake.

"Dexter, what I do is none of your business. One night with you doesn't give you the right to tell me who I can go out on a date with!"

"I didn't say it did, but you should know that I own your pussy. This asshole won't fuck you the way I have, he won't feel the same when he sides into you, he won't make you wet like I do".

"Mate, I suggest you—"

"Shut up fuck up dickweed, no one is talking to you "mate." Her sweet pussy belongs to me and only me," Dexter roared, cutting Alistair off and taking a step towards him, with anger burning in his eyes.

Oh boy, this is just great.

Two men were eyeing each other like two lions during mating season, ready to rip into each other's throats. I was partly flattered and partly angry that Dexter thought that one night with him gave him a right to tell me with who I could go out with.

Alistair 's face flushed red and my pulse sped up with anxiety at how Dex was behaving.

"Alistair come on, let's go," I hissed knowing that Dexter was ready to punch my date. I shot him a furious glare and started dragging Alistair away, before this whole thing got out of control.

Dexter slammed the door to his apartment, swearing under his breath. I decided to take the stairs to avoid any other surprises. I wanted to disappear into the ground with embarrassment.

Alistair was silent all the way back downstairs, but he stopped me just before I wanted to get into the taxi.

"Did you really sleep with that guy up there?" he asked, looking at me like I'd beaten up his dog. I sighed and wondered what was I supposed to say to him? I couldn't lie. Alistair was sweet and decent, but my body craved bad mouthy Dexter.

"It was just one mistaken night that meant nothing to me. I don't normally do that and I really want you to take me out on a date, if you still want to that is?"

I saw hesitation in his eyes that was soon replaced by smile. Alistair was handsome and well mannered, the kind of guy that I should have gone for in the first place.

God, what was wrong with me?

"Of course," he said confidently.

We jumped into the waiting taxi in absolute silence, I was trying to act like earlier encounter with Dexter had never happened, but deep down I knew our date was already spoiled. The conversation in the taxi was stunted and awkward, although Alistair managed to make me laugh a few times. My head was somewhere else and things hadn't improved when we got to the restaurant. The waiter mixed up our orders, so we had to wait an extra hour for food, and by that time we were both starved and pretty annoyed.

He dropped me home by ten and gave me a quick kiss on the cheek. I kept apologising, trying to tell him that I normally didn't do one night stands, but he kept saying that he wasn't judgmental. Alistair was a gentleman, but he didn't say if he wanted to see me again or not.

When I took the lift back to my apartment, the corridor was silent. I had no idea if Dexter was in or not. At least he wasn't waiting for me this time. After I drank a glass of white wine I went to bed, thinking about the feel of Dexter's skilled hands on my skin.

He woke me up early the next morning; his bedroom shared a wall directly next to mine, so I heard as he slammed the door back and forward. When I glanced at the clock, I saw that it was only 4.00 am. I tossed and turned drifting back to sleep half an hour later.

I finally got up around eight. It was Tuesday and I knew that if I didn't talk to him right away, my whole day would be ruined. I knew a really great coffee place a couple of miles away from the complex. This was a good way to bring him back to being my friend. I thought that we both needed to set things straight and talk about Dexter's expectations of me. We hadn't set any particular rules, and we had only slept together once, so I didn't understand why he was so angry that I went out on a date.

I pulled on an old pair of jeans and T-shirt, took my car key and headed out. I decided to walk through the concierge area to check if there was any post for me. I was waiting for a few papers from the solicitor.

It was just after eight and I wasn't expecting anyone in the concierge this morning, but there was a dark haired woman talking to Duncan. She looked pretty pissed off. I started reading the flyers on the desk, waiting for her to leave. When I looked closely I finally recognised her from Harry's party. She was the brunette that Dexter disappeared with just before my dance.

"Mr. Tyndall is my bloody fiancée. I don't understand, how could I not be on the list?"

I slowly turned around, knowing that I couldn't have misheard what she said. Dexter was engaged. I stepped towards them feeling like all the air was suddenly punched out of my lungs.

"Dexter, you want to speak to Dexter Tyndall?" I asked, just to be sure.

"Yes, finally there is someone here that understands what I want," she complained, glaring at Duncan.

"In that case, I'll take you to him. I'm sure he'll be glad to see his fiancée," I chipped in, a fake smile forming on my face even though I was ready to scream, shout and scratch her face with my sharp nails.

I hadn't had the chance to really look at her at the party—I was too busy avoiding Dexter—but now she was standing right in front of me and I hated to admit that she was stunning. Her thick black hair fell in luscious waves around her shoulders, her skin was clear and bright, and she wore a white dress that hugged her slim body amazingly well. Her manicure was perfect and she wore hardly any make-up, which was even more annoying.

I would never look like that, not even after hundreds of plastic surgeries. I knew that it was just sex between me and Dex, but I despised stinky, slimy lies. I thought that finally, after so many years of listening to the same bullshit, I had found a guy who was upfront about everything. He wanted to screw me without any expectations and I was okay with it, but the freaking fiancée? *Hypocrite!* How dare he be angry about Alistair?

"And you are?" she asked with an indifferent tone of voice. She was English, a Londoner just like me. This couldn't get any worse.

"I live right next to him. We're neighbours. I bet he will love the surprise," I added and started walking away. She strolled casually after me, but didn't say anything else. The ride in the lift was long and very awkward. She was doing everything she could in order not to look at me.

"Okay, I'll take it from—"

"Hold on." I cut her off and barged into Dexter's apartment. I didn't have a clue if she was following or not, but I wanted to serve him the best wake-up call that I could think of. He was up at 4.00 am, so now he was probably back in bed, catching up on his sleep. He wasn't in the living room, so he was probably still asleep. I proceeded to the bathroom.

I found a tall glass and filled it with ice water, not even thinking about what I was doing. Anger was crashing through me like the tall waves on the shore. This time I didn't plan to simply walk away and bury my head under the sand—I was ready to give him hell.

"What on earth are you doing?" she shouted when I came out of the bathroom, heading towards his bedroom.

"Oh, nothing. Sleeping Beauty is still in his comfortable bed, so we need to wake him up," I sang and barged through the door. The model was saying something to me, but I wasn't listening. I poured the water straight onto his gorgeous, lying, deceitful face.

He roared like a tiger on the prowl, jumping off the bed still naked and soaked right through, shaking his head. My insides turned into mush, but that wasn't the time or the place to look at his glorious tanned body. Dexter was a bastard and a liar.

"What the fuck, Sasha? Have you lost your fucking mind?" he shouted, not paying the slightest attention to the fact that he wasn't alone. I refused to acknowledge his massive, slightly erect dick.

"Oh sorry, did I wake you?" I asked sarcastically. "I just wanted to let you know that your fiancée is here to see you!"

Dexter's face went wild, the muscles on his jaw tightening. Finally, his eyes registered the stunning brunette in his bedroom. I was ready to smash his windows with a baseball bat.

I wanted to tear him apart, not because I was weak enough to have slept with him, but because he was a fucking liar.

"Hello, darling. My pussy has missed you," the model said with that sweet tone that made me nauseous. I was out of the door before I had a chance to listen to their bitter exchange, but I still heard his loud roar.

"Get the fuck out of my apartment, you stupid bitch!"

He seemed angry, but I bet that he was ready to fuck her in the same bed where just the other night he had fucked me. I couldn't stand there. I wasn't jealous, just really pissed off with the fact that I fallen for his charms. I should have gone out with Alistair weeks ago, before Dexter came along.

When I got into the car park I wasn't thinking straight. A year ago I probably would have cried in shame and horror, but right now I needed to drive for a while to think about what to do next.

Memories of that day from nine months ago were pulsing through me like a drumbeat, every thought pounding in my brain. Kirk was the guy I had been ready to spend the rest of my life with. I loved him so much that it physically hurt.

Betty was sick, so she had cancelled my training session for that night. I was more than disappointed, as I was hoping to try a new advanced routine on the pole. She didn't know that I had been practising at home. Kirk was out catching up with a friend from work. I didn't want to be stuck in front of the TV for the rest of the evening, so I decided to head to my best friend Jessica's house.

Over the past few months, Kirk hadn't been the same. He was acting cold and distant, like we were strangers, not two people sharing their lives together under the same roof. We hadn't talked much and I felt neglected when he didn't want to have sex. Whenever I asked him about it, he kept saying that it was just stress. Apparently, he was working on a new project at work.

I was worried about him, so I gave him the space that he needed. It was all right to feel worthless once in a while, but this had been going on for months now. No relationship was perfect, but we were going through a pretty rough time.

Jess was probably sewing tonight and I needed a friend that I could talk to about this stuff with Kirk, so I took the bus to her place. It was a freezing cold November night; there were supposed to be snow showers that evening.

When I finally got to her street, my fingers were numb. I wasn't even sure if Jessica was home. Luckily for me, there was a dim light in her bedroom. We had been friends since kindergarten—she had eaten and slept in my parents' house often enough. Mum always treated her like another daughter. So I didn't knock, but walked in knowing that she wouldn't mind.

Jess was such a messy freak. There were clothes on the stairs: a pair of underwear and a man's shirt. The living room was in a bit better state, but it was empty. I put my hands to the radiator, hoping to warm up a little. I was just about to shout when I heard noises coming from upstairs.

I hesitated, wondering if maybe I shouldn't have just barged in unannounced. In the past few months she had been acting weird, asking me to call before I showed up. I stood on the bottom of the stairs for about thirty seconds, wondering if I had the guts to check out if she had company. Jess didn't have a boyfriend. She was a party girl and she liked her independence.

"Fuck, Jess—you're so fucking amazing. I want to come on your tits."

I froze, wondering if I was having hearing problems. I knew that voice, but something was wrong. Kirk didn't swear and he didn't talk dirty in bed. I laughed nervously to myself, not wanting to believe they were capable of hurting me so viciously. I picked up the man's shirt and smelled it. My stomach revolted and my heart started skipping beats.

No, no, no—this wasn't happening to me. Not again and not with my best friend.

I shot up the stairs; I had to know for sure. When I opened the bedroom door I saw Kirk pounding himself into Jessica, the sweat gathering on his back, her head thrown back in ecstasy as she gripped the back of his head with one hand and twisted the sheets with the other. I stood there staring at their display, feeling as if all the air had been sucked out of the room leaving me dizzy and nauseous.

My best friend and my boyfriend were fucking. I had no idea how long I stood there watching them, but eventually she noticed me and screamed. Kirk jumped out of the bed.

"Sash, what the fuck? What are you doing here?" he shouted. *No stuttered apology, no hasty explanation, just a stupid question barked at me like I was in the wrong for interrupting them. This was just getting better and better. I was shaking, sinking into a deep, open black hole of pain. Three years ago my life had fallen apart and now it was happening to me again.*

"How long? How long have you two been sleeping together behind my back?" I asked, tears streaming down my cheeks. I didn't want to cry. Kirk was unmoved, staring at me with cold indifference on his face.

"What the fuck do you want me to say? You're so boring, always whining that no one cares about you. And the sex. God, Sasha, always the same, monotonous. At least Jess is adventurous."

My mind snapped back to the present. I knew that I shouldn't be driving and thinking about the past at the same time, but I couldn't stay in the apartment. That night, Kirk had moved out of the flat that we had shared together. He hadn't become violent then—oh, no. That was a few weeks after I caught them. Kirk was my third serious boyfriend. The one before that also cheated on me, also with a girl that I was friends with.

I put my foot down and drove around the coast, feeling depressed about this whole thing. With Dexter it was just sex, and now that he had managed to bang me, I was ready to find a cash buyer and sell the apartment. I'd had enough of being treated like a punching bag. This time I was stronger and Dexter was going to regret that he had lied.

Dexter

"Are you fucking deaf? Get the fuck out of my apartment, Victoria!" I roared, ready to hit her. I was so fucking pissed off with her shit that I didn't care anymore that she was a woman.

"Go on, throw me out, but I remember what you did six weeks ago at the party. I'm sure that the police would be very interested in my statement," she sang, looking over her nails.

I was in front of her, still naked, before she had a chance to hiss. My face was inches away from hers. "What the fuck are you talking about, you bitch?" I demanded. My head was clear as a whistle. For the first time in ages, my thoughts weren't fucking racing. The party in London—yeah, I was there with her, but I had no fucking idea what she was talking about.

"You did something really, really bad and I bet that you don't even remember it," she whispered. She wasn't intimidated by me for some reason. I'd never laid a finger on a woman, but Victoria was testing me. I wanted to rip her face off with my bare hands. "I'm not like the rest of your women. You can't just toss me away when you've had enough. You will regret that you ever got rid of me."

"Are you fucking threatening me?" I asked, not backing up. I could just wrap my hand around that little throat and squeeze it. My brain was trying to bring up that party in her house, but my head was blank. I'd had some pills and probably a whole bottle of whisky. I didn't remember shit.

She started backing away from me towards the living room, still smiling. Why did I have to bang her? She was sending me off the rails and she had scared Sasha off.

"I'm reminding you of what you're missing out on," she snapped. "I want you, Dexter, and I'll have you in my bed again."

"Fuck off or I swea—"

"Go on, finish it. Bury yourself further with threats," she challenged, then turned around and walked out of my apartment. The water was dripping off me and I was staring at the fucking door. What was she accusing me of? A rape? An assault? I had no clue. The problem was that I didn't remember that night at that party.

My head had been screwed—I drank to shut down the voices in my head. I might have had sex then, but hell, I had no idea what I'd done. The bitch wanted to bring me down.

Sasha and me—fuck.

She'd poured cold water on my face. I was ready to kill her, but then images from the other night began floating in front of me. Her soaking wet pussy and me, fucking her slowly. It was the best sex I'd had since I could fucking remember.

I almost forgot that I saw her last night with that asshole. She had arranged a fucking date with some ginger haired douche and I had nearly lost my shit. This woman was infuriating and I didn't know why I even cared. She was just like others, but every time I closed my eyes I had her in front of me. The sex was better than I anticipated, Jesus that was an understatement and I wanted to do it again; have her again, possess and devour her body. When I glanced down at my cock I realised that it was already at full mast. I was pissed that she ditched me so quickly for someone else, furious with the fact that I was being replaced. She was the only girl that stunted that crippling hollow feeling. She was my healer.

Fourteen

Dexter

Victoria's threats didn't scare me, I had no idea what she thought she could achieve by blackmailing me. She didn't need money; she wanted to feel important again, and to undermine me. I was supposed to meet with one of my clients earlier on, but after the unexpected visit from Victoria, I couldn't focus. I was so uncomfortable when I saw Sasha with some loser that I had managed to sleep in and that fucking meeting had completely fallen out of my head. The guy was probably raging. This investment was important to me, but now my whole day was fucked and I needed to take the edge off my bad mood.

When I closed my front door I had an urge to knock on Sasha's door, but I was sure that she wouldn't want to listen to what I had to say, besides I was still pissed off with her about last night.

Fucking fiancée? Who did she think she was, accusing me of being a fucking pussy?

I had told her that I didn't do relationships, but she thought that she was a clever beast. I'd never had to explain myself to anyone, and that wasn't going to change anytime soon. I could fuck whoever I pleased. I banged her and it was time to move to the next one, but deep in my stomach I knew that she wasn't like the others. Sex with her brought me back to the living world.

The problem was that since that row in my apartment, I couldn't stop thinking about her pussy and her sassy mouth. It was like one time wasn't enough. When I had her in my arms begging me to fuck her harder, it was fucking bliss. I had never listened to anyone else's needs before and we did end up fucking eventually, but I went easy on her, devouring her pussy very slowly.

When I got into my car, the text messages began to come through. It was probably the client from earlier on. Too bad I didn't give a fuck.

It had been days since I visited Mum. She was still angry with me. A couple of weeks ago I missed a family dinner, so I lost the status of favourite son. She didn't believe my bullshit anymore, but I wasn't prepared to sit through the whole meal and listen to how everyone was concerned about me.

Mum ran the house, cooked for my brother and hadn't looked at another man since Pap died. She insisted that she still had to work. I paid off her mortgage and took care of all her bills, but she still refused to quit her job at the school, saying that it was because she needed to get out of the house once in a while.

The house that I grew up in was situated in south Gyle. My younger brother, Connor, still lived at home, playing his stupid video games all day long. I just didn't get it. What was wrong with him? He seemed determined to become a loser. He was fucking twenty, not fifteen, and I was fed up with trying to get him to do anything with himself.

"Dexter, is anything wrong? What are you doing here?"

"There is absolutely nothing wrong, Mum. You said you wanted to see me more often, so here I am," I said, trying to sound like I was perfectly fine. Victoria was the reason I was pissed off, but right now Sasha was the bigger problem.

My mother was a short, petite woman with brown hair and kind eyes. Even now, her looking at me like that made me uneasy, bringing up unspoken subjects that weren't worth talking about. Like the fact that I didn't have a girlfriend.

I grew up in this house, but after Pap's death, every time I walked through the door I felt haunted. Every corner hid a memory and even after so many years, the house affected me in certain ways, inflicting emotions and feelings that I tried to push away. My father killed himself in the attic. I was the one that found him. I had stood in the door, watching as he swayed back and forth.

"Do you want something to eat? I have a cottage pie," Mum asked, snapping me back to reality.

"Okay, Mum, I'll have some."

I sat in the kitchen while she started moving around, preparing food for me. We used to talk like that all the time. I did miss her cooking. I missed my old simple life, when I didn't have many responsibilities.

"How are you feeling? Still waking up early?" she asked innocently. Once I had made the mistake of telling her about my sleeping pattern; since then she kept bringing it up every time we were alone, asking me to see someone. That wasn't happening and I didn't need to see a specialist.

"Not since Joey passed away," I replied, lying through my teeth. I scrolled through my phone, deleting all the messages from Victoria. She could go and fuck herself; she had nothing on me.

"He was a good man, Dex, so I know it must be hard for you having no one next door now."

I didn't have to pretend in front of Mum. She knew that I didn't get on with many people and never had many friends. Joey was an exception to that; we were very close and his death took a toll on me. We used to talk about politics, women and whatever the hell was going on in the world. It had been three months and since then, I've been on a slow descent into destruction.

"There's a girl that just moved in next door. Sasha, his niece," I muttered as Mum put a plate of her awesome pie in front of me. My tone was indifferent, but Sasha's name stirred something in me, pulling me away from the gloom. I needed to have her in my bed again.

"A girl—so you met her? Is she nice?" Mum began her interrogation. I was twenty-eight and since Pap passed away, I hadn't brought any women home. I started stuffing my face with the pie, distracting myself from Sasha's moans that I could hear in my head. Fuck, this was getting out of control. She was no one; just a woman I'd fucked.

"Annoying. Blonde, not my type."

"So you talked to her then?"

"Yes, we talked, but she isn't like Joey, Mum. The apartment is on the market, and when she sells it, she'll be gone," I explained.

"This Joey—his death was unexpected and it was such a shock for you. Maybe you should see someone, Dexter. When your father died you slipped away and I don't—"

"God damn, Mum, this isn't the same! I'm fine; talking to a shrink won't help me. Stop pressing me."

"I kept telling your father to go and see someone. He never did, and then it was too late. I keep blaming myself because I wasn't more persuasive. I'm worried about you and Jack and Connor. You more than anyone, because you just lost someone close to you again."

I didn't know what to say to her. Pap was weak; there was nothing that she could have done. The stress and problems had been eating him for years. I was determined not to become like him. All right, so she was right. I had been smoking, drinking and taking more pills since Joey's death, but I wasn't planning to take my own fucking life because of him. That wasn't how I dealt with grief.

Mum was concerned and I didn't want to worry her more than she had to. I took her hand and squeezed it. "That girl,

Sasha—maybe she will become a friend, who knows. She is helping me a bit, so please don't stress, Ma. You couldn't have helped Pap. He's gone, so stop blaming yourself."

"All right, I'm sorry," she said and sat down next to me. I had to tell her something, anything, to stop her worrying about me. "I can pack you some of that to take with you if you like?"

"No, I'm good. I have to go, it's just a flying visit," I said and smiled. That lightened up her mood a bit and I felt better. Deep down, I knew that I was lying to her. Me and Sasha, we would never be friends. I wanted to possess her again—this time body and soul. I wanted her to ditch other guys for me. I knew that she was going to be gone soon.

Sasha

Eventually, I had to go back. The agency rang asking me to cover a shift in another hospital and I agreed. Dexter's car wasn't there when I arrived back at the apartment. I changed, picked up some stuff for tonight and had a quick bite to eat. Alistair didn't call or text and I honestly wasn't expecting him to. We had fun, but I couldn't take my mind off Dexter and the fact that he lied to me.

I reached the hospital by half six and put my head down, working hard, forgetting about everything that had gone on today. There was no point thinking about it. He took the act of fucking like bunnies to the next level. I simply couldn't get that kind of night out of my head.

The kids on the ward were great; they kept me on my toes, so the night passed quickly. I left at six, exhausted and with a blister on the sole of my foot. Stupid me; I wore new shoes to work and now my foot was in agony. It was useful enough to know Dexter's parking space. He was in and I didn't want to hide. Fortunately for me, I got into my apartment without any kind of interruption. For the first time since I'd moved here, I went to bed with a headache. It bothered me that Dexter was so quiet; normally he made a lot of noise this early in the morning.

I swallowed painkillers and after an hour I finally drifted. The nightmares about that night when Kirk lost his temper flared up again, and at some point I woke up screaming. My heart pounded as I looked around disorientated, and my t-shirt was drenched with sweat. It'd been a while since I'd dreamed about him. When I glanced at the clock, I realised that it was time to get up. I had slept straight through a long eight hours.

The bedroom was a mess, but I wasn't in the mood to do anything about it. The estate agent had yet to call about another viewing. It had been what, almost four weeks and I still didn't have a buyer.

I decided to skip the shower and head to the pool. I put on my blue bikini, planning to stay in the sauna for a bit. My life was still under control. Soon I was going to forget about Dexter and his filthy mouth. It was just a matter of time.

Duncan kept staring at my boobs when I signed in to use the facilities. I had pole-dancing training tomorrow, so I skipped the gym and headed to the pool.

The pool and sauna were completely empty. I guessed that it was the time of day when everyone was at work. It was great to get in and just relax in the water. This week I was planning to start over again, maybe put some adverts online and wait for a buyer.

I had my goggles, so I started doing a few laps underwater. The pool was small, but lengthy enough for a workout. When I reached the other side I grabbed the edge and broke the surface of the pool. Someone's feet were right in front of me. Gasping for breath, I took my goggles off and my heart kicked me right in my chest.

Fucking Dexter was standing on the edge of the pool looking down on me, wearing red shorts. As usual, my eyes couldn't help but wander over his smooth well-muscled chest and sculptured legs. Damn, why did he have to be here now? Any other day he worked out at six in the morning. This was just my luck.

"Hello, Barbie. Enjoying your swim?" he asked. It was a good thing that I was in the water; otherwise I might have melted into the floor. The memories of our night together suddenly clouded my mind and I couldn't work my mouth again.

I didn't answer him; I just turned around and began swimming in the opposite direction, hoping that he might just leave.

He didn't. Instead, he got into the pool and swam towards me. I didn't want to do this. We fucked; he cheated on his fiancée; that was the end of story.

"Ignoring me, are we? Let me remind you how much your pussy loved my tongue, shall I? I'm ready for another round."

I splashed him. I couldn't help myself; I was so angry all of a sudden. It took me less than thirty seconds to get wound up. It looked like he wasn't that bothered about Alistair after all.

"Fuck off and get back to your fiancée, fuckface," I snapped. I had no make-up on and I must have looked pretty rough. He was unbelievable, still talking about sex with me when he was committed to someone else.

"Shut the fuck up, Barbie. I wasn't planning to explain myself to you, but I guess now I have to, because you're so unbelievably stupid."

My jaw was hanging open. No, he didn't... He didn't just call me stupid. We were both standing by the edge of the pool. I was considering drowning him. It was a shame that he was so hot.

"Yes, Dexter, I'm stupid because I fucking slept with you!" I shouted, splashing him again, but this time he grabbed my wrists, holding me in place.

"Once I can tolerate, but the fucking second time you might want to be careful or I will cut your hands off," he hissed. The heat from his touch sent a wave of surging warmth down between my legs. I was in the water, but I could still feel it.

"Get off me," I shouted, trying to pull away, but his grip was firm. When he brought me closer to his chest I wasn't sure if I remembered how to breathe.

"I didn't want to insult your intelligence, but how stupid can you be, thinking that I had a fucking fiancée? Victoria is a slut that has been spreading shitty rumours about us since I ate her pussy for breakfast. Yeah, I fucked her, but then I got bored, so I swapped her for someone else. End of story."

Fifteen

Dexter

Sasha was a woman of needs and like other women, she made assumptions about me in that sassy little head of hers. Fuck, an explanation wasn't on the cards, but she was behaving like a child, splashing me with water and shouting. Nothing was going my way today and this fucking drama was stressing me out. Ever since that night, I couldn't stop thinking about her. I'd managed to oversleep today, waking up at seven, forgetting about my usual six a.m. workout altogether. I kept seeing her with that asshole in the corridor. I was still pretty fucked off that she had balls to ditch me for someone else straight after we had sex.

"Bullshit, Dexter. I heard her; she said that you two were engaged," she said quietly, finally stopping her struggling, so I loosened up my grip. I noticed her blue bikini and her hardened nipples. Her magnificent tits were a throbbing reminder of that night in my apartment. When I was sucking on them I felt like I was conquering the world, her whole body. Hell, I wanted to have her again, hear her loud cries. What the fuck was wrong with me? I did enjoy repeat sex with the same woman, but no other had ever affected me this much.

"Barbie, you obviously didn't pay attention to anything I said. Dexter Tyndall does not do relationships! The bitch is blackmailing me. We aren't fucking engaged, so get over it!" I yelled, bringing her face closer to mine. We were only inches from each other. This wasn't a game any longer. Sasha was at my mercy and I had this huge urge to violate her mouth again.

I let her go, knowing that I couldn't force her to do anything. I was done with her if she wouldn't believe me.

"Why is she blackmailing—about what?" she asked, swimming away from me. She was going to make me work for it.

"Oh, so now you're fucking interested? It finally got into your head that I'm not a man that likes to be tied down?"

She looked lost and I was ready to dive underwater and give her a quick orgasm. I bet she would love it. Underwater sex sounded exciting. It was one the things that I hadn't yet tried—at least not yet.

"You wouldn't trust anyone either if you found your girlfriend cheating with another man, not once but twice, right?" she asked, looking uneasy. This wasn't an answer that I was expecting.

I've fucked lots of women, but I'd never hidden anything from any of them. That wasn't my style. They all knew that I liked sex.

Her huge tantrum that morning and pouring fucking freezing water all over me—okay, so it all made sense now. More than just one fucker had betrayed her.

I swam to her again and brought my arms around her waist. She was reluctant, fought with me for a little bit before I made her look at me.

"You were the one that found a replacement fast enough. Who the fuck was that guy the other night?"

"Alistair , my co-worker, he had been asking me out for ages," she explained. My blood started to boil. She didn't need to know that I was raging inside, even thinking about another guy touching her sexy body.

"So you thought that you could catch two birds with one stone right? Had a fuck buddy on the side and do the dating thing with someone else?" I challenged. She rolled her eyes.

"We had sex Dexter, that's all. You didn't tell me that I wasn't allowed to date anyone else."

"Dating and sex that's two different things. We both know that no one will come close to making you come the way I have, so you might as well forget about dating other people. Our "session" was pretty hot and I wouldn't mind doing it again. I don't have a fucking fiancée, Sasha. Victoria is just some pissed-off woman that I had obviously been fucking for too long. We went to a party, but I don't remember what went on there. I woke up in the morning and she was lying naked next to me. My head was fucking blank."

She frowned, probably analysing what I said, taking short breaths, pretending like she wasn't affected by how close we were. I smiled wolfishly, wanting to stick my face between her tits. We didn't need to discuss why I behaved the way I did that night when she was going out with that asshole. My feelings weren't relevant at that moment.

"No fiancée or a jealous girlfriend of any kind?" she repeated.

"Told you, I don't do the girlfriend thing."

"I did enjoy that night in your bed, but then in the morning you were so angry when I tried to sneak out. I agreed to go out with Alistair that night because I was pissed off," she explained. "It pains me to admit, but you were right. You are great in the sack."

Something in my stomach turned and a shot of heat began travelling down to my fucking bones, spreading faster than a flash of light. I was getting turned on just by speaking to her and yet I'd already fucked her? I hated playing nice Dexter, but I liked that she wasn't afraid to say how much I'd pleased her the other night. Still, when she was angry she made me want her even more.

"See, I told ya, Barbie; women never complain and you talking about us fucking is a big turn on. Let's get out of this pool before I lose the rest of my control and violate you in here," I growled, reaching out underwater and brushing my finger over her sex. She flinched and looked at me with heated eyes. I was hard again and being in the water didn't help at all.

My finger slipped further under her swimming suit, but she quickly shoved my hand away and started moving through the water.

"I came here to do a few laps, Dex, so hands off!" she warned me, swimming away. We could play hide and seek all day long if she wanted to. I had all the time in the world.

I was lucky, meeting Sasha in her tight little bikini. I could simply pull on it and her rack would pop out. My lips would be sucking those pink nipples in no time at all.

"Shut up, you love being teased and fucked by me. I might be an asshole, Sasha, but I'm not stupid," I laughed, swimming next to her. She rolled her eyes at me, then put her goggles back on and started doing laps under water.

My cock was still a problem; anyone could walk in here. I was the fucking landowner and parading about with a hard dick amongst pensioners wasn't going to help me in any way. I started thinking about two dudes without clothes on and continued to swim. I pretended that she wasn't there, that I was alone. I told myself that if I behaved, she would let me fuck her later in my apartment. That was pretty much enough, because now I had something to look forward to.

Half an hour later I suggested a quick fifteen minutes in the sauna.

It was hot and steamy, but the best part was that I had Sasha there with me. I couldn't fucking stop staring at her beautiful tits, which made me throb with need like no time had passed.

She wasn't even my type, but my cock, as ever, had a mind of its fucking own.

Sasha

I agreed to the sauna, but when I sat down, I realised that I was locked in a small, steamy space with Dexter Tyndall, a guy

114

that I was strongly attracted to, and suddenly this wasn't such a good idea. My breathing was shallow, my heartbeat sped up, and I was ready to get out after only a minute or so. He was sitting next to me with only a small distance between us, but my body was still going through turmoil. I glanced at his boxers and cleared my throat.

"You're hard again, Dex. I mean, I haven't even touched you yet," I said, trying to break the tension that hung between us. Since the moment he had cornered me in the pool, I'd had streams of inappropriate thoughts passing through my brain every few seconds. I blamed it on him; every time he looked at me, it was like we were back in his apartment.

He looked down at his impressive cock and winked at me. "It's your fucking fault. Your bikini doesn't leave much to imagination."

"What? It's not really tiny or anything," I complained.

"That's debatable," he muttered, closing his eyes. "Distract me, Barbie. Tell me something about you, so I don't have to think about how much I want to fuck you right now."

I sighed, looking away. My mind had gone blank and he wasn't helping by stretching out on the steps with his amazingly hard and sweaty chest. "Tell me about Joey. He was my uncle, after all, and so far I don't know anything about him."

"He bought the place couple of years ago. I don't know why, but we got on straight away. As you probably realise, I don't usually get on well with many people, but he was patient with me, tried to talk to me. He suggested golf. I fucking hated it, but he insisted that I stick with it. Within months he turned me around and we started playing together. I fucking liked him, but he had to go and die on me."

I was staring at him, shocked that he admitted to that. I had to tell him about the letter, but this wasn't the right time. I didn't want him to get angry again. It was a real shame that I never met Joey; it seemed he was Dexter's good friend. I had to get it out of Mum what happened all those years ago, why she had never mentioned him before.

"He liked travelling," I said. "I found so many pictures in the drawer in the bedroom and I don't know what to do with them all. It's so strange; apparently he was my mother's stepbrother but I'd never heard of him."

"Yeah, it's baffling. Joey always insisted that he had no family. As far I could tell, I was the only person that he was close to. Maybe your mother is hiding something embarrassing. How about your father? Have you had a chance to ask him?" As he spoke he moved closer to me, his moist skin brushing against mine. It was like an electric shock passing through me, burning my skin with scorching heat.

"I doubt it; Mum isn't like that. She's been married to my father for over thirty years. Besides, Dad doesn't know much about her family either."

Tense silence stretched on for about a minute until he finally asked, "When is the next viewing?"

I felt beads of sweat running in a trail down between my breasts, disappearing down my abdomen.

"Sorry, what?" I asked, forgetting his question. He'd said something about the viewing. His body was so close and it was all too much. It felt like I was being pulled to him by a strong magnetic force. When I glanced at him, his eyes were on me again, heavy and filled with lust. I had never thought that much about sex, not until I started living here. Not until Dex.

He reached out and ran his finger over the swell of my breast, and my voice hitched in my throat.

"You're shit, I can't fucking trust you to behave," he growled, leaning over and tracing his lips over my arm. My mind was getting clouded and my body was shaking with anticipation.

"Excuse me?" I breathed out, lifting my eyes to him.

"The distraction—it's not fucking working. I want to thrust my cock into you now and let everyone hear your screams."

"Bring it on, Dex," I whispered.

Why the fuck did I just say that? Good little Sasha didn't do this kind of thing. Thinking about sex in the sauna where anyone could walk in on us. This was stupid.

He stopped and brought his face closer to mine. "You may regret this, Barbie," he growled and then covered his lips with mine so eagerly that I was on my back within moments and he was pressing himself over my trembling body. The kiss took everything out of me, consuming me like a spreading fire. His hands dived under the bikini, and when I felt his fingers inside me everything became blurry.

"Good fucking, Barbie? Ha, you like being a dirty little slut, don't you?" he whispered into my ear and for some reason his words didn't shock me, only turned me on more. I wasn't the same person from a year ago. I wanted him to slide his dick deep into me until I lost the feeling in my limbs.

"Ahhh Dexter, I want you to fuck me now," I ordered, losing whatever reserve I had. I ran my hand over his hard cock. His head was in my cleavage; his teeth were pulling material away, nibbling and sucking my nipples. He'd flipped a switch deep inside my core, turning me into a river of desire. I moaned, moving my hand up and down his thick hard shaft.

His fingers were inside me, pulsing and thrusting. Everything stopped when he pulled away suddenly. He jumped off his seat, looking like a madman. His eyes were on fire, taking my body in.

I was disorientated, staring at him with shock. "Why did you sto—"

"I want you in my apartment in two minutes. Otherwise, I'll fuck you on the stairs or in the lift, where everyone will hear us," he said cutting me off, and then left the sauna.

Trying to catch up with my own breathing, I started pulling my bikini back into place. His raspy voice rang in my head. I shot through to the changing room and started putting my clothes on. *Stupid, stupid girl.* Dexter was a man of his word and if I wasn't upstairs in two minutes he was going to have sex with me outside, right in front of the concierge's office.

I decided to wrap myself in a towel, not wasting time on clothes, and ran to the lift. Thirty seconds later the lift was taking too much time, so I decided to use the stairs, running all the way to the third floor. I was taking two steps at the time, my chest was burning and I was losing half of my clothing on the way.

"Time is up, Barbie," he said standing in the entrance to our floor.

"What? You can't—"

He brought me to his chest and dragged us down to the floor, slamming the door to the entrance. It took me a second to realise that he was still pretty much naked, already wearing a condom, and I thought, this was going to be fun.

Sixteen

Dexter

Good girl, my ass. She was a fucking tease, pretending that she didn't know what she was doing to me in the sauna. I wanted to see if she liked the challenge. The neighbours, my reputation—I didn't fucking care. I wanted her and I was prepared to take a risk.

Staring straight back at her innocent wide eyes, I was done with being the other Dexter.

She was panting, bending over to catch her breath; she must have run all the way up the stairs. It was good that she was taking me seriously. I grabbed her by the elbow and dragged her back to our joined corridor, pushing her against the wall. Her towel fell on the floor and my eyes took in her impressive rack in a wet swimming costume. Her tight little nipples created a fire deep in my groin, awakening hunger for more. I had thought that I could take control, but seeing her like this had crushed whatever resistance I had left within me.

"We aren't having sex here—"

"You lost, so you have nothing to say, Barbie," I snapped and dug my lips into her neck, pressing my cock down between her legs to her entrance. It was fucking bliss. I just couldn't think straight when she was around. She had her head arched away, exposing her neck to me, breathing heavily. This wasn't right, but it felt fucking amazing.

"Dexter, someone might see us here."

"I can smell your desire, baby, so drop this good-girl attitude and let me fuck you. This will be quick and you have to keep your mouth shut," I warned and bit her earlobe. She hissed. My cock throbbed, digging inside her entrance. Her swimming suit was blocking the way to that moist irresistible pleasure.

I had a feeling that this wouldn't shut her up, so I grabbed her shoulder and spun her around. It was a huge risk taking her here on our floor, but it was exciting and I loved being in total control.

She mumbled something when I dragged her bikini bottom down. Her ass was right in front of my cock. I kicked her legs apart, stroking my hard shaft, licked my fingers and then ran them over her slick sex.

I didn't want to give her time to think about it when she shuddered. My hands were on her hips as I lined my dick up to her entrance and shoved my full length inside her as hard as I could. She moaned loudly and my head spun. I could listen to that fucking sound all day long.

"Fuck, Sasha, you feel better than the first time," I growled, pulling her hair so she arched closer to my face.

"Yes, yes, so much better," she sighed.

I started to move inside her, losing control of how fast I was going. My hips were pushing and before I fucking knew it, she was screaming. My skin was burning, my pulse speeding as pounded my cock into her wetness. She was moaning loudly, arching her hips to me. Fast and aggressive, I didn't want to fucking stop.

I wiped the sweat off my forehead, feeling as if my body was slowly coming apart, but I didn't slow down.

"How do you like this, Barbie? Too fast for you?" I panted, losing my fucking mind. She was coming undone for me, her wet pussy pulsing and tightening around my cock. Sasha was loud, shouting words that didn't make any fucking sense.

I bit on her shoulder as I came, filling her up with my hot, sticky semen. It was like all my Christmases had come at once. I was taking in long pulls of air, my heart thumping deep in my chest. I pulled away from her and then slapped her ass.

She looked at me, eyes glazed over, and I laughed. She was the hottest pussy I could ever remember having. There were women at parties, in offices, clubs and bars. I needed sex to push the deadly voices in my head away.

Sasha was fucked, literally and physically, so I picked her up and strolled inside my apartment. No, I wasn't done with her yet, but I was fucking starving. That was just my starter; I still wanted a main course.

I slammed the door, expecting a phone call from the concierge at any minute. All the neighbours had probably heard her screams. Fuck, I had to stop making life difficult for myself.

"That was awesome, but you didn't have to fuck me in the corridor. We could have made it to the apartment," Sasha said. She was putting her wet bikini bottoms back on when I came out of the bedroom dressed in a t-shirt and black trousers. I lifted my arms and stretched.

"It was necessary to teach you a lesson. Next time you won't even make it to the stairs," I said with a wink, and went to the kitchen. The cleaner was coming tomorrow afternoon, and shit was lying everywhere. I hated tidying up.

"So how does this normally work? Do women leave after sex or do you make them stay?" she asked standing behind me, her hair all ruffled and sexy. The deep red flush on her cheeks was a total turn-on. She didn't look nervous being around me and she wasn't scared. For some reason, I didn't want her to leave just yet.

"Do you have to be anywhere?" I asked casually, pulling some vegetables out of the fridge.

"My pole-dancing lesson starts at seven," she said, moving around the kitchen. My imagination started to go wild just thinking about her body moving around the pole. Fuck, I was just inside her. How could someone get me worked up so fast?

"Stay and I'll make us some dinner."

"All right. I like hanging out in your place."

For the next hour I was busy preparing food. My women normally visited me in the evening, after six. We fucked, made small talk, and they were out by eleven. Some of them stayed for the night, but that happened rarely. I thought it might feel weird with Sasha, but the conversation between us flowed. I told her more stuff about Joey, asked her some questions about her life in London. By five, dinner was ready and I was having fun watching her eating my pasta dish. She seemed impressed by my culinary skills.

"I wasn't expecting that you could cook," she muttered, crossing the fork and spoon on her plate. It baffled me that I had a blonde woman in my apartment, eating my food.

"I guess I'm just full of surprises," I chuckled.

"Do you know what you're going to do about the supermodel brunette?" she asked, getting up and taking out the plates.

"The supermodel brunette?"

"Your fiancée," she said sarcastically, walking back to the kitchen.

"No, I haven't thought that far ahead. I'll get my solicitor involved if she ever shadows my motherfucking doorstep again."

She laughed, shaking her head. This wasn't fucking funny. I watched her put plates in the dishwasher. She bent down to do that, giving me a great view of her ass. Pole dancer—who would have fucking thought it?

"But you must remember what happened at the party, even when you were drunk?"

"Whatever the bitch is implying won't matter. She can threaten me as much she wants."

Sasha seemed to be mulling over what to ask next. Why did she have to bring Victoria up?

"Why do you have so many pills in here?"

Sasha

I didn't want to sound nosy, but there were pills everywhere, in small unlabelled containers and in a bowl right by the dishwasher. Next to the fridge I also noticed a pipe and could smell weed. I wasn't judgmental, and Dexter didn't look like someone who would enjoy getting stoned, but I was a nurse, after all. I thought I needed to ask these questions.

He was on his feet before I knew it. He shoved me to the side, picked up the bowl and put it in the cupboard. When he looked back at me, his nostrils flared. Okay, so he was angry.

"That's none of your fucking business," he barked.

Yes, the sex was amazing, adventurous and maybe I was finally coming out of myself, but I was concerned. I hoped that all these medications were prescribed and he didn't just get them from anywhere. "Are you ill or something? You don't need to be an asshole about it, I'm just trying to have a conversation," I said, not wanting to sound annoyed, but it surely came out that way.

"Then have a conversation about something else. Like, for example, how much you want to suck my cock."

Shit, this was getting absurd. He shifted so fast, switching into some other Dexter. I hated when he sounded like he was only using me.

"You wish. I don't know what your problem is. I was simply showing you that I'm concerned about you. None of these pills are in the proper containers. How do you know which ones to take?"

The muscles on his jaw started twitching and he stood up straight, like he wanted to do everything in his power to intimidate me.

"Are you going to get on your knees and suck my cock or not?" he asked with that familiar superior tone. Anger pushed through me and I stepped towards him.

"You're behaving like a child. We both know this isn't about sex. You're simply refusing to address the issue and talk about the random fucking pills."

"We fuck, Barbie, and that's all there is to it, so fucking stay out of my business and get down."

I was normally very patient and understanding, but Dexter pushed me over the edge. His mood swings weren't funny anymore.

"Don't you ever try to treat me like a whore. From now on I want you to stay away from me until you grow the fuck up!"

I marched back to my apartment, not even looking back at him, slamming the door behind me. I tried to take a few deep breaths. He could so quickly make me lose control. Pills—I had dug in where I wasn't supposed to, so he automatically shut me down. He had many issues, but it was just sex, I wasn't supposed to get involved.

I made sure that I locked my terrace doors that night. I thought that we would make up, and have more mind-blowing sex. Okay, so I was wrong about the part with the fiancée, but the pills, weed and his lifestyle was scary. He was either going through a rough time or he was ill. Maybe Dexter wasn't acting; maybe he was an arrogant prick that treated women like possessions.

After our fight I took a hot bath, easing the thoughts about the past few days. I had to sell the apartment. Now that Dexter wasn't a problem, the whole process shouldn't take that long. He was done with playing me. Once I was out of here I was ready to start over in Edinburgh.

I wasn't surprised that I didn't hear from him. At six I changed, packed my training gear and then I was out, heading for another pole-dancing lesson. Gina knew about my performance and this week we were trying more advanced routines. I was ready to do it again, but I had no idea how often Harry organised these sorts of parties.

That evening I could barely catch my breath by the time the hour-long training was up. Gina had pushed me hard and my legs were trembling. The spins were more complex and really challenging.

It was just after half past eight when I got back to the complex. The girls wanted to go out for a quick drink and I'd agreed. After almost a year I finally felt like I had friends again, women that I could talk to. This kind of warmed my mood a little.

I was still pretty pissed off with Dexter. I needed and expected an apology. If he wanted to form any sort of relationship, he had to start acting like a normal human being. The pills were really worrying me now. He was right, this was none of my business, but I had a feeling that he was self-medicating, and this had proven to be dangerous before.

When the lift stopped I stood by my door for some time, fighting with myself. He had disrespected me, but I had to check that he was all right. The deep worrying feeling hadn't left me since I'd stormed out of his apartment earlier on.

I stepped out on the terrace and crept over to his side. Luckily for me, the curtains in his place weren't shaded and I could clearly see what was going on. He was on the sofa, just lying there, looking like he was in pain.

I was ready to push aside our stupid argument from earlier on and find out what the hell was wrong with him. I slid open his door and went inside uninvited.

Seventeen

Sasha

I instantly smelled a strong odour of weed coming from the kitchen and living room. Dexter was lying on the sofa with his eyes closed. I spotted a joint on the table with a half-empty bottle of whisky. I guessed he must have drunk quite a bit already.

I shouldn't really have cared about him and his well-being. As he'd pointed out several times, it was just sex between us, but after this morning I couldn't stay away. I was concerned that he was mixing too many unregulated medications just for the sake of it, causing more damage than good to himself.

"Hi," I said softly.

"What are you doing here, Sasha?" he asked. I was expecting him to be his usual self, acting superior like this morning, but his question was quiet and guarded.

"I was worried about you," I said, knowing that there was no point in making stuff up about why I was here. I got an impression that he liked to put on an act, and I wasn't buying it anymore. All I wanted to do right now was to find out what was wrong with him.

Tomorrow I had another viewing that he probably didn't know about, and there was a strong possibility that I could gain a sell out of it. The estate agent had mentioned that his client was very keen. But this wasn't the time or the place to bring it up.

He ran his hand over his face, then looked at me. For the first time I noticed dark circles under his eyes.

"I have a really bad fucking migraine. So sorry, but I can't fuck you right now," he growled. He lifted himself up, hissing as he did so, probably as the pain in his head escalated. People who suffered from migraines had to lie still for several hours, mainly in a darkened room.

Dexter picked up the joint from the table and lit it up.

"Does this happen often, the migraines?"

"Too fucking often, and after years of using it, the weed doesn't seem to be working as effectively as it used to," he snapped, sounding angry.

I bit my lip, trying to come up with something, anything. The silence stretched for several minutes. "A nurse that I work with knows a very good neurologist in Glasgow," I said and then paused, not even sure if I knew what I was saying. "I can arrange an appointment for you tomorrow; we can drive there together if you want?"

He inhaled sharply, dropping his head down. "My mother has been dragging me to doctors since I could fucking remember. All these fuckers are the same, doing tests, but never knowing what the hell is wrong with me."

I shook my head, understanding why he was resistant. I sighed and walked to the bathroom, and an idea popped into my head. In the bottom of a drawer I found a black towel. My own muscles were tense after the workout and I didn't want to fight with him anymore; we were past that now. I ran the towel under cold water and then squeezed it out.

"Sasha, what the hell are you doing here right now?" he repeated when I walked towards the sofa. It was a positive sign —he wasn't using that stupid nickname again, but my real name. Maybe arsey and arrogant Dexter had finally left the room.

"Helping. Now lie down on the sofa again," I ordered.

He didn't argue this time; he looked like he was in a lot of pain. I placed the towel over his eyes and forehead and told him to stay still. For the next twenty minutes we didn't say anything. I sat down on the chair opposite, thinking about Joey and my mother. I'd been meaning to visit her and if Dexter agreed to go to see a neurologist, I could kill two birds with one stone.

Sometimes migraines were very severe. I didn't want to ask him about the pills, alcohol and whatever else he was taking. Those kinds of personal questions seemed to anger him. In time I was certain that he would eventually explain what was going on. I bet he was the kind of guy that if pushed, would withdraw further and close up completely, so I had to be patient.

After some time I thought that he finally had fallen asleep, but then his husky voice vibrated through the room. "Tell me about the saddest day of your life, Barbie?"

I dragged more air into my lungs and closed my eyes. I didn't want to talk about it. Since that day three years ago, I'd thought about that terrible day only a handful of times. I had been suppressing it inside for years now; maybe it was time to finally share it with someone else. I had refused to talk about it, remembering how long it took me to put the pieces back together again. That deep wound always remained inside me and I was afraid to scoop it out with my own words, in case I fell apart all over again.

"It was three years ago. It had been raining all day in Glasgow and I was eating curry that my boyfriend had cooked for me. Two hours later I was sitting in the hospital and the doctor told me that I'd had a miscarriage."

I swallowed the tears, not wanting to break down in front of him. For several minutes we didn't say anything. I don't know why I decided to tell him about the fact that I had lost a baby. He didn't care and it wasn't like we were going to end up together anyway, but I felt comfortable being here with him. That hadn't happened since I left Glasgow.

"How did you feel then?"

His voice was comforting for some reason. My little baby had meant the world to me and I was in denial for so long after that. Kirk had been so happy when I announced that I was pregnant. My limbs went numb as an old pain started pulsing through me again, reminding me of how I felt then. It was only the beginning of everything that went wrong in my life. When I found out that I was pregnant it was the happiest moment in my life, but then it was taken away from me in a heartbeat.

"It was like someone had scooped out the last bits of joy left in my body and thrown them away. There was nothing after that; just emptiness that I had to face every single day. No comfort, no solace, no anything."

He took the towel off his eyes, but I refused to meet his gaze. There was no point. He wouldn't understand it anyway. Dexter had never loved anyone, and I had burned myself so many fucking times.

"Maybe the baby was not meant to be. Maybe the guy was an asshole and it spared the baby and you any future pain," he said.

Tears fell down my cheeks and I still refused to look at him. The past version of me temporarily replaced the real me, the happy me that I was then, pushing in dark twisted memories of what happened, so I shut myself down. Dexter was right, Kirk had turned into a monster, but we'd both wanted that baby back then. He was hurt and the whole relationship had gone downhill from there. I didn't want to imagine what would happen if I'd stayed with him.

I got up and headed to the door, wiping the tears away. I couldn't let him see me like that, so lost and damaged. I liked playing strong. Why did I have to be so honest all of a sudden?

"Hey, Sasha," he called after me and I stopped and turned around. "Whoever he was, he wasn't worth your time and I'm sorry about your baby. It must have been hard."

Dexter

I didn't sleep that night, thinking about what Sasha had said to me. Whatever shit came my way didn't fucking matter, because it looked like she had gone through a lot more than I could ever comprehend. When I'd lost my father I was a mess, but Sasha was hiding more scars away from me I could tell.

I shouldn't have cared, but I fucking asked the question, which meant that I did care. She was the hottest pussy I had slept with and I got hard every time I thought about her pole-dancing moves at the party.

One second I was calm, relaxed, thinking about our steamy sex in the corridor; the next minute she was walking into my life with her muddy shoes, wanting to know why I needed pills, asking uncomfortable questions.

The demands of her going down on me had come out of my mouth before I could stop myself. I behaved like a complete ass sometimes. We'd had good times together and I enjoyed her being around me. Three years ago, she got pregnant, probably with some douche, and then she lost the baby. Maybe I pushed the boundaries, but I felt comfortable around her and when I was in pain I didn't think much about what I was saying.

The intense headaches started after Joey's funeral. I used to have migraines before, from when I was fifteen. My mother dragged me from one doctor to another, but no one could ever find a reason behind it. I learnt to deal with it, distracting myself with a lot of sex and weed. I didn't really like getting stoned, but my brain switched off then. It was great not to feel anything.

I woke up later than usual, at five a.m. The headache had finally gone away, so I got some work finished. Sasha was at the apartment today and I was ready to take her up on her offer from yesterday. I wanted to make amends for treating her like she was a whore, so I made a few phone calls and cleared my schedule.

Despite the restless night I had shitloads of energy and I was knocking on her door at ten o'clock in the morning with a coffee. Yes, I wanted to fuck her again, and I was hungry for more information about that asshole that fucked her life up.

Really? I needed to get a fucking grip.

She opened the door wearing white shorts and a red top. My mouth watered, but I forced myself to keep my eyes on her face, not her glorious tits. She folded her arms over her chest and raised her left eyebrow.

"Morning, Barbie. Coffee?" I asked, imagining her naked. No—I had to shut off my stupid fucking sex drive. She took it from me, looking wary and slightly uncomfortable.

"Thanks, but I'm confused. You must want something if you bought me a coffee?"

"Well, sometimes I am a human. Besides, I wanted to take you up on your offer from yesterday," I said, hardening my eyes on her. She wasn't wearing a bra—fuck, again teasing me like that.

"Offer? What offer?" she asked.

"The neurologist in Glasgow?"

"You want to go with me?"

"Yeah, I can't take this shit anymore. The headaches are getting worse," I said. I didn't normally ask women out—not that this was a date or anything—but for some reason I trusted her. She was a nurse.

She switched her weight to the side and bit her lip. My dick twitched.

Focus, Dex. You can fuck her later in the car.

"No, that's cool, but I need to pop in and see my parents first. My mother needs to sign some paperwork for the solicitor. Besides, I haven't seen her since I moved here," she replied. "You know, I can introduce you to her as my boyfriend. Maybe it's time. We have been seeing each other for a while now, you know. What do you think?"

I looked at her like she was crazy while panic invaded my body. I wanted to have her in my bed again, but meeting the parents—what the fuck? I wasn't ready for heavy shit like that so early in the morning.

Then a huge smile broke over her face and she shouted, "Gotcha!"

"What the fuck?"

"The look on your face! God, it was hilarious. You were shitting yourself," she laughed.

I shook my head. "You know that you will regret that, Barbie."

"Shut up, Dexter. I needed to mess with you a little. Anyway, on a serious note, I do need to see my mother. You can wait in the car or come in, whatever. I don't care."

"All right, but do you always talk this much? I cleared my schedule so we can head off early, but now we are discussing pointless crap."

"Charming as always. Just give me five minutes. I need to change first," she muttered and disappeared inside. I didn't want to meet her mother, but I was curious enough. Joey had never mentioned any close family and after all, Sasha was his niece. Maybe I was ready to break all the rules.

Sasha was holding a stack of papers under her arms when she came back. She looked sexy as fuck wearing black leather pants and the same white top from earlier on. How was I supposed to keep my hands away from her for a whole hour?

The drive to Glasgow was going to be interesting. Sasha was serious about helping me, but I was thinking about all the places we could have sex. I fucking hated meeting with women for dates or going to their apartments, but this was different. I actually wanted to hang out with her.

I insisted on driving, because I didn't like to fuck around. Surprisingly, the conversation between us flew nicely. Sasha was talking most of the time. She seemed nervous and I had no idea if it was because of what she had revealed to me yesterday or because I made her uneasy. I was barely listening to her, thinking about sucking on her wet sex.

It was hot and humid and that didn't help, because I was hard most of the drive. Half an hour later I pulled up outside a semi-detached house in an all-right neighbourhood. I had bought a house around here a couple of years ago, so I knew the area quite well. Sasha's parents weren't rich—that was obvious—but I wasn't judging. It wasn't like I always had shitloads of money, and Sasha was supporting herself, and that was what mattered. My mind clouded as I imagined banging her in some swanky hotel in the city.

"I shouldn't be long," she said, tossing her blonde hair behind her.

"So? You won't invite me in?"

"You want to come in? To meet my mother?"

"Why not? It's not like you're going to introduce me as your boyfriend—but we both know that you want to," I chuckled and leaning over, I caught her lower lip and sucked on it. She gasped, but I pulled away, knowing that this was bad fucking idea, because I was ready to rip her clothes off and fuck her right there on the driveway of her parent's house.

She was breathing hard, trying to tame her crazy hair.

"Whatever. Me and you as a couple is never going to happen," she said and got out of the car. I strolled after her, thinking about some old dudes having sex. It must have helped because my dick went flat. After all, I still wanted to make a good impression.

Eighteen

Sasha

This was bad idea. Dexter wasn't behaving like himself; he was simply too nice and I didn't know if it was because we were going to see my parents or because I had told him about my precious baby. Last night he looked so vulnerable and lost. Normally my coping mechanism would've stopped me and shut the truth away, but yesterday everything was so different. I felt as if I wanted to share my secret with him.

Now I was standing outside my parent's home, anxious to have him next to me. Mum knew that I had sworn off men for good, and I didn't want her to think that there was something going on between us. He was the exact type of man that I didn't want to get involved with, and this trip was just a favour.

I knocked a couple of times and then walked inside, feeling slightly nervous. Dexter was standing right behind me with that unusually calm expression.

"Hey, Mum, it's me. I brought someone, a friend," I shouted. When I looked back at him he was smirking behind me. What was I supposed to say? A boyfriend?

Mum came out of a room wearing a green long dress. She was off today and she was probably in the middle of baking. Being in the kitchen relaxed her. Mum worked hard, normally a fifty-hour week, while Dad drove around Europe. I learnt from an early age that both my parents were proper workaholics.

"Sasha? Are you okay, hun?" she asked.

"Yes, I'm good. I need you to sign some paperwork. I think we forgot to complete this one form." I then pointed at the

Scottish sex god standing behind me. "By the way, this is Dexter, my neighbour."

My mother smiled widely. "Hello, Dexter. It's nice to meet you," she said, eyeing him intensely.

Dexter looked puzzled, staring at her with some sort of recognition in his eyes. "Mrs Scott, it's lovely to finally meet you," he said, finally snapping out of it and shaking my mother's hand. "I'm sorry to be so forward, but I recognise you from one of Joey's photographs that he had in his apartment."

Mum's face paled and her eyes went wide with shock. For about a minute no one spoke. Tension mounted in the air and I felt like someone had dropped a large stone between Dexter and Mum.

She grabbed my arm suddenly and said, "Sasha, can I please have a word with you in the other room?"

Before I had a chance to say anything, she was dragging me upstairs. I shot Dexter a confused look, shrugging my shoulders. She shut the door to the bedroom quickly, like she was afraid that he would follow.

"Mum, are you okay? That was quite rude," I pointed out.

"You should go, and take that boy with you. I told you that I don't want to talk about Joey," she stated, rubbing her hands over her thighs nervously. This was getting silly now. I had no idea what had happened in the past, but the guy was dead and he was my uncle. I needed to know the truth.

"This is the man that I was telling you about, remember? Dexter. He knew Joey and apparently they were close. What's going on? What are you so upset about?"

"Nothing, it's nothing. I'm not going to discuss this with you or him. Find a buyer as soon as you can. I don't want anything to do with this whole thing," she insisted.

I folded my arms over my chest, trying to figure out what she was hiding. I'd never been interested in family drama, but she was keeping stuff from me—stuff that was obviously important.

"These things take time. I won't be able to just sell it overnight, Mum. And I'm not leaving until you tell me what Uncle Joey did to you or what happened."

"This has nothing to do with you, Sasha, and I won't be digging out any crap right now."

"In that case, I'll ask Dad. He should know more about—"

"No, don't you dare! I don't want to worry your father; he's on the road. Sell it as fast as you can. Tell that man downstairs that I'm not feeling well. I don't want to see him."

If my mother convinced herself about something, then that was it. She was stubborn as a mule, and she wasn't prepared to talk about it. I wished that we had the same connection we used to, before I'd moved to London. It was my fault that we had drifted apart.

"Fine, but eventually you'll have to tell me what's going on," I muttered and left the room. I felt like a complete idiot. It looked like I didn't know my family after all.

I went back downstairs and told Dexter to wait for me in the car. He didn't question me. Mum signed the paperwork and fifteen minutes later, I was walking away from the house.

Thoughts about my childhood and school were moving through my mind. I was trying to remember family gatherings, events that mattered, but nothing came to mind. No one had ever mentioned Joey before.

"Are you all right, Barbie?" Dexter asked me when I got into the car.

"No, not really. I'm confused. Something is wrong. My mother has never behaved like that. She was perfectly fine until you mentioned that photo."

"I'm not wrong—she *is* the woman from the picture. It should have clicked earlier. Joey carried it with him all the time. It was pretty fucking important to him."

"She bluntly refused to explain anything. This doesn't make any sense," I muttered.

"I don't know what to say, Barbie. Joey was a very private person. I never asked him about the picture," Dexter said. I sank back to my seat, knowing that I had to tell him about the letter.

"Dexter listen, at Harry's party, after you showed up when I was changing, you dropped a letter. I think it must have been in your jacket pocket," I began, wondering how he was going to react when he found out that I have read his private correspondence.

"Letter, what fucking letter?"

"A letter that Joey wrote to you while he was on holiday. I read it, so I know about his epilepsy attack and the way you reacted that night."

Dexter looked at me, taking a short sharp breath. I was moved when I read that letter, and I wanted to get to know the real Dexter.

"We were friends Sasha, very good friends."

"Dexter, you saved him that night. I don't get it. Why do you have to hide under that selfish act, like you don't really care and–"

"I was lucky that I knew what to do. Joey was a decent man, but he's gone now. End of story. I don't want you to dig into this shit now," he cut me off, sounding angry and frustrated. There was no point pursuing this subject any further with him. I learned from early on that he was stubborn and uncooperative when it came to questions like that. We hadn't just met and yet he still wasn't ready to open up to me about the way he behaved.

He drove off the estate in silence. I was glad that I finally told him that I read that damn letter, at least I didn't have to hide anymore than I had to. My own past was in pieces and I didn't want him to see me as a victim.

"My mother wants me to get rid of the apartment as soon as possible," I said. Dexter tightened his palms on the wheel, but didn't say anything. The estate agent had scheduled a viewing for today, but I didn't mention this to him. Suddenly I felt really sad. I wasn't ready to leave. He was insisting that this was just sex, but at the same time he was breaking a lot of rules for me. Maybe there was something between us, but I was fully aware that Dexter wasn't boyfriend material.

We reached Glasgow Royal Infirmary within twenty minutes, riding in complete silence. As we parked the car, I noticed that Dexter had tensed up. We weren't together—hell, we weren't even friends—but I felt that this was a big deal for him. Going to the hospital with someone else, trying to break the usual cycle.

Doctor Boyd had agreed to see him on such a short notice as a favour. Maria, my old friend from uni, had managed to schedule the appointment for him that morning. Boyd was a quite well-known neurologist with many years of experience, and I had a feeling that Dexter had never seen such a renowned specialist before.

It took us a while to find the right building, but after a frustrating search we managed to locate Boyd's consultation room. We didn't talk at all, but Dexter was obviously nervous. I was only there for moral support, but every time I glanced at him he looked agitated and anxious. I didn't think that it was appropriate for me to go into the room with him, so I said I'd wait outside.

Dexter

I didn't know why I had agreed to see this fucking specialist. He wouldn't tell me anything new. He asked me questions about my medical history and requested some pointless tests. I got a prescription for a new drug that I was supposed to try out for a few weeks. In my opinion it was a complete and utter waste of time, but Sasha wanted to help me and I was playing nice Dexter for a bit.

Dark thoughts began to invade my mind. I couldn't fucking stand hospitals; the smell reminded me of my miserable teenage years. My mother was determined to prove that there was something wrong with me. She couldn't save Pap, so she wanted to run every possible test on me, making my life even more miserable. Doctors were running test after test, but they couldn't find anything wrong. For a couple of years I blamed Mum for my getting into fights and heavy drinking.

I was fucked off with the way everyone treated me. I didn't have a brain tumour or a cancer. It was the same with my brother. Mother was so overprotective about everything.

The dark thoughts were slowly embracing my mind, pulling the strings of self-preservation away. I didn't have any fucking pills on me and the stuff that the neurologist had prescribed was new. I drove on knowing that I needed to get stoned quickly, but I was out of weed.

I could call Penny or Courtney again, but they were both pissed with me and besides, I wasn't in the mood for fucking anyone else apart from Sasha.

It was always a vicious circle, the act of sex. Yeah, I needed to fuck someone, but Sasha wouldn't want to be used. She cared that I was in pain yesterday and she did tell me about her miscarriage. Fuck, yeah, I was attracted to her, and I wanted to taste her pussy again, but at what cost?

After my appointment, we didn't talk. I couldn't believe that I lost that letter from Joey. I must have left it in my suit jacket. She thought that we could talk about it, hell I didn't want to bring it up or think about Joey at all. We were close, but he was dead. I didn't quite come to terms with the fact that I couldn't talk to him anymore.

When I was passing the Hilton, I took an abrupt turn to the left and drove straight to the swanky car park filled with shiny new cars. Sasha looked at me, surprised. She was beautiful and at this moment I didn't understand my obsession with fucking brunettes. I had never been sexually attracted to blondes; even in college, all my girlfriends had been dark haired.

"And we stopped here because?" she asked, sucking on her bottom lip. I leaned in, inhaling the same perfume that she'd worn the first time we met outside in the corridor. My johnson started twitching uncontrollably. This was the only fucking way; I had to stop the encroaching darkness and her loud moans could easily cure me.

"Here's what's going to happen, Barbie. You want me and I'm horny as fuck, so we are going to get a room in the hotel and we are going to fuck," I said and closed her mouth with mine, fast, so she couldn't say no. Besides, I had been meaning to kiss her since I shut the door on my car. I brought her closer and moulded my hand around her boobs. She moaned and that was enough to send me to another planet.

My groin burned and I made a deep sound in the back of my throat, pushing my tongue inside her mouth and kissing her like she was the only woman that ever existed. I didn't even need to check; I was confident that she was wet. Her pussy would be dripping for me.

"Dex," she moaned when I pulled away, my chest rising and falling in rapid movements. "You could have just asked me and I would have said yes."

"You talk too much, so I just made a decision for you," I said and got out of the car.

Just outside the building I stopped, pulled her into my arms and abused her mouth until she couldn't catch her breath. We got looks from posh hoity-toity people who probably found touching in public a disgrace. I didn't care anymore. Right then, I wasn't in my complex and I was planning to fuck her hard until I was numb and she was satisfied.

The woman at the front desk was taking too much time. She seemed nervous, blushing when I asked how fast she could give us the room. While she was trying to figure out how to use a fucking computer, I brought Sasha in front of me and shoved my hand inside her knickers. A group of Asian businessmen were surrounding us, and no one was paying attention to us.

She looked at me, trying to pull my hand away, but I slapped her wrist, grinning.

When I delved my finger into her wet folds, my cock strained against my trousers. I pressed my erection into her bum cheeks. At that point I didn't have much control left in me.

"How would you like to pay, Mr. Tyndall?" the receptionist asked. She smiled at me. Yeah, yeah, yeah. She wanted my cock too, but I was too busy taking care of my Blondie. The dark-haired receptionist needed to get in the queue.

"Here, try this," I said and threw my bank card over Sasha's shoulder. The woman went back to the computer screen and I plunged my finger inside Sasha's wetness again. My pulse was racing, and I ran my other hand through her hair, gently kissing the back of her neck. I started massaging her clit slowly, my cock digging against her perfect firm ass. She dropped her head to the side, biting her lip hard. I wondered how long I could torture her like this. Her thighs tensed and I ran my tongue over her neck, forgetting for a second where I was. She was arching herself forward and I smiled to myself.

This was just the beginning, baby.

Nineteen

Sasha

"Here is the key to your room, Mr Tyndall. I hope you enjoy your stay," the receptionist said, winking at Dexter. What the hell was wrong with her? Did she not see that he was with me? Dexter still had his hand in my knickers, so I couldn't make a sound. When he finally pulled his hand away, the muscles in my stomach tightened and I groaned silently. I felt like I needed a slap. My knickers clung to my soaking-wet pussy.

"Thank you, Laticia," he replied with his serious tone. Good that he didn't encourage the flirting, because I was ready to punch her. I rolled my eyes when he grabbed my hand and proceeded to drag me towards the lift. My head swam with delight, but I was also questioning myself, cautious about his fingering me in public. I let him manipulate me like this. Deep down I was excited, trembling with anticipation. Dexter was like a wild adventure: scary, thrilling, but deeply satisfying. An adventure that could come to an end at some point, but right now he was here and I wanted more.

He was tapping his foot impatiently and when the lift arrived, he pushed me inside.

"Why are you so—"

"Shut up and tell me what you want me do to you," he growled, cutting me off. He pushed me against the mirror, so I was locked in his strong grip. His chest was crushing my breasts and the temperature of my body skyrocketed to about a hundred degrees Celsius. My knickers were drenched and I wasn't thinking straight.

"Sex would be good, you know," I said, trying to be funny. He narrowed his eyes at me and kicked my legs apart with his foot. When I felt his hard length between my legs I hissed with pleasure.

"That sassy little mouth of yours will get you in so much trouble. I want details, Barbie. Tell me what you want." He began kissing his way down to my cleavage. His cock was pressing itself over my pussy, which was throbbing painfully. What was it with this guy that I liked his games so much?

"Strip me and then fuck me hard," I growled and he went down and started unbuttoning my trousers. The lift stopped and he quickly covered me with his body, smirking. We were lucky enough that the floor was empty. I couldn't wait for us to get inside the room. I thought that he was fiddling with the key just to piss me off more. Finally, we barged inside kissing passionately, moaning and panting loudly. When I managed to pull away and look around, my jaw dropped. This wasn't a room, it was a presidential suite with sofas and a bar. The bedroom was triple the size of my own bedroom in the apartment.

"Wow, this is amazing," I gasped, but he didn't give me much time to admire the place. He picked me up and threw me on the bed like I didn't weigh anything at all.

"Did I tell you that you fucking talk too much?" he asked and started stripping off. His jacket, shirt and trousers went flying around the room. My heart began to pound when I took in all of him, standing and watching me with fire in his eyes. This wasn't how I imagined this afternoon would go, but I wasn't complaining.

"No, but did I tell you that you should be nicer to me?" I asked. I got on my knees and started crawling towards him. He laughed, shaking his head and dropping his boxers to the floor. My breathing sped up, and I kept my eyes glued to his erect cock. I was so turned on that I couldn't think rationally.

"I hate to break this to you, but you only get the asshole Dexter from now on. I'm done being nice. You like me rough, don't you, Barbie?" he asked as I licked my lips.

His cock was just level with my face, so I started caressing his rock-hard shaft softly. He pushed his head back and when my mouth covered the tip, he growled with approval. Everything started speeding up. My heart pumped faster as I wrapped my lips around him and began sucking him off. Dexter wrapped his fingers in my hair as I continued to move my mouth over his length.

I liked it that I was controlling this. I could stop it at any time and he would go mental. The thought of it turned me on even more, my lips sucking faster, pulling and massaging as I added my hand.

Boiling heat shot through me, igniting the fire deep in my core. I wanted to make him come, or maybe torture him a little for what he had done to me in the reception area.

"Fuck, that's enough, Barbie. I'm going to sink my cock into your wet pussy. I bet you can't fucking wait," he rasped.

I was on all fours before I took another breath. He was crawling behind me, pulling my leather trousers down and ripping my knickers off. I gasped and tried to look behind me, but he only laughed.

"No peeking," he whispered and then I felt his fingers sink deep inside me. I cried out, knowing that I wasn't going to last long. All of it was happening so fast and I thought I was going to explode, but then he pulled his fingers away.

He was ripping something, probably a condom packet, and several seconds later he was thrusting himself inside me. He was so hard, but I took him all. He grabbed my hips from behind and began to fuck me fast. Within a moment I was out of breath, panting as he pounded his hard cock into me. My thighs were numb, my pulse rocketing as I moaned and screamed for more.

"You have such a perfect ass, my Blondie, and I want to hear you come hard for me," he growled, picking up the pace.

I was coming then, just as he said, so hard and so fast that I couldn't control it. My orgasm shattered through me and I did scream then because he didn't slow down, digging his fingers into my skin, running his lips over my back.

I was loud and held nothing back as his cock kept thrusting into me faster than ever. He came and then we both collapsed on the bed, breathing hard.

Dexter

I liked having sex with Sasha; she was so responsive. We were like a match made in heaven. I brought her into my arms and we lay there for several minutes, panting heavily.

Fuck, normally I would have thought about sex with other women, but she was more than satisfying, bringing me to the edge of insanity every time. I fucking liked holding her close to me, knowing that she was no one else's, just mine.

I had no idea where this thought came from and all of a sudden I got scared, petrified that I was going to end up like my father, fucked up and dead. That wasn't on, so I pushed her away and jumped off the bed. I'd been planning to fuck her all day long, but I didn't want to use her just because she was willing. We had some sort of connection.

When I glanced at her I couldn't help but run my eyes over her magnificent breasts and wide inviting hips. Sasha was a real woman. Fuck, why have I always wanted to fuck scrawny skeletons?

"What are you doing?" she asked, yawning. I'd worn her out good. She looked delicious and when she'd sucked my cock earlier, I thought I had died and gone to heaven.

"Ordering us room service; I'm fucking starving," I growled at her. I was getting too comfortable. It was time to call someone from the old crowd tomorrow, just to be on the safe side.

She was behind me, tracing the lines on my back, and I liked it. I shouldn't have, but I did.

"I want a mango sorbet, pretty please," she sang, fluttering her eyelashes at me. Like this shit was going to work on me—but I couldn't help but smile.

I grabbed my bank card and picked up the phone. Something had changed. My thoughts weren't rushing like they had when we left the hospital. My head was normally busy with ideas about different business investments, but the sex with Sasha had calmed me down.

"Let's see what they have on the menu," I muttered and then ordered a few different items. After I slammed the receiver down, Sasha was smiling at me.

"Thank you, I appreciate that you listened," she said. We were both naked and the food was going to be a while. Might as well go down on her... I couldn't resist.

I smiled and jumped back on the bed. I didn't think I had ever done this before: paying for a room just because I couldn't wait to get home. That was a first.

"The sorbet is for me, not you, Barbie," I said and started kissing her neck. She had smooth skin and I wondered if she would continue to fuck me even after her move.

Where is this coming from, Dex? You're not monogamous.

"Tell me about your family. What are they like?" she asked.

I pulled away and took a deep breath. She wanted to talk now, when all I could think of was her tight, moist pussy. "What difference does it make if I tell you about them?!"

"Hey, it's not like I'm asking you to fucking marry me. It's a conversation, Dexter. This is the way people communicate with each other," she snapped and folded her arms together. Feisty Sasha—yeah, I liked her.

"I was never very good with conversations; I prefer to fuck and that's something that I definitely know how to do," I said with a smirk.

She rolled her eyes. "You'll have to try harder then, because now we're here and waiting for food, so we might as well talk."

"Or we can fuck, which is a much better way of spending time," I suggested.

"We could, but we won't. Besides, what are you afraid of? That I'll fall in love with you or something?" she snorted. "Don't be fucking stupid."

First marriage, then love? What is she trying to say, that it's impossible to love me or something?!

I was angry again; it took her about thirty seconds to piss me off.

"Barbie, I could make you fall in love with me if I wanted to, but to answer your question, no, I'm not scared. After my father hung himself, I haven't confided in anyone. Joey was the only person that knew what was going on with me."

"Have you got any brothers or sisters?"

"One younger and one older brother. Jake is married and has two kids, and Connor—well, the little shit still lives at home. He fucks me off so much, playing computer games all day long."

"He'll grow out of it eventually."

"He'd better, but he's stubborn like my mother. I paid her mortgage off and she barely has any bills, but she still insists on working."

"You paid your mother's mortgage off?" she asked with disbelief.

I didn't get it, what's the big deal? I had a plenty of money and surely I wasn't going to just splash it on my fucking brother. He needed to get a real job.

"Yes, I did. After I purchased the complex and turned it into luxury apartments, I was bored and my mother needed to chill."

A knock on the door startled both of us, jerking us into reality. I jumped off the bed, put my boxers on and opened the door. It was a good thing that it was a waiter at the door. I hated women giggling and blushing around me. It was so pathetic.

I took the tray and put it on the big wooden table, which was in the middle of the room. I insisted that Sasha eat naked. Everything was fucking delicious. A tomato, basil and mozzarella starter, followed by steak and Barbie's choice of mango sorbet. We ate in silence, polishing everything off in good speed, and then I insisted of feeding her the final course.

Sasha

I knew that he didn't want to feed me; it was another game for him. He was supposed to put the spoonful of delicious sorbet into my mouth, but most of it ended up on my boobs.

"I'll take care of it," he growled and before I knew it he was licking the sorbet off my chest, swirling his tongue around my nipples. He had me hot and bothered again and within a few seconds he was fucking me again. This time he took his time, making me come slowly, but with so much intensity that I nearly passed out. When I was with him, I felt detached from problems and worries. Reality didn't seem that harsh. I couldn't move by the time he was done with me and an hour later we both had fallen asleep.

I woke up in the early morning and found him snuggled into me. I stared at him for several seconds, wondering what the hell I'd got myself into. Dexter was difficult and he protected his privacy like a lion. He was letting me in slowly and with caution, but I wasn't delusional, thinking that we could ever work as a couple. This was a nice situation to be in for now, but I needed to remember that I had a big heart and I couldn't let him break it.

I took my time with my shower and make-up. The room was beautiful; the bathroom was finished to the highest standard. I was planning to take all the small toiletries away with me.

When I came out Dexter was fully dressed, packing his stuff away.

"Morning, sunshine," I called out.

"Hurry up, we're leaving," he barked at me. Right, so he wasn't a morning person. Our perfect honeymoon was over. He threw me out into reality so fast that my head was spinning.

"All right," I muttered.

There was no point in arguing and I guessed I had to forget about morning sex. He looked like he was in a hurry. We were out of the room within few minutes and by the time we got to the lift, his silence was bothering me. I thought that I had pretty crappy mood swings, but he was just so inconsistent. One minute he was tender, the next angry and withdrawn.

The atmosphere had shifted, and the tension was making me uneasy. Dexter was tapping his foot against the floor and checking his phone every five seconds like he couldn't wait to get out of this hotel. I had no idea what had happened while I was in the bathroom, but I was fed up with trying to keep up with him.

The lift opened and just as I was about to get inside, I looked up. The air whooshed out of my lungs and I thought I was going to go down on the floor right in that moment. I was staring at a face from my nightmares.

Twenty

Sasha

Kirk was staring at me with wide startled eyes. I swallowed past the large lump that formed in my throat. Pain from the past poured through my heart as I remembered him coming at me with those vicious hate-glazed eyes. I was trying to move, to do something, but I was glued to the spot.

"Sasha?" he asked, like he didn't recognise me, the fucker.

Dexter began to shift next to me and his eyes took in Kirk. My ex-boyfriend had short brown hair and he was wearing a suit. He looked sophisticated and it seemed that after a year, life was treating him pretty well. This wasn't fair and I wanted to vanish. I grabbed Dexter's elbow. Panic was invading me quickly like an unexpected avalanche, washing over my body, threatening to suffocate me. Dark thoughts began rippling through me as I stared at the man I had been in love with for years. It had taken him only a second to betray me.

"We need to take the stairs, right now," I hissed.

"Sasha, wait. I want to talk to you. I've been meaning to call your mother," Kirk said, taking a step towards me. The corridor was slowly closing in on me; the panic attack was approaching as my heart rate escalated. This wasn't happening. He wasn't here, he couldn't be. His voice had haunted me in my dreams until this day.

"Sasha? What the fuck is going on?" Dexter snapped, annoyed. I couldn't just stand there like that and let Kirk manipulate me into a conversation. I span a hundred and eighty degrees and started marching away.

"Hey, wait. Come on, Sash, I think I deserve at least a minute of your time."

I felt his hand on my shoulder and nausea hit me. The pain washed over me, reminding of that fatal day in our flat when I was trying to make amends, to understand why he did it, picking up the pieces from the past four years. Then came the humiliation and his hidden cruelty when he began turning everyone against me, kicking me while I was still down.

"Don't fucking touch me, you piece of shit!" I screamed, whipping around.

In the next moment Dexter was right in front of Kirk's face, shoving me aside. In other circumstances I would have told Dexter to mind his own business, but seeing Kirk again drained all my energy and courage from me. My whole body was shaking and I knew that I had to get out of this building; otherwise, I was going to start screaming.

"Sasha, who would have thought. You got yourself a body guard, how ab—"

Kirk didn't finish what he wanted to say; Dexter had him pinned against the wall, his face a couple of inches away from Kirk's. My ex wasn't weak. He was taller and bulkier than any other man I knew. I gasped when I saw Dexter's face. He looked like a madman, his eyes filled with escalating fury.

"Say one more word to her, shitface, and I will rip your tongue out of your mouth!" Dexter growled and shoved his elbow over Kirk's neck, pressing it until my ex-boyfriend's face paled. There were other people moving through the corridor and Dexter was making a scene. Bile rose in my throat. I couldn't get him involved—not then or ever.

"Dex, please. He's not worth it. Let's just go," I said quietly and touched him.

He listened, letting go of Kirk, who slid down the wall like a sack of potatoes. I was going to throw up, but then Dexter grabbed my hand and started dragging me away, heading for the stairs. All the while he was talking to me, but I wasn't really listening. The voices from that night were alive in my head. I felt like the new confident part of me had died and I was left with my old mousy self.

"Listen, stay here for a second, I'll be right back," he told me in the car. I knew that he had to go back and check out.

Shivers tingled down my spine as memories of previous encounters pushed right through my head. The stabbing panic threatened to seize control of my brain. I didn't know how much time passed, but eventually Dexter came back. He shoved something cold into my hands.

"Eat. This should make you feel better."

I looked down and saw that he had brought me a mango sorbet like the one we had shared last night. Tears threatened to splash out of my eyes, but somehow I managed to push them away. Several deep breaths later I had my body under control, but my mind still wasn't functioning quite as well as normal.

"Sasha, seriously, eat. Otherwise I'll feed you. The sorbet will distract you from whatever the hell is going on in that sassy head of yours."

I sighed loudly, counted to ten and looked at him. Dexter grinned. I couldn't let him see me like this, broken and shattered. Kirk was a psycho and I should have known better; we were back in Glasgow. I didn't even think that I could bump into him—the city was massive—but fate was a total bitch.

I lifted my hand and started eating. As my taste buds registered the amazing sensation, my brain started to switch off. Dexter was right; the sharp taste of sorbet could turn any negative thoughts away. I emptied the bowl within minutes. My breathing was coming back to normal. Maybe there was still a chance for me.

"Nice one, Sasha. You didn't even offer me a bite," he grumbled.

"Shut up, you didn't say that you wanted any." I inhaled slowly and let his eyes travel over the tight white top that I'd worn today. When I met his gaze, instead of desire I saw troubled concern, and that put me on edge. I didn't think he cared about my feelings.

"Who was he?" he finally asked, switching on the engine.

I'd told him something that I hadn't shared with anyone else before, but my past was fucked up and very complicated. I was afraid that if I told him the whole truth, he might not look at me the same way. "My ex-boyfriend," I said.

Silence stretched on for some time until Dexter began to drive off the car park. I assumed that we were going back to the complex. The wild adventure was over.

"I could kill him for you if you want," he offered.

I glanced at him, smiling widely. "And what would you do with the body?"

"Barbie, why are you even asking that question? I've enough money; I would hire someone to do the dirty work for me. I'm too good-looking to be messing with shit like that."

"Too good-looking, huh? How are you so sure?"

The car stopped at the traffic lights and Dexter leaned over and kissed me, deeply and sensually. "I'm sure. I'm the best-looking man in Scotland and probably England too," he said, pulling away.

I couldn't stop laughing, trying to hide my uneasiness.

"Kirk was the father. He did care when I got pregnant, but then things went downhill fast."

"Why do you hate him so much?"

I was staring down at my fingers, aware that Dexter wanted the real answer. We weren't in a relationship, but I wasn't done with sleeping with him yet. I didn't want to dive straight back into the gloom, like my first few months in London, where I was the loneliest person on earth, broken and battered

"He hurt me, but I don't want to talk about it. I know that I never want to see him again."

"I can still hire a hit man to kill him."

"If you kill him, that means that you care too much about me, Dexter, so cut it out."

I didn't need to look at him to know that he didn't like my statement. The light changed to green and the car moved forward. The silence was awkward, but at least he had done a good job with lightening my depressive mood; his, too, for that matter. I still had no idea why he'd behaved so strangely when we woke up.

"I do care about you, Barbie; more than you realise. This isn't a fucking game anymore."

His words rang in my head, spreading warmth down through me, igniting my body with heady emotions. Neither of us said anything else for the rest of the drive, but I was wondering if he really meant what he said. Was Dexter sending me some sort of encrypted message? Was this more than just sex between us? He was so cold, and the next moment he was Prince Charming.

I was hoping that the prescription would give him some relief from the pain. There were many causes of migraine. Dexter used a lot of other drugs and he smoked; this wasn't a good combination.

An hour and a half later, we arrived back to the complex. I was in a much better mood. Dexter was quiet. I had another pole-dancing training session tonight and I needed to take it easy before the class. I was hoping that he'd had enough sex today and would let me rest.

Unfortunately, there was a sour surprise waiting for us outside the entrance. Victoria stood by the doors, looking even better than the last time I saw her. She wore a tight red summer dress that showed off her figure, high heels, and barely any make-up. Fuck, I really wanted to smear mud all over her face. It hadn't taken her long to come back.

"Well, well, well. Who do we have here? A mouse and a prince," she said

Dexter

"Get the fuck out of my property," I said, stepping right in front of Victoria. I thought that I had settled this with her the last time. I wasn't in the best of moods today. Sasha had woken me up and it didn't take me long to realise that I had snuggled up to her in my sleep. When she'd disappeared into the bathroom I felt like I was ready to explode. I was scared, afraid that I was getting too close to her, and it was time to abandon the sinking ship. Then our encounter with the ex, and now I had to deal with this crazy bitch again.

"I'm going inside, Dexter," I heard Sasha saying. Victoria was staring at me with that stupid smile on her face.

"So, you and the chubby blonde? What are you now, a charitable shagger? No one would fuck her, so you offered?" She chuckled.

I lost it then. It was the combination of anger from earlier on and something else… the darkness that inflicted more violence. I grabbed her shoulders and pushed her against the entrance doors. Hitting women wasn't my thing, but she turned me into mad Dexter.

"It's not your fucking business where I stick my dick, so get the fuck out of here before I stop remembering that you're a woman," I growled, pressing her hands over her head.

"There's a video that you should see. Check your e-mail lover. And start treating me well; otherwise, I might accidentally leak it to the authorities or the press. I bet they would be very interested in what I have to say," she whispered and then licked my ear lobe.

I stepped away from her. Video? What the fuck she was talking about now?

"You have five seconds to get your ass out of here; otherwise, I'll call the police myself," I snapped and then went inside.

Five minutes later I was upstairs, scrolling through my e-mails. Victoria's was on the top, so I opened it. A shudder began moving through my spine. This couldn't be good, but I had to see what she was threatening me with. The screen was black at first and the sound quality wasn't too good, but I instantly recognised myself in one of the bedrooms at the party. Loud music was blasting in the background and I instantly knew that song.

"Fuck, babe, you're so tight, so fucking tight."

I didn't remember fucking anyone at the party. Victoria had invited me and when I got there I was in really shitty mood, so I started drinking heavily. The camera was shooting from the side while I was fucking someone in the missionary position. A blonde girl. I didn't recognise her or remember her moans. Nothing rang a bell. She came and then told me that it was the best night in her whole life, but I was already out, snoring next to her.

She giggled to herself, then got up and took the camera with her as she walked to another bedroom. She brought the camera to her face. "Hi. My name is Jenny Rogers and I'm fifteen years old, and this was my first time."

I fucking lost it then. I threw the laptop from the table and roared like my head was going to explode. A ton of bricks dropped into my stomach. I started pacing around the room, trying to remember everything I'd done that day, but my mind was blank.

I hated crowds, loud fucking music and socialising, but Victoria had insisted on going. We met at the train station and she picked me up. I hit the bottle instantly, because I didn't want to talk to anyone. Everything became blurry when I took some pills.

Sex with an underage girl—hell, even I wasn't that stupid, but the video seemed authentic. I couldn't get my head around it. I was breathing deeply through my nose. After a few moments I started going through the photos on my phone. The party was almost four weeks ago.

I scrolled through and then stopped, and the colour drained from my face. I saw my own selfie with the blonde girl from the video.

Twenty-One

Dexter

The confirmation was in the photo, but I still couldn't fucking believe it. I began opening the cupboards and pulling out whatever pills I had left on the counter. My mind started chasing one thought after another; a sign that I was just about to lose the last bits of self control that I had left in me. The world started spinning, turning me into another person, the violent Dexter. I was ready to beat the crap out of someone just to relieve my frustration.

I had no idea what to do, who to fucking call. They could lock me up for this shit, and I could get a good few years in prison. The pills were supposed to stop making me feel like I was losing the ground under my feet.

I always slept with whatever woman came my way, but a fucking fifteen-year-old! I had crossed the line this time, and I didn't even remember anything. My head was blank; I had no memories or recollection of anything that had happened at that fucking party. Someone must have dropped roofies in my drink, but now it was too fucking late to prove anything. The shit would be out of my system by now.

I was just about to swallow a dozen pills when my phone started to buzz. The number was unknown, but I answered it anyway.

"Tyndall," I barked.

"Told you, I'm not like everyone else. You can't just toss me aside and move on, Dexter," Victoria purred. I clenched my fists so hard that I cut the circulation to my fingers.

"What the fuck do you want?"

"Just this and that. Don't worry, you will know soon. For now, you can do whatever you like. Just remember, I'm the one that's squeezing your balls slow, but tight."

"You're full of shit. You used someone to drug me."

"Don't be ridiculous, darling. The video is real—Jenny couldn't stop talking about that night. Besides, I've missed your cock."

I tossed the pills on the floor, roaring with frustration. I could take the risk and just tell her to go and fuck herself, but I had been building my business and reputation for years, and I couldn't afford to toss it away. My track record wasn't exactly in my favour. I had been quite violent when I was younger, but this could jeopardise everything—my whole fucking life. I had used an underage girl for sex.

"Victoria, you want sex? Is this what this is about? I fucked you so hard and no one else came close?"

"Yes, I want sex, but I also need a date for a party."

"A party? What fucking party?" I shouted.

"Oh, calm down. It's something that I'll use you for, a date for a party and some other functions."

"I'll end you for this, Victoria. I can fuck you up so bad that you will never lift yourself up again."

She laughed. We had only been fucking for a couple of weeks, but I always knew that there was something off about her. I shouldn't have messed with her, especially after the freaky shit in the bedroom that she wanted.

"Promises, promises. Just wait for my phone call, baby. You will be going to that party with me whether you like it or not."

She hung up and I wanted to smash my phone, but somehow I managed to toss it on the table. I had shitloads of money and I could make this go away, but how? It was time to make some phone calls.

"Hey! Are you all right?"

Sasha was just walking through the terrace doors. I was furious, but she was probably the only person I wanted to see right now. Yeah, this was none of her business, but right then I needed a good fucking distraction.

"Victoria sent me a video from this party we went to together couple of weeks ago, and this shit isn't good," I announced and scrolled through the e-mails. I handed her the phone when the video started playing. She watched it in silence, but the shock came straight after the girl announced how old she was. "The bitch is blackmailing me," I said.

Sasha exhaled and spotted the smashed laptop on the floor. She shoved her hands into her pockets, her eyes darting at me. "So you didn't know how old this girl was when you slept with her?"

"No. I think that bitch Victoria drugged me, because I don't remember anything at all. That evening I told her that I was done with her, but in the morning I woke up in her bed, and not in bed with the girl from the video."

"Does this happen often, that you don't remember stuff?"

"Of course not. I like women to be fully aware of what I'm doing to them. I was in a shitty mood then, and at the time I thought that the party would be a good distraction."

She was asking too many questions. Fuck, maybe she didn't believe me. She seemed so calm about this whole thing.

"Call your solicitor, Dexter. You can't let her get away with this."

"And say what? That I was too fucking high and drunk to remember anything? No, I'll deal with this shit and then I'll destroy her. This is a game to her; she only wants my cock, nothing else. She likes to be in control."

Sasha

159

I didn't know why I was so calm, talking about it like he didn't do anything wrong. I should have been freaking out; he'd slept with someone's child. He'd brought this on himself. Maybe with Victoria he finally crossed the line and she wanted to teach him a lesson. But I couldn't just leave him on his own with this. The video definitely seemed genuine.

The girl looked really young, but we couldn't be sure that she was underage. He needed to check this to make sure that he had actually committed a crime.

"Dexter, don't do anything stupid. I'm here if you need me, but we have to be careful who we talk to about it," I said.

"Thanks, Barbie," he muttered and then he cradled me to his chest, resting his face in my neck. For a moment I couldn't move, I was so shocked, but then I closed my eyes, enjoying that one rare moment of affection.

It all ended when my own phone started vibrating in my pocket. He let go of me, clearing his throat, and nodded for me to take it.

"Hello," I answered.

"Miss Scott, it's Jeremy from Thomas George."

My stomach sank and I glanced at Dexter, who was watching me.

"Hey, how are you?"

"Good. I just had a phone call from the client that viewed your property earlier on. He would like to offer you the full asking price. Also, Mr Clement is a cash buyer, so it looks like everything can be sorted within a few weeks."

I couldn't believe it—I finally had an offer.

"That's fantastic news! I'm happy to take the property off the market, and you can let your client know that I'll accept the offer," I said, trying not to sound too happy, knowing that Dexter was listening. His eyes narrowed and he clenched his fists. This wasn't good. Was he pissed that I'd sold the apartment?

I told Jeremy to call me back with more details. When I hung up, an awkward silence stretched on for some time. I had no idea why, but I felt like I'd betrayed Dexter. I wasn't ready to move out, but at the same time I couldn't turn the cash buyer away. Mum had called after I left Dexter with Victoria outside. She was insisting that I needed to speed things up.

"You fucking should have told me that you had a viewing," he snapped, leaning over the kitchen table and digging his hands into his hair.

"You knew the apartment was on the market, Dex, and since we had stopped fighting, I assumed that I didn't need to tell you about everything little thing I do. The guy viewed it when we were in Glasgow and I couldn't turn him away. I'm sorry that you had to find out like this, but I had no choice. It's my mother's inheritance," I explained. I didn't even know why I was saying this to him. He had known that sooner or later, this would end.

Fooling around one night in a hotel and a sad confession on my part didn't make us a couple. We were fuck buddies, and that's all there was to it.

"Fuck, Sasha, I'm not ready for someone else next door. Call this fucker back and tell him that you don't want to sell it. I need more time," he said, pacing around.

I frowned, confused. "This isn't about you, Dex. My mother is freaking out; she wants me to get rid of it," I insisted.

"Who is the buyer?"

"Don't know—some old guy and he's offering cash."

Anger rippled through his face, and his jaw tightened. I really had no idea what the big deal was.

"Get out, Barbie. Get the fuck out of my apartment!" he shouted suddenly. I took a step towards him, wondering what the hell his problem was. Only a moment ago I was in his arms, and the apartment in question didn't even belong to him.

"God, Dexter, stop it! You knew why I was here. He won't be moving in tomorrow; we still have time. We could—"

"What, Sasha? You thought that everything would be same once I knew that you were leaving? I'm fucking pissed. You should have told me!"

"Dexter, calm down. I'm not moving out tomorrow. Why do you have to make such a big deal out of it?"

He laughed, but it wasn't his normal cheerful laugh. He looked like he was crazy.

"I don't fucking care if you stay or leave. You are one of the wettest pussies that I have fucked, but I'm not someone that you can mess around with!"

I didn't want to stand there and listen to his bullshit. I was so convinced that we were past that. I walked away and slammed the door behind me, angry that we were back to square one, that I let him get to me again. Why were we always arguing about stuff that didn't matter? It was pathetic.

Maybe I shouldn't have taken that phone call in front of him, but I couldn't pretend that I would live next him forever. It was my parents' apartment and I had no say in the matter. Mum needed a buyer. My job wasn't paying enough to for me to take out a mortgage for three hundred thousand pounds.

I threw up when I got inside my own apartment. Now he wasn't only making me mad, but also ill. Dexter was self-destructive, but he didn't need to take it out on me. I was trying to convince myself that he got angry because he cared about me.

It was early and I didn't want to stay inside knowing that he was next door. Several minutes later I heard him beat me to it, leaving first. I exhaled with resignation and then decided to go to bed.

I took some sleeping pills. With the visit to my mother, the intense sex with Dexter, my encounter with Kirk, Victoria showing up and then the phone call, I was utterly drained. I needed to be on my own for a bit to digest everything that had happened today. The pills worked their magic and I drifted within minutes.

After our fight, days passed and Dexter didn't come around. I heard him in his apartment, but we were living like we didn't know each other. Our argument gave him a good excuse to stay away from me, probably for good. I was waiting to see other women coming and going from his apartment, to show me that I was really just one of many.

Gina was pushing me harder during pole-dancing training, so I went to work on Friday night a little sore. She mentioned an upcoming competition in London in a couple of weeks and she wanted me to sign up for it.

I always dreamt of competing, but I never thought that I was good enough. I knew that I was ready, but Dexter occupied my mind and I couldn't quite focus, knowing what he was going through. I couldn't help someone who didn't want my help in the first place.

On Saturday I was done with arguments and fed up with waiting for Dexter to come over and apologise, so I signed up for the pole-dancing competition that Gina was talking about. That night I went to bed angry and pretty stiff from earlier training. It looked like Dexter wasn't going to apologise, and I was fine with it. Sunday morning I wanted to sleep in late, but a loud knock to my door woke me up. I got out of bed, wondering if Dexter finally had decided to pull his head out of his ass. I opened the door ready for a big rant, but it wasn't Dexter; it was Harry from number thirteen.

"Hey, beautiful, how are you?"

I threw myself at him, not caring for the world that we didn't know each other that well and this was a bit forward. When I pulled away, he looked relaxed. "Good. How are you?" I asked.

"Are you alone? Sure I'm not intruding?" he asked, looking around.

"Yes, I am. Why? Did you think that I had company?"

"Dexter..."

I lost my smile then. He probably thought that Dexter was a changed man and now we were madly in love.

"That bad, huh?"

"No, I'm fine. Dexter is next door and he's still himself."

Harry came in and sat on the sofa. Looking at him, I began to wonder what was wrong with me. Harry was a much better choice than Dexter: handsome, well mannered, and he was into me. I should take him up on his offer just to piss Dexter off, I thought.

"So how is it going anyway?"

"Good. I found a buyer, so it looks like I'll be out of here within the next couple of weeks."

Harry looked surprised. "Really? Wow, I wasn't expecting that. Where are you moving to?"

"Probably Edinburgh. I work in the city, so that makes more sense," I said and then began telling him about Joey and how I ended up in the complex. We talked for a while over coffee about his work and my pole-dancing competition. Harry was a good listener and two hours later we were still on the sofa talking about his business.

"So, what's happened to the madman next door? I know that it isn't my business, but I saw the way he was looking at you during the party," Harry finally asked.

"It was just sex between us; nothing else and nothing more," I said, looking away.

"And you wanted more?"

I laughed. "No, of course not. I had no expectations. Dexter is a complicated man with a lot of issues. Yes, we had a great time together, but it's not love, just sex. He seems to be pretty pissed off with the fact that I'm selling the apartment."

Harry nodded. "Well, it's obvious; he's crazy about you, but he's too stubborn and self-centred to admit to it."

I was shaking my head. Dexter was crazy about my pussy, not about the fact that he wanted to be with me. I didn't want to dig into why he was so afraid of love. His old girlfriend was blackmailing him and my own past was too fucked up to make this work.

"Don't be silly. Dexter only cares about himself. We both know that," I said.

"You don't know him very well then. He cares, Sasha, but he has a strange way of showing it. I don't know why. I never asked about his problems."

"Let's just change the subject. This is too depressing and the world doesn't revolve around Dexter Tyndall."

"No, you're right," he said, getting up. "I need to shove off anyway; I have something that I have to take care of. "

"It was great seeing you. Thank you for stopping by," I said, hugging him. I walked him to the lift. When it arrived, Dexter strolled out. He stopped instantly when he saw us.

Twenty-Two

Dexter

Harry had his arms around Sasha. What the fuck was going on? A shot of raging jealousy singed my chest, but I tried to ignore it. I hadn't seen her since she got that fucking phone call. Fuck, even now she looked sexy as hell, wearing skimpy black shorts that exposed these well-defined thighs.

I was frustrated sexually and mentally. In the past few days I had been trying to figure out why I got so pissed off the other day. I'd always known that she was going to move out, but we weren't done playing yet.

"Hey, Dex, how are you?" Harry asked.

"Fine."

That's all I said, then I opened the door into my apartment and slid inside. I couldn't be bothered talking to him, not right in front of her. We were close and we had stuff in common, but the situation with Victoria hadn't really sunk in yet and I had a lot to think about. I kept insisting to myself that me and Sasha, we were done—this whole thing had gone too far—but I still wanted to have her in my bed. I regretted that I had thrown her out of my apartment right after telling her that I didn't care.

In the past twenty-four hours, I had been fighting with myself, wondering if I should just go to her and apologise. Fuck, Dexter Tyndall didn't show any signs of weakness.

Several minutes later there was a knock to my door. I wondered who it was this time.

"Hiding in our bunker, are we?" Harry asked, standing at the door. I should have known that he would show up here, but why did he go see Sasha? He had no business with her.

"Not in the fucking mood. What do you want?" I asked and started walking away. I heard him closing the door behind us.

"What's with you and Barbie?"

I ignored him and picked up some Jack Daniels from the cupboard. My head was racing again, and I hadn't fucked anyone else since Sasha. This was getting out of control.

"Nothing. We fucked, fought, made up, fucked some more. It was fun," I said, laughing it out, but I sounded like a total asshole. My body was craving her for more than just sex.

Harry didn't look happy with me and yes, I got it. I hated myself right then. I'd fucked up. And then there was Victoria and her emotional blackmail. I had no idea what to do.

"All right, so if you're done with her then can I have a go?"

I lost my shit then. I got up so quickly that the chair fell back onto the floor, and I grabbed Harry by the collar. I was ready to beat the shit out of him, but Harry was taller than me, and he reacted faster than I expected. He wrestled with me for a bit and then slapped me like I was a girl.

"For fuck's sake! Calm the fuck down, Dexter. I'm your friend. Do you really think that I would tap that while you can't even get it together enough to admit that you want to keep her for yourself?" he shouted and let go of my shirt.

I didn't say anything. He was partly right; I went into a rage even thinking about her and another guy. But then she had just made a decision and fucking accepted that offer.

"It's complicated," I muttered.

"Funny, because when I asked her about you, she said the same thing," Harry replied. He seemed angry and my own head was wrecked. I didn't know what I wanted anymore. "She said that you aren't the boyfriend type, so she isn't holding much hope."

Barbie was right. What did Harry want from me anyway? To go to her and declare my love? That wasn't happening—this wasn't a fucking Mills and bastard Boon book.

"She's right and there won't be any happily-ever-after. I like her, but that's about it. I don't work well in a relationship."

Harry sighed and sat on the sofa. I was hoping that he would leave, but he stayed and began asking me about the business and the complex. I was sensing that he wanted to know what went on between Sasha and me, but I wasn't ready to talk about what was really niggling at me. This whole thing was complicated enough between us.

An hour later he was gone and the buzzing in my ears started, so I took a bath. A few hours later, I was still hearing the buzzing noises and I couldn't pinpoint them, so I stayed busy rearranging the paperwork in my office, looking through properties and my finances. That didn't help, and I started going through my apartment, trying to find the insects that must have been making that noise that I had been hearing all day. My pulse was speeding up and I couldn't sit in one place, so I put running shoes on and went out. A few miles would do the job. The imaginary voices should eventually go away.

I passed through the entrance to the complex and ran through the grounds. The gate to the beach was unlocked. I kept looking behind me, feeling like someone was following me, but each time I stopped there was no one there.

I ran for miles, longer than I should have, stopping from time to time and glancing behind me. My breath was coming in short ragged pants; I was pushing myself hard with no real purpose. At some point I turned around and then walked back. The buzzing noises followed.

This time the physicality of hard exercise didn't seem to be doing me any good. Sex and women were the best solution to all my problems, but I didn't want just any pussy; I needed Sasha's.

I wasn't so much anxious as agitated and tired. There were still many hours of the day left. The thought of coming back to the empty apartment plunged me into consuming despair, but this was what I had always wanted. Pap died because he couldn't handle life. I'd rather stay alone than be dead.

"Dexter?"

I lifted my head and stopped, seeing Sasha in her tight running shorts and sports vest. She was walking towards me from the other side of the beach. Now I had no choice; I had to come up with some sort of apology, because I wanted to get lost with her, shade the windows in my bedroom and bury my cock in her slick wetness. "What are you doing here?"

It was a lame question, but I didn't know how to act around her anymore. She made me uneasy. I was normally very confident and aggressive, even with clients. I knew what I needed from them, but being with woman I cared about—that was an entirely different thing.

"Right now, nothing. I'm going home," she replied and walked past me. Okay, so she was still pissed and she didn't want to talk to me. That was understandable after the way I had treated her.

"Barbie, wait. I need you to hear me out, so stop running," I barked.

She glared at me. "I'm not running away Dexter, I'm going home."

"Listen, I'm fucking sorry, all right? I shouldn't have thrown you out of my apartment," I said, massaging the nape of my neck.

She sighed and shook her head, then walked up to me. Why couldn't I just say that I wasn't ready for her to leave, that I liked having her around? *Stupid fuck!*

"Just don't say something that you don't mean, Dexter."

"Shut up, Barbie. I mean every fucking word. I was pissed that you were going to leave, so please let me make it up to you," I said.

She raised her eyebrows, looking apprehensive. "How?"

"Let's go down to the beach. Walk with me."

"Dex, I'll be moving to Edinburgh soon. This won't last forever," she said, reminding me about that fucking sale.

"I know."

It wasn't that bad; Edinburgh, I could live with that. All I wanted was to keep her with me for a bit longer. I insisted on going closer to the shore. The tide was out tonight, revealing muddy rocks and seaweed. We were still a distance away from the apartment, but all I could think of was her body in those tight athletic clothes. I found a nice private space between the rocks. It was a fucking heaven and I knew that no one could spot us here, unless a boat passed by. I didn't care. I wanted listen to her panting, moaning my name again.

"Dexter, this isn't a good idea," she said, her voice strained.

"Shut your sassy mouth and let me fuck you. Consider this my way of saying fucking sorry."

Sasha

Alarm bells started going off in my head when he brought me into his arms and kissed me, his tongue instantly connecting with mine. This was so wrong, but it felt so good. His touch and calming words shocked me. The savage desire I felt reminded me how much I had missed him over the past few days.

He took off his t-shirt, exposing his wide gleaming chest. He must have been out for a run around the same time as me. It was funny that we had gone in opposite directions. I was angry when I saw him, but still pretty worried.

"Sexy, you're so fucking sexy," he said, turning me around and running his tongue over my spine, then my bum cheeks. I gasped, feeling his fingers stroking me. I was wet for him, and angry, and turned on all at once.

"Dexter, maybe we should talk about—"

"No, no talking, Sasha. I need to be inside you and you will love every second of this sweet torture," he said, cutting me off, and I shut my eyes feeling his fingers working their way into my wet knickers. His mouth was kissing my shoulder, biting at my neck. Tingles of heat lashed down the base of my spine. He had so much control over me. I tried to glance around to make sure that we were alone, but I was shaking with anticipation and need.

Dexter sank his finger into me and I thought that I was going to explode. Normally it took him a bit longer to make me come, but I was already crying out, wanting him to carry on, feeling like my heart was going to pound right out of my chest.

"Oh, now please, I need you inside me," I croaked, losing touch with reality.

"So wet for me—fuck, I missed this."

His erection was pressed against me, then suddenly he was inside me. My breath hitched and Dexter pulled my hips closer to his.

"Shit, don't stop, just don't," I said and he laughed.

"You ordering me around, Barbie? Bad, bad girl," he rasped and thrust himself into me fast and deep.

He pulled out, then pushed his hard erection back into me. My eyes were screwed shut as he pounded into me.

I couldn't tell what was different this time, but I exploded straight away as his hand moulded against my breast, hearing his heavy panting. I felt dizzy from the sudden orgasm. He didn't stop, but only fucked me harder. He was saying something, but I was too lost to listen.

When he turned me around I was on the verge of losing my mind. His teeth claimed my hard nipple and he sucked it, groaning, then continued to fuck me as I bent over the rock.

I knew that I was going to have bruises, but right then I didn't care. Dexter came quickly while I was shaking, gasping for air. I collapsed on top of his chest, panting.

I felt him pulling my leggings and underwear back on. When I opened my eyes, he was smirking.

"Maybe we should go out more often," he said.

I rolled my eyes. "Maybe."

We went back to the complex together and I offered to make him dinner. It was obvious that he didn't like staying anywhere else than in his own apartment, but I wanted him to break the routine. This was nice and different.

We ate talking about Joey again, not touching the subject of the sale or us at all. I was shocked when Dexter wanted to sleep in my bed that night, since he had work in the morning.

I thought that he was going to run away, but he stayed and then went down on me, giving me another mind-blowing orgasm. We fell asleep tucked in each other's arms. I didn't want to think about the future and what was going to happen when it was time for me to move out. I knew now that Dexter did care, but he had to think about how to deal with Victoria. Fear began creeping its way into my head, but I pushed it away. It was better to believe that everything was going to be all right.

I was awakened by screams. For a brief second I thought that I was dreaming. Something wasn't right and the space next to me was empty. I rubbed my eyes and sat up in bed.

"Ants and fucking cockroaches everywhere!"

"Dexter? Are you all right?" I called out. There was a light on in the bathroom and the shower was running. I got out of bed and opened the door. The bathroom was steamed up and I heard Dexter talking loudly.

"Crawling everywhere... Sasha, you see them? Little fuckers," he kept saying.

I swallowed hard and slid the door to the shower open.

He was standing by the wall, his eyes wild and scary, darting everywhere. "There are bugs everywhere, Joey. Can't you see them? Crawling up and down, all over me," he kept saying over and over again.

My heart stopped and I just stood there for a second, frozen. I was unable to move. The water was surging over him, his skin was mottled red from the heat of the shower and his hard scrubbing, and for the first time in my life I had no idea what to do.

Twenty-Three

Sasha

"Bugs, cockroaches…"

I was staring at him, wondering what the hell he was talking about. He pointed at the walls and ceiling like there was something really there, crawling up and down. I swallowed hard. He was hallucinating. I didn't know how to act, so I stepped inside and switched off the water.

"Dexter, hun, come on let's get you out of here," I finally said and touched him. His wet skin was burning. I needed to stay calm, but deep down I was freaking out, wondering if he had finally lost it. Eventually he listened to me and stepped out of the shower, shaking wildly. He kept mumbling that there were insects everywhere, on his legs and arms, and he tried to flick them off. I closed the shower doors and put the towel around him. In the bedroom I realised that it was shortly after five in the morning. Dexter didn't have to be at work until eight. This was getting stranger with every passing second.

It took a few minutes for him to stop talking. I knew that I had some Valium in my apartment, so I told him to go to his apartment and get dressed and went to fetch it.

I began throwing stuff around on the floor, searching through my bag frantically. It took me ten minutes to finally find it. When I barged into his apartment, he was already in his suit.

"What are you doing?" I asked, bewildered.

He shrugged his shoulders, adjusting his tie in the mirror. The pupils in his eyes were still dilated, but he looked more like himself. "Getting ready, what does it look like?" he snapped.

"Dexter… you can't, we have to go to the hospital," I stuttered, pushing him down on the bed.

Was it possible that he was pretending the incident in the shower didn't happen? He seemed annoyed.

"I'm fine, Sasha; I freaked out. Don't stress. I thought that I was seeing things," he said calmly.

I wasn't buying this. "No, Dex. You were convinced that there were bugs everywhere. You can't go to work; you need to see a doctor. This isn't normal," I insisted.

He shoved me away and stormed back to the living room. "Don't be fucking stupid. I'm going to the office."

"Dexter, it's five a.m.," I shouted.

He glanced at his watch, then at me again. "Bullshit, you fiddled with the time," he growled.

I opened my mouth to say something, but no sound came out. There was something very wrong with him, with this whole situation. He sounded like he thought it was me that was acting crazy. I needed to call his mother or someone from the family.

"No, Dex, I haven't. The noise from the bathroom woke me up and you were inside—"

"Sasha, I don't have time for this bullshit. I need to go. Just lock the door behind you. I'm fucking fine," he snapped and stormed out of the apartment.

I couldn't catch my breath. My panic was rising. Now I was going to go through a meltdown because of him. I thought that he would realise that it was only just after five a.m. and come back. He didn't, so after an hour I started looking through his drawers. All his numbers were listed on his landline handset. I found the contact that said Mum and exhaled with relief. I didn't want to call her just yet, but I was on the verge of losing my sanity, so I saved it to my mobile just in case.

I locked the door and went back to my own apartment. At six fifteen I had a phone call from the agency asking me to do a day shift instead of night. I agreed, not even knowing why.

I knew Dexter was very moody—it was part of his bad-boy appeal—but I've never seen him like that, almost psychotic. It was the first time and I didn't want to pretend that it hadn't happened. I went to work an hour later, knowing that this was very serious. I was worried—really, really worried.

Dexter

"Sally, get me another coffee," I barked at my secretary. I was pissed off with the world and convinced that Sasha was playing games with me. She must have changed the time on my iPhone and the clock in the kitchen, but when I got to the office, no one was there. Something clicked then. But I wasn't crazy; I had just lost track of time.

"Here you go, Mr. Tyndall," she said, placing a fresh cup on my desk.

I managed to get the number for pest control. There were bugs in her bathroom; how could she not see them?

The morning meeting didn't go too well either. Robert and the others were staring at me, bewildered, as I sped through my presentation. It was only nine fifteen when I finished, and it seemed that they hadn't been keeping up with me.

"Dex, buddy, are you sure that you're all right?" Robert asked straight afterwards.

"I'm great, why?"

"You were going too fast; the clients won't be able to follow you. Maybe you should slow down."

"It was slow, Rob," I muttered.

He laughed and patted me on the back. "No it wasn't, mate. You were going like two hundred words per minute. Just take your time next time."

This guy had no idea what he was talking about. My thoughts were racing frenetically when I went into my office. I was taking the pills that the neurologist had prescribed, but they didn't seem to have any effect on me anymore. I needed some weed, but I still had a whole day to get through. Was Sasha working tonight?

I stayed in and asked Sally to fetch me lunch. By the time the day was over I had completed twenty reports, responded to over a hundred e-mails, and planned three new projects. I deserved a reward, so on the way home I went shopping. I had this urge to spend shitloads of money today. I went into the Armani store and saw a plain blue t-shirt, so I bought the same one in every colour that was available. Then I bought twenty new ties and a couple of expensive watches.

Sasha wasn't at home when I got back, so I sat down and rolled up a joint. I didn't want to move, but I was horny. Maybe it was time to call someone else—a new girl—but no, Sasha wouldn't like that.

I didn't know what time it was, but I stayed up until three o'clock in the morning. Sasha came back around eight am. She'd had a phone call in the morning to do a day shift in the hospital.

"Dexter, we need to talk about this morning. You thought that you were seeing things," she said softly, starting in again. This woman was relentless.

"There is nothing wrong with me Barbie. I'm good, so stop worrying about me. Let's fuck. I really want to fuck right now," I told her.

"I'm knackered. And sex isn't a solution for everything."

We fought then, so I told her to get lost. It was the same thing all over again, but I didn't want to listen to her banging on about my health. I had never felt better in my life and I was filled with endless energy. I didn't understand why she needed so much sleep.

In the evening there was a knock on my door. She was dressed in her robe and it looked like she had just woken up.

"Missed me already?" I asked, leaning out of the door.

"No, I came to check on you."

"I'm fine and ready to fuck you again," I said and wrapped my arms around her waist, lifting her up.

"Dexter, if you want to keep me happy, then let me take you to the hospital. You need to see a specialist."

I put her down and dragged my hand over my head. "I'm done talking about this, Sasha. For fuck's sake, why can't you let it go? We have been through this already!"

"Because you are acting strange, seeing things, like you have psychosis, Dexter. Using sex as a distraction—"

"Shut up, just shut up and leave me alone! Come back when you get your shit together and want to have sex!" I shouted at her, cutting her off. Then I slammed the door in her face. I heard her door close moments later. That night I stayed up again, feeling angry and frustrated. She didn't get it that I had lived with this shit since I could remember. No one had ever found anything wrong with me and I felt great right now, so what was the problem?

I went to bed for an hour or two. At three in the morning I was up again working, drafting e-mails and creating exciting new projects to work on. I felt invincible, accomplishing all this work by five and then driving to the office at seven

Wednesday and Thursday went flying by and I hadn't heard from Sasha at all. I was bloody raging, but I wasn't planning to knock on her door. Instead of sitting in the apartment and waiting for her, I spent my evenings shopping. I bought new suits, new shoes and splashed some cash on a new car. It was an impulse; I drove past the Range Rover showroom and decided to pop in. I wasn't worried; money wasn't an issue.

On Friday afternoon I was working from the office downstairs in the complex, going over some paperwork. I had just picked up the phone and dialled a number to speak to Robert when I heard a buzzing, scratching sound in the receiver.

My heart began to pound faster and I knew that something was very wrong. Someone was listening in to my private conversations. I stared at the phone for some time, remembering the story that Joey had told me. He said that the government could bug the phones to spy on people. Now everything made sense; now I knew why I was losing the bids for properties. There was a possibility that my phones were bugged.

I ran my hand through my hair and paced around the office, thinking, trying to calm the racing thoughts. I deleted the files I was working on and shot back upstairs to Sasha's apartment.

She had made me give her back the key to her terrace doors, so I started banging on her door. It took a while, but finally she opened up.

"What the hell, Dexter? I was sleeping. I had an extra shift," she complained.

"All my phones in the office are bugged," I said.

"Dexter, what are you talking about?" she asked, yawning. Fuck, she wasn't getting it. Everyone was slow, talking slow, acting slow. I was the only one that understood what was really going on.

"Someone has planted bugs in all my phones; probably in the entire complex. We are being spied on, Sasha. That's what's fucking going on."

Sasha

I was staring at him with confusion. Was he going through another episode? I had tried to make him go to the hospital during the week, telling him that he needed help, but he acted like he didn't have a problem.

"All right, okay, Dexter. I won't use the phone. Why don't we go to your apartment and check it out?" I said.

"Fuck, finally someone believes that this shit is real," he growled. I shut the door and we strolled back to his place. We hadn't seen each other properly since Monday morning after the episode with the bugs in the shower. We had fought outside in the corridor when I insisted that he needed to see someone—a specialist. I couldn't let him distract me with sex, so I kept my distance. He was very stubborn and he slammed the door in my face. I wanted to get him diagnosed so he would get the help he needed and we could move forward, but I wasn't getting anywhere.

One of the paediatric wards of a neighbouring hospital had closed down, so more children were being admitted to the hospital I worked in, and the agency was on at me to do more shifts. I'd had a really difficult night and Dexter woke me up. I needed a few extra hours of sleep.

We went into his living room and I stopped abruptly. There were bags and bags of shopping all over the floor. New designer stuff spilling out of bags. A lot of t-shirts that were exactly the same style, but in several different shades, new suits, watches and ties. His table was covered with empty bottles of whisky and dirty plates and cups. I was trying to get my head around this, knowing that I needed to get him help.

Dexter handed me a phone. "Listen to that buzzing sound, Sasha. Everything is just—"

He started talking so fast that I couldn't follow him. Half the time his speech was slurred and fragmented. Something in my head began to click. Methadone—the neurologist had prescribed him methadone. I had seen it briefly when we were in the hotel and I remembered reading somewhere that the drug worked as a mood enhancer. There was a possibility that the pills were causing his hallucinations.

Dexter was still talking, pacing around and pointing at his phone. I couldn't take this any longer. I had to get him to the hospital. The past few days proved that he was getting more and more psychotic.

"Dexter, I'm really concerned about you. Please let me take you to an ER to see what's wrong."

He stopped talking then and looked at me, his eyes moving from the phone to me. "You know that I fucking hate hospitals, but you look worried, so I'll go."

I was shocked that he said that, but more with the fact that he wasn't fighting with me anymore. I had been expecting a full-blown argument. He was chaotic, talking without much sense at all, but I was happy that he finally he agreed.

"Okay, hold on. I'll get changed quickly."

I didn't want to leave him, but I had to use the phone to call his mother. My heart was pounding in my chest and my hands were shaking when I dialled her number. It was time to cut to the chase and tell his family what had been going on.

Dexter

She insisted on driving because apparently, I wasn't capable. What the fuck? I argued with her about this outside, but she didn't budge. The phones were bugged, I knew it, but I couldn't deal with that because all of a sudden I had all different thought streams rushing through my head. My eyes and ears were too sensitive. The world behind the window was blurry and I felt dizzy, but I kept talking. Sasha was nodding, agreeing with me as the words poured out of me for some time.

We found the car park and then got to the reception area, which was filled with other sick-looking people. Sasha asked me to wait on a bench while she went to speak with the nurse.

People were staring at me, so I grabbed my head and pulled it down, not wanting to look at anyone. I needed to have sex or start smoking a joint. It was like someone had poured a stack of ideas and thoughts into my head and then began adding more and more to it. My head felt heavy, my body was burning, my pulse pounded and I felt like I was slowly suffocating.

Sasha came back. "We have to wait," she said. She didn't ask me how I was or anything. When I looked at her, she smiled and took my hand. I exhaled with relief, feeling safe. In that moment I realised that I never wanted her to leave me ever again. Her comforting hand sent a tremor of warmth all over me, slowing down my heart rate. I felt happy, euphoric that I finally had someone who gave a fuck.

Then an image of my father swaying from side to side appeared in front of my eyes. I remembered the arguments, the late-night drinking, and Mum's tears. That euphoric feeling disappeared like a flash of lightning and then I came to the realisation that I was in love with Sasha. I absolutely fucking loved her, and suddenly that thought petrified me. Panic cooled my veins, freezing cells in my body, thrusting me into oblivion. A bitter ball of fear coursed down my spine. This wasn't happening to me; I couldn't love her.

I pulled my hand away and exhaled. "You know you were a good fuck, Barbie. Great," I began.

She laughed, not getting what I was trying to say. "Right now, Dexter, really?"

"It was always just sex for me, nothing else. You were a quick, pathetic fuck. I think I have to tell you the truth: I always knew that you were easy," I said leaning over and whispering the last word into her ear. It was time to end this bullshit, time to stop it.

She paled and pulled away from me. "Dexter, you don't mean that. We both know that it wasn't just sex; we spent a lot of time with each other."

"You passed the time, but I guess that I'm done with fucking you. We are done and I don't care about your shitty past. It was a mistake and I should have stuck to my rules. I never fuck blondes, especially not curvy, whiny blondes."

She got up then, probably upset about what I said. I didn't want to end up like my father, dead and forgotten. Her wide eyes filled with tears, but I only laughed and continued to laugh. The love for her was ripping me apart, tearing my insides. I couldn't take it.

Suddenly I spotted my mother approaching us. "Dexter, hun, are you all right?"

"Good, you're here. I'm leaving. This man really needs your help," Sasha said to my mother and then turned around and walked away.

"Who was that, Dexter?" Mum asked.

"No one, Mum. Absolutely fucking no one."

Twenty-Four

Dexter

As soon those bastards placed me in that small hospital room I was on my feet, banging at the door. Panic overtook my running thoughts and I wasn't sure if anyone could hear my screams. It took me ten minutes to realise that I was alone in this locked room and no one gave a fuck. I was petrified; my thoughts were racing like hell, speeding faster than ever before. Sasha had left me; she walked away when my mother showed up. I knew that it was all my fucking fault. I insulted her, pushed her away and told her to get lost, but couldn't she have stayed?

Suddenly the door swung open revealing a doctor and a nurse standing in the doorway with small smiles on their faces. It was difficult to read what they were thinking. I didn't think I could cope with a million questions being thrown at me by Smug One and Smug Two. My eyes roamed the room and focused on Lady Death, who stood in the back of the room staring at me. She was the only one that understood what I was going through. I saw her passing me a rope to end this all, like she did with my father.

The guy in front of me took a seat and opened a file with my name on it. Why did he have a file with my name on it? He looked young, barely in his twenties, and I kept thinking that he was an actor, not a real doctor. Someone from the government had found out that I discovered the bugs. Now they were after me.

"Dexter, my name is Dr. Cole. Why don't you tell me what has been happening to you?" He looked at me with an easy smile. I didn't trust the fucker. Despite that, I talked, going over and over what happened in the office, about my phones being bugged, about cockroaches in the bathroom. I talked until I was exhausted, noting that Cole wrote a few notes now and then. I asked about my family and was told my mother was outside in the corridor with my brother Connor. I could do this on my own. I didn't need them.

"Okay, let's talk about what I think is happening to you, Dexter."

"No!" I shouted, jumping out of the hospital chair. "I haven't fucking finished yet!" None of these fuckers knew what was going on.

"Dex, I need you to focus on me. I can help you feel better, but you must try to hear what I am telling you. From your symptoms and your family history, I think you are in need of some support and we can provide that." His voice was assertive, but it smoothed my rage ever so slightly. "I believe you have a mental condition known as bipolar disorder. Do you know what that is?" he asked, looking at me with dark penetrating eyes. What the fuck was he talking about? I didn't get why he thought that I was mentally ill. I was seeing this shit for real.

"I'm not fucking bipolar!" I shouted.

"I understand that this is strange for you, but we need to help balance your medication so you will feel better and you can go about your normal life without the current levels of stress that your mind is creating. Your headaches, your lack of a normal sleeping pattern, your anger issues—all of these symptoms are caused by a chemical imbalance that creates this chaos in your life. Wouldn't you like to sleep properly without a headache just once?"

I said nothing, only stared at him. How the fuck did he know this about me?

He stood up and nodded to the nurse with him and said, "We'll be right back."

He was gone for about ten minutes, and then my mother came crying and saying that I had to stay in the hospital for a bit. Soon everything turned into a nightmare. No way was I going to be committed to some loony bin. I started to get really angry, and more nurses began showing up the louder I became. The young doctor that interviewed me told me that I needed to be hospitalised to get the methadone out of my system because it could dangerously destabilise me further, but I knew it was a load of bullshit. Apparently, someone prescribed me the wrong meds, which caused hallucinations. This wasn't fucking possible. Sasha had made contact with that noted neurologist. He couldn't have prescribed me some shitty pills that didn't work.

"Dex, stop fighting them. You need to do this, bro," Connor shouted after I tried to push away one of the nurses. The woman wanted to stick a needle into my arm. I tangled my fingers into my hair, pulling it taut with frustration. I shouted that they were all wrong, that they didn't know what they were talking about. My brain felt like it was slowly melting and it was going to blow up within a moment. Sasha had betrayed me, left me alone, and my mother was sobbing, looking at me like she didn't know me.

"It's bullshit. I'm not fucking sick. My phones were bugged. Fuck!"

"Son, please let them help you. Don't fight. It's for your own good," she said.

"Mum, listen to me: talk to Sasha and ask her about the bugs in the bathroom. She will tell you that I'm not crazy."

I fought when they tried to escort me to the psychiatric ward. I wasn't going anywhere without a fight. Everything was moving so fast—my thoughts roiled, shooting through my brain like bullets from a gun.

They put me into a small room with two windows reinforced with wire mesh. It had a bed, a small table, and a small loo. The doctor wanted to put me to sleep for a few hours to help with the detox and to relax me, but I refused to take anything. I was furious with myself, with my mother, and fucking Sasha. My head was banging and anger was seeping out of me, smashing through my body like a tsunami ready to destroy everything in its path. Everyone had turned against me.

It seemed like hours had passed before anyone turned up. Half an hour later, some guy unlocked the door to my room and walked in like he owned the fucking place. A large, bulky nurse was standing next to him.

"Good afternoon, Dexter. My name is John Bishop and I'm going to be your doctor whilst you are in this ward. Dr. Cole from ER told me that you had several episodes recently that have caused you distress," he explained.

"I need to get out of here. There has been some sort of error. Check my files. I'm not crazy," I insisted.

"I'm not saying that you're crazy, Dexter. You need help from healthcare professionals who understand how to treat someone with bipolar disorder; it's a common illness and nothing to be ashamed of. If you break your leg, a doctor operates to pin it, and a few months later you are healed. The brain isn't like that. It's a very precise balance of chemicals and hormones that need to be delicately looked after. Almost like if you forget eggs in a cake recipe. If you leave them out, the cake just isn't right. You could still eat it and it would taste okay, but it just isn't quite right. People with bipolar disorder are the cake without eggs. The problem we have is that someone with bipolar isn't supposed to take methadone. This medication caused your psychosis and hallucinations. Your mother said that this has been going on for a while."

"My mother doesn't know anything about my life, Doc. I'm always in control."

"Your mother seemed to be convinced that you hadn't been sleeping much at all. There can be many symptoms of bipolar disorder. Some of them include psychosis, slurring speech, anger, euphoria and sometimes even memory loss. I can go on and on, Dexter. I have looked into your medical history records.

No one has ever given you a proper diagnosis, and from what I can understand, during your teenage years you were treated for various ailments, but that hadn't improved your well-being. We aren't against you, Dex. I am not the enemy. Depression might have been one of the reasons that your father killed himself, as it can be genetic. He had similar symptoms throughout his life, and he was never diagnosed either."

I was looking at this smart-ass doctor, hiding my head between my legs, trying to breathe. I wanted him to stop talking. Fuck, depression. Was I that sad that I developed a mental illness? I needed to speak to Sasha, find out if this shit was real, but she hated me.

Then Bishop began telling me that I was going to stay in the ward for a couple of weeks. I was under observation to help me detox and stabilise. What pissed me off the most was the fact that he kept saying that he wanted to help me, that things were going to get better. I told them straight that I wasn't going to take any meds. I was done with this shit. For years weed and my own pills worked, and now all of a sudden the doctors finally figured out what was wrong with me?

Whatever.

The nurse that was with Bishop tried to convince me that the pills would calm me down, but I told her to go to hell. She was English, with a double chin and fat chunky fingers. After ten minutes she finally left me alone. The buzzing sound in my ears eventually went away, but I felt trapped, betrayed. No one was going to help me. My mother and brother, they fucking locked me in here, and Sasha, she didn't mean shit. I had fallen in love with her, but I couldn't be chained up by some crawling emotion, so I decided to erase her out of my head forever.

Sasha

I was in the solicitor's office, finalising what seemed to be more unnecessary paperwork, but I simply couldn't focus on the

188

text that was in front of me. It had been a hell of a week. Dexter hadn't come home since the day I left him in the hospital with his mother. For days I'd been thinking about what he said to me. I hadn't shed any tears for him and I wasn't planning to, but I felt guilty because I left him there and walked away.

I bumped into Harry by the concierge downstairs and we had a little chat. It was a shock to find out that Dexter had been transferred to the psychiatric unit. Harry didn't know any more details and I didn't want to press him. I felt guilty that I hadn't acted sooner. Extreme mood swings, weed, pills and his strange behaviour. I didn't know if they'd managed to diagnose him, but I suspected bipolar or schizophrenia. My medical knowledge was quite limited in that area. I'd always perceived a person with clinical depression as someone locked in the house for days, withdrawn and isolated from everyone. In a way, Dexter was the complete opposite. Maybe I should have called his mother after the incident in the bathroom. Although I felt for him, he had used me, made me feel like I was one of his brunette whores. The stuff that he said to me in the hospital was deliberately hurtful. For a moment I thought that he hadn't meant any of it, that he had said it all in anger, but as it turned out, he was lucid enough and determined to push me away. I had been patient with him, tolerated his extreme mood swings for long enough. I wasn't responsible for him. I didn't need another Kirk to fuck up my life.

"And there," said the secretary, pointing at the paper, pulling me away from my thoughts. I forced a smile and signed whatever was needed.

"Is that all?" I asked.

"Yes, now we just need to wait for the buyer's solicitor. The whole process shouldn't take long. You probably have another three weeks in the apartment, so enjoy."

I thanked her and left. Three weeks was not a long time. Even so, I was still planning to move out sooner. I needed to get out of there before Dexter's release from the hospital. I was trying to figure out how I felt about him, but I couldn't quite reach a conclusive answer.

My rational side was letting me know that I had developed feelings for him. We were with each other for a short time, but I couldn't love him. Men like Dexter were far too toxic and too selfish to love. I thought that after Kirk I was incapable of falling for someone new, but Dexter was something else, and in time he became something more to me.

I drove back to the complex half an hour later. Every cell, every nerve had been missing his passionate touch. Despite that, my feelings meant nothing. I couldn't bring myself to visit him. In the end we both used each other for sex. Love, as he said often, was for pussies, and I was done with being one. He wanted nothing to do with me and I had my own life that I had to get on with.

Mum was ecstatic when she heard about the offer, and with the money that was suddenly available she offered to help me with a deposit for my own flat in the city. My parents were planning to pay off their mortgage and finance part of their dream holiday in the Caribbean.

When I parked my car next to Dexter's new Range Rover, tears welled in my eyes. I didn't know why I was upset. I had been doing so well this past week. Dexter had lied. He didn't care about us. I was no more than a challenge. He only wanted to prove that he could have me. I slapped myself hard and said loudly that the old Sasha had died. I was a new, confident and strong person, and I didn't waste tears on assholes.

I strolled inside the complex and took the lift to my floor. There, the memories slipped in. Even if I had the opportunity to stay, I couldn't, because he still owned me.

"Sasha!"

I turned around abruptly, seeing Dexter's mother standing outside his apartment. I'd only met her once, but I recognised her instantly. She had the same wicked smile as Dexter. It was slightly inappropriate, but like him, she probably didn't care. I started fiddling with my keys to distract myself from troubled thoughts that suddenly crept into my head. This was going to be awkward. I'd shared the most passionate moments with her son, and she didn't even know me. I was just like one of his other playthings.

"Hi, Mrs. Tyndall. How are you?" I asked in a small voice.

"Oh, you know, it's been hectic, but mostly good. I was wondering if I could speak with you, Sasha?" she asked, giving me the same intense look that Dexter usually had when he wanted something.

"Sure," I replied, knowing that I needed to know if he was all right. "Come on in."

This was a bad idea, but I had a feeling that the Tyndalls always got their way. Mrs. Tyndall was much shorter than I; she had silver hair and kind eyes. She asked me a few basic questions about my work and the apartment, and then thanked me for looking after Dexter. Our conversation was awkward and stiff, but I couldn't tell her to leave. She was here for a reason. Finally I couldn't help myself and asked.

"How is Dexter doing? I mean, is he coping on the ward at all?"

Deep down I was afraid to know or acknowledge that I cared. Dexter was so shut down; he protected his privacy like a lion. Also, I did miss him like crazy, but no one was supposed to know. There was a strong possibility that I did love him a little.

"He fought with the nurses and punched the care worker when they escorted him. It was a mess." She sighed. "Then he refused to accept what's happened, refused to take the medication. He didn't want to see me at all."

My heart sped up. Of course he probably thought that it was a sign of weakness. I'd only known him for a month or so, but I knew that he wasn't ready to accept that he was mentally ill.

"Oh, no."

"I don't know how it happened, but after constant battles something finally changed. Doctor Bishop called it a breakthrough."

Twenty-Five

Sasha

"What do you mean?"

"Well, apparently Dexter accepted the medication and finally opened up. That was only two days ago, and everyone is still wary about any progress."

"Did he say anything about it?"

"I'm not quite sure. The nurse said that he probably realised that he wasn't getting out of the hospital any time soon, so he gave up. Decided to act like a grown man for a change."

"Thank God," I muttered.

"You know, I need to tell you—Dexter does care for you a lot."

I inhaled, feeling as though my heart had stuttered in my chest.

Crap, where did this come from? I felt the usual warmth rising in my body. I wanted to forget about him and move on with my new life. Dexter said some crushing things to me, things that I couldn't simply forget.

"Mrs. Tyndall, when I moved in, Dexter had many female visitors and he wasn't particularly discreet about it. I believe that he used sex as a distraction, an outlet for his bipolar issues. He won't have changed—I haven't tamed him. He showed me his true colours in the hospital and said some very hurtful things that I can't forget. Now, with proper medication, his illness can be managed. I'm moving out in two weeks and I–"

"I believe my son has fallen in love with you, Sasha," she cut me off.

I went silent, staring at her as if she handed me my still-beating heart on my palm. I needed to get up, but I flopped back on the chair. Love—that word sounded funny even to me. Dexter didn't believe in love or emotional attachment.

"Did he say that?" I asked.

She didn't reply. Okay, so it was clear that he didn't drop on his knees and reveal to her that he finally found the love of his life. Besides, I couldn't imagine him even saying something like that.

Mrs. Tyndall cleared her throat. "No, not exactly."

"He doesn't love me, Mrs. Tyndall. It was just sex between us, that's all."

"Dexter shared with me what he said and the way he spoke to you in the hospital. I believe that week gave him some time to think and now he regrets what he said."

I needed more air, because all of a sudden I felt like I was suffocating. He called me a fat, whiny lay and told me he was done with me. This whole thing went too far. I wasn't ready to hear that he finally came to his senses, that he understood that he'd done wrong. Whatever. He had weeks with me and never once told me that he wanted me to be anything more than a quick fuck.

"Dexter believes… I won't directly quote him, Mrs. Tyndall, but to him love is for wimps, so it's impossible. He doesn't love me and there won't be any reconciliation between us."

"He's a man, Sasha, and it takes them longer to grasp something so obvious. I'm not here to convince you to give him another chance. That has to come from him. I just wanted to thank you for looking out for him. My husband took his own life. He, too, went to the doctors and they never looked into his mental well-being. This illness could be genetic, and now after so many years I can finally begin to understand what had been going on."

I felt like I was betraying Dex and myself. I couldn't go to visit him, because I knew that if I saw him, I couldn't deny that I was in love with him. Dexter needed to get back on his feet on his own. His mother could say whatever she had to, but we both knew that Dexter wasn't willing to change.

Mrs. Tyndall didn't stay long. We chatted a bit more about his behaviour and the fact that the doctors believed that finally he had the right medication to control his illness. All I wanted was to move out before he returned, but I wasn't sure if I was ready to start over without saying a proper good-bye.

Dexter

It had been two and a half fucking weeks and I was still stuck in the ward. It didn't take me long to grasp that Bishop was a self-important asshole. I couldn't fucking bribe him and the big nurse wasn't falling for my charms. They were relentless, trying to convince me to take the meds, but I knew better. For months I had been taking my own drugs, and I didn't need Prozac to feel like a new me. I spent most of the time in my room, staring at the wall, thinking and analysing what happened to be me.

For about a week I refused to see my mother and brother. Jack was in the army and he was away somewhere in Germany. I was glad. He didn't need to see me like this. I knew that I was a stubborn fuck. My own inner darkness had been mounting since the moment Sasha had walked away from me. This place wasn't helping. Nights were the worst, because then I had dreams. Shit—so many intense dreams that pulled me back into the oblivion.

One morning, I woke up abruptly after dreaming about my father. I missed him and I still hadn't come to terms with the fact that he made that selfish decision to leave us. I was just a kid then, but I should have known that there was something wrong. Now I remembered all the symptoms, the outbursts of anger, the mood swings. I always did what he asked me because I wanted to make him proud.

I remembered very well that day when I found his body. He had been drinking in the evening and arguing with Ma about her talking to the neighbour next door. He thought that she was having an affair, that she was cheating on him. I couldn't listen to him, so I went out to see a girl from school that I desperately wanted to date. I spent my last pocket money on some shitty flowers and chocolate, thinking that if I impressed her she would finally choose me. Dad always taught me to show people how much you cared for them, so that's what I did. When I showed up she was standing outside her house with a popular kid a year older than me, and they were kissing. I couldn't believe it. I had been helping her with homework, bringing her tea and sweets during breaks. I thought she was the one.

She didn't even notice me and I was devastated, furious with the fact that I wasted so much time with her. Back then I was naive enough to believe that I had a better chance of going out with girls if I treated them well.

That evening I stayed up until the early hours of the morning, walking around the neighbourhood waiting for my father to find me and give me hell about being late. He didn't come, so I went home. Mum's car was gone. I knew she was probably out looking for me. I headed straight for the attic, planning to stay there and wait for Mum, wanting to be somewhere else. The attic door was stuck, but I managed to open it. As soon as I stepped inside, my eyes took in my father's swaying body. He was hanging from the ceiling. For a long moment I just stood there trying to snap out of my shock, the darkness slowly consuming me. A cold chill invaded the marrow in my bones, and I couldn't catch my breath. I had no idea how long I stood there. Maybe half an hour, maybe an hour. Finally, I heard my mother's car and I went to get her. For about half an hour everyone in the house was screaming, crying, trying to deal with the shock. I went back to my room and clenched my fists. Before I knew it, tears began falling and didn't stop. My father had left me; he took the path of death and despair.

I didn't even realise that I was crying now too, as I sat here in the hospital ward. Warm tears were streaming down my ugly face and I squeezed my eyes closed, breathing hard, trying to stop this fucking nonsense. I never cried, not since I buried my father. He was the man that I looked up to. He'd taught me to treat everyone with respect. We had shared some incredible moments together, and I always tried hard to please him so he could be proud of me.

Right now these fucking tears were making me weak—I hated being that guy from the past. I achieved more acting like I didn't give a fuck. Women preferred the other me, the hardcore Dexter, the dirty-talking man that fucked them hard. Dad's death broke me and I was never the same after that. All of a sudden he was gone and I had no one to talk to, no one to go camping with, no one to go fishing with. People paid no attention to me when I was polite and caring, but they did when I was obnoxious.

I stayed in my room, thinking that the hospital itself was making me unstable. The only thing left for me was to sit and think about my shitty life all day long. When I was alone, Sasha was standing next to me, naked, giving me her usual attitude. When I was eating the shitty hospital food, talking to that asshole Bishop, or hanging around the ward, she was with me. I saw her face all the time. I thought about her more than I was supposed to and I was angry, fucking furious with myself. The doctors, the nurses, my mother and my brother—they all wanted me to take meds. They were all saying that I wasn't going to get better until I understood that they were with me, not against me.

"You will never get that girl back if you refuse to take your medication, Dexter," said Nurse Jones when I was pacing around the corridor in the evening. This drove her mental and I liked winding her up; it felt like a small victory in this place.

"What fucking girl?" I snapped.

"The one that you keep screaming for every night."

I stopped and glared at her. She couldn't have known about my nightmares, but she probably had heard me. Bitch. I tried playing nice Dexter with her, charming Dexter, arrogant Dexter. Crap, nothing was working. She wasn't taking my bullshit.

"Whatever. I have no idea who the hell you mean," I barked, feeling sweat run down my back. I hated my dreams, hated Sasha and the whole system, and at some point I hated my father. Nurse Jones smiled, revealing her grey teeth.

"The woman, Sasha, she must mean something to you. I heard you, honey-bunny. You ain't getting out of here if you won't start taking your meds," she added, smirking at her own cleverness and turning her eyes down to her magazine. I hated the fact that I didn't get my way. I clenched my fists and strolled up to her window. Every night I had the same dream. I saw Sasha walking away from me, never responding to my shouts of protest. Maybe I had pushed this whole asshole attitude too far. Life was better if I was obnoxious and rude, but Sasha meant everything to me. I wanted her to love me, the true, real me.

Okay, I'd had enough; I was done with Bishop and this whole thing. I needed to get out of here.

"Fine, give me the tablets, woman. I'm fucked off by your snide little comments," I snapped at her.

Nurse Jones grinned like she just lost half of her fucking weight when she handed me the pills. I swallowed them with water and walked away dejected.

That was about a week and a half ago. My thoughts kept racing away, but within days I started feeling better, more like myself. From that day I began taking six different pills every day. Bishop called this progress, I called it a weakness. Either way, I didn't want to stay in the hospital longer than was necessary. I needed to get out.

Mum showed up and I agreed to see her. As usual there were tears, a lot of tears, but then we talked like two normal people. She kept telling me that I was good person, that deep down I cared for people, but I wasn't sure if I believed her. She started blaming herself, so I opened up to her and told her my innermost thoughts, stuff about Sasha and the fact that she was the only woman that I found tolerable. I didn't like showing the real me to other people, but I was done hiding and for sure I couldn't hide shit from my mother.

"Bipolar disorder can be genetic, Dexter, and I'm sorry that I didn't see it. It was my fault. I had been dragging you to all the wrong doctors for no reason."

I grabbed my mother's hand, remembering the shit that she was talking about. Yeah, she was right. There was no need, but I didn't want to make her feel worse.

"Don't be absurd, Ma. Those stupid assholes didn't know what they were talking about. Bishop is an idiot too, but apparently he knows the shit. The pills are working. I could be out of here in no time."

"Maybe you should stay with me for a bit then. I don't think—"

"No, Ma, I'm not disabled. I need to get back to my own life."

"But Dexter, you can't be alone."

"There are no buts. The meds are doing me good. I'm ready to get out, so stop it, please."

We argued about that shit for a bit, until I got my way. My mother couldn't do that to me. Besides, I had to speak to Sasha. I wasn't fucking delusional; I knew she would probably curse me out, but I had to at least try.

Two and a half weeks later, I was finally getting out. Bishop wanted to see me for a consultation next week and I was supposed to be taking the meds for the next six months minimum.

I had to admit—at last some doctor had done something right. I didn't feel like I was high, but I didn't feel down either. I felt stable for the first time in years. I didn't have the same amount of anger coursing through me; I wasn't trying to filter through a million thoughts at once. I wasn't thinking about what I had to do next, later, tomorrow, next week—I was happy to just be in this moment right here without the chaos my mind created. He suggested I join support groups, to talk to people who'd had to live with this fucked-up condition for years, but I wasn't ready. All I wanted was to get back to normal.

The day that I got out, Mum insisted on dinner in her place. Jack and Emily were visiting with their twins and I had to play a family man. Everyone was acting normal, or at least they tried. The dinner turned into a supper. Mum was doing everything she could to keep me in the house longer. By the time I was able to finally get back to the apartment, it was after eight.

I was fucking nervous when I drove up that road towards the complex. I had run through different conversations with Sasha in my head a few times, but I had no idea if I was doing the right thing. Sasha was feisty and she didn't take my bullshit. I messed up, fucked everything up, but I was hoping that she would at least listen to what I wanted to say.

My new Range Rover was parked in the usual spot. I walked to the other side of the car park to check if she was in. As far as I remembered her shift pattern, she didn't work on Tuesdays. I dragged my hand through my hair, feeling the familiar burning in my groin. This whole thing was getting out of control. Bishop mentioned something about sex. I didn't listen to his usual bullshit, but one thing stuck. I used sex to mask and suppress my emotions. Maybe there was something in it. I fucking loved sex—I mean I am human—but I'd been sleeping with a different woman every week. I wasn't planning to just give sex up, but since they locked me up I was no longer consumed with the thought of it. Sasha's tight pussy was the only pussy that I wanted.

Even without my illness I wasn't the monogamist type, but for her I was willing to give it a try, even change a little just to be with her.

Duncan in concierge was ecstatic when I showed up. Apparently he had no idea that I had been in the hospital. He gave me some updates about what had gone on when I wasn't around, and then I headed upstairs.

My corridor was empty and my stomach made a funny noise when I looked at Sasha's door. I couldn't just go inside my apartment. I had to talk to her, see her, fucking touch her again. My palms were damp when I approached her door and knocked. Almost three weeks had passed and now I was finally going to see her—and I was freaking out because I realised that I really cared about her.

Twenty-Six

Sasha

I was putting the last few books into boxes when I heard someone at the door. I had been packing all day; the apartment was supposed to be vacant by tomorrow. All week I had been anxious about completion day. Harry mentioned that the doctors wanted to keep Dexter in the hospital for another week and that thought had been playing on my mind since I found out what happened. I ran to the door and opened it. My heart leaped in my throat when I saw Dexter right in front of me.

I was ready to slam the door in his face, but instead I lost the feeling in my limbs. My heart let me know that it was aware he was there, only a step away, by stuttering and then speeding up. He looked as handsome as always, but he looked better, healthier, whole, wearing a plain white T-shirt and old worn-in jeans. We hadn't seen each other for more than three weeks since that fateful day at the hospital.

"Hello, Barbie," he said. That voice sent a tremor of boiling hot lust right through me. Damn my libido and my stupid over-the-top hormones. As his eyes slowly took in my body, I recognised the invisible pull between us that weakened my knees instantly. Although turned on, I wasn't ready to see him. It had been three long emotional weeks.

"Hello, Dexter," I said, my voice giving away my uneasiness. My attraction to him could overshadow the pain if I let him walk through my door again. I had to stay strong and be vigilant. We had screwed, but now we were simply neighbours, nothing else. Despite my internal battle, my body craved him immensely. I couldn't put my finger on it, but there was something different about him. For starters, he didn't have that usual arrogant smirk on his lovely face. "What can I do for you?"

He took a step towards me and pulled the breath from my lungs. I didn't plan to back away; I stood firmly in the same spot with a pounding heart. Dexter's eyes were heavy, and shots of heat brushed my hardened nipples, but his gaze didn't roam my chest like it used to. Strange. Maybe the time in the hospital did change him a little.

"Can we talk?" he asked gently. Beads of sweat ran down the back of my neck. I needed to back away from him to regain control.

"Dex, we have nothing to talk about. Besides, I'm in the middle of packing, so I don't have time for you or your drama," I said and opened the door to let him see that I was indeed moving out.

His eyes were still on mine. He still hadn't glanced at my boobs, not even once, and I had on a low-cut top. My mouth went dry. God, he looked good and smelled even better.

"Barbie, please. I said some things that I didn't and could never mean. Invite me in or as a landowner, I'll be forced to inspect the apartment," he pressed, narrowing his gorgeous eyes at me. I had to stay calm, but that was almost impossible because his body was so close. I couldn't deny this any longer— I had feelings for him. Deep penetrating love fluttered through me, gripping me tightly, and my heart stuttered continuously. None of this mattered. We were done playing games.

"I guessed that you'd still be yourself. Don't bullshit me, Dex. You meant every word that day. Leave me alone. I have shit to do," I snapped.

"Do you know how much you turn me on when you're so feisty?"

203

I sighed and tried to slam the door in his face, but he put his shoe on the threshold. This was getting absurd. I really wasn't ready for this conversation. For once I didn't care how I was feeling.

"Dexter, please don't be an asshole. I don't want to talk to you. I don't even want to look at you. Leave me alone. I'm trying to put my life back together," I said, ignoring the vivid images of him sucking on my clit. I was so wet and he hadn't even touched me. Fiery heat crept in, up between my legs. I had to kick him out and then leave.

"We have unfinished business, Barbie. In the hospital, I thought about you a lot, and I need you to understand that I was fucking wrong. At least hear me out... please."

I was just about to open my mouth to tell him that, whatever he was planning to say, it didn't matter anymore, when I saw Victoria coming out of the lift.

"Dexter!" she barked, which got his attention. "I'm not the kind of woman that you ignore."

I was ready to move on, forget that he ever existed, so I slammed the door in his face and locked it. I didn't want to walk away. I really wanted to hear their conversation. I bet that Victoria had no idea that he was in the hospital.

"Victoria, I'm in the fucking middle of something," he finally shouted.

"That's okay, darling. I can hand the video to the police whilst I wait for you to not be in the fucking middle of something."

"What the fuck? Do you want me to fuck you, right now, right here?" he snapped in anger.

My stomach contracted with a hot dose of jealousy. I didn't want him, but I couldn't let her take advantage of him. My rational side told me that it had been three weeks, that he wasn't my business anymore. Deep down I wanted him for myself, but I knew that wasn't going to happen. The moment he told me that he was done with screwing me, he broke me.

They went inside and I knew that I had to let him go. Victoria gave me the perfect opportunity to get out of here. Most of my stuff was already in my new flat in Edinburgh. I picked up all the boxes and started moving them to my car. Today I only collected some of the last bits and bobs, at the same time saying goodbye to the place where I spent the past two months. The new owner was willing to take the furniture from me. It was now or never. I was leaving the complex for good.

Dexter

My palm was itching badly, and even though I was saner than ever before, I still wanted to hit Victoria. I hadn't had time to think about how I was going to deal with her. Deep down I was silently hoping that she would leave me the fuck alone, but she had other plans.

We went inside my apartment. Sasha was packing, moving out. I had time before she was going to disappear on me completely; first I needed to know what Victoria wanted this time around. Back in the hospital, Bishop had refused to give me my phone. Apparently it was a distraction and I wasn't ready to connect with reality. It was true, and I discovered shitloads of missed calls from Victoria, but I hadn't bothered calling her back.

"I have a charity function tonight and I need a date," Victoria said, playing with a lock of her brown hair.

"Can't tonight. I'm busy," I snapped, thinking about my Barbie next door. She narrowed her eyes at me and took a step towards me. I was playing with fire. This woman had my balls and I couldn't fucking piss without her permission.

"I wasn't asking. I'm telling you. Be ready for tonight, tuxedo and the whole shebang. I've been trying to get hold of you all week. One wrong move and your gorgeous ass will be behind bars," she said.

"I was fucking busy, Vic."

"One phone call, that's all it would've taken, Dexter. Eight o'clock and don't make me come back here."

Then she began telling me what she wanted to do to me in detail. I stood there bouncing ideas around in my head, thinking about how to destroy her. I'd had a little chat with Ronny before I went into the hospital, but he refused to get his hands dirty. For the first time in years my head was completely free, my thoughts controlled and ordered. The bullshit was over and I wasn't going down for something that I'd done when I'd lost my fucking mind. At some point my illness had conquered me, but I was in control now.

Victoria left ten minutes later and I began scrolling through my contacts, thinking about the people that I could call, but all these assholes were useless bankers, stockbrokers and investors. They had no idea how to deal with a crazy bitch like Victoria, who had absolutely nothing to lose. After not coming up with anything useful, I took the stairs and ran to the other side of the wing. I had three hours before this crazy bitch would show up and I needed help. After banging on Harry's door for some time, the bastard finally opened up. In this situation he was my only ally.

"Dexter, couldn't you be any louder?" he asked with only a towel around his waist. I strolled inside. "Yeah, come on in. Maybe I can't get you a cup of get-the-fuck-out-of-here tea?"

"Listen, I need your help; better if you sit down for this," I said, ignoring him.

"I was in the middle of taking a shower, Dex," he snapped. "Let me put some clothes on. I'll be back in a minute."

Ten minutes later, I had him sitting down at his swanky dining room table. I wasn't a very good friend. Harry always made the fucking effort and I'd pretended that we were close as a means to an end. I didn't know why I hadn't thought about him before. Harry had contacts all over Scotland and I knew for sure that he was into dodgy shit. He'd brought Victoria to the party and right now I was running out of options. I had to start from the very beginning, tell him about my screwed-up illness.

"Right, so what's up?"

He knew me well, better than I gave him credit for, but I never told him what exactly was wrong with me. Harry did ask me a couple of times about the pills and weed in my kitchen, but it was easy enough to brush it off, like it wasn't a big deal.

I told him about my years in the darkness, the sex, the drugs. Then I moved on to Sasha and our time together, my mania, the pills from the neurologist, and finally Victoria and that story from the party, the sex with underage girl, and everything else. By the time I was done he was staring at me in shock, shifting from one side to the other. I judged people all the time, but this wasn't easy, talking to someone else about my own problem.

"Depression, psychosis. Wow, Dexter. I had no idea," he finally said.

"I'm on meds, good meds that are actually helping, but I need your help with Victoria. If this thing gets out, I'm screwed, so for now I have to do what the bitch says."

"Victoria is a hunter. She doesn't want money. She wants you to be her plaything, to be in control of you. You are essentially her prey."

"Don't I know that? Fuck. I can't talk to anyone else about this. I don't remember anything. I was high most of the night," I argued.

"First, go to that charity bullshit with her and I'll make some phone calls, see what I can dig up. We need to find out if that girl is actually fifteen."

"I fucked up with Sasha. I can't go to this party with Victoria."

"You've got no choice, mate. Sasha sold the place. She will be out of her apartment tomorrow," Harry stated and lit up a cigarette.

He had my attention again. Tomorrow? What the hell was he talking about?

"What do you mean that she sold the place? It's only been…"

I didn't finish because suddenly I realised that it had been three weeks. I didn't really notice the time in the hospital. The cash buyer, she had a cash buyer. How could I have missed the fact that she was moving out today?

"What? I thought you knew."

I was on my feet then.

"Find whatever you can on Victoria. I have to go. I need to talk to Sasha before she leaves!"

"First, stop acting like an asshole. Sasha is a gem and the shit that she had to put up with when you were around, God. I don't even know what to tell you."

"You're not fucking helping for sure. I'll deal with Sasha. I know what I have to do."

Harry nodded, and a minute later I was running down my own corridor, knowing that I had only one chance to make this right. Victoria had distracted me before.

I banged on her door, shouting, "Sasha, open up. I need to talk to you!"

My heart pounded in my chest. It was too quiet in there. She must have already left by the time I went inside with Victoria. I paced around in the corridor for some time, hammering at her door, just to be sure. When I realised that she wasn't there, I took my phone out and made a call.

"Russ, I need to know if the sale for apartment twenty-one has gone through yet?" I barked into the phone. I was the owner of the land and the building, so every transaction had to go through my solicitors.

"Mr. Tyndall, I believe that the completion date is set for tomorrow," he said. I cursed and hung up the phone, scrolling through more contacts. The ground underneath me was slipping away and I was falling back into the oblivion. I needed to get a handle on this.

Finally I found the right person. It fucking rang and rang for ages. Angus was a busy man, but he could make it happen. There was just so little time left and this was going to cost me.

"Dexter, my boy. What can I do for you?" he asked with cheerful voice. A bunch of ice-cubes were cascading down to my center.

"I need you to make a phone call with an offer. It's the lowest transaction that you've probably ever come across, but I need you to do it anyway, Angus."

Twenty-Seven

Sasha

The day I drove away from the complex, I found myself howling in misery. I kept telling myself that I wasn't crying over Dexter, but over that gorgeous, stunning apartment. It finally had been sold and I was never going to get that kind of opportunity ever again. My life in the Grange was over.

After I got on the road to the city, it finally hit me. I had fallen in love with Dexter Tyndall, a man that had screwed enough women to fill the whole of Edinburgh, most of the coast, and probably halfway to England. He had bipolar and many problems, but he loved his uncomplicated lifestyle. He could sleep with any woman he chose and the fact that he might have to care about anyone else's feelings never entered his head. He made the choice to be this person and he wasn't going to change.

After my drama with Kirk, I promised myself that I would never ever fall in love again. The timing couldn't have been any worse. I had gone through that terrible breakup, I had experienced so much sorrow and beatings and abuse. I was too old for this crap. Dexter wasn't my Prince Charming. He was the Prince of Darkness. We all had issues. It was probably straight after his father's death when he began slipping away from reality, self-medicating and using alcohol to make himself feel better, but I had an ugly past too. He wasn't the only one who'd been suffering.

That was a few days ago. Now I was coping again, living my own better life.

"Hello, Earth to Sasha, are you even with me?" Gina asked. We had arranged to meet up for a drink and she wanted to see my new place. We were discussing the upcoming pole competition in London. Gina had taken part in it years ago and she offered to train me for it. I jumped at this opportunity straight away.

I shook my head and smiled, knowing that yet again I was driving myself crackers with thoughts about Dexter. I left a few days ago while he was busy with his "fiancee." Correction. I ran away to avoid the confrontation. That part of my life was over and he was wrong. Our business was finished, even though I bloody loved him, but that was a small and unimportant detail.

"Sorry, what were we talking about?" I asked.

Gina took a sip of her wine and peered at me. Her crazy red hair seemed to have a mind of its own today. She looked like her head was on fire.

"Come on, spill it: what's his name and what did he do to you?" she asked. I learned that Gina was very intelligent. She had a master's in psychology and some other qualifications, but her own life was a mystery.

"Oh, it's no one. Don't worry about it. No one worth talking about," I said, brushing it off.

"You're competing in about two week's time, darling, and if you aren't focused enough, this won't work. Tell me—who is this guy and what's he done to you?"

"His name is Dexter and he won't ruin this for me this time around. I'll be all right," I stated with determination.

Gina didn't usually discuss men and their problems with me. She thought that it was the biggest waste of time. As far as I knew, she was single and too busy with work to even consider being tied down. I had been going to pole-dancing training often, at least four times a week, practising whatever new routine that Gina had given me. Tonight we were discussing my plan for the competition. Most of the time I was listening, but it was impossible for me not to think about Dexter.

"Have lots of sex before the competition. That should solve the problem straight away," she said, winking at me.

My heart was shattered, but I had a new flat in the city, new friends, and everything was slowly moving in the right direction. I needed to look at the bright side.

A week ago, I had applied for a permanent job in the hospital and I was hoping to get an interview. I needed a full-time position and I wanted a normal social life again. These were just small steps. I made the decision that I was going to live my life the way I wanted, not like I used to.

Gina picked up a gossip magazine from her bag and started turning the pages. The wine was slowly going to my head, and I thought that for a moment I spotted Dexter's face on some of the pages.

"Sorry, can I have a look at this for a second?" I asked, pointing at the magazine. Gina nodded and handed it to me. I started turning the pages frantically until I found what I was looking for. There it was: Dexter Tyndall with Victoria Cross at some kind of charity banquet. My jaw dropped and I stared at his face for several seconds in disbelief. The bitch looked stunning wearing a white low-cut dress, posing with Dex outside the building. Dexter was in his tuxedo, looking gorgeous. He wasn't smiling, just staring blankly at the camera. I read the note underneath.

Victoria Cross and her partner fundraising money for starving children in Africa.

She must have blackmailed him into doing that. Dexter wouldn't just agree, but then he wasn't ill anymore, so maybe he had gone back to his usual self. I felt guilty that I escaped without discussing anything, without even a goodbye. Victoria was a leech and he had to do what she said. I couldn't really get involved. His illness and his overactive libido brought him into that mess.

"What's wrong? Who is he?" Gina asked, snapping the paper away from me. I ran my hand through my hair, breathing harder than I should.

"That's the guy that I've been trying to forget," I said.

"Dexter Tyndall. Holy moly, he's hot and looks like a real asshole. Care to tell me what happened between you two?"

"It's a long story. We had the most amazing sex. It was my fault, though. I thought that I was ready for a no-strings-attached relationship, but I was wrong."

"Wrong? What, were you stupid enough to fall for that prick?"

"Something like that, but he's in the past now. We are done and we don't have to see each other ever again."

"Rubbish, you're still badly hung up on him. I'm going to set you up with someone."

I was trying to pretend that I was fine, but deep down I was raging. Dexter and Victoria. I wasn't supposed to care about them.

"What for, a date?" I asked, ready to get that thought out of her head.

She patted me on the shoulder and took the magazine away from me. It was strange, but after spending so much time together we had grown unexpectedly close.

"I think so. You need one night with a hot random stranger to forget about this Scottish sex god forever."

"No. I'm done with casual sex and I was supposed to be done with men as well."

"A date is what you need. Let me see what I can do." Gina giggled and I rolled my eyes, knowing that she couldn't be serious.

Dexter

I was standing in the shower, trying to wash away the memories from the party that Victoria forced me to attend. It was a hell of a night and I chose not to touch any buzz during the party. I could drink, but as that asshole Bishop said, alcohol and antidepressants were a lethal combination.

The water was streaming down my body while I massaged my shaft, trying to make it work again. I hadn't had sex since I was locked up in the psychiatric ward. The party didn't go well and Harry still hadn't come back to me about Victoria.

I thought about last night, how I dutifully put my tuxedo on and an hour later Victoria picked me up outside the complex. She was chatting to me like everything was fine, like she wasn't blackmailing me. She hadn't brought up that stuff with Jenny. Bitch was sweet as candy, trying to act like things between us weren't fucked up.

I was out of buzz and on the meds, but I was raging inside that I was so fucked up by some chick who had more money than sense. I wanted to track down that girl from the party myself to check if she was really fifteen. Victoria could have made this whole shit up. I couldn't let her beat me at my own game. The truth was that I brought this on myself. I should have stayed sober that night.

The charity banquet was held in one of the hotels in Edinburgh. Once we were inside, Victoria started introducing me to all the celebrities in the room. I didn't give a fuck. I was ready to get out of there, but she glued herself to my arm and didn't let go.

We were posing for photos, chatting with her wooden friends as she splashed her cash to help poor African kids. Most of the night I was trying not to explode. Victoria kept saying that I was her date when all I thought about was Sasha. My Barbie was in my head all the time: the way she laughed and teased me, the way she smiled and that naughty twinkle that appeared in her eyes. She was gone from my life because I had managed to drive her away with my stupid mouth.

"Dexter, let me introduce you to Mr. and Mrs. Rogers and their daughter Jenny," Victoria said, nudging me for the tenth time. I lifted my eyes and looked at the couple in their late forties. When my eyes darted at the girl I realised that I wasn't dreaming. Jenny Rogers, the fifteen-year-old girl that I had fucked during the party was standing in front of me. Blood rushed to my ears when her father shook my hand.

"Hi," I muttered. Jenny smiled, blushing. My stomach revolted and I thought that I was going to lose it. Victoria had crossed the line.

"Mr. Tyndall, Victoria mentioned that you own the Grange complex. We were thinking about moving to a similar idyllic location. Are there any apartments on the market at the moment?" Rogers senior asked. Anger was burning my skin and I took air into my lungs, trying to calm down. Jenny had her finger around a lock of her hair and was still grinning at me. She didn't look like fifteen, for sure, but this wasn't the time or place. I felt disgusted that we'd shared a bed together. Victoria had me and I couldn't move. She was squeezing my balls tight.

"I don't think so, Mr. Rogers. These apartments tend to be very popular," I grumbled.

"Please do let Victoria know if anything goes on the market. See, we want to be closer to our daughter's college. The city can be so hectic."

I nearly threw up my drink and Victoria patted me on my back. I was so fucked.

I'd lost. The bitch had me.

She didn't say anything about the girl for the rest of the night. When the evening was finally over, Victoria forced me to go back to her apartment in the city. The drive was long and I was losing my head, wanting a proper drink.

We didn't even get through the door before she was on me.

"Dex, I want you to fuck me hard, the way you usually do," she purred.

"You got anything to drink?" I asked. I had to get wasted if I was going to fuck that bitch.

"There's some wine in the fridge."

I pushed her away and strolled into the kitchen. This was absurd, but I couldn't do this sober. I didn't need a glass. I opened the bottle and drank straight from it, emptying half of the bottle in one go. Ten minutes later, I was back in the bedroom where Victoria was fingering herself, beckoning me over. At any other time I would have been hard in an instant, ready to fuck her brains out. Right then, though, my cock hadn't even twitched.

I took my clothes off, knowing that I wasn't drunk enough, but I had no other choice. She pulled me towards her and started kissing me, her tongue moving inside my mouth. My head was completely screwed; all I could think of was Sasha's amazing body. My skin crawled when Victoria started running her claws down below, caressing my skin. Blood rushed through my veins, but my cock was lifeless.

Sasha's movements on the pole. Sasha's smile and her feisty mouth. Victoria had her sticky fingers in my boxers. She looked down on my dick, licking her lips. This wasn't fucking happening.

"Dexter, what the hell is wrong? Why aren't you hard for me?"

I was pissed, frustrated and heartbroken. Sasha was in my head. Her orchid perfume was still on my skin and I couldn't sleep with the woman in front of me. I pulled away from her and dragged my hand through my hair.

"I can't fuck you. Sorry, babe, but my johnson isn't working for you."

She took my hand and brought it between her legs. Her pussy was soaking for me, but I couldn't do this. I was numb from head to toe. The alcohol made me feel sluggish and worthless.

"It's wet and ready for you. Come on, Dex," she urged me, but I slapped her hand away.

"You're revolting. The last thing I want is to stick my cock into your fucked-up cunt."

She went mental then, calling me an asshole, screaming and threatening to call the police. I started putting my clothes on, knowing that this was probably the end of me, but I was done with this shit, with her threats.

That night I expected to get arrested, but no one came. That banquet was two days ago and I was still free, still sitting in my apartment feeling sorry for myself. I had a text message from Victoria in the morning. She was giving me another chance to prove that I was cooperating with her demands. It was straight after I read the text message from Harry.

I might have something. Just call me when you get this.

Twenty-Eight

Dexter

The banquet with Victoria was three days ago. Her demands were childish. I didn't get why she was so obsessed with me and my cock. Since that day in her swanky apartment my dick hadn't gotten hard unless I thought about Sasha. Harry had some good ideas, and we were planning to execute them soon. I had never wanted to end up like my father, so emotionally bound to a woman, but I knew if I behaved like I have in the past few years I would drive everyone away from me. It was time to bury the obnoxious and lethal Dexter deep in the ground. I missed Sasha. All of a sudden I wasn't interested in any brunettes, just one particular blonde.

At work, in the apartment, everywhere I went—all I thought about was Sasha. I missed her curvy body, her sassy mouth, and that wet silky pussy that I enjoyed screwing so much. I fought with myself over what I wanted and what I felt. I did love her and I didn't want to be alone anymore. She was the only person that made me happy. Love terrified me and I was scared that I had lost her. Like everyone else I'd really cared about. In one moment Dad was with me, in the next he was gone. I'd always guarded myself, afraid to get too close. Joey was the only one that understood me, but then he was gone too.

Victoria wasn't happy with how things ended between us the other night. I was afraid that she would change her mind and just snap. I bet no one had satisfied her the way I had, but someone needed to let her know that the old Dexter had died. The moment I said those shitty things to Sasha, I was done with being a train wreck.

I'd fucked up badly and now I wanted to fix it; I needed to. When I woke up on Saturday morning I was done with thinking about our times together. It was time to get her back.

My mother gladly reminded me about my appointment with Bishop on Monday. No one apart from close family, Sasha, and Harry knew about my issues and I was hoping to keep it that way.

After a strong cup of coffee, I grabbed my car keys and left the complex. I knew exactly where I needed to go, but I wasn't sure if she would want to listen to me. Our last meeting wasn't particularly successful. I'd said some things that weren't relevant to us. Now things were even more complicated.

It took me over an hour to drive to Glasgow. Traffic was terrible. Besides that, I was a nervous wreck: my palms were sweaty and my pulse irregular.

When I arrived on the familiar street, for a brief moment I thought that Sasha might be here, but I didn't see her car anywhere. But she wouldn't go back to Glasgow to live with her parents. She had talked to me about Edinburgh.

I'd chosen casual, not over-the-top clothes, and I had practiced my smile in the bathroom mirror earlier on. I had Ronny; I could pay him to get me her address, but I wanted to fix this the right way. Sasha needed to see that I had made some changes in my shitty life, and if this was going to work, I had to start from the bottom.

I cleared my throat and knocked three times. There was a small Fiat parked outside, so someone was definitely at home. My fucked-up heart skipped a beat when I heard footsteps, and a few seconds later Sasha's mother opened the door. She was in her jeans but had no make-up on. Her eyes took me in, widening slightly. She didn't look happy and I hadn't even opened my mouth yet.

"Kath, please, I need to talk to you. This is very important," I said, switching straight to her first name. It was a huge risk, but Sasha's mother looked like she didn't take any bullshit.

"Is my daughter with you?" she asked, opening the door wider and glancing outside.

"No, she isn't. I screwed up and she left. You're the only person that can help me. I need her new address."

I sounded like a complete douche, but I knew that if I convinced her mother, then I stood more chance at gaining Sasha's trust. This could go either way—she could invite me in or throw me off her property. The second option wasn't very appealing.

She took a sharp deep breath and looked up the road, like she was afraid that someone would see us.

"I'm not going to talk about Joey."

"I'm not here about Joey. All I care about is your daughter, Kath."

She hesitated for a moment, probably weighing her options. Then she opened the door wider, nodding to me to get inside.

"Let's go to the kitchen. My husband is upstairs. He's sleeping and I don't want to wake him up."

The house looked old; the kitchen needed updating. I probably had only five minutes to convince this woman to give me Sasha's address. I bet she'd moved to Edinburgh like she planned.

"Dexter, right?" she asked when we sat down at a small table in the kitchen.

"Dexter Tyndall. I used to be Sasha's neighbour before ..."

Shit, I wasn't supposed to bring Joey up. This was a really, really bad start. Kath was just watching me. Her expression was detached. I needed to show her that I did care about her daughter, that I wasn't some douche ex.

Get it together, you stupid fuck.

"Sorry, what I meant to say was that me and Sasha—we lived next door to each other, but I was stupid enough to drive her away when she tried to help me. I have been in the hospital in the past few weeks. The sale of the apartment went through a few days ago and now I don't have her new address. She moved out before I had a chance to speak to her."

Silence. Fuck, why wasn't the woman saying anything? Her hazel eyes were looking straight through me. I couldn't bullshit her, even if I tried.

"My daughter went through hell, Dexter. Her ex-boyfriend ruined her life. It took her a year to pick up the pieces and start living again. Sasha doesn't need another Kirk. He was a disrespectful, selfish man that couldn't keep his dick in his pants. Why would I help you?"

I tried to breathe, containing my anger. I still had no idea what happened with her douche ex, but this wasn't the time or a place. Besides, what was I expecting? A warm cup of tea and sympathy? No. Sasha's mother didn't like bullshit.

"Did Sasha tell you what happened between us?" I asked.

"She didn't have to say anything. I know that haunted look on her face. She talked about you a couple of weeks back. She said that you had women in and out of your apartment, that you were making her life—"

"Kath," I cut her off, risking everything. "I'm not going to bore you with my crazy messed-up life. I admit, I made some bad choices, but all I need is a shot, another chance to make things right. Your daughter is a wonderful woman and I want to make her happy. Yes, I did sleep around before Sasha, but I was always open and honest about my lifestyle choices. I had never promised anyone a relationship. Your daughter changed me after we started hanging out together. Sasha helped me to get my life straight. She pulled me out of my own misery. Please, I beg you. I need to talk to her."

"You know, you remind me of Joey a little. He wanted to make me happy, too, more than thirty years ago," Sasha's mother said all of a sudden.

Crap, this wasn't something that I needed to hear. I thought she didn't want to talk about Joey.

"He was a good guy and probably the only one that understood me."

"Dexter, Sasha moved to Edinburgh. I want her to be happy and… I think I'm done with lies," she said, pausing. Right, I was losing her. "This whole thing with the apartment and Joey, it only pulled us apart. I think I owe you and her an explanation."

"Honestly, Kath, I really don't care about Joey. I want Sasha. You don't need to explain anything," I said. This wasn't going the way I planned. I was a pretty screwed-up guy with a fucking mental illness. Joey was a good guy, with a complicated past.

"I'm afraid to talk to her about this. My husband doesn't know and I want to keep it that way, but my daughter... she deserves an explanation and I want you to tell her everything when you get the chance to. I'm scared that she will push me away once she knows the truth."

"Kath, I'm sorry, but you're confusing me."

"I'm going to tell you a story from the past, so please listen. You can judge me after," she said firmly. "My father remarried when I was fifteen. Mum had died of cancer years earlier. We had each other and we were happy... well, that's what I thought. Dad met a woman, things developed quickly and he married her. Joey became my stepbrother and he came to live with us just after a year. Things weren't easy. I didn't really like Gill, my step-mum. I hated Joey with a vengeance, but soon that hate turned into something else, something that neither of us understood. Cutting this story short, we ended up falling for each other. Years later, Gill divorced my father and Joey went away to university. No one knew we kept in touch, but as usual, life got in the way and I found myself engaged to Sasha's father. Joey never promised me anything, and when he came back to Glasgow he asked me to run away with him, to leave Robert. That day, my father caught us in the garden. He went ballistic and he threw Joey out. My family didn't want a scandal, and my Dad didn't want me to break the engagement. Our love was crazy, but it remained unfulfilled. Joey became very successful and he came back for me. A few days later I found out that I was pregnant with Sasha and I decided to go ahead with the marriage, with my new life. Joey and I saw each other a few more times after that, but then he stopped visiting me. He only wrote letters. Many letters sent from different places in his travels, but he never said if he was still living in the country or not."

She paused and I stared at her in shock. I wasn't expecting this. When I came here today I thought that I could get Sasha's address and disappear. It looked like Kath was a dark horse after all, falling for her own step-sibling.

"Then almost two months ago I received a phone call from the solicitor saying that Joey had left me a property. It was such a shock. I had thought about him over the years, but I never looked for him. We drifted apart, but he made sure that I'd remember him even after his death."

"Kath, I don't think you should be telling me all this. Maybe you should ex—"

"No, Dexter. You knew Joey yourself, and you understood him. Sasha won't just give up. She will eventually dig the truth out of me. All these years I've been questioning myself, asking if I made the right decision. I was always worried about other people, about my father and family. I sacrificed my own happiness and I don't want this to happen to my daughter. It's not my place to tell you about what happened to her with her last boyfriend. She ran away from the city, from the drama. If you want her, you need to be open and honest."

I nodded, getting what she meant. I didn't know what I was supposed to do. My head felt overloaded with information. Love was so fucked up, and yet I was still pursuing it. Eventually I got what I came for.

Now, everything finally made sense. Joey had talked about Sasha's mother, but I never asked for any explanation. He took that story to his grave.

When I said my goodbyes to Kath, I didn't head straight to Sasha, but I went to one of the stores in the retail park. This was something that I felt I needed to do first. The hospital pushed some bad memories through, but Bishop and Jones had helped me. They pushed and pushed until I agreed to take the meds and admit to them that I needed help. I paid upfront for a flat-screen TV and asked the guys in the store to pack it into my car.

My palms were damp with sweat when I arrived at the psychiatric ward. Everything looked the same. The TV wasn't too heavy, but I still managed to get into a fight with a fucking security guard who didn't want to let me through. In the end, I made a hell of a noise and disturbed the usual deadly silence on the ward.

"Dexter, what the hell are you doing here?" asked Jones, as I barged into the staff room carrying the box. There were other nurses and caregivers there, all looking at me like I'd lost my fucking mind.

"I was in the neighbourhood and I thought I'd pop in to see if you all missed me," I said sarcastically, putting the TV on the table. I should have paid people to do this shit for me. They were all still staring blankly, like I was going through a complete relapse.

"What's all that?" asked someone that I didn't know.

"What do you think it is?" I asked back, wondering what the hell was wrong with these people.

"A TV," Nurse Jones said.

"Well done, Jonesy. You scored. Now tell us all, what do we use the TV for?"

"Dexter!" she shouted, getting red. "This isn't funny. You aren't supposed to be in this room. Why did you bring this TV in here? I'm going to call secu–"

"Chill, Jonesy, and listen for a second. I can't fucking stand you sitting in here reading the same fucking magazine all the time, so I decided to get you a TV for entertainment. Think about this as my going-away present."

I expected her to start shouting again, but for a really long and awkward moment she just stared at me. I didn't like that look on her face. The other nurses and caregivers in the canteen looked equally baffled.

"You bought us a TV?" she repeated.

"Yes, Jonesy."

"Oh, darling, that is so sweet of you."

Before I knew it, Jonesy was putting her weight on me, attempting to hug me. Shit, I wasn't ready for that. I had lots of money and finally one doctor had done something right for a change, so I thought I could show my appreciation.

"Okay, okay, that's enough. You have to set it all up yourself. Tell Bishop I'll be here on Monday," I blurted out, pushing her away from me. I couldn't bloody believe it. Tough Jonesy had tears in her eyes. After all this time, I finally cracked her.

"You're good man, Dexter. Let other people see it sometimes," she said when I was leaving. It was funny, because I felt good. Nurse Jones wanted me to stay and talk, but I couldn't waste time on pointless chitchat. I was ready to head over to Barbie.

Within minutes I was back in my car. I had the address, but Sasha didn't want to talk to me. Last time, fucking Victoria had interrupted us and complicated everything even further. Now all I needed to do was to tell Sasha how I felt. This sounded easy, but that thought fucking petrified me, because I had no idea if she felt the same way.

Sasha

The interview for the job in the hospital went well. I couldn't do anything else; now I had to wait for their decision. Gina had set up a blind date for this evening, but I still hadn't confirmed if I was going or not. I needed more time or more sex to forget about Dexter, like I did with Shaun and Kirk. It was hard to deny that I didn't like being with Dex, but I didn't want to be one of many. I wanted to be the one.

After the interview, I went shopping and bought a new dress for this evening. My new place had one bedroom with an open-plan living room and kitchen. It was nothing fancy, but I had everything I needed. After living in the Grange it was hard for me to get used to this small space. When I arrived outside on my street and headed straight to the door, I stopped in my tracks. Was I was hallucinating, seeing Dexter at my door? Colour drained from my face, and my heart betrayed me. Four days and it felt like no time had passed. The pull was there; it didn't disappear as I had hoped it would.

"What the hell are you doing here?" I asked, nearly dropping all my paperwork on the pavement. He wore a black polo shirt that exposed his sculpted muscles. His hair was longer, and he had a slight beard, which only made him look sexier. Damn, me and my oversensitive libido.

"You ran away when I told you that we needed to talk," he said, smiling, as if things between us weren't awkward enough.

"Dexter, I asked you to leave me alone. We have nothing to talk about."

"We have plenty to discuss, my darling Barbie. We can do this the hard way or the easy way. The choice is yours."

I shoved the paperwork into his hands and searched for my keys. I'd gotten to know him pretty damn well, so I knew that he wasn't about to let this one go. My hands were trembling and my pulse sped up when he was near. Yes, sex with him was pretty awesome, but that was over. He hurt me and I was in the process of falling out of love with him.

"So you won't leave me alone until I'll have a conversation with you?" I asked.

"We both know that I'm not planning on it."

"Fine, we will talk, but not here. In a restaurant," I snapped at him, opening the door to my flat. He lifted both of his eyebrows, looking at me with astonishment and hidden excitement. My skin itched for him, for the warmth from his body. I wondered how he found me, if he had paid someone to stalk me all the way here.

"You want to have a conversation in a fucking restaurant?" he repeated.

"Yes. Invite me to dinner or we ain't talking at all."

His eyes were glued to mine. Yet again, he didn't look down at my boobs. I was getting wet thinking about our last encounter on the beach. Sweat gathered between my boobs. Was it possible that he was done with running after other women and only wanted me?

My inner voice laughed at me. Dexter Tyndall couldn't simply change. He was still an arrogant, self-centred bastard.

"Whatever you want, Barbie," he said, shrugging his shoulders.

"All right, wait in the car. I'll be back in ten minutes."

"Are you afraid to invite me in?" he asked, leaning over.

A dramatic shudder passed through me and my heart kicked me right in my chest. After weeks of not being in my life, he still melted my knickers right off.

"I'm not afraid. I'm just careful," I replied and slammed the door in his face.

Twenty-Nine

Sasha

I didn't want to make too much effort, but my heart beat loudly in my chest, letting me know that Dexter had come back to rip apart the last piece of my broken soul. He'd said some unforgivable stuff in the hospital, stuff that wrecked my confidence, reminding me about the past. I knew that if I invited him in we could end up in bed, back to square one, so I had to demand we talk on neutral ground.

I changed quickly, dressing in a pair of leather pants and navy top, making sure that it was low cut. Despite everything, I liked making him needy and frustrated. Dexter needed to see what he had lost and I wanted to make him as uncomfortable as I could during the whole dinner. He hated being around other people and he was going to feel uneasy in a busy restaurant. It was a test: I needed to see if he had been taking to his meds, that the episode from weeks ago and the following time in hospital had taught him anything at all.

Several deep breaths later I went outside, looking sexy. The humid, sticky air wasn't helping with my overactive libido, but I told myself that I could get through this.

When I jumped into his car, wearing my black heels, his eyes were glazed with lust. I swallowed hard, reminding myself to keep my distance.

"You look gorgeous, Barbie."

"Really? Complements, Dex? Have you bumped your head or something?" I asked, laughing.

"Actually, I have never been better, thanks to you."

I didn't know what to say to that. Was he thanking me for locking him in the psychiatric ward? Impossible. Dexter had never been grateful for anything before. I glanced at him, wondering if I had missed something. For some reason he looked tense, nervous and not like his confident usual self. Something was definitely different about him. My hormones were going into rapture, preheating and lubricating my core. Our sweaty bodies in that hotel room, in his apartment, it was perfect and sexy and I wanted more. My inner voice reminded me that it was the past.

"What are you thinking about, Sasha?"

His voice drew me back and I flinched, feeling the familiar flush creeping over my cheeks. Fuck, we were at the traffic light and he was staring at me with those gleaming brown eyes.

"Nothing that you should be concerned about," I replied in a low voice.

He smirked and the car moved. "You're terrible liar, Barbie. You're turned on and you want me to fuck you again. I can tell by the way you're squirming and clenching those thighs."

Bastard. I shifted in my seat and looked away, knowing that I was so freaking wet that it was uncomfortable.

"And I thought that you had changed." I snorted, shaking my head.

"You love when I talk to you dirty, you sassy liar."

He knew me better than I knew myself, but I refused to acknowledge it. Something was definitely off about him. This new, different Dexter, this calmer and civilised one was much more frightening than the dirty and arrogant one, and he was less predictable.

He parked the car somewhere in the city centre and winked at me when I crossed my arms over my chest. My gut was telling me that I was making a mistake, that I was stepping into dangerous territory. Dexter was destructive and I was supposed to start over, away from him.

"We need to hurry this up. I was supposed to have a date tonight."

Dexter

I stopped and looked at her. She was fucking with me. The only date that she was having tonight was with me and my cock. The other asshole, whoever he was, could go to hell for all I cared. Her words made me feel like she was slowly slicing my skin apart with a razor. She was only punishing me and I couldn't let her get to me.

The restaurant wasn't too far. I had picked out a decent Thai place in the centre of Edinburgh and demanded their best table by the window, away from everyone else.

"I'll let that one slide, Barbie. You ain't seeing anyone else tonight. We both know that your pussy belongs to me," I muttered. "I'm asking nicely, so hear me out."

She raised both of her eyebrows, folding her arms over her gorgeous chest.

"Is this what you call nicely?" she asked, shaking her head. "What do you want from me, Dex? You told me that you were done with fucking whiny fat blondes, and now you're here acting like nothing happened, like everything is all right."

She cut me down to size with that statement, but all I could think of was her tight wet folds. This was getting out of control. I had to get down to business and stop thinking about sex.

"I owe you an apology. I wasn't fucking thinking straight then. In the hospital, you took my hand and I got scared, petrified of having someone in my life, someone that gave a damn. Barbie, you mean the world to me and I want to try this whole monogamous relationship thing with you," I said, looking straight into her green eyes, so she knew that I was being honest.

She stopped smiling and looked at me like I was still psychotic.

"Don't blame this on your mania, Dexter. You meant every word that day."

I reached out and took her hand, and my cock strained in my jeans. *For the love of God, instant hard-on for my Barbie.* It looked like my cock did work after all. I was ready to strip her and screw her on the table in front of everyone here, but I had to make her believe me first.

"Sasha, for fuck's sake. I'm sorry. I can get on my knees and apologise and beg forgiveness if you want me to, but you're the best thing that happened to me. I want more. I want to fuck you so bad, but not just today. All day, every day, any time of the day or night. I don't want any other pussy, Sasha."

She was holding her breath and I was wondering if this whole prepared speech would do me any good. I couldn't treat her like shit anymore, but I was inexperienced with this whole vanilla emotion talk. My feelings right at this moment weren't relevant. She didn't believe me, and until she did, I wasn't ready to reveal how I felt.

"But you don't believe in love or relationships. We had fun, Dex, but I can't do this. I can't pretend that we can make this work."

Stubborn to the extreme, but she was more than that; she was relentless in believing that I still wanted to fuck the whole city.

"I didn't before you, but now I want to make you come every day. I want you and only you," I insisted.

"Any drinks?" asked the waiter, interrupting my cheesy monologue and pissing me off. Sasha pulled away her hand, tossing her blond hair behind her. I really wanted her in my apartment tonight, but she was wary, apprehensive. Maybe this wasn't what she wanted to hear; maybe she was expecting a marriage proposal. Christ, I wasn't ready for that.

"Champagne, the best you got, and now get fucking lost," I barked. The waiter mumbled something and disappeared.

"Charming, as usual, Dex."

"So what do you say, Barbie? Please forgive me for being a dick and let's start over."

"What about Victoria? I saw your picture in the magazine. You were together at a charity event."

I exhaled. Victoria and her stupid games. Cold sweat seeped over me, zipping me with fresh fear at the mention of that psychopath. At that banquet, there were paps everywhere and she forced me to pose with her and smile like we were married. She kept ruining everything. I'd had enough.

"I'm taking care of her. She won't be a problem."

Sasha sighed, looking like she didn't believe me.

"Yes, you're being nice and promising a lot, but what is going to happen once I spread my legs for you?" she asked and I was ready to answer, but she beat me to it. "I want proof, Dexter. Show me how much you care and I'll think about it."

The waiter came back with champagne. I grabbed it away from him and poured her a glass.

I was hoping that this would be an easy fix, that maybe I could just woo her with an apology and then we could fuck. Even now, I was hard for her.

"Sasha, is that you?"

Some woman approached our table. She was tall and slender, holding an obscene number of shopping bags. I should have insisted on the table in the back, so we wouldn't have to be disturbed. I looked at my Barbie, who suddenly shifted on her seat. Her eyes grew wide with shock and horror.

"Hi, Sharon," Sasha replied, sounding uneasy. She glanced at me in panic, then at the woman.

"Oh my God, what are you doing in Edinburgh?" Sharon squealed with excitement. She was pretty enough and it looked like she knew my Barbie well. She quickly turned to look at me, flashing me a flirtatious smile, which I didn't return. Something stank here, something big. Sasha's body language changed. I couldn't say that she was relaxed with me, but now she was pale, trying to hide the panic and nervousness.

Who the fuck was this cheeky bitch? They obviously knew each other from Glasgow.

"I don't think that it's any of your business. You're interrupting my date," Sasha shot back.

"Why don't you introduce me, darling? I'm sure—"

"Sharon, have you forgotten how you treated me when I showed up at that dinner a year ago? I don't want to talk to you. Get the fuck out of my face before I lose my temper."

Sasha

My world was falling apart all over again. Sharon stood in front of me acting like we were still best friends, like she hadn't humiliated me enough. I couldn't just sit here and take it. She thought I was still that old broken, naive Sasha that couldn't stand up for herself. Well, I'd just proven to her that I wasn't.

I was done with being treated like a stupid mousy bitch that everyone was taking the piss out of. The emotional scars of my past were messy and Sharon deserved hell for her part in them.

"But, darling, don't be so mean. It was you that kept spreading those silly rumours and—"

"Shut your ugly lying mouth!" I yelled, losing control. I was ready to jump right at her and hurt her. "Kirk stuck a fork in my cheek, Sharon—a fork! Then, because he wasn't satisfied with merely stabbing me with a kitchen utensil, he slashed half of my face with a broken bottle, because I dared to ask him for the money he owed me. Why did you think I was in the hospital for two weeks?"

Sharon was too stupid to believe me. We'd been friends, but she'd always had a thing for Kirk. After that traumatic day, he started spreading lies about me, telling our friends that I couldn't handle the breakup, that I'd ended up in psychiatric hospital, and she believed him. Bastard got out on bail. His mother had to take out a loan to finance it. She had some powerful connections and apparently he'd never gotten in any trouble before.

233

"You twatbag, get the fuck out of her face," Dexter growled, getting up. Everyone in the restaurant was suddenly watching the whole scene unfold. Sharon had never seen me angry and out of control, so she was staring at me in complete shock. I had always been a good little yes-girl with low self-esteem, but a lot of things had changed within a year.

After Kirk's attack, everyone had turned their backs on me. That was straight after I was released from the hospital. All our supposed joint friends backed up his filthy lies. I was afraid to go out on the street; I was scared of my own shadow.

"I knew you were crazy. Kirk was–"

"One word, say one more word to her and I swear to God I'll shut that mouth for you, and trust me, it will fucking hurt," Dexter shouted.

People were staring in shock at us, the snickers and whispers traveling around the room quickly. I didn't care that we were making a scene. I was livid. Sharon brought those crappy memories to the surface and they made my whole body tremble with rage. I couldn't let her break me; it had taken me twelve months to lift myself up. First Kirk talked shit, now her—I'd had enough.

"Dexter, come on, let's go. The bitch isn't worth it," I said. Sharon hadn't said another word. She was clearly startled, staring blankly at me. Pure fury rippled up and down my body. I wished that I was the same person back then that I am now, when all those people that used to call themselves my "friends" were abusing me, calling me a liar.

I rushed out of the restaurant, not waiting for Dex. I couldn't breathe, so I stuck my head between my knees, dragging air into my lungs. He had his arms around me before I knew it. The warmth from his body spread slowly, waking up the lust that I'd buried when he hurt me in the hospital. At that point, my defence mechanism shut down. Sobs escaped me and I simply started crying into his chest. I was so ashamed of all this. For months I'd done so well.

"Fuck, Sasha, stop this bullshit. Don't let that bitch get to you," I heard him saying. I inhaled the musky scent of his cologne and wiped the tears away. After a few more seconds, I was ready to pull away from him. I had to get it together and stop using him to make myself feel better. After all, he was still a bastard and a liar.

When we got to his car, I said, "Just take me home," and buckled my seat belt.

Dexter gripped the steering wheel and inhaled loudly. "I just want to know one thing, Sasha. That fuckface from the hotel, did he really do those things to you that you said in the restaurant?"

I didn't have to say anything; my eyes had already given him an answer. My feelings were transparent. Pain from the past grew rapidly, reminding me how worthless and broken I'd been back then when I couldn't stand up for myself.

"Fucking prick. Fucking bastard. I wish that I'd beaten the shit out of him in that corridor. I–"

"Dexter!" I shouted, shaking all over. "Stop it. Please, stop it. Enough. Don't say anymore. I can't do this right now. Just take me home."

"Fine," he said and turned on the engine.

Thirty

Sasha

I didn't want to see him at all, but he had to pick up his stuff. Our three long years together meant nothing to him. I had been sitting on pins and needles all day, wondering how he was going to act when he showed up.

My heart was shattered, broken, and I hadn't stopped crying since the moment I realised that it was truly over. It was the second time it happened. My last boyfriend had cheated on me with my roommate and now Kirk had done exactly the same, but with my childhood friend.

I packed whatever I could into boxes. We had stuff that we'd collected together and I wanted to be sure that he wouldn't take anything that didn't belong to him. Our relationship had been intense and at the time I thought it was also real. I couldn't believe that it was over. I felt betrayed, betrayed and lost. The contract for the flat was coming to an end next month and I didn't know what I was going to do after that.

I heard the car outside and looked out the window. Kirk got out, looking like his usual self, and a few minutes later he was upstairs. He knocked. It was funny, because this flat was still under his name, but we had to act like we were civilised.

I opened the door and let him in.

"Here's your stuff. I packed it up for you," I said, trying to sound strong, but it came out like I had swallowed a wooden stick. I was so weak when he was around, always ready to fulfill his every need.

"What about the stuff that we bought together?" he asked and then I noticed that he had been drinking. His voice had that familiar hard edge to it, like when he enjoyed provoking an argument. I shouldn't have let him in.

"Kirk, how much have you had to drink?" I asked shyly.

"It's none of your fucking business. I do whatever I want now that we aren't together," he shouted straight into my face.

"What happened to us? Why did you do this?" I whispered to myself, knowing that he wouldn't listen, but he took a step towards me.

"Nothing. Nothing happened. I got bored of you telling me what to do all the time."

I dragged some air into my lungs, not even realising that he had heard me. This wasn't how I imagined our last meeting would go. I thought he would at least apologise to me, but it looked like he had other plans.

"We were happy, Kirk. I can't under—"

"There is nothing to understand, you stupid bitch. You were boring, always worried about what our friends thought about you. Jessica seemed like a better candidate all along."

"She was my best friend!" I shouted.

"And a very good fuck!"

Tears began streaming down my cheeks then. I couldn't believe he was behaving as if I meant nothing to him.

"We need to discuss the money now, Kirk. You've been avoiding talking about it for some time."

A couple of months ago, I took a loan from the bank for eight thousand pounds so he could get a new car. Kirk had bad credit, so he asked me to apply for it. I agreed, but so far I had been the only one paying it back.

I don't know what happened then, but Kirk's eyes shifted and I saw a mad gleam in them. His fists were clenched. Before I knew it, he had pushed me over to the sofa.

"I ain't giving you anything. We are not together!" he shouted and then stormed to the kitchen.

Something snapped in me. I was done with being pushed around, done with being treated like an idiot. I went after him, knowing that I couldn't let it go. I was going to get this money back from him no matter what.

He was searching through the cupboards for something, probably for more money. I had a tendency to hide some emergency cash in the kitchen, away from him, but he could always find it.

I wiped the tears away from my face and picked up a fork, my hands trembling.

"Stop going through my stuff. I want you to leave now."

I kept my voice calm and controlled. I needed him to go and sober up. Kirk was working and he could afford to pay back the loan. He didn't stop opening and closing the cupboards, talking to himself, so I nudged him with the fork.

"Take your stuff and get out!"

He turned, launched himself at me and grabbed my wrist. Everything happened so fast, so unexpectedly. He was so much stronger that I couldn't do anything. Next thing I knew, I felt excruciating pain in my cheek. A warm and sticky liquid poured down my face.

"You stupid bitch. You were always weak. Don't you fucking dare talk to me about money. I took care of you when you were in the hospital, so you owe me."

I opened my eyes and realised that he had stuck the fork into my cheek. Then he knocked me to the floor and was standing above me, his eyes wild, unrecognisable. Although I was in pain and shock, I couldn't let go of the fact that he was cheating me out of my money.

"The car is mine, Kirk. I paid for it!" I yelled, trying to get up, but then he kicked me, knocking over the bottle that was on the kitchen counter. It smashed next to me.

"Stupid fucking bitch. Whiny cow. I made you! It was me that created you. You would be nothing without me," he kept saying, picking the pieces of glass off the floor. I screamed when he launched at me again, realising it was just the beginning of his rage.

"Sasha. Hey, Barbie. For fuck's sake, snap out of it. You're scaring me."

Dexter's voice drew me back to my shattered reality. He wasn't driving anymore and we were outside my new flat. I was so caught up in my past that I didn't even realise we'd arrived back on my street. I didn't know why I brought these awful memories back up. It had been a long year and I'd transformed myself, became a different Sasha, a stronger one.

Kirk broke three of my ribs that day and he slashed my face with pieces of the broken bottle. I was in agony for days from the corrective surgery. My parents insisted that I press charges, so I did. He was arrested for domestic assault and actual bodily harm, but he was bailed a week later. That was just the beginning of my nightmare.

"I'm all right, Dex. I just want to go home," I insisted.

"If that bitch was telling the truth, then why is that asshole walking free?" he asked.

I closed my eyes, knowing that there was no point hiding the truth anymore. No one apart from my parents knew exactly what I had gone through. I looked at Dexter, then took a deep breath and started explaining what happened that night. I told him about Kirk, about his drunken episodes, about what he did to me and about the fact that I'd been ready to do anything for a guy that I loved. By the time I was finished, Dexter's fists were clenched, his face unrecognisable, twisted with anger and rage.

"I had him in my hands. Fuck, I wish—"

"Dex, stop it, please. That isn't everything. There is more," I managed to say, dropping my head in my hands.

"Jesus Christ, Sasha, more?!"

"He was bailed and started spreading rumours about me, telling people that I had a breakdown because he broke up with me. He pushed it too far, made out that I became aggressive and started stalking him. Everyone believed him and because we had the same circle of friends, it was easy for him to convince them. I was very insecure then, not the person that I am now. People assumed he was telling the truth, that I was a liar. My friends stopped talking to me, and everyone turned their backs on me. I started getting threatening messages and emails. I had lost everything. I couldn't work, so the hospital had to dismiss me. It was a total shambles."

Dexter was shaking his head, cursing Kirk out. I felt good that I finally got the truth off my chest, that I came clean. I'd found things out about Dexter, pushed him to go to the hospital and he didn't hate me for it. Still, Dexter had to earn back my trust, show me that he changed.

"It was a nightmare and Kirk only got a few months. I didn't get any justice."

"I wish you would have told me earlier. I could have cut off his balls and dick in that hotel. Fuck, I was so close," Dexter growled. "What about that woman from the restaurant? Was she your friend?"

"She used to be our mutual friend, but she knew Kirk first. He went to prison for a few months after the hearing. His mother hired the best solicitor in Glasgow and he made up that he was under a lot of pressure at work, that he was stressed and depressed, which culminated in an unprecedented attack. He had all his friends telling the judge that we loved each other, that I slashed myself with a broken bottle for attention, because I couldn't take it that he broke up with me. Sharon had a thing for him and spread rumours about me."

"Fuck, Sasha, you should have punched her. At least you'd make yourself feel better."

I smiled and closed my eyes. "I don't want to talk about this anymore. It hurts too much. I moved to London because I couldn't take Scotland anymore. That's why I stopped dancing and socialising. I needed to get away, to start over, to bury myself in a new environment. Kirk ruined my life. I haven't had much luck in love or relationships. With you, it was just sex and I enjoyed it. It was fine that we didn't have to label anything, but now I'm done with being a plaything. I'm starting over, so just respect that. Show me that I can trust you, and then I might consider forgiving you."

Dexter

I couldn't fucking believe what I was hearing. That fuckface from the hotel, that pig, dared to lift his hand to my Barbie. He violated her and then turned everyone against her. I'd had a chance to kill him, to pull his eyes out of his sockets, but I let him go. I fucked up. I'd known Sasha for over two months now and I never tried to find out more about her past, never asked any questions. I was so blind, so obsessed with sex that I didn't dare to look further. I hadn't recognised her pain. And now I couldn't fucking get my head around the fact that she had done so much for some douche. I'd guessed that she was damaged, but I'd chosen to ignore it, because I was a coward.

I wanted to take her to my fucking apartment and hold her, tell her that she didn't have to think about this shit anymore, but I had lost my chance. This whole fucking love and emotions stuff was new to me. I had never paid enough attention to her feelings. Or my own. Straight after Pap's death, I shut out my inner turmoil with sex and drugs. It worked, but I drove myself crazy trying to numb the grief. I promised myself that I would never let anyone else in because I couldn't take the pain. Dad had his flaws, but I always wanted him to be in my life.

Now it was a different story.

I couldn't just tell her that I had fallen in love with her. This shit wasn't going to work, not after weeks of convincing her that I wasn't capable of loving anyone.

Later that evening, I was so wound up by her story and the fact that her asshole ex got away with hurting her, that I made a phone call to Ronny. There was no way I was going to let this shit go.

"What's up, brother?"

"You know the info that you managed to pull up for me a few weeks ago, on Sasha Scott?"

"Yeah, what about it?"

I hesitated for a split second. This wasn't the best way to start over, but I was furious and that fucker needed to be punished. Barbie's past was shattered. It looked like she had been prepared to do anything for this guy and he simply used and abused her in every possible way.

"Her ex-boyfriend. Dig deep. I want to know if he's clean or if he has something in his pocket, anything that could help me to bring him down. I'll pay you double rate for it if you get me something tonight," I said, knowing that Ronny was the best. Either way, that douche was going to pay. I had no idea how, but I could get in touch with people who could find something on anyone. It was just a matter of time and I had the available funds to make him suffer.

I went back to the complex and spent the rest of the night on the laptop waiting for info from Ronny. It was still early, but I needed to study the guy, find the best way to break him.

It was going to be a while before I'd have Sasha back in my bed. The old fucking Dexter had died in the hospital and a new one had been reborn. I was still stubborn as fuck, but now I had a new motivation. I had to get Sasha's trust back.

Ronny did give me something to work on, but around eleven he sent an email, saying that he needed more time. Apparently Kirk Adamson was clean, so I told Ronny to keep looking.

In the morning, my alarm went off at seven. I did my usual workout, but an hour later than I used to before I was admitted to the hospital. I didn't have to be in the office until nine. In the beginning it was hard to get used to this new routine, but now I didn't have to deal with my overactive mind. Sasha wasn't working tonight, but she had pole-dancing training. The hours in the office were dragging, and after countless meetings with my solicitors, I left early.

Mum was on the phone to me, checking if I was all right yet again. We chatted for some time while I waited in the carpark outside the leisure centre. My mother was relentless. She kept saying that I needed to find myself a new hobby. I said my goodbyes when I saw Sasha coming out of her training with a hot red-haired woman, probably another pole dancer. She was more Harry's type than mine.

I stepped out of the car and decided to meet her out front. Three weeks was a long time for me to go without sex. I had a twitch in my pants when I spotted Sasha wearing tightly fitted yoga pants.

The red-haired woman shot me a murderous glare. She didn't look too happy to see me, and I bet that Sasha told her what kind of dick I used to be. I waited patiently until they said their goodbyes. Sasha didn't know that I was planning to see her tonight. This was meant to be a surprise.

"Dexter... hi," she said. "What are you doing here?"

"I was in the neighbourhood, so I thought I could see you," I replied. "Are you hungry?"

She looked like she didn't believe me. "Yes, I am, but we aren't having sex tonight, Dex. I thought that I ma—"

"Jesus, Sash, you're obsessed with my cock." I laughed. My imagination went wild thinking about her and my cock.

"Whatever. I'm letting you know that I'm sticking to what I said earlier."

"Yes, ma'am," I said, saluting, and she rolled her eyes. "Just get in and shut up. We are going out for dinner. I promise that won't touch you unless you want me to, and trust me, you will want it soon."

She snorted and glanced around the street, like she was expecting that I was pulling some sort of trick.

"Where are we going?" she asked, folding her arms over her amazing chest. I wanted to wrap my tongue around her nipples. I couldn't focus when she looked so sexy.

"To the complex. I need you to see something." I could see that she wasn't happy, but she went along with the idea. We were silent for most of the drive, and I was hard. My dick was getting out of control around her. That sexy body was right next to me, but I couldn't even touch her, because I'd ruined everything, but I planned on fixing it.

"Did the new resident move in?"

"What resident?"

"The older guy that bought the apartment from me? Did he move in next door yet?"

I smiled, remembering her moans when I was licking her soaking pussy. "No, not yet." This was partly true, but I wasn't ready to say any more just yet.

"What happened to your new car?"

"I returned it, along with about fifteen suits and ties."

She didn't say anything until we were passing through the concierge. Duncan went purple when she asked him if he'd missed her. Fucking tease. She loved making men uncomfortable. Yet all those months ago, she let some douche take advantage of her. I began to realise that I didn't know her at all.

"Dexter, we won't have sex today," she reminded me when we were in the lift. She probably noticed my euphoric smile as I remembered our hot sex in the corridor. I had to stop thinking with my dick. She needed to see that I'd buried old Dexter deep in the ground.

"Barbie, you're obsessed with fucking me. I haven't said anything about sex since we got into the car."

"I'm aware of your tricks," she muttered when I opened the door and let her inside.

"Stop talking like that, because I'm really going to lose my shit and bang you in the corridor again. Let's go to the kitchen."

"I've been in your kitchen before."

"Smart-ass. No, I need you to see that I got rid of all the drugs, weed and buzz. I brought you here for you to see for yourself that I'm not fucking around, Sasha. I'm starting over, clean and honest. You and your tight pussy are the only natural high that I want."

Thirty-One

Sasha

He let me in and I went straight to the kitchen, wanting to see it for myself. All the containers were gone. He'd even gotten rid of the weed and whisky. He started opening the cupboards and drawers, showing me that there was nothing in them.

All right, so he was sticking to his medications, but drugs and buzz were just the tip of the iceberg. Depression didn't just go away; it fed on a person, waiting for that one unexpected moment to strike back. I couldn't just jump back into a relationship. We both needed more time, and if he wanted me, then he needed to show me that he wasn't throwing out any empty words.

"Dexter, that's great you're not going back to your old ways, but—"

"Hold on; that's not all. I need to show you something else."

I followed him to the table. He typed something into his laptop. His elbow brushed over my stomach, accidentally, but I felt tingles running over the base of my spine.

"All right, so what do you want me to see?" I asked, feeling warm all of a sudden. All the windows were shut and it was humid outside. He winked at me and typed something else on the address bar. I leaned over when a new page popped up. It took me a few seconds to realise that I was staring at a support group website for people who suffered with bipolar disorder.

My mouth opened, but no sound came out. I was shocked, not quite believing that he would join something like that.

When I glanced at Dexter, he was watching me with nervousness in his eyes, like he was afraid that I would take his honesty the wrong way.

"What is this, Dex? What does this mean?"

"I'm going to go to this support group meeting. Sticking to meds is easy, but that asshole Bishop said that I could have relapses. I don't want to screw this up."

The emotions that started floating back to me were dangerous. I didn't want him to see that I was moved. Dexter Tyndall and a support group. This was the last thing that I thought he would do. All this time, he didn't want to let me in, pretending that it wasn't a big deal when he saved Joey's life. I didn't want to believe that he would sit in a circle of other people discussing his private life. A warm tingle began crawling its way to my heart. Shit, I wasn't expecting it. Dexter was trying hard, probably because of me.

"Have you got the date of the meeting set yet?"

We were standing so close to each other. Sweat broke out on the nape of my neck, and a slow burn spread across the skin on my breasts. My knickers clung to my wet pussy, building a familiar desire deep in my core. I was always so weak around him, but now it was torture, because I loved him. It was a bad idea, coming here. It made me realise that I needed to feel him inside me again, that I wanted him to devour my mouth.

"Barbie, I want you to come with me. You know how much I can't stand being around people, but I want to be clean for you."

Tears forced their way to my eyes, but I didn't let him see that these words melted my heart. We were discussing the possibility of being there for one to another, not the possibility of spending life together forever. The reality hit me like cold rain on a humid summer day.

"Come here, you knob," I said and brought him closer to me, needing to satisfy that craving for closeness. I didn't want him to see through me, to sense that I had developed deep sincere feelings for him, and now he was wrecking me from the inside out. There were endless possibilities, many other men, but Dexter was the first one that restored the idea that I could be loved again.

He didn't waste much time; he wrapped his arms around my waist and started brushing my neck gently with his lips, barely even touching it. He was too much; this whole thing was too much. My resistance against him, the steel fence around my heart began melting, like ice in Hawaii.

"Argh, fuck it," I rasped, bringing his lips down to mine quickly. I needed to taste him again, feel him heat the blood in my veins. Dexter's hands were in my hair, his lips tasting, caressing mine. I moaned into his mouth, rubbing my thighs over each other. I was soaking wet, throbbing between my legs. He cradled me closer to his lean body and grabbed my hand, directing it down to his impressive erection. I imagined him making love to me this time, rubbing my clit while I was on top of him. I knew that I had lost this battle when he grabbed my hips and sat me on the table, spreading my legs apart.

"This is fucking happening," he stated and claimed my neck with his mouth, moulding my breasts at the same time.

I moaned when his forefinger caressed my hard nipples, as he rubbed himself over my sex. I shut my eyes, arching my neck back, ready to forget about my own promises and resolutions. Dexter took off his T-shirt and pulled my trousers and knickers down, plunging his fingers inside me. I cried out with pleasure and the need for more. I didn't know where I was and what was happening, but I loved it.

"All mine again," he growled. I bit his shoulder, feeling that I was going to come apart when I heard the tiny voice of sweet surrender, as well as the voice of reason.

"No, Dexter, we can't do this. I'm sorry, it's too soon," I rasped out, pushing him away. He pulled back, breathing hard. His eyes were crazy hot. I tried to fix my hair, buttoning up my shirt. The desperate throbbing was so freaking uncomfortable.

It was going to take me countless hours of masturbation to forget about him.

Dexter exhaled sharply. His massive erection was popping out of his trousers, and a slap would have been a great reminder that we were still working on this whole "fucked-up relationship."

"Told ya, Barbie. You can't help yourself, can you? You want me so much." He chuckled, leaned over and blew air into my cleavage. "I could motorboat these bad boys all day long if you would let me."

Bastard, he knew how to get to me with that dirty talk. I never thought that I had it in me, but I liked rough sex.

"It was a moment of weakness, Dex," I said, trying to laugh it off. "I'll happily go to that meeting with you. Just let me know when and where."

I kept my eyes steady on his eyes, not on his perfect, sweaty, muscular chest.

"And you're coming with me to have dinner at my mother's this Sunday," he prompted, handing me a glass of water.

"What? Your mother's? Why?" I asked.

"Because I want you to be there. It's part of the plan, you know—to show you that I'm deadly fucking serious about us."

He was annoyed now, and yet again, I was stunned. I needed to remember that Dexter was still himself and I needed to keep him on a short leash. This whole thing with sex was going to be very difficult, because I wanted him badly, but the desire for him was what got me into trouble in the first place.

Dexter

This woman was going to fucking give me a heart attack. She needed to see that I was taking my illness seriously. The whole thing with the support group went better than I expected and I even had a chance to grip her superb toned body against mine. That was a bonus, but then she panicked and pushed me away. I dropped her at her home a few hours later, waiting for some news from Ronny, but he had nothing. It looked like, apart from the initial charge for assault and ABH, Sasha's ex was clean. I was getting anxious, but Ronny hadn't given up yet. I offered him more money and he asked me to give him a few more weeks. He had to reach out to his connections. Ronny was working on it and that was the main thing.

"I have news," Sasha said when I picked her up on Saturday night, a week from our heated-up meeting in my apartment. I made a mental note that if I wanted to make her fall in love with me, I had to make a huge fucking effort, which meant going out on dinner dates, the cinema, romantic walks and all that bullshit. I missed sex more than I thought I would, but Sasha's pussy was worth the wait. Sasha was still wary of the new me, so who knew how long it would be?

Last week had been long and frustrating. I took her out almost every evening and I was getting agitated in the bigger crowds of people. We chatted, had dinner, and then I would drop her off. She knew how much I hated this whole dating thing, but she was testing me to see if I was good enough for her. Now I was beginning to understand why there were so many problems with women and relationships. People had too many expectations.

For a whole week I couldn't touch her, kiss her or even slide my finger into her. She was driving me fucking insane with these stupid rules; I was going to die of blue balls. Sasha was a terrible liar, and I knew that she wanted me too. Sometimes I could smell her desire heavy in the air when we sat close together; it was a complete turn-on. She allowed me to tease her, so I took advantage of that wherever I could.

"I bet your pussy is so wet that it can't wait for my cock," I said when she got into my car on Friday evening.

She rolled her eyes and when she was fastening her seatbelt, I took the time to check out her rack. We were made for each other. I kept talking dirty to her and she kept showing up wearing low-cut tops and short dresses. I knew exactly what she was doing, driving me to an early grave.

"I went for an interview the other day and I had a phone call today. They offered me a permanent full-time position in the Royal Infirmary hospital in Edinburgh," she explained, beaming.

"In that case, I'm taking you out. We need to celebrate it."

New job, new flat—she was really starting over. I didn't want her to live in the city; I wanted her with me in the complex, but we weren't even a proper couple, thanks to my fuck-up from a few weeks ago. Besides, I wanted her to see her ex being punished, so she could gain some justice.

I hated crowded restaurants and our first non-date proved that we could get interrupted at any time. Today I wanted this dinner to be spectacular, so in the morning I made some phone calls and secured a private table on the roof terrace in one of the best places in Edinburgh.

The first support meeting was next week and I was scared to death. Even thinking about any kind of deep and meaningful conversation with other people freaked me the fuck out. I didn't bother to tell Sasha, but in the middle of the night when I was alone in the apartment, I had been getting cold sweats. All my distraction and avoidance techniques had been taken away from me, so I was desperate to have her in my bed. Not just to fuck, but so I wasn't alone.

I parked the car outside the Chester Residence, one of Edinburgh's most stylish hotels. I wanted to have her to myself tonight, forgetting about nosy people around us. A couple of times I insisted on going back to the complex and cooking for her, but every time the answer was the same—a resounding no.

In the concierge there was a tall waiter that welcomed us with a glass of champagne. Earlier on, I'd reminded her to grab a change of clothes, because we were going to stay for a night.

Sasha was quiet once we sat down at the table. We were on the terrace on the top floor with our own apartment that I had hired for the night. I knew that I could forget about fucking her here, but a man can dream.

"Dex, I don't know what to say."

I poured her a glass of vintage champagne and smiled. "We're celebrating, Barbie. Just eat, drink and think about my cock. That's all I'm asking," I said with a wink.

"Still trying, huh? Thinking that all that dirty talk you will get you laid?"

"There is no doubt about that, Barbie. We are made for fucking and you love my dirty mouth."

She laughed and winked right back at me. For a bit we talked about banal stuff—her new flat, my work—until the food was brought up.

"I spoke to my mother today—you know, about my new job," she chimed in all of a sudden. I was alerted straight away. Fuck, in the past week I had been trying to find the right moment to tell her about Joey and her mother, but that right moment never came. "She said that you came to see her to get my new address."

She never asked how I found out where she lived. Now it was time to come clean and tell her everything.

"I was desperate, Barbie, and I knew that if I charmed your mother, my job with you would be much easier."

Sasha smiled, shaking her head. "She sounded strange on the phone, like she was reluctant to talk about it," she explained, looking confused.

I took a deep breath. I couldn't keep this from her any longer. "We spoke quite a bit. She told me some stuff about Joey, stuff that she was hiding from you," I said. Sasha opened her mouth, but didn't say a word. This wasn't how I wanted this evening to go, but I couldn't hide this shit from her anymore.

I went ahead and explained what her mother had told me. It was a big deal, but we were both done with keeping secrets from each other, and she needed to know. Joey was a decent guy and I missed him. If it weren't for him, I would probably never have met Sasha. She deserved the truth.

She took her glass and emptied it in one go, not taking her green eyes off me.

"You knew about this for a week and you didn't say anything?"

"I was planning to tell you in that fucking restaurant, but then we got interrupted. You were too upset, Barbie, and then we never had the right moment."

"This all makes a bit of sense now. My mother used to go away every so often and every time she came back she was different, happier. They didn't lose touch; they had been seeing each other behind my father's back!"

"Wow, hold on a minute. You don't know this. They fooled around a bit when they were younger, but that doesn't mean that your mother had been cheating on your father."

"I need to talk to her about this. I can't believe that she waited all this time to tell me." Sasha turned away, looking for her phone. She wasn't making much sense and her mother had asked me to take care of her.

"Sasha, listen to me carefully. Everyone has secrets. Joey is dead and there is nothing that you can do about any of this now. Neither of us knows what happened with them. Let's—"

"I have to speak to Mum, to find out why she lied to me!"

"No, Barbie. Sleep on it and talk to her tomorrow when you've had a chance to process this. Don't be rash," I insisted.

"All right, fine. In that case, distract me, Dexter. Let's go to the room. I've kind of lost my appetite."

"What for?" I asked, confused and still pretty hungry.

She smiled. "To fuck, of course. Is there any other reason to go there?"

Thirty-Two

Dexter

I was back on my feet before she ended that sentence.

"You better not be fucking with me, because I swear to God, I'll go through another nervous breakdown if you're joking," I growled. She giggled and something flickered in her eyes. I spotted her lust straight away. She was turned on while I was worried about her emotional well-being.

I bet her pussy was already soaking for me. Flaming desire blinded me for a second and I lifted her off her chair. She was hanging on my shoulder, laughing hysterically.

"Get the fuck out of here," I snapped at the waiter when he walked through the door with another bottle of wine. He grumbled something under his breath and disappeared shortly after that. I was already imagining what I could do to her. This time I was planning to proceed slowly, strip that lovely dress off her and devour every inch of her body—and keep going until sunrise, until neither of us could take any more.

"That wasn't very nice," she pointed out.

"Shut up, Barbie."

I barged through the door and threw her on this enormous bed covered with silky cotton sheets. There were endless possibilities of what I wanted to do to her, but her pleasure was a priority. My cock was already rock hard and I now knew for sure I couldn't ever see myself with any other woman. Sasha was perfect and she was mine.

She went on her hands and knees, exposing her magnificent boobs and biting her lip. Slowly crawling to me, she began unbuttoning my expensive shirt that I bought especially for her. This fucking woman was going to ruin me, but in a good way. My heart had never beat so fast, thumping in my ears. Her eyes looked hungry and my dick was hurting because I was so hard. I didn't think I was going to last for more than ten seconds once I was inside her.

"Dexter, you're so freaking hot. Numb me, please. I don't want to wait any longer," she purred, pulling me down to the bed. I claimed her mouth like a starving man, slipping my tongue deep inside, teasing and caressing her tongue. It was fucking heaven and I needed to be inside her.

I started pulling her dress off slowly, trying to catch my fucking breath and savor the moment. Soon she stood only in her underwear, a red lace bra and matching skimpy thong. I couldn't cope; she was so beautiful, ready to spread herself wide for me. Sasha smelled like a musky wildflower and sex, her scent made me drunk with my own desire. My cock was throbbing when I lowered myself over her, sucking on her nipples and caressing her hot, wet sex.

"You have no fucking idea what I'm going to do to you," I growled, tearing off my shirt as if I were in a race. My trousers flew across the room while I kept my gaze on Sasha. I played with her tits, sucking and nibbling until she was moaning, trying to hurry me up. My mouth started moving down her stomach to her pelvis. I laughed and looked at her. Her hips were shaking with anticipation. I couldn't wait to hear her loud screams. I was the master of her pleasure tonight; I owned her.

She bit her lower lip and arched her hips forward; I flicked my tongue out slowly to lick the length of her slit. When I got a taste of her honeyed sex, I started licking her greedily, kissing her opening deeply, showing her what she had missed. My cock shuddered, and all I could think of was fucking her into endless orgasms. Her pussy was flowing with arousal juices. She had been ready since I showed up on her doorstep again, asking for forgiveness.

"Dex, more, oh please, more," she begged. I smiled wolfishly, ready to fulfill her wishes, when something shifted in me. I had no fucking idea why, but I suddenly stopped. This whole thing didn't feel right. Only a week ago she'd hated me, claiming that she didn't trust me, and now she was spreading her legs for me, straight after I told her about her mother being in love with Joey. This was fucked up, and for the first time in my life I didn't want to do this. It didn't feel right.

"Dexter, what the hell? Why did you stop?"

I crawled next to her to be closer, and my eyes never left hers.

"You're using sex to tame the anger for your mother, Barbie. You aren't ready for full blown-up fucking tonight," I said, wrapping my fingers around hers. My cock was ready to burst, and I wanted her, more than ever, more than I'd ever wanted anyone, but I couldn't go through with it. Not like this, not right now. I went a month without sex, so I guess I could wait a bit longer.

"What are you talking about? Of course I'm ready," she yelled, taking my hand down to her sex to finish what we started.

"Don't bullshit me. I am the king of denial. You just found out that your mother had an affair with her stepbrother and you threw yourself at me to avoid thinking about it, like it's perfectly normal. I can be an idiot sometimes, but I'm not fucking stupid."

She slid off the bed and picked up her dress. Great, so now she was pissed at me. That was the fucking reason that I avoided relationships for so long. Women were still an enigma to me. I was an asshole when I wanted to fuck her brains out, and now I was an asshole when I wanted to protect her.

"I want you to take me home," she said, now fully dressed, staring down at me. I got up, pressed my palm over my crotch to rearrange my dick into a more comfortable position. The area around my groin was on fire.

"Stop acting put out, Barbie. I want to bend you over my knee and spank you so hard that you won't sit for a week for the shit that you've just pulled on me. You're hurt and angry that your beloved mother hid a secret from you. Maybe we should have talked about this first, before jumping straight to sex."

"Dex, she lied to me, and I can't just forget about it. My first boyfriend cheated on me, then Kirk, and now my mother has betrayed me. Things would have been different between us if she'd said something, anything. Instead, she tricked me into this whole apartment business, pretending like she wanted to help me, but all along it was a cover-up."

"Maybe she had her reasons, Sash. He was her stepbrother; I don't know, maybe she was ashamed and scared that you wouldn't understand. I made the same mistake. I didn't want to talk to my own father," I said, opening up about my feelings for the first time. "I avoided everything that had been going on for so long, and I regret it now. I wish that I had reached out to him more, to fucking try to understand what was wrong. Sasha, just don't use sex to deal with whatever shit you feel. It doesn't work. As you know, I'd been doing it for years and look where it got me." We were both damaged and miserable, but we had each other. We didn't need to make the same mistakes as our parents.

"All right, I'm sorry. I was angry. Let's just sleep here tonight. I don't want to go home."

"All right, Barbie, but only because I said so."

Sasha

Dexter knew about Joey and Mum. I couldn't comprehend why he hadn't said anything; he'd kept this news to himself for nearly a week. I thought that if I let him have sex with me, I could forget about everything for a while.

After the trauma with Kirk, I had drifted away from Mum. We used to speak daily, but after my move, things changed. In London our conversations became more and more rare and always brief. I had visited my parents during Christmas break, but I was too afraid to go anywhere and I went back to London on Boxing Day. Kirk was still in my nightmares.

For years, Mum had been hiding this crushing secret. She could have been with Joey, they weren't even related, but she still chose Dad. I was always convinced that my parents loved each other, but I never actually saw them in love. Yes, Dad had joked that she was the only woman for him, but looking back, I had no idea if they were truly happy. Maybe all these years she wondered how different her life would have been if she had married Joey instead.

Dexter saw right through me and refused to fuck me, claiming that I wasn't ready. It was kind of sweet, but it annoyed me anyway. We talked a little, and he even managed to open up about his own father. After I wiped my tears away, we finished our meal. Then he ran me a bath. An hour later I was asleep, snuggled into his chest.

I woke up before he did. For a moment I just lay in bed, thinking about our conversations over the past few weeks. Last night I'd pushed him. I thought that sex would solve most of my problems. With anyone else he probably wouldn't have stopped, but I wasn't just anyone else anymore.

The apartment we were staying in was enormous, designed with passion. The main wall was a rich purple, which matched the sumptuous, deep-pile carpet. The sofa and chairs were a soft cream colour and they were all puffed up with soft, gold-accented cushions. The chandelier and matching side lamps had ornately cut crystals that refracted the light so they cast their beautiful shadows around the room artfully. All the wooden furniture was antique and yet fit well in the modern scheme. Everything was finished up to a really high standard. I decided to sneak out to the terrace to make a phone call. My parents were going on their dream holiday in a couple of hours' time. I needed to clear the air before they would be gone.

"Hi, Sasha bunny. How are you?" Mum asked, sounding excited, much different than yesterday.

I dragged more air into my lungs, knowing that this would be hard. "Hey, Mum. Are you alone?" I asked calmly. She would not talk to me if Dad was in the room.

"Your Dad is out, doing the last shop for the trip."

"Dexter told me about Joey," I said quietly.

"So you have forgiven him?"

I looked at the phone. It sounded like Dexter had told her everything. This wasn't something that I expected. Deep down I felt a little betrayed that she had shared this with him first, rather than me. We used to tell each other everything, but that was before my move to London. After that traumatic time I shut myself down and stopped talking to my own mother. Kirk not only ruined me as a woman, but he also damaged my relationship with people close to me.

"Dex is... trying, Mum, but I didn't call to talk to you about him. I called because I wanted to know why you lied to me."

There was a silence on the other side of the phone for a while. Then I heard her heavy breath.

"I was young and stupid. I felt ashamed that I didn't make the right decision, that I didn't marry him. Things were different then; people wouldn't have understood. Your grandfather was strict, and he had a good reputation. He told me straight that he would disown me if I chose Joey."

I had never met my grandfather. Her explanation sounded reasonable, but still. She could have told me the truth.

"Did you see him after I was born?"

"A few times over the course of twenty years. He made sure that I never forgot about him. Maybe that's why he never got married. He wrote to me for years, but I never replied to any of his letters."

I had to pull the phone away to breathe. I'd judged her too soon, but I still felt betrayed. "If you weren't happy with Dad, then why didn't you divorce him?"

"Because I couldn't do that to him. As partners, we understood each other. I was a coward, afraid of a real love. Sasha, bunny, I don't expect you to understand. The attitudes were different then and he was my stepbrother. This wouldn't have been easy. His mother never really liked me."

"You should have kept the apartment. You would have loved it."

"I'm sorry, bunny; I'm sorry that I made you do this." She sobbed into the phone.

I tried to breathe, forcing the tears away. "Just don't lie to me anymore. I can't take it."

"I promise. I'm sorry, darling. Tell me. How are things with Dexter? Have you forgiven him yet?"

"I'm trying. He's changed, but I think I need more time. We're having dinner with his family today."

"That's good, Sasha. Always remember to follow your heart, not your head. He loves you... I know that he does. When he was here, we talked. He never said it, but his eyes gave it away. At first I thought that it was all too soon for you, but I think you need to be happy. You need to move on."

My mother couldn't be serious. Dexter didn't love me; he liked the idea of loving me. We had known each other for two months and everything was so fresh.

"We will see, Mum. It's early days. I don't want to get my hopes up. We both carry scars that are deep and sorrowful."

"You will do what you think is best. I buried this secret years ago and I thought Joey was behind me. Maybe it was destiny— if it weren't for him, you would have never met Dexter."

Funny, this was the same thing Dexter said. She was right, but I needed some time to think about her lies, to digest this whole secret. She had broken my trust. We said our goodbyes and promised to talk in a couple of weeks. I was still angry that she'd manipulated me like that and I missed Joey's apartment.

"Fuck, Sasha, don't scare me like that. I thought you left me," Dexter said appearing at the door. He had sexy messy hair and he was shirtless. I walked up to him and took his hand.

"I'm hungry. Let's have breakfast."

Dexter

I panicked for a moment when I woke up and she wasn't in bed. For a split second I thought she fucking left me. Then breakfast was absolute torture. She had on a very skimpy and sexy nightie. Her boobs were on display nicely with her hard little nipples showing through the silk, teasing me. I could barely think about eating while she was talking about serious shit, her mother and Joey.

Sasha wanted to try out the spa in the hotel and I needed to get distracted. My thoughts about taking Sasha over the table and fucking her brains out were going to get me into trouble. She needed some alone time and I thought that if I worked out, I could forget about her sweet pussy.

My cock was semi-hard, and I was raging with sexual frustration. I killed myself on the treadmill. I jogged around fifteen miles and then abused the free weights. By the time I was back in our room, Sasha was already there looking so fucking delicious. She wore a long, deep-red dress with a high split that exposed her gorgeous legs as she walked or sat.

"You're fucking going to kill me, you know that?" I barked, changing my clothes. "My cock has been painfully hard since yesterday when you pulled that fuck-me-now shit in the bedroom."

"I fully appreciate your patience, darling," she said winking at me. "You know they say patience is a virtue?"

I'd had enough of this shit. I got to her before she had a chance to take another breath. My mouth was on hers and my fingers dug into her soft flesh. I wanted her to remember this kiss, so I worked my mouth eagerly around her until she was breathless. The kiss was rough, but sensual. I placed my fingers over her round ass and squeezed it. She moaned into my mouth and I was ready to strip her naked and thrust my cock inside her wet folds.

Luckily enough I pulled away, grinning like I hadn't just come in my boxers.

"That's all you're getting from me, darling. You'll be sitting through dinner at my mother's house wet and needy for my cock."

Her eyes were blazing hot and I knew that she was very wet for me, but I was good Dexter, patiently waiting for my turn.

"Fine, I get your point. Let's go, we don't want to be late," she snapped, picking up her bag.

I was planning to tease her a bit more during dinner. My mother's house needed to be updated, but Mum was stubborn. She didn't want to listen when I talked about increasing the value. She liked her old-school kitchen. She even refused to use my old room. All my teenage stuff was still on the walls.

Sasha kept asking me about my father while we were driving. In the past, the subject had angered me, but now I knew that I had to talk about him. I'd made a deal with Bishop: he let me out early, and I was supposed to open up, talk about my feelings.

I was glad when we arrived, because she finally gave it a rest. Jack was there with the twins and his wife, Emily, teasing me like always. Sasha was the first woman that I ever brought home, so everyone was taking the piss. Lunch went better than I expected. The twins loved Sasha, and Emily was already planning our wedding. The conversation flew; even Connor dragged his sorry ass from upstairs. I kept teasing Sasha under the table, moving my hand over her thigh. I couldn't wait to get her alone in my room.

"You keep this girl close. She's the best thing that's happened to you," Mum said when I was putting the plates in the dishwasher.

"I know that, Mum."

"Do you love her?"

Wow, my mother didn't beat around the bush at all. Crap, no one knew how I felt.

"I'd rather not label anything yet, Ma. We haven't really known each other for long," I said. That was bullshit, but I was waiting for the right moment. My mother didn't need to know anything before Sasha did.

"Dexter, don't be stupid. Stop hiding and tell her how you feel. I've been waiting long enough for you to bring someone home."

I nodded. This sounded fucking easy, but I had no idea how was I supposed to tell Sasha that was in love with her. She wouldn't believe me. I had burned myself in her eyes. I had to regain her trust first.

Later on, I followed her to the bathroom. She was pissed that I kept teasing her at the dinner table, whilst my family was asking questions about her work in the hospital.

"Not so fast, Barbie girl," I said and slid in after her. She was giving me an easy access with that sexy red dress of hers.

"Get out. Someone will hear us. Don't be disrespectful," she hissed. I pinned her against the shower door, flashing her my charming smile.

"I can't help myself. You're too sexy to resist," I murmured and lifted her dress, pressing myself closer. There wasn't much space in the bathroom, but it was enough to drive her insane.

Thirty-Four

Dexter

I started kissing her neck, inhaling that heady scent of her orchid perfume. She was wearing my favourite red slutty thong. I wanted to torture her, slowly, until she snapped and begged me to fuck her. It had been too long since the muscles of her pussy were clenched around my dick. The building frustration was taking a toll on me. Sasha's sexy body was like a magnet to my cock.

My fingers crawled over her thigh, moving in a teasing motion until they reached the heat between her legs.

"I didn't give you permission to touch me yet," she said. I laughed and traced my thumb over her clit. She shuddered under my touch.

"Funny, I didn't think that I needed an invitation," I muttered. "Fuck, Barbie, you're so wet. Your pussy is dripping for me."

She arched her head back as my finger began caressing her mound, slowly at first, barely even touching it. My head was clouded with her incredible scent, my pulse speeding. All I wanted was to tease her.

"Oh, Dexter, keep doing that," she moaned when my lips were between her huge breasts, my fingers picking up the pace, sliding inside her wetness, the inner muscles clenching around my fingers. I was done with this bullshit, done with waiting. This was what she was making me do.

She moaned and I slipped another finger inside her, alternating with teasing and caressing her swollen clit. I captured her mouth with mine; my blood boiled when her body was close. I started moving my fingers in and out faster. I curled them upwards hitting her G-spot, making her writhe. She was pinned to the wall, and when she was just about to come on my hand, I spun her around and slapped her ass.

"Dexter, please, baby."

I loved hearing her begging for release.

"Spread your legs wide," I ordered. I could get off just by looking at her round ass. She bent over and I thrust two fingers back inside her. She came instantly, biting her own hand to muffle the sound. I was rock hard, stroking my own shaft. Her juices drenched my hand. I was so fucked. Sasha had broken me completely.

Sasha

Dexter took me home after the lovely dinner with his family. He had an early-morning appointment with Dr. Bishop in the hospital and Dex said that he didn't want me in his apartment, as I was too distracting. Things were going great and I didn't particularly want to sleep alone, but we didn't want to rush into things. Sex with Dexter would be mind-blowing, but it would also lead to letting him know that I had forgiven him.

In all my previous relationships, guys had to work hard before we passed second base. I would wait at least a couple of weeks, after I was certain that they weren't playing with my emotions. With Dex, it was all unconventional, but I just needed to be sure that he went to his appointment and didn't crumble under the pressure.

I had an early shift on Monday, and I was planning to drive straight to the gym. The pole competition was early next week and I needed more intensive practise. My body was flexible and I had trained really hard, but there were women out there that trained every single day.

I woke up on Tuesday morning stiff and very horny. Since he'd given me that amazing orgasm in his mum's bathroom, my body craved more. There was a surprise for me the next day at ten a.m. Dexter had sent me the most amazing bouquet of red roses and some French croissants for breakfast, with my favourite coffee. I couldn't freaking believe it. He'd transformed from the Prince of Darkness into a real Prince Charming. We both were holding off, and with each day he'd been convincing me that he'd kicked the old Dexter out for good.

The appointment went well, the meds are keeping me in the sane world.
—Your really fucked-up boyfriend-to-be

I smiled, feeling the warmth slowly filling up my heart. I freaking had fallen in love with this man without even knowing it whilst he was in the hospital. He was probably really frustrated and I wanted to thank him for being so patient. We were done with playing silly games. We both wanted each other, so I grabbed my phone and sent him a quick text, letting him know that I wanted him to meet me at the studio tonight after my practice.

That night's session was hard. I went over my routine a few times, and by the time the hour was over, I was exhausted. Gina and the rest of the crew left straight after, leaving me alone. The day of the competition was approaching and I desperately wanted to do well. Since breakfast, I had been thinking about Dexter, wondering if he was missing me and getting turned on thinking about me. He wasn't free of Victoria just yet, and my own insecurities were planting doubts in my head. I didn't need another useless man; I couldn't afford to get burned again. Kirk had wrecked me and Dexter had showed me that he was destructive enough. His illness had pulled us apart, but we had this deep crazy connection and I did love him. I was willing to risk it.

Apart from worries about "what if," I was horny. Dexter had showed me that he did care that I was satisfied, and I was planning to reward him with a little pre-show of my pole routine.

"What the hell, Sasha? I thought we were having dinner," he grumbled, walking into the empty studio. I learnt the hard way that he was very impulsive. If things didn't go the way he wanted, Dexter turned into a spoiled, annoying brat.

"Sit down. I need to show you something," I said.

"We have a fucking reservation at the Hilton. This better be quick."

"Trust me, you will love this," I whispered, kissing him softly when he finally sat down on the bench.

"As you know, I'm competing next week in London and I wanted to show you some of my moves. Just sit tight and watch me," I said, innocently approaching the pole. He shifted on the chair, probably only now noticing that there was an actual pole in the room. I pulled my hair in a tight knot and glanced at him. Finally, his sharp brown eyes fixed on me, and I knew that our reservation at the Hilton wasn't important anymore. This whole thing was going to be messy.

I began with walking around the pole with my inside arm holding onto the metal bar. I brought my opposite arm into a split grip. I was ready for the most complicated moves. My muscles were aching after the earlier killer session, but I was getting turned on as Dexter's eyes followed me. I lifted my legs up from the floor, bending my knees behind me. Heat began travelling down, igniting the fire inside me as Dexter's gaze slid down my body slowly. I was sure that he stopped breathing altogether.

Raging heat sank into my bones, spreading around my body like molten lava. Thoughts about him making love to me were distracting and I had to stay more focused. Shortly after that I did a basic inversion, my body shaking with the need for release.

I pulled myself together, and once my body was inverted, I unhooked my legs that were around the front. Then I used my leg that was hooked around the back and, with my arms, I lifted my back up into the bar. I slid down and spread my legs, holding onto the pole. I was certain that was enough to get him all worked up.

When I glanced back at him, Dexter was walking towards me fast, unbuttoning his shirt.

"I'm only just warming up, Dex. You have to wait for more," I said when he approached me with fire brewing in his eyes.

"No fucking way. I'm done with this shit. I've been playing the nice and understanding boyfriend, but my limit has been reached. We are going to fuck, hard. I am going to be inside you. Right now and right here."

"What? No, anyone could walk in here. Let's go back to my flat."

"Fuck that. I'm done with this shit. Take off your clothes," he ordered. I hesitated, knowing that this was a really, really bad idea. Dexter's shirt was on the floor within moments, then mine followed along with my shorts. I was alarmed and excited at the same time, knowing that the doors were unlocked.

"Dexter, please. We can't—"

"Shut up, Barbie, I can't wait. I want you," he said, cutting me off. He lifted me up and carried me to the padded mats in the corner of the room, right in front of the mirror. He removed my sports bra, leaving my knickers on. Each hair on the back of my neck stood up straight when he stood looking down on me with that familiar heated desire in his deep brown eyes. Then he pulled his boxers down, without concern that anyone could walk in on us.

"Like what you see?" he teased when I admired his rock-hard cock, which was level with my face. He went down, distracting me for a second. My nipples were fully erect when he suddenly bit the left one, and I was fired into waves of pleasure and pain. The nice Dexter was gone—he had been replaced by the domineering lover, the one that I had fallen for so easily.

I brushed against his cock, but he pushed my hand away, licking my nipples until I was moaning. He used his teeth to remove my lace knickers, exhaling his warm breath over my needy pussy. The thrill of excitement and anticipation grew; my core was on fire. The deep rhythmic throbbing between my legs allowed me to forget about the unlocked doors. Dexter smiled and started licking me, slowly at first, then faster and greedier. Heat began ravaging my body, and my pussy was desperate for his hard shaft to fill it.

I cried out when his tongue began swirling up and down my wetness. His fingers were digging into the skin on my thighs, trying to keep me in place. I was so close to orgasm and he had only just begun. I gripped the side of the mat, my heart pounding. Just one more stroke and I was going to come undone—when it all stopped. Dexter pulled away, and when I glanced at him in desperation he was tearing the condom wrapper off.

"Oh, you have no idea how much I missed that delicious pussy," he rasped and shoved his throbbing cock inside me a moment later. I cried out, pulling him into me. Dexter pushed the hair away from my face, his eyes meeting mine.

"Are you ready for this, Barbie?" he asked.

"Christ, Dexter, just fuck me already. You've made me wait long enough," I snarled. He laughed and started moving inside me, and I screamed with pleasure, already worked up by his earlier tortures. He lifted me up so I was sitting on him, and my tits were bouncing up and down as he sped up, ravaging my greedy pussy.

It didn't take long for an orgasm to build inside of me, begging for release, and just before I reached that glorious cliff to fall off, he stilled and turned me around.

"No. What are you doing? I was—"

"So impatient. This will feel so much better if I make you work for it." He laughed, the bastard, and then took me by surprise and pounded hard into me again. I had no idea how long he was planning to play with me like that, but after only few more hard thrusts that slammed up into my body, I was coming. My whole body tingled, my eyes rolled back. My muscles turned into a jelly and I collapsed on the mattress quivering, trying to catch my breath. Even my toes were tingling. I had just experienced the most intense orgasm of my life.

"Get dressed. We're leaving."

I couldn't move. He had to drag me back on my feet. I didn't want to think where we were going, but I really hoped for another session of hard-core sex.

Dexter

I was a fool fucking her in the gym when anyone could walk in, but in the end, seeing her coming for me like a firecracker had been worth it. She was worn out, but I wasn't done with her yet. I was planning to take her back to my apartment; there I wanted to devour her pussy all night until she begged me to let her sleep. It was her fault: she'd made me wait and she knew how much I fucking hated waiting around. Tomorrow, during a romantic dinner with candles, I wanted to reveal to her how I felt. But tonight I would ravage her till dawn.

I was breaking every traffic rule on the way to the complex. Sasha kept telling me to slow down, but I wasn't listening. I was already picturing what I could do to her in my own apartment, behind closed doors. She'd woken me up from the nightmare, healed me, and I couldn't let her go.

"Come on, Barbie, let's finish what we started," I said, locking the car.

"I need at least a half-hour nap before the next round, Dex."

"No fucking way. The session at the gym, that was only foreplay, Barbie. We have a lot of catching up to do."

"Whatever, Dex. I'm tired."

I smiled to myself and then took her hand, and we strolled towards the complex. I had never done this before, walking with a woman and holding her hand like we were a real fucking couple. This was a first.

We were just about to step into the building when the door opened up and Harry nearly enough walked into my face.

"Dexter! Victoria is upstairs," he said with a grave expression on his face. The bubble burst, and my good mood faded as soon as I heard that fucking name. Sasha glanced at me. She didn't have to say anything. Victoria had ruined our time together once before and it looked like she had done it again.

"Sasha, I'm going to take care of that bitch. I promise," I said.

"How are you going to take care of her? One phone call to the police and you're finished. You have to do what she says," Sasha reminded me.

I was ready to scream. I was so angry I could hire a hit man and get rid of the problem straight away. Why could I not remember anything from that fucking party?

"I have a better idea," Harry said with a wink and started talking. Slowly I started seeing the light at the end of the tunnel.

"I'll drive Sasha home. Victoria won't be happy if she sees her," Harry suggested. I tensed straight away, wanting to disagree. My plans for this evening were ruined, but she had work tomorrow and I couldn't let Victoria know that we were close. Harry had a plan, a good plan. Sasha didn't want to go upstairs, and for the first time, I had to agree with her. Victoria couldn't see her with me if Harry's idea was going to work.

"All right, Barbie, I'll call you tomorrow right. Don't worry, I won't forget about my promise."

"Fine, but don't let her manipulate you into sex, because I won't be happy," she said with a flash of anger in her eyes.

"Barbie, are you jealous?" I asked, amused.

"I'm not jealous, just careful. Besides, Harry is taking me home. You stick to your side of the bargain and I'll stick to mine." She kissed me on the cheek and started walking away. Harry shook his head, muttering something under his breath, and strolled after her.

Sassy-mouthed Sasha… I was ready to spank her, but first I had to take care of Victoria. I went into the building, thinking about Harry's plan. Victoria was obsessed. It was all a game to her and I was fed up with playing by her rules.

"Why do I always have to wait for you?" she snapped when she saw me approaching.

"My cock doesn't get hard for you, bitch, so get to the point and tell me what the fuck you want," I demanded, not moving. I couldn't let her inside; it was safer to talk outside. She ran her tongue over her red lips and smiled.

"Isn't that obvious?" she asked. "I think it's best if we get back to the original setting. That should sort your problem out, right?"

Harry had mentioned that she wanted him to organise another party and to invite us both to it.

"How much longer are you planning to play me?"

She smiled and touched my cheek. She had a cold hand. "Until I get bored," she sang.

"Fine, whatever. Obviously I can't fucking say no to you, can I?"

"No, darling. I have your balls, remember?"

"A party—that's what you want? Do you think that if you corner me in Harry's apartment, my dick will miraculously get hard?"

"I hope so. You were always my favourite one. As soon as I get you in that room, you'll forget about that fat blondie."

"You brag too much, Vic. I have shit to do," I said, trying to stay fucking calm. I wanted to slap her for calling Sasha fat.

"Saturday night, Dex. I'll be waiting. You won't get away from me. We are made for each other."

I laughed and called the lift. I needed to keep my mouth shut, but I wanted her to suffer badly for all the shit that she managed to pull on me. Just a few more days; I knew that I needed to be patient. She was going to pay for this, and she would regret that she had ever tried to fuck me over.

Thirty-Five

Sasha

"Harry, I'm not sure about this. What if she won't come with us?" I asked, feeling like my stomach slowly wanted to empty itself, heaving with nerves. Harry was crazy and his idea was risky. Jenny was still only a child and I didn't want to use her to catch Victoria in her slimy lies.

"She has a huge crush on him. When I chatted with her yesterday, she wouldn't shut up about him," he argued, looking at me with his clear blue eyes. We were in his car outside Jenny's college in the north side of the city. Harry had managed to track Jenny down. I didn't ask how, but he had his ways, his dodgy contacts. My hatred for Victoria grew with each passing moment, but I was still reluctant to approach this girl. I knew that Dexter couldn't go to the police. Our choices were limited.

"I don't know about this. What if someone sees us?"

"That's why you need to speak to her. She'll believe you... right, there she is," he hissed and nearly enough pushed me out of the car. Indeed, Jenny was coming around the corner. She was alone, and she didn't even notice me. Her eyes were glued to her smartphone. She still had her school uniform on and I was surprised to see her without a bunch of girls. Everyone in high school had friends.

I rubbed my damp palm over my jeans and approached her from the opposite direction.

"Hey, Jenny. Hey, hold on. I need to talk to you."

She stopped and glared at me with mistrust, putting her phone away. My heart was accelerating and all of a sudden I had no idea what I wanted to say.

"Who are you?" she asked.

"I'm a friend of Dexter's. We live next door to each other. Harry said that you were dying to see him. I thought that we could chat for a bit," I said, not quite sure if this approach would work. She was a child, but she wasn't a freaking idiot. Excitement glittered in her eyes, but it was quickly replaced with reluctance. She was fifteen, but with his looks and that arrogant mouth, Dexter Tyndall was able to charm anyone, even a naive girl just past puberty.

"Aunt Victoria was supposed to organise our date, but she isn't answering her phone," Jenny complained.

"Victoria is your aunt?" I asked, losing my breath. Damned Victoria and her manipulative games. She needed to be hospitalised. She was using a child to bend Dexter to her will, to make sure that he was under her complete control.

Jenny made a face. "She isn't my real aunt, but my mum knew her for years. Victoria always insisted that I call her auntie."

I had to remember to try and look like I wanted to help her. This wasn't the time or a place to freak out. "All right, listen," I began, trying to stay calm. "I can take you to Dexter tomorrow. There is a small party in the complex and he's going to be there. What do you think?"

"Really? Oh my God, he's so gorgeous! Victoria promised that he would date me, but since that night she hasn't been in touch. I don't even have his phone number."

Nausea hit me and my stomach heaved with disgust. I didn't want to believe that Dexter had had sex with this girl and that Victoria had no qualms about using Jenny's innocence to get what she wanted.

"So it's true then—you slept with him?" I asked quietly, trying to keep the strain from my voice.

"Yes, of course. He was so passionate and loving. It was the best night in my life!"

I really was ready to throw up then, but I couldn't risk Harry's carefully prepared plan. I had to keep it together if I wanted to help Dexter in any way. I glanced at Harry, who was watching us from the car.

"All right, I can pick you up from town tomorrow around seven and take you to him. What are you going to say to your parents?" I asked.

She smiled, waving her hand. "Dad is away and Mum will be out, so it's fine. Am I really going to see him tomorrow?"

"Promise, but remember—it's between you and me. No one must know."

"I'm not an idiot," she snapped. We exchanged our numbers and then she strolled back towards the centre. My heart was pounding and I felt guilty. This girl was really enraptured with Dexter, and I wasn't capable of breaking her heart. This was cruel, but she was too young to be mixed up in this sort of company. We just needed to get a confession out of Jenny. In order to get anywhere, we needed to have this on tape.

"And?" Harry asked.

"You're right, she is completely blinded by his gorgeous face," I said, shaking my head. "I don't know, Harry. He did sleep with her, so they will arrest him anyway."

"Victoria has too much to lose. She won't let this leak to the media or press. This will work, trust me."

"I hope you're right," I muttered.

Harry drove me straight home. Dexter wanted to see me this evening, had insisted, but I needed to clear my head, to think about what I'd committed myself to doing. We were going to meet tomorrow at the party. The plan was straightforward, but I had a bad feeling about this. Dexter was really trying for me. We had attended a meeting with a support group for bipolar disorder a couple of days ago and I was still amazed that he actually had gone through with it.

I went to bed anxious and really worried about tomorrow. Even Dexter's sexy phone call didn't take the edge off my mood. He described in detail what he was planning to do to me, once this whole thing was over. I was frustrated, but dark thoughts overshadowed all my emotions.

When I finally fell asleep it was late, probably around two. The next day I was exhausted and then the day was very hectic. Harry came to visit, going over and over what he wanted me to do.

The time dragged until four in the afternoon. Dexter called a few times, asking me if I was ready. In the end I hung up on him and then texted him, saying that he needed to chill the fuck out. Jenny rang exactly at seven, telling me where she was waiting in town. I took the car and drove over fifteen miles to pick her up from the centre of Edinburgh. On the way to the complex, she started telling me that her mother was constantly out, partying with friends and leaving her alone most of the time. Her father didn't know; he travelled around the world, trying to make up for his absence with expensive and lavish gifts. Deep down I felt sorry for her, and kind of understood that she wanted to find love anywhere she could.

"Are you really taking me to him?" she asked after some time. "This isn't any sort of joke?"

"No, of course not. He lives in the Grange complex," I assured her, feeling like I was committing a crime myself.

"So you live next door to him?"

"Yes," I lied.

"I bet his apartment must be gorgeous. I can't wait to see it," she sang. My stomach was churning badly and I was dreading the moment when I had to tell her why exactly I'd brought her to the apartment. She was going to hate me.

Dexter

"Hello?" I snapped into my phone, standing in the middle of Harry's apartment. His guests were already there, chatting and drinking, searching for the perfect partner for one glorious night of fucking.

"Dex, we need to meet," Ronny said, sounding on edge. I glanced at the phone, realising that he had called from different number. This wasn't like him. I'd tried calling him a few times in the past few days, but his phone was constantly switched off. Sasha was already in my place with the girl, trying to prepare her for what was about to happen. Ronny couldn't have picked a worse time.

"I can't right now. I'm in the middle of something."

"This can't wait—that guy Adamson, he isn't as clean as I thought, but I have to run this shit by you first. The sooner the better."

"All right, give me a couple of hours," I said and hung up. Maybe this was my lucky day. Ronny usually didn't talk in code, but I was hoping that he had found something that would send that asshole right down. It was time for him to be punished and pay for what he'd done to my Barbie. Payback was a bitch and I hoped he found that out soon.

I'd put my best suit on for tonight and taken my meds as usual. I had one glass of champagne just to keep me going. I wasn't planning to touch any more than that. Everything was working as we'd planned and I was waiting for Victoria. She was running late. That bitch wasn't even here and she was already putting me ill at ease. I needed to concentrate, forget about Ronny for now. Victoria was the bigger problem.

"How you doing?" Harry asked for the tenth time tonight. I swear to God, I was ready to slap him.

A few hours earlier, Harry's guy had put a wire on Sasha. I let him touch her only this once with the hope that this girl would talk; otherwise, I would have to deal with Victoria for the rest of my miserable life.

"Told you already, I'm fucking nervous. Where is that bitch?" I looked around, ready to drink a whole bottle of whisky, but that wasn't wise. I needed to be focused. A few regular brunettes were smiling at me, giving me the right signals, but I ignored them. My fucking heart was taken by a curvy, sexy-as-hell blonde. Sasha owned me.

"Just calm down. She won't miss this party. She sounded excited on the phone," Harry said. "By the way, how are things with your Barbie? Have you landed on your knee yet and told her how much you love her?"

The bastard was teasing me and he knew, but how? Fuck, I couldn't keep anything to myself when he was around.

"I would have, but now we have more important things to worry about," I barked.

"Mate, Barbie is special, so I wouldn't wait around if I were you," he stated, sipping champagne. "I can't believe it. A woman that tied up Dexter Tyndall. I think I'll have to write a book about that. I would make shitloads of money."

"I dare you." I laughed. "And since we are on the subject, what about you? I haven't seen any women here that caught your eye so far."

"I won't get my own happy-ever-after, Dex. My soul is too tainted. There isn't a woman out there that could handle me," he said and finished his drink. I was just about to ask him what he meant when I saw Victoria at the door.

She glanced at me but pretended that she didn't see me. I kept glancing at my watch, wondering how long she was planning to play this game. Sasha was in my apartment on the other side of the wing. Somehow I had to get Victoria back to my bed and start this whole shit show.

It took her another twenty minutes and a few more drinks to finally pull me into an empty room. I spoke to a few women myself, trying to make her jealous. Two brunettes were ready to suck my cock in front of everyone here, but I politely declined. Victoria was drinking and it was a good sign. We went to one of the empty bedrooms.

"I have missed you, Dex. I hope that you recovered from our last encounter, because I really want you to fuck me. Will you?" she asked, running her fingers over my arms and biting her lip, trying and failing to be provocative. Victoria loved games—she loved the tension, the real build-up to the finale.

I grabbed her hand and put it on my cock. Thoughts of Sasha's ass began circling in my mind and that worked, because my dick twitched in my trousers. She squeezed it hard, brushing her rancid lips over mine.

"Well done. See? You just needed a little time to recover. It's time to fulfill your duty, darling."

"Fine, let's go to my apartment. You know that I don't like an audience."

"Okay, come on. I'm glad that you finally came to your senses. I want you to break me tonight, fuck me so hard that you ruin me for all other men."

I finished the champagne and shortly after that, we left Harry's apartment holding hands like old-time lovers. All the women out there in the main room were disappointed. I was tense. I needed a drink, but I'd promised Sasha. Playing games was one thing, but doing shit like this with Victoria was an entirely different reality.

Harry was supposed to let Sasha know when we were on the way to my apartment. That would give her enough time to hide and record everything. I unlocked the door to my place and didn't give Victoria much time to think about the act or my cock. I couldn't let her get suspicious, so I brought her into my arms and started kissing her. Her perfume was too sweet, vile and overpowering, and I hated the way she was digging her nails into my stomach, deliberately trying to put me off.

"I'm going to fuck you hard, because that's what you want, right?" I rasped, ripping her dress off her in the living room.

"Tie me up!" she ordered.

I inhaled when she started playing with my trousers. This was going to be the longest few minutes of my life and it was just the beginning.

Sasha

"See, I told you. She doesn't care about you. Victoria only wanted him for herself," I whispered to Jenny. Harry had phoned ahead, giving us enough time to hide. This wasn't easy in the beginning. The girl kept asking about Dex every five minutes and she didn't believe me when I told her that her precious auntie used her that night to blackmail Dexter and now was threatening to send the video to the police if he didn't do what she wanted. She cried, then blamed me, then cried some more. I felt like shit when she looked so heartbroken.

Before we arrived at the apartment, Dexter had moved the old swanky cabinet for us to hide behind. Victoria wasn't paying much attention to what was going on around her. Jenny needed to see everything that was happening in the living room. She pressed her mouth in a hard line, watching as Victoria tried to take off Dexter's pants. I couldn't look. I wanted to murder that bitch, touching him like she owned his body.

"But she promised. She said that if I slept with him at the party, he would be mine. All the girls in the class would be jealous that he was going to date me," Jenny hissed back, tears filling her eyes.

"I just wanted you to see this for yourself. She knew that you were underage; she knew that this could ruin him," I kept whispering. Dexter had had a professional wire me up, and apparently Harry was recording everything.

"But I love him. She knows that I love him," Jenny whispered, hiding her face in her hands.

"Come on, I think we should stop her," I said and I dragged her away from our hiding place. I picked up the heavy statue off the table and dropped it to get Victoria's attention on us. Dexter's eyes found mine quickly and he pushed her off, dragging his hand through his hair.

"What? Jenny, hon, what are you doing here?" Victoria said, looking at her fake niece with her eyes wide, finally noticing us.

I couldn't believe that she was so stupid, that she believed this whole thing would work.

"How could you? You promised that he was going to be my boyfriend. Sasha told me that you used me to get him for yourself." Jenny was shouting hysterically.

I placed my hands on my hips, smiling. Dexter picked up his shirt and put it back on.

"Yes, Victoria; explain to your niece why you asked her to drug Dexter at the party," I said, pausing to give her time to think about this. "Jenny was a fifteen-year-old virgin. You made her do this just because he hurt your stupid ego by rejecting you."

"Jenny, honey, don't listen to her. We talked about this, right? I had to bring Dexter here first. I was planning to call you—"

"No, Sasha has told me everything. You used me because Dexter didn't want you anymore."

"Shut your mouth, you stupid little whore. This is a grown-up world. Men like Dexter would never want a little girl like you. He belongs wrapped around my little finger." Victoria took a sudden step towards Jenny. I reacted instantly, as the anger overtook my usual reasonable thought process. With a sharp intake of breath, I launched at the bitch and slapped her, as fast and hard as I could, not even knowing what had gotten into me. My palm burned and for a second everyone in the room froze.

"You stupid fat slut, who—"

"Shut up, Vic!" Dexter yelled, stepping between us both just in time, as Victoria looked like she was ready to rip my face off. She was glaring at me with fury, holding her cheek.

"Touch me again, whore, and I swear to God, I'll destroy you," she rasped.

"Let's get back to the point, Vic," Dexter said. "You convinced Jenny to sleep with me when I was high and incoherent?"

Victoria didn't take her eyes off me and Jenny, but she relaxed slightly, smiling with satisfaction. "It was the perfect way for Jenny to lose her virginity. Trust me, you did her a favour. Besides, what are you trying to prove? I have the video. You still have to do what I say and I'm planning to squash that little cunt of yours with my bare hand."

"Actually, Aunt Victoria, I didn't... I mean, Dexter didn't take my virginity. I made him pretend."

Thirty-Six

Dexter

"I'm sorry, Jenny—what did you just say?" I asked, barely forming a coherent sentence.

"We didn't have sex. I was embarrassed that you weren't all that into it, but I knew that there was a smartphone in the room, recording me," she added, blushing.

I swallowed hard, wondering if this shit was happening for real, that I was being saved by some supernatural force. Someone upstairs must really fucking like me. Victoria paled and I was looking straight at Jenny, wanting and praying that her tale was real and I hadn't gone ahead with fucking her.

"Tell us what happened exactly," I said gently.

"You were dozing off, and your... you know, instrument wasn't working, so I told you to pretend," Jenny said, dropping her gaze to the floor. I was ready to embrace her, but I knew that it wouldn't look right, so I forced myself to stay still. For the first time in my life, I was glad that my cock hadn't worked the way it was supposed to.

"Of course you slept with him, Jenny. What are you even talking about? The video is genuine, you stupid little bitch!" Victoria screamed.

I stepped towards Victoria, euphoric. Sasha kept opening and closing her mouth in a state of a shock.

"Shut the fuck up, Vic, and don't you dare speak to Jenny like that; otherwise I'll unleash Sasha on you. Every single word from this conversation is being recorded. You can go to hell for all I care, but from now on you leave us alone," I said with a smile, pointing at my Barbie. Sasha finally snapped out of it and unbuttoned her blouse, showing Victoria the wire. "So I'll tell you what is going to happen now. First, you will get the hell out of my life forever and you'll stay away from Jenny. If you won't comply with these conditions, I'll destroy your reputation so badly that you won't be able to do business anywhere in Britain. You'll be truly and utterly screwed."

"You can't —"

"Oh yes, I can and I will. Harry is on my side, and you know what kind of contacts he has, right?"

The colour drained from her face. We both knew that no one would want Harry as an enemy. He was lethal.

"This isn't over, Dex," she warned through gritted teeth, then picked up her bag and stormed out of the door. I collapsed on the sofa, hiding my face in my hands, feeling like all of a sudden all my strength was gone. The bitch was gone and we were finally free.

"Dexter, are you all right?" Sasha asked, walking up to me and touching my shoulder. I wanted to pull her down to my lap and kiss her, but Jenny was still in the room. Sasha was the best thing that ever happened to me and I was ready to fucking spend the rest of my life with that woman.

I cleared my throat and stood up. "I'm sorry it had to come to that, Jen, but you probably already realise that I'm not the guy for you," I said, looking straight into her eyes. What was I supposed to say to a fifteen-year-old girl that wanted me to take away her virginity? She deserved someone better than me, someone closer to her age.

"You could go on a date with me. I might be fifteen, but I'm not a child."

Jesus Christ. These women are going to kill me.

"Yes, that's right. You're fifteen, but even if you were twenty that wouldn't make a blind bit of difference," I said.

"Why not?"

"Because I'm in love with the woman that is standing next to you and I can't imagine living my life without her," I said, darting my eyes towards Sasha. "I'm really, really sorry."

Tears filled the girl's eyes. There wasn't any easier way of doing this. I couldn't promise her anything; she was only a child. Then the door opened up and Harry barged inside, looking like he had been running.

"Jenny! Come on, let's get out of here. There is someone that I really need you to meet," he said, winking at me. Bastard, he had heard everything, even my admittance to undying love for Sasha. Jenny looked devastated as she walked out with Harry. She shot Sasha a murderous glare before Harry shut the door behind him.

"You broke that poor girl's heart, Dex," Sasha said with slight edge in her voice.

Damn, I knew I fucked up again, dropping that bomb on her in the most awkward moment. This wasn't how I wanted to tell Sasha that I was in love with her, but I had no idea about romantic shit at all.

I walked up to her, feeling nervous and like my abdomen was in knots. "She'll get over it," I muttered.

"So you love me, huh? Did you just realise it or have you known it for a while?" she asked, smiling.

I dragged my hand through my hair, knowing that she wanted the whole truth.

"Barbie, at the moment that's irrelevant. All I want to know is if you're going to say this shit back to me."

She laughed. "This shit? Charming, Dex, and so romantic —you sweep me off my feet. You really know how to be subtle," she said, running her finger over my chest. "I don't know. I think I might keep you in the dark for a little while, at least until I'm sure that you're serious."

Fucking tease. I grabbed her and brought her close to my chest, narrowing my eyes. "I do love you, Sasha, but I love fucking you more. As long as your pussy is wet for me I don't care about anything else."

She chuckled. "That's good, because that makes me love you a little."

"Maybe you'll love me more when you find out that I bought the apartment next door, just for you." I knew how much she enjoyed living in Joey's place.

"What? That's impossible. The sale has gone through. That old man—"

"You forget something: I'm the landowner. Everything has to pass through me," I cut her off, kissing her gently. "Besides, I couldn't let just anyone live next to me. The apartment is yours. It always belonged to you."

"Okay. In that case, I love you too."

"For fuck's sake, I always knew you were after my money."

"Shut up and kiss me like you mean it."

***

"Where the hell are we going, Dex?" Sasha asked for the fifth time as we drove through the busy streets of Glasgow. She'd tensed when we passed the sign outside the city half an hour earlier, and shot me a questionable look.

I ignored her, trying not to think about her gorgeous lips wrapped around my cock. "To a special show. It's a surprise, Barbie, so quit asking," I muttered, knowing that I was taking a huge risk, hiding this shit from her, but I wanted her to gain her own personal closure. Ronny's unexpected phone call at the party had sounded promising, so I went to see him that evening when the thing with Victoria had finally blown over. Hell, my trip to his place was fucking worth it. By the time I got back to the complex, my brain was completely fired up.

Sasha folded her arms over her chest, pretending that she wasn't uncomfortable with being in Glasgow. Our trip had probably brought some unexpected memories back, stuff that pushed her out of her comfort zone and wreaked havoc on her confidence. But she was strong and it was time to put her past completely behind her.

We drove in silence for another fifteen minutes until we reached an industrial park filled with office buildings and some retail stores. I bet she had no idea what was happening. Her ex's company had expanded in the past year and his office had moved to a new location. The thing that pissed me off the most was that he was living it up, enjoying himself like he deserved everything he had. But he only had a few more minutes of freedom left.

Once we arrived outside the stylish building, I sent Ronny a quick text message.

"Dexter, what is going on? What is this place?" she asked, chewing on her bottom lip.

"We are paying a final visit to your shameful ex," I said gently. I knew she was going to freak, but that prick needed to pay for what he had done.

The colour drained from Sasha's face, and she stared at me like I'd lost my fucking mind. "No. Drive off. I don't want anything to do with him," she insisted.

"Baby, trust me. It's time. Come on," I said and got out of the car. I glanced at the building, seeing that someone was walking towards us. He was just in time; it looked like Ronny needed a pay rise.

"Dexter, please. Why are you doing this to me?" she asked.

"Because you need to get that eight grand back. He ruined your life and it's your fucking money," I explained.

"We both know that he won't do it. Come on, let's go back —"

"Sasha?"

Finally the prick noticed us. Sasha shuddered next to me, glaring at him with bitter anger and fear. I was ready to beat the shit out of him, but that wouldn't really satisfy me. I wanted him to experience real pain, the kind of pain that he would never forget. One lousy punch wouldn't cut it.

"Right, that's close enough, asshole," I snapped at him, when he tried to approach her.

"What the fuck do you want?" the asshole asked, glaring at me with interest. He took a pack of cigarettes out and lit one. He was taller than me, wearing some cheap suit with over-the-top shoes. Pathetic. I glanced at Barbie, who looked frozen, and I nudged her with my elbow. She cleared her throat, finally landing her eyes on that piece of shit.

"I want my money back, Kirk."

The guy started laughing, so I joined him. This was only getting better and better. It took him another thirty seconds to stop.

"Fuck, Sasha, do you think you can come up here with some asshole and that I'll return the cash that technically belongs to me? How stupid can you be?"

"I'd be careful if I were you, fuckface, or I'll forget my manners and teach you how you're supposed to speak to ladies," I warned him.

"Dexter, what are—"

"Crystal's accounts, asshole. I know all about your dirty dealings, hidden transactions and transfers from last year. You better get that checkbook out before I make some phone calls to your fucking boss and put you in prison for at least five years," I said, inhaling the cold air.

Sasha shifted next to me, but I didn't look at her. I was watching that prick as what I said slowly registered. His eyes narrowed, and that familiar smirk disappeared, quickly replaced by anger.

"Sasha, who the fuck is this guy?" the asshole asked with panic in his eyes.

My Barbie touched my arm, sending a twitch down to my cock. "You heard him. I want my money back, Kirk. Now!"

"Hurry up, shitface. We haven't got all day," I rushed him. He hesitated, glancing around. I was enjoying watching him as he nearly shit himself. Ronny had done well. This asshole thought that nobody knew and he had gotten away with it. It took him fifteen seconds to write Sasha a check. I didn't want Barbie to touch him, so I walked up to him and grabbed it. A minute later we were strolling back to the car. I didn't let go of her until we were inside.

Her raspy breaths were bothering me, and I wanted to tell her that this wasn't the only surprise that I'd prepared for this evening.

"Watch this now," I said to Barbie seconds later. A few cars passed us and sped up to the building. Within moments a few guys went up to Kirk, surrounding him. We both watched as he got arrested on the spot. He put up a fight, shouted, cursed Barbie off, but shortly after that he was handcuffed and led to a police car.

"Dex, what the hell? What just happened?" Sasha finally asked. Her hands were shaking as she witnessed the whole thing in stunned silence. I brought her closer to me, wanting to ease her discomfort.

"Your ex has been fiddling with some accounts for years now. A few weeks ago I asked my good friend Ronny to find out if he could get something on that piece of shit. At first everything looked fine. All his accounts were clean, but he was living above his means, placing lots of money on bets, going to casinos, buying stock that he couldn't afford. It looked like the rat bastard had accrued quite a number of debts over the last few years. He was earning a basic salary, so Ronny got suspicious. He started investigating all the accounts in the company that Kirk worked in. It looked like his manager was also greedy. They started with small sums, using his PA's accounts to cover up the amounts that they were transferring around the country."

"Oh my God, but how—"

"I wanted him to give you the money first. With Harry's contacts, he will be sent to one of the worst prisons for a good few years. The shitface will pay for what he did to you, Sasha. By the time he's brought before the judge he will have a few more charges under his belt. He's done, baby. Don't worry, he will never bother you again."

Sasha was staring at the car as it started slowly driving away. Then she glanced down at her feet.

My heart was pounding with excitement. I'd really wanted to hit that prick, but I knew that prison was going to teach him a much wiser lesson.

"Okay. In that case, the dinner is on me tonight," she said, smiling through the tears in her eyes.

Thirty-Seven

Sasha

The end of my performance on the pole needed to be spectacular. My legs were trembling, sweat dripped down my back, and I took long, shallow breaths, trying to concentrate on what I was about to do. Dexter was out there in the audience watching me, but I couldn't see him. The loud burlesque music blasted all around me, encouraging me to take that last move to the next level, to show everyone what I was capable of.

I'd spent the past two hours watching the others perform. Some girls were really good, but we were all on an amateur level, competing against each other for fun. After another breath, I climbed to the top of the pole and crossed my legs at my ankles. There I leaned into a position called Cross Ankle Release.

I arched my back as far as I could and reached both arms over my head to grab the pole. As my back continued to arch, my legs were closed tightly. My whole body was trembling as I began sliding down the pole until my body was in the shape of crescent moon, seductively trying to connect with the audience. Every part of me knew that I'd done well, that I was good enough.

Then I finished the whole show with a couple of extreme spins, hooking my legs in the middle and bending my back backwards. My breath was short and I was exhausted but pleased with myself. I hadn't made any mistakes throughout the whole half hour.

Applause broke out when the music died down and I smiled widely, bowing. The judges weren't giving anything away. I spotted Gina in the front row. She was whistling and clapping like crazy. She had supported me all the way. Dexter was nowhere to be seen and I was slightly disappointed that he hadn't seen my whole performance.

I ran backstage and grabbed a bottle of water. My heart was still pounding away. Other girls started congratulating me, telling me that I was great. We chatted for a bit, discussing the moves and my routine. I didn't know if I had a chance of winning, but this competition had always been something that I wanted to try.

I was just about to walk towards the changing room when I felt someone's hand on my mouth. Within moments I was dragged behind the curtain. I yelped, panicking, my heart in my throat.

"Barbie, you were fucking incredible," Dexter rasped in my ear. I relaxed, knowing that I wasn't in any danger. Bastard scared the shit out of me. "It's time to fulfill your duties. I have been waiting long enough."

Desire scorched through me and I instantly felt his smooth fingers tracing my exposed thighs.

"Have you been watching from here?" I asked when he spun me around. Dexter's brown eyes were ready, filled with fire, and my heart melted when I saw that I'd made him proud. In the past week we had barely left his bedroom and although I was tired, I wanted him to fuck me now.

"Of course. You gave me a raging hard-on arching and bending like that. I had to leave before anyone noticed."

I laughed, knowing that he was right. We had gone to the cinema the other day. Shortly after the film began, security had to throw us out because Dexter was trying to go down on me in the back row. He was out of control around me, and I loved that about him.

"You talk too much, Dex. I thought that you brought me here to fuck me," I complained, smiling seductively.

"Oh yes, fucking is in the cards. I want to hear your screams," he growled and spun me around again, slapping my ass. "Put your hands on the wall and bend over."

A shudder of excitement rippled through my body, but I did what he said. My pussy was aching for his cock as his fingers slid down the front of my knickers while he moved his other hand down between my legs. Within moments he'd dragged my latex shorts down and was running his fingers over my naked ass.

"Fucking beautiful and all mine."

He didn't give me much time to think about what he was going to do next. He thrust himself inside me and I yelped, seeing stars burst behind my eyelids. My legs were trembling, my muscles overstretched, but I felt his every rough thrust. My orgasm was building up, and I bit the skin on my arm, trying to suppress my loud moans.

"Oh, Dex," I gasped.

"This is going to be fast, so shut your mouth and take it."

He did go fast, pounding his hard erection into me like he was in a race, and I was trying to catch up with him, screaming. Dexter's nails were on my hips and our moans vibrated, letting everyone near us know what we were up to. I was coming undone for him and I didn't care that we had an audience or if we were heard. I needed it, after the stress that I'd just gone through.

He came inside me, cursing at first, then cradling me into his arms. I was panting, barely standing on my feet. He took the last bits of my energy, fucking me like there was no tomorrow.

"Move in with me."

"Come again?" I asked, wondering if I'd misheard him.

"I want you living in my apartment with me. Do I have to spell it out for you?" he asked with impatience, drilling his eyes into mine.

My head was clouded from the intensity of my last orgasm and I could barely gather my thoughts. I couldn't make this

kind of decision right now. I was a mess. "Dex, let's talk about
—"

"You have nothing to say. I have already moved your shit in with mine, so it's been decided. Anyway, are you ready for another round? I'm horny again…"

Thirty-Eight

Sasha

Sweat was trickling down between my breasts. I knew that I was going to suffer later, but we were leaving tomorrow and this was my last opportunity to enjoy this glorious weather. We never had that much heat in Edinburgh. Mum said that it had been raining for over a week and it was bitterly cold. I really wasn't ready to return to Scotland just yet.

I was lounging in thirty-two degrees Celsius around the pool area in Spain with Dexter Tyndall, my sex-obsessed, dirty-talking, long-term boyfriend. I had managed to pick up a fantastic tan already, but today I was topping it off. We arrived a week ago, booking the last minute trip in order to relax and recharge our batteries.

I opened my eyes and noticed that Dexter was done with sunbathing, and now he was watching me.

"How long have you been staring at me like that, you freak?" I asked. Dexter smirked and winked at me, trying to get the attention of the waiter who was hovering at the bar. I knew that look on his face, the one that burned my insides with a beat of steady desire. He was horny.

"Long enough for you to give me a boner," he muttered, pressing his hand over his red shorts to re-adjust himself whilst scanning the pool area for another waiter. I felt so relaxed being here with him. He drove me mad sometimes, well, most times, but we both needed this break. He knew that I hated it when he kept watching me like a total creep.

"There is a time and a place for stuff like that, Dex," I replied, smiling.

"Not with me. You should know that. I'm always ready to sink my dick in you," he disagreed. "Anyway, what do you want to drink?"

"A martini with lemonade."

"I ain't getting you that shit," he sneered, shaking his head. I rolled my eyes. Dexter hated when I drank martinis. Apparently I got too flirty after just one.

He had picked one of the best hotels in Barcelona. This swanky place had one of those beautiful infinity pools on the roof terrace. In the past few days we had been walking around the city, sightseeing and partying into the night. Today it was just about chilling. Our room was large and it gave us enough privacy. Dexter made sure that we didn't have anyone directly next to us. When we were in our crazy sex zone I usually had to really keep it down because he made out that I scared people off with the noises I made when he made me come.

There was something going on around the pool area. I noticed that some guy in a pair of speedos suddenly went down on one knee after one of the waiters handed something to him. His girlfriend was lounging on the chair unaware that he was trying to get her attention.

"Oh my God, he's not going to—"

I didn't finish what I wanted to say, because the German tourist was already proposing to her. Well, I didn't speak the language, but from the context I understood that he was asking his girlfriend to marry him.

"What's going on?" Dexter asked and looked at the couple. When the girl finally realised what was happening, she started shouting something in German, then crying, and then shouting again. There was a loud "ohhhhh" around the pool. She must have said yes, because people started clapping. Me, on the other hand, I burst out laughing. This was one of the most absurd proposals that I had ever seen.

"Jesus, I'll have to find a better place for holidays next year," Dexter muttered. "Waiter! Where the hell is he now? A marriage proposal in public, fucking pathetic."

"You have to step up your game a bit, darling," I said, smiling as I turned on my side so I was facing him. He looked gorgeous with a deeply bronzed tan, shining chest and even with that annoyed expression on his face. It had been three long years since we put our differences aside and committed to be in a relationship. We'd had our ups and downs like any couple, but I had never been happier.

"What? You want me to propose to you here in public, like this loser?" he asked, his jaw tight. I loved winding him up and pretending that I didn't care about love. We were great together, but even to me, the whole idea of marriage was still quite overwhelming. I mean, I was certain that I wanted to spend the rest of my life with him, but we were still young. Dexter had his mouthy and obnoxious moments, but he had a good heart.

"Maybe you should start thinking about these things," I hinted, trying to mask my amused tone. I wasn't in any hurry, and I liked my life just as it was. There was no point in rushing anything, messing this up, especially since Dexter had done so well keeping himself sane and healthy.

"You're out of your tiny blonde mind, Barbie. First marriage, then kids, and before I know it, I'll be fucking you only on Sundays. That's not happening," he snarled with annoyance. A couple of older women glanced at him disgusted and I laughed hard. Dexter always forgot that there were a lot of Brits in our hotel.

The waiter finally showed up.

"Beer for me and martini for the lady with lemonade and lots of ice," he barked at the short Spanish waiter. This was hilarious; Dexter looked worried about settling down, about moving our intense relationship to the next level. That was so cute, and I was getting excited. Wrong, I was getting wet, thinking about his hopeless emotional side. In the past three years he had proven to me that he cared for me very much.

"I don't think we would have time to have sex at all," I added, and started rubbing sunscreen all over my legs. "You know, when you get married and have kids, there is just no time for anything else."

"No fucking way, Sash. Forget about marriage and that whole shebang. Get your sexy ass to the room. I need to fuck you again," he growled and stood up. "I've had enough talk of this bullshit."

I laughed when he grabbed my hand and yanked me to my feet.

"Hold that order for drinks, Pedro," he shouted at the waiter.

"I was only joking, baby, and yes, the proposal was lame. Come on, let's stay here for a bit longer," I urged, marching after him. "I need to work on my tan a little more."

"I'll be tanning your pussy with my cock for the next hour, Sash," he stated when we reached our floor. "You're an evil bitch, pissing me off, winding me up with that whole marriage bollocks. Now it's time to pay!"

Okay, so he was a little pissed off now, but still, I couldn't stop laughing. It was obvious that Dexter did care. He was nearly thirty and a couple of times I heard how his mother reminded him that he needed to get a grip and propose. I didn't care much either way. I was happy with the way things were. Everything was going great. I had a permanent job in Royal Infirmary Hospital as a paediatric nurse and I used my pole dancing lessons as a stress reliever. We complemented each other and I didn't want to ruin our blissful life together.

Dexter grabbed my ass when he shut the door, slamming me into his chest. My breathing sped up, and desire overtook my normally clear thought process.

"How do you want it?" he growled, kissing my neck gently.

"Dexter's style, pretty please," I whispered, enjoying each time his tongue caressed my skin. He grabbed my neck and continued to move his mouth, until my knees gave out and I was lost in unbelievable sensations that skittered over my whole body.

"On all fours, baby, it's time to spice things up a little," he said, slapping me and spreading my legs to open wider. He began licking my wet pussy from behind. This was going to be a memorable afternoon.

Dexter

I was sitting at the bar exhausted, drinking whiskey. A band was playing a well-known song on a stage that had been set up temporarily for this evening. I had not long since finished fucking Sasha. I couldn't get enough of her. After an hour we dropped onto the bed exhausted but extremely satisfied. After I had given her two multiple orgasms, and fucked her senselessly for most of the afternoon, she finally shut up about this whole marriage thing.

The German loser who proposed to his girlfriend by the pool was here too, looking drunk but happy. Women were checking out the girl's ring, wetting themselves with excitement. No one could see that this was one of the lamest things that anyone could do. I couldn't believe that the girl actually said yes.

I was still angry and I had no idea why. Sasha was mine and I had nothing to worry about. If someone had told me five years ago that I would be on holiday with the girl that I had been seeing for over three years, I would have flipped out, completely lost my temper. I was a different guy then with emotional issues that were slowly driving me insane. Since Sasha had put up with my shit for that long, well, in my opinion she deserved a fucking medal.

"Come on, let's go dance," she sang, looking flustered, wearing a mini skirt that exposed her fantastic thighs—that I had gripped while pounding my hard cock into her earlier on. "I love this song; it's our song."

"No fucking way. You know I don't do this shit," I growled, checking out her cleavage. I needed to get hammered first in order to get up on that dance floor.

"Loser," she snarled and ran to the dance floor where other men and women were already dancing. I watched her as she started moving, laughing hysterically. She was a bit tipsy, so I needed to make sure that she didn't do anything stupid.

I wasn't supposed to go overboard with alcohol because of my meds. I had a few small episodes last year, but Dr. Bishop said that it was due to pressure in work. I'd invested money in a couple of properties and some of the contractors had fucked up the labour, causing several problems. I knew it would have been easier to get back to being the old me. It was exciting, shagging whatever bird I wanted to, but I was in love with Sasha. Every day I when I woke up next to her I couldn't believe how fucking lucky I was.

"Your woman knows how to move!"

I glanced back at Pedro, who was moving to the rhythm of the music while making a drink for someone else. His dark eyes were following Sasha's body and I knew what he was thinking about.

I nodded without saying anything and looked straight at my woman. The tables were set around the stage and it was pretty packed. We'd decided to spend our last night in the hotel. In the past week, we had been out almost every day, eating, partying and fucking like rabbits. All right, I had to admit. I lusted after her all the time. She would tease or touch me somewhere when she shouldn't and my dick would react.

Right now Sasha was bending, swaying her hips. She looked delicious and she was looking at me whilst she danced. I swallowed more whiskey and looked around. One thing got to me: all the fucking men were watching her. Most of them had women by their sides, and they were still paying more attention to my Barbie than them. This wasn't something that I wanted to acknowledge, knowing that they were admiring the way she moved.

I thought that I would never bother with jealousy, but Sasha was incredibly sexy and she was like a magnet for cock. Men checked her out when we were together, and I was aware of that but tried to ignore it. During our three years together we had never discussed it, but this sudden realisation was pissing me off.

Her short skirt was showing too much of her sexy legs, and that was part of the problem. Sasha laughed loudly and started spinning herself around a Portuguese female tourist she had chatted with before. We had met a few people here, but I hated socialising.

Even the guy that proposed by the pool looked mesmerised by my girlfriend. Slowly I started getting uncomfortable. She was mine, and now I was beginning to think that I needed to make us official. I couldn't imagine being with someone else. I fucking loved her, cherished her; she was the best thing that happened to me.

Deep down I knew that a proposal was going to be tricky, because I wasn't a romantic man and I didn't want any of that cheesy staged shit. Fuck, it was time to stop messing around and ask her to marry me.

Mum had been busting my balls in the past year. She wanted another wedding. Connor didn't even have a girlfriend and I was the next in line. I bet she was scared that I would have a relapse, that my bipolar would strike again.

We were flying back to Edinburgh tomorrow morning. There I would have plenty of time to think about how I wanted to seal the deal. This whole thing was going to be in Dexter's style, to the point, intense and memorable. Sasha would say yes; there was no doubt about that.

"Another one?" Pedro asked.

"Nah, I'm taking my woman back to the room. She has had enough," I replied and headed to the dance floor. Women were glancing at me, sending seductive winks. Yeah, yeah, they all wanted my cock, but I was already taken. Hopefully in a couple of weeks' time both Sasha and I would be officially off the market.

"Your time is up, Barbie. You know how much I hate when you tease me like that?" I told her, grabbing her by the hand. People started clapping; the band was finishing another song.

"Oh come on, just one more. I'm having a great time," she begged, giggling. She was drunk now. Fuck, how could I not see that? She swirled her sexy body around me. I hated dancing, but all the men around us needed to know that this girl was mine, so I didn't mind giving them a little show.

I brought her closer and started moving with the rhythm, grinding my hips against her, keeping her close.

"Come on, baby, guide me," I whispered in her ear.

Soon, I realised that this was a bad fucking idea. Alcohol was coursing through my veins loosening my control and I was instantly hard. Her orchid perfume swirled around my nostrils, her hips and the eyes that I had fallen for.

We danced together easily moving with the rhythm, but once the song ended, I grabbed her and started dragging her back to our hotel room. My groin was burning with fire and I needed to sink my cock into her sweet pussy, teasing her mouth with my tongue.

"I want you," she growled, slurring her speech, barely standing straight. If I wanted to make her my wife, I had to take care of her. She was in no fit state for sex right now.

"You might want me, but you have had enough of my cock for today. It's an early night for you," I said as I pulled her inside the room.

"Noooo … I want to dance and make love—"

"No, Barbie, shower and bed," I whispered and crawled into the bed next to her.

"I love you so much, Dex," she said and then closed her eyes. Within a few minutes she was out cold, sleeping. I glanced at her and dragged my hand through my hair.

"Me too, baby, me too…"

Thirty-Nine

Sasha

I wasn't feeling well on the plane, my head was spinning and I started getting cold sweats halfway through our journey. It was a short flight and I was already missing Barcelona. I loved the sun, the parties and wild fun and no moody Dexter that could make me crazy. We hadn't been on many holidays because of his demanding work schedule. He knew how to spoil me, but he didn't have to work that hard. We both earned enough to enjoy ourselves.

He woke me up with breakfast in bed very early this morning. Last night I had drunk at least four glasses of sangria and then I danced, until Dexter insisted on going back to the room. My head was banging, and on top of that, I had a dodgy tummy. I didn't say anything to Dexter; he was already in one of his moods. The holiday was over. Now it was the time to get back to reality.

Once we landed, it took ages to get us through passport control. There was a long queue ahead. Dexter was already scrolling through his phone, checking his emails. It was late October and the weather in Edinburgh was terrible. The rain was pouring from the sky. All I wanted was to get back home and sink into our comfortable bed. After standing in line for about half an hour, Dexter's phone started ringing.

"It's Rob. I need to take this," he said. I just waved my hand. I wasn't feeling well. I didn't want to be sick in front of him and all these people in the queue. We had way too much fun in Barcelona, or maybe it was the food that I ate on the plane.

"Tyndall," he answered, a bit more aggressively than usual. It turned out that Robert needed Dexter's help with one of the projects that they had been working on for the last several months. I was used to this by now. His business took up a lot of his time. It took another half an hour to get outside.

"I shouldn't have told him that I was back today. There is a problem with one of the clients and he wants me in," he explained, pushing the trolley with the luggage.

"Just go. I'll take the next taxi and make us dinner for later. We still have a whole weekend together."

"Leave the suitcases at the concierge. I'll pick them up when I come back," he ordered. "I want you to be in bed, naked and ready for me when I step through the door."

He kissed me, pressing his mouth over mine greedily, caressing my tongue with his. The kiss curled my toes and sped up my heartbeat.

"Don't be too late; otherwise I might be asleep already," I teased him.

"Whatever. You can't get enough of my cock, Sasha."

He picked up his bag and strolled back towards the door. Ten minutes later I was in the taxi, driving back to the Grange. The nausea came back as we were arriving at the complex, and I felt a little dizzy. My parents were visiting us next week and I was looking forward to catching up with them. Since Dex gave me the apartment next door, I used it as crash pad for my family and new friends that I had made in the hospital.

Duncan from concierge helped me with the smaller carry-on luggage, and by the time I walked through the door I felt exhausted. My stomach revolted. I ran to the bathroom and threw up the food I'd eaten on the plane. I blamed the alcohol last night and the hectic holiday. We should have gone to Maldives and lay on the beach for two weeks. That way I would have felt more rested.

I ran the tap and washed my face, wondering what the hell was wrong with me. My tan looked awesome, but I felt like crap. This sickness should pass by tomorrow, and once I had a good night of sleep I would probably feel like myself again.

I started looking in the cupboards, searching for something for my stomach, when I spotted my tampon box that I bought a couple of weeks ago. In my head I started calculating weeks. All of a sudden, my heart stopped because I realised that I'd missed my period last month.

I placed my palm over my stomach, shocked like someone had poured freezing cold water over me.

"No, I can't be ... No, we didn't ..."

I couldn't finish the sentence as sweat gathered on my forehead. Dexter hated condoms and we ditched using them last year. I had been having a hormonal shot since then, but when I checked my diary a few moments later, I realised that I missed it last month. Mum had been in the hospital and she had to have surgery on her knee, so I spent quite a lot of time in Glasgow. I remembered rescheduling my visit at least twice that month.

Now everything was coming back to me. I put some clothes on and drove to the nearest chemist with my heart in my throat. This wasn't the end of the world; I was still convinced that it could still be food poisoning. Maybe I wasn't pregnant, although since my last miscarriage, I secretly hoped that maybe in the future God would bless me with another child.

Me and Dex, we never talked about our future and kids, but judging from yesterday's conversation about marriage, he wasn't up for such a dramatic change in our lives. I was dreading knowing, and I was already imagining how Dexter would react.

I bought three tests and arrived back to the complex half an hour later. There, I headed straight to the apartment next door. Dexter didn't like going there anyway, so it was a good place for me to escape sometimes. I couldn't catch my breath when I waited for the results. My whole body shook when the test came out positive. I did two more to be certain, and it was official. Dexter had knocked me up. I was pregnant.

Suddenly an anxiety attack shot through my bones, as I tried to steady my heartbeat. There was no way I was telling him anything until I'd confirmed it with the doctor. Dexter never said that he wanted a dog, let alone kids. We loved each other, but a baby could complicate everything. Seven years ago I'd had a miscarriage. At the time I was with Kirk, a man who was now rotting in prison. Now I was in the perfect relationship with a man that loved me dearly, but I felt overwhelmed.

I sat down in the bathroom, staring at the test and wondering how I would break this news to him.

The voice of reason told me to wait for the right time, until we settled back into our daily routine. We just came back from Spain. Maybe I should sleep on it for the next couple of days. I had no doubt that Dexter loved me and he wouldn't do anything stupid, but for the first time in my life, I was terrified at the prospect of being a mother

Dexter

Rob needed to get a life. He was much too obsessed with this new project, and by the time I finally managed to get away, it was seven o'clock in the evening. I had a woman waiting for me at the apartment that hadn't seen my cock since yesterday, which was long enough.

The idea that I had been thinking about over the past twenty-four hours had been burning my fucking mind. Tomorrow I was planning to do something about it. First I needed to get a ring, but I couldn't pick up any ring. Sasha deserved something really special and unique. We hadn't talked about our future. The past three years we both lived day by day, never thinking ahead. Sasha hated when I left my clothes around and when I didn't clean up after myself. She hated the fact that all the girls that I used to fuck kept calling me, demanding to see me. No one could believe that I had turned into a monogamist. Eventually this had stopped. We argued a lot about stupid stuff, then made up. Hot sex was always a winner.

I was falling more in love with her every day. Some day's pressure got to me and I used alcohol to get to sleep. Sasha didn't mind me drinking, as long as I didn't go overboard.

The idea of settling down and having kids was appealing, but I didn't want to give up on Sasha's pussy just yet. We had plenty of time to make babies. Our whole lives were ahead of us.

I arrived back at the complex exhausted; Sasha was the only person that could make me feel better. Thank God that I managed to get Sunday off. Robert ran all the projects when I wasn't there, but he wanted me to go in to the office tomorrow. He was a real pain in the ass, but he was very reliable.

Sometimes I panicked when I thought about our future, that Sasha was suffocating me, that I couldn't be committed to her for the rest of my life. Thoughts like that scared me. Bishop kept saying that I needed to stick to my meds, that I was looking for faults in my happy relationship to punish myself for my imaginary failings. I knew he was right. All I knew was that she belonged in my apartment.

I was ready to marry Barbie. For the first time in my life it was clearer to me than anything else.

When I shut the door, the living room was empty. Something smelled nice and I knew that she had made dinner for both of us. When I walked into our bedroom, the shower was on. I stripped as quickly as I could, stretched my arms above my head and slid inside the bathroom. Surging desire spread down to my dick, and I was ready to push the exhaustion aside and enjoy a quick romp in the steamy shower. She was standing in the cubicle with her eyes closed, not moving.

I slid the door open and stepped inside, bringing her ass closer to my stiff cock. She turned around abruptly.

"How long have you been back?" she asked. Warm water began travelling down our bodies.

"A moment ago, right on time for a big O." I smirked and brought her closer, staring at her green eyes. There was some wariness and sadness there that was quickly replaced by desire. Maybe it was just the fact that we were back, the relaxing break was over.

"Shall we move to the bedroom?" she asked, biting her lip playfully.

"How about we stay here, Sash? I would really like to fuck you in the shower for a bit," I muttered and trailed my mouth over her tits, taking her left nipple into my mouth.

Sasha leaned back against the shower wall, spreading her legs apart and allowing me to massage her superb breasts at the same time.

"Can I ask you something, baby?"

I slipped my fingers in her tight pussy, discovering that she was already soaking for me, which only turned me on more. I wanted to cut the foreplay and thrust myself deep inside her.

I lifted my head to meet her gaze.

"You wanna talk now?" I growled pushing my fingers in and out. She closed her eyes, arching her head backwards, moaning.

The waters surged down over her boobs and my head. For a moment she was enjoying my tortures, and then she opened her eyes and asked, "Do you think that our relationship is serious enough?"

I stopped inside her, snapping back to reality.

Fuck, where the hell had this question come from? Was she having doubts about us?

"Barbie, why are you asking this question right now?" I snapped, moving up, so my eyes were level with her face.

"I don't know, Dex. We live together and we love each other, but we have never talked about the future. I just want to be sure that we are in the same boat," she replied, but I had a feeling that this wasn't it. There was something that she wasn't telling me, something important.

"I fucking love you, Sasha; that should be enough," I said, thinking about my secret plan. I didn't want her to suspect anything and this wasn't the right time for a serious talk. "And I'm going to prove that to you in just a moment."

I didn't let her ask me any more questions, and when I started pleasuring her with my fingers again she quickly forgot what we had talked about. I focused on her mouth, then went down on my knees and began licking her slick sex, as the water surged down my back. Sasha moaned, and I knew that I could keep fobbing her off as long as she was distracted.

Her clit was in my mouth and I sucked on it, nibbled it and licked it until she was panting. Blood shot down my cock, as her hands moved in my hair. I could keep doing this all day long. She cried out when I picked up the pace, fucking her with my tongue. With my free hand I stroked my hard cock, while Sasha's hips began to tremble.

I could stay in this position forever, feeling the muscles in her core, pulsing and gripping my fingers tighter. She was such a turn-on, and I intensified the sensations and the movements of my mouth when she was just about to come for me.

"Dex, oh God, just don't stop now, don't—"

She cursed when I pulled away all of a sudden. I stood, leaned over her and bit her neck. My skin was numb to the water that flowed down our bodies. I abused her mouth and continued to stroke her until she came hard, screaming at the top of her lungs.

"Sweet, now it's time to make it more fun. Are you ready to take my hard, stiff cock?"

"Ready, arrh, yes, yes," she mumbled, so I had no choice then, but to thrust myself inside her and, oh sweet Jesus, she felt amazing. Because of this gorgeous woman I was going to end up in an early grave and I couldn't wait to make her mine.

All those fuckers that were looking at her ass better be backing off. Once there was a wedding ring on her finger, no one could touch her.

Her pussy was slick and wet. I kept going fast, gripping her hips tighter, until she was coming again. The warm water was stinging our bodies, adding pleasure to unbelievably explosive sensations. Our bodies melted together and I was kissing her and coming inside her at the same time, filling her with my hot seed. Shower sex had its advantages. I needed to remember it for the future. I had to make a habit to shower with her more often.

Forty

Sasha

I was throwing up right, left and centre this morning. Dexter was out at seven, so luckily he didn't see me hanging over the toilet. He normally didn't work Saturdays, but because of our holiday he had a backlog of things that he had to take care of. The pregnancy news came like a storm in the middle of a sunny day and I wasn't sure what to do, how to feel about the fact that there was a tiny part of Dex inside my womb. I should have told him last night in the shower, but I got scared. He was doing all these wonderful things to my body, distracting me from my erratic thoughts. Maybe I was deluding myself, thinking that we were together forever.

Dex was going to lose his mind, panic or run away. We hadn't discussed the subject of family or even marriage. First things first, I needed to see a doctor and find out if everything was all right. I felt like I was in a right mess, forgetting about that hormonal shot last month. After my miscarriage I'd dreamt about this day for months, and now that it was here I was panicking, because the timing wasn't right.

On Saturday we normally hung out in the city, if Dexter didn't have to work. After the shower, I cleaned the apartment, ate some breakfast and then called Gina, asking if she would meet me for a late lunch later on.

Mum would have known what to do, but I didn't want to tell her anything yet. Dexter deserved to find out first, before anyone else did, but Gina was a good friend and I could use her advice. I was happy and scared at the same time, not knowing how to deal with the shock. After my last miscarriage I wondered if I would never be ready. Dexter was a grown man. He'd proved to me that he had changed. It was time to show me if he was still the man that I had fallen for.

The weather had improved a bit, but it was cold. Edinburgh was busy and many people were out, rushing around. Dexter's office was in the north part of the city. We were going out for a dinner tonight. Apparently he was celebrating finishing another big project. Since I started working in the hospital, I made quite a number of friends, but I didn't want to speak to any of them about this. Gina was the right kind of person and I just needed to lay out this whole situation for her. I still had no idea what had been going in her own love life. She always managed to avoid talking about herself.

"Wow, look at you, Miss Tanned. So how was the holiday?" she asked, joining me in the restaurant. Her fiery hair was sticking out and the short bob suited her.

"Great. We both loved Barcelona. Spent most of the time partying. The weather was gorgeous."

The waiter approached us and took our orders. I needed to remember that I couldn't touch alcohol. I drank so much in Barcelona, not even realising that I was expecting. Now I felt really guilty and lost. This whole secret all of a sudden felt daunting.

"Well, in that case we should celebrate it. We should order some cocktails." Gina laughed, calling up the waiter again, but I stopped her.

"No, no, I can't have any alcohol. This is why I called you. I'm going through a crisis," I said quickly.

She lifted her left eyebrow, and after about five seconds, her jaw dropped.

"Fuck! Your mouthy boyfriend knocked you up. Didn't he?"

I covered my face in my palms, taking a few shallow breaths. She pulled my hands down, widening her wide eyes.

"Does he know?" she asked.

"No, I just found out yesterday and I'm petrified to say anything. I thought that I was still all right. I missed that hormonal shot last month," I explained, shaking my head. My and Dex's relationship was very physical, and we had always had a lot of sex. It was how we stayed connected. He didn't like showing his feelings too much and I felt that he wasn't ready for kids or even marriage. "I asked him last night in the shower if we were serious, and he didn't really give me a straightforward answer."

Gina knew everything about Dex. She was my complete confidant, but she had never showed up at any of my parties in the apartment or hung out with me and Dex. I stopped trying to figure her out after a few months. She just liked being secretive.

"You have to tell him. I guess it's time for him to man up."

"What if he doesn't want this baby? What if this will break us?"

"For fuck's sake, Sash, when did you become insecure? Dexter Tyndall is the father of your child. You said that he changed, so it's time to see if he really has balls."

The drinks came in and I sipped some water.

"All right, fine. I'll tell him tonight, during dinner," I assured her.

"Sasha, don't worry. He's your man and you're done with playing now. This is serious shit."

We talked then about my holiday and about seeing the doctor. Dexter paid for a private medical insurance even though I was happy with NHS. After lunch and more telling off from her, we drove to the private surgery in another area. This was just the beginning and I was freaking out myself, because my man was still wary of being fully committed to me

Dexter

I managed to get out of the office at two o'clock. The next week was going to be stressful. We were purchasing two big developments in one of the council estates areas.

Sasha's question in the shower kept playing in my head and made me a little nervous. It came out of nowhere and this kind of stuff always concerned me. Maybe she wanted to stop living on an impulse and needed to know what I wanted in the long run.

Now wasn't the time to worry about it. I took an afternoon off, leaving Rob alone. I paid him enough and I didn't want to listen to his nagging today. I headed to one of the best jewellery shops in the city. Women were smiling at me. There was no doubt that I looked good with a tan.

I took off my sunglasses and walked into the stylish boutique where I was planning to pick up a ring for Sasha.

A very tall, slim woman approached me wearing an elegant, expensive two-piece suit.

"Can I help you?" she asked with a wide smile.

"I need to pick out an engagement ring for my girlfriend. It needs to be special, of exquisite quality and unique," I said with my sharp and demanding tone. She blushed, and a few other women in the store looked disappointed. Yeah, I was taken; they all had to get used to it. "It's better if we do this in the back. I have money to spend, so you need to show me your most desirable pieces."

The woman was nervous but tried to act professional. She showed me a few rings and I rejected them all. Sasha had to have a ring that wasn't available anywhere else. We had a long discussion about some of the things that I wanted. She took notes, but I left disappointed and on edge again.

My plan wasn't going how I wanted it to, and I drove to the complex thinking about the execution of it.

When I arrived, Sasha was sitting in the living room, changing channels on the TV. Maybe I was being paranoid, but yesterday there was something off about her, about the way she asked that question in the shower.

There was something bothering her, and that shouldn't be the case, because we just got back from a relaxing holiday. Maybe we needed to have another getaway.

"Hello, gorgeous. I managed to get out early," I said, kissing her forehead. She had my favourite white shorts on and a tight green top. Such a tease, I wanted to lock myself in the bedroom for the rest of the afternoon.

"Hey, do you want something to eat? I can make a salad."

"Nah, I had a bite to eat in the city. All I want is to chill. It was a stressful day. That asshole Rob is going to kill me with that schedule of his," I complained. She was watching some reality TV. I hated that shit.

"I thought you were the boss," she teased.

"I am the fucking boss, but I made a mistake and put him in charge of some of this project, thinking that I could offload some work from my own schedule. I need to find him a pussy. That should chill him out a bit."

She laughed and I got up, crawling up closer and staring down at her stunning tits.

"What are you doing, perving over my cleavage?" she asked with amusement.

"I can't get enough of these bad boys," I said, trying to lick her nipple, but she didn't let me, pushing me away.

"Dex, be serious for once. I need to talk to you about something," she said and stopped smiling. I dragged my hand through my hair and looked in her eyes. Sasha was relaxed when I walked in, but she seemed tense now, like she wanted to hide what was really going on with her.

"Talk to me about what, Sash?" I asked, not even sure why I was suspecting that there was anything wrong.

When she was just about to tell me what was bothering her, my phone started to ring. It was the jewellery shop. I left my number with the manager earlier on, telling her to call me as soon as they had something special. I wasn't expecting it until tomorrow.

"Sorry, I have to take this," I told her with a wink and walked to the other room where she couldn't hear me.

"Hello," I snapped to the phone, ready to tell her to stop wasting my precious time unless she had something special for me.

"Mr. Tyndall, I believe we have found something extremely rare. I understand that you told me that the price is irrelevant, but this ring is very expensive. One of our private collectors sent a few samples an hour after you left," she said, sounding more excited than me.

"What kind of stuff are we talking about here?"

"The ocean paradise diamond, Mr. Tyndall. The original diamond has been shaped to 1.5 carats. That's a wearable size. It's rare, practically unique. Unusual but beautiful. We could arrange a private meeting in our boutique. When do you think you would be available?"

"Next week sometime, during the working week. That would be less suspicious," I replied, imagining how the stone would look on Sasha's finger. The whole idea was fucking crazy, but I wanted to execute it in style, my kind of style without cheese and stupid romanticism.

"Excellent, Mr. Tyndall. How about Tuesday afternoon?"

"Tuesday sounds fine. Get the package ready. I don't want to waste time."

She assured me that she had everything under control.

"Who was that?" Sasha asked, looking at me. Lies, fuck. I hated lying to her, but my plan was precise and she couldn't suspect anything.

"Harry. I have to run upstairs to see him for a minute about something and when I'm back I want you to see waiting naked for me in bed."

She rolled her eyes.

"We aren't having sex. We have to talk first."

"Barbie, I'm not going to repeat myself. Just be ready. I'm hard already. Look at this."

I had to drop my pants for her to show her my dick. She shook her head, and told me to get lost. I bet she wanted to bring up the conversation from the shower, about commitment and shit like that.

"Grow up, Dexter, and hurry up. I hate waiting around for you."

Sometimes I hated it when she didn't like to play with me. We couldn't talk about us, because whenever we did, we ended up fighting. God, she just needed to give me a few more days. Besides, I was convinced that something was off about her. She was probably worried about my hectic schedule. The past few months were really busy.

I ran to Harry's apartment, wondering if he was going to be in at all. The guy was still an enigma to me. Since Sasha and I got together, we avoided his mixer parties. Harry wasn't a guy that I would want to get tied up with. After so many years, I still had no idea what his deal was, but it wasn't my business to get involved.

But I needed his help to execute my plan for this special proposal.

I knocked a few times, louder than I was supposed to. For some reason I didn't want to wait to arrange things. Sasha was sulking and I had to go through this whole serious talk with her tonight if I wanted to get laid. Maybe she could suck me off in the shower tonight. God, I was getting hard even thinking about her.

"Dex, hey, what's up?" Harry asked when he opened the door.

"We can't have this conversation outside," I said and invited myself in. If Harry had company, then that was too bad. Lucky for me, his apartment was empty.

"Yeah, come on in as usual. I'm not busy," he said sarcastically. Okay, so I pissed him off again, but I wasn't doing well when I had to take care of such an important matter.

"I need a stripper, Harry, badly and like now."
That kind of got his attention instantly.

Forty-One

Sasha

Dexter was lying to me. He had never before taken a phone call in the other room, so last night I stood by the bedroom door and listened to his conversation. He was talking about some sort of package, about me being suspicious. My heart had been beating the whole time, as I wondered what had changed between us in the past forty-eight hours. Maybe my gorgeous, bipolar boyfriend was done with being good. Maybe he was bored and needed to boost up his ego in the arms of another woman.

There was a possibility that he was buying drugs. He hadn't touched any dodgy pills or weed since he had been hospitalised. Yesterday, my doctor had confirmed that I was four weeks pregnant. He talked me through what would happen over the next few appointments. Everything was happening so fast. Gina tried hard to cheer me up, but I felt lost. I thought that I could wait until dinner with the news and I was ready to tell him, but then he took that phone call. We were both pretty honest about everything. He knew how sensitive I was about lying. I waited for him to tell me about this mysterious package, but straight after he was done talking, he vanished to see Harry for some reason. Bad vibes began stirring my mood.

"Have a good day and think about my cock," he said when he was leaving today at 6:00 a.m. My shift in the hospital wasn't starting until eight, so I had a bit more of a lie in.

Normally I would have replied with something snarky, but I was too absorbed with my own worrying thoughts. Feeling like a right possessive girlfriend, I started checking his office in the spare bedroom. Opening drawers, the cabinet and in his desk, looking for anything that could tell me what was going on.

I exhaled sharply when I found nothing. This wasn't normal behaviour. Dex had proven to me time after time that he loved me and now I was carrying his baby.

An hour later, I dressed and went to work unable to shake off that annoying feeling that hung over my shoulder.

***

Days started to pass by and I couldn't seem to find the right moment to tell him that he was going to be a father. It was a good thing that he kept leaving early, not seeing me throwing up in the mornings. Nausea shook my body and weakened me a bit, but my work in the hospital kept me going. Things began shifting. Since that conversation in the bedroom, Dexter began shutting himself inside the office for at least two hours every day after he was back from work.

When he didn't make love to me for two days I started to become paranoid. He never ditched sex, so something was definitely going on. Then on Thursday we had a quickie in the living room, which should have put things back to the way they were. I still felt left out. My head was all over the place. I was wondering, deciding how best to bring up the subject, but the time didn't seem right.

None of this was good for us and I was slowly freaking out. My parents were visiting this weekend. Dexter was either cheating on me or he was taking drugs again.

I managed to get out of work early enough on Friday. Gina didn't want to see me in her class. I was told that I had to rest and tell my loving boyfriend what was going on.

Maybe I was selfish keeping the news about the baby from him, but since Spain it seemed we were living separate lives. Drugs were not acceptable and I was considering speaking to Bishop.

Dexter had another secret phone call last night. This was the second time that he lied to me this week, fobbing off my nagging questions. I could have talked to him about it, but in some ways I needed to see for myself what he was up to. Last night, he confirmed that he was picking up the package today. Stupidly enough I talked myself into going to the street that I overheard him talking about. This was stupid and naïve, but Dexter was hiding something.

I drove to the city, trying to justify to myself what I was doing. The area that I parked in was filled with clubs and bars. Dex and I had really liked a restaurant nearby.

My heart leaped in my throat when I spotted my beloved walking along the Greyfired Road, looking as handsome as always. My reasonable side screamed to get out of here, but instead I started following him.

I wasn't the kind of girlfriend that spied on her boyfriend, but sure enough I was turning into one. I had to fight for my happiness. He walked for another hundred yards, glanced around and then disappeared inside a strip club.

I had to stop and take several breaths. My hands were trembling, pulse speeding. There was no point jumping to conclusions about anything yet. Maybe he was meeting a client. The possibilities were endless, but I wasn't planning to hang out on the street.

I stood there a couple of minutes desperately waiting for him to appear. When he didn't, I went inside. A couple of men inside turned to look at me as I passed through the narrow entrance. It was early afternoon, and the club was quiet. The objective was simple: he couldn't see me. He couldn't know that I had followed him here. Well, until now I had never really bothered checking up on him or gotten jealous about other women. I had always been secure in our relationship. We were a good team and I thought that he could be trusted.

The club was a small, stylish and discreet place. I quickly sat down at the back where I had a great view of the bar area in front. I hid myself at the back in the shadows, where no one could see me. Dexter stood by the bar talking to a woman while she poured him a pint of beer.

My internal voice of reason reminded me that I was being stupid. He wasn't meeting anyone here; he simply stopped for a quick drink. His grey, expensive-looking suit looked good on him and waves of desire shot down my spine. I smiled to myself, knowing that I was turning into an obsessed girlfriend. He wasn't doing anything wrong. Then, I saw a very tall brunette approaching him. She was definitely a stripper with long legs, dressed in a short shiny dress. Dexter smiled.

They started talking, in my opinion, too comfortably. I didn't like that stupid smile on his face. It simply said that he was ready to fuck her. I kept breathing, watching them like a hawk. When the woman started touching his arms I was ready to scratch her eyes out. I had no idea how much time had passed, but when she started playing with his tie, I was ready to throw up. I thought that the last three years had changed him, that he wouldn't go back to being a total manwhore.

There were a few other people inside, mostly men and a few other girls sitting by the bar, watching my boyfriend's exchange with this other girl. Dexter laughed loudly when she whispered something into his ear. Then he took something out of his pocket.

I couldn't see what it was, but he handed it to the dark-haired woman. I waited for him to kiss her, or do something, anything proving that he was a cheating, lying bastard. The woman lost her smile and I didn't know if I should have felt relief or anger.

They talked a bit more until he finished his beer and left, using the other entrance. There was no way that he noticed me. My thoughts spun. The meeting was strange and I had no idea what was going on or what he was lying about. And what was it he showed that brunette slut?

I sat there trying to pull myself together and stop shaking. His mother had warned me that I was supposed to keep an eye on him.

I waited an hour, asked for glass of water at the bar and then left knowing that I had to confront him tonight and reveal the truth. The problem was that I had no idea how he was going to react.

Dexter

My plan was coming together nicely, but Sasha was acting odd. In the past two days she barely spoke to me. I tried to ask her a few times what was wrong, but she kept blaming work, saying that she had a stressful shift.

Harry nearly hit me when I asked him to recommend me a good strip club. It took a while to explain what I was planning to do. He knew all the dirty details about me and Sasha, and he liked her.

When he finally calmed down and allowed me to get my words together, he patted my back and said, "You're the most fucked up guy that I have ever known."

"But do you think this would work?" I asked, feeling nervous.

"Not sure. This is supposed to be about her, not another woman," he added.

That kind of made me thing twice, but I didn't say anything else. In the end I decided stick to my original settings.

Harry had done what I asked him and put me in touch with Lorraine. She was a stripper and lap dancer. She was very beautiful, sinful, and in any other circumstance, I would have fucked her, but Sasha had stolen my heart.

Lorraine understood what she needed to do. She tried to flirt, offered me a free dance, but I declined. I was focused enough and I still had a lot of things that I needed to take care of.

Once I was done with the most important arrangements, I drove back to work. It was still pretty early, and I wasn't in a working mood, so instead of heading back to the office, I went shopping. Sasha had a short shift, and it was my turn to cook tonight.

Blood rushed down to my cock when I thought about our shower sex the other night. I wanted to take her in the kitchen and then the bedroom as well. Sex with her was always adventurous and the past two days I had neglected her.

I was definitely one lucky motherfucker.

"I'm home, baby, so first things first. Get in the bath before I change my mind and fuck you hard on the kitchen worktops," I shouted, walking in with all the shopping bags.

She emerged from the bedroom, wearing yoga pants and a low cut top. Shivers trembled down my spine when I thought about her pussy, but her expression was alarming.

"Where have you been all afternoon?" she asked, looking like she was ready to rip my balls off.

"In the office, why?" I asked, trying to embrace her with my arms, but she pushed me away. Okay, she was pissed about something, but I couldn't think what I'd done this time around.

"I popped into the office to see you earlier on, but Robert said that you left at two o'clock," she stated, placing her hands on her hips. "So you can stop lying to me, Dex."

Shit, I wasn't expecting that she would visit me, and I had no choice now but to make more lies. Barbie wasn't stupid, and she figured out that I was hiding something from her. I thought that I could get away with being secretive for at least another day.

"I had to check out a few projects. The traffic was terrible and this took much longer than I anticipated."

She pressed her lips in a hard line and narrowed her eyes. She didn't believe me. We hadn't had sex for two days. I gave her space, thinking that she needed it.

"Stop it, Dexter. I heard your secret phone call the other day. Is it the drugs? You're back in contact with your dealers."

I took a few steps towards her, keeping my neutral expression. Her perfume swirled my senses and my dick twitched when I wrapped my arms around her waist.

"Drugs? Are you out of your mind, sexy?" I asked calmly. I didn't want to spoil our evening together with my short temper. "You know that I haven't taken anything since I was hospitalised."

She pushed me away and avoided looking me in the eye. We argued quite a lot, mostly because I was a messy fucker, but she had never looked at me like she was right now. She looked furious, disappointed even.

"No, Dexter, you're lying to me. I have always accepted the way you were, but I want the truth now. What is going on with you right now?" she pressed, looking tense and worried.

"Have you been through my phone or something?" I demanded. "What's happened? This isn't you, Sash."

"No, Dex, stop turning this around. I went to see you today and you weren't in the office. Are you seeing someone else? Just tell me. I think I deserve to know the truth."

"For fuck's sake, Sasha, I'm not seeing anyone else. Haven't I proven to you already how much I love you?"

"Just tell me—where have you been this afternoon?"

Someone must have said something to her. There was no doubt about that.

"Okay, Dex, you can have it your way. I'll be in the other apartment until you decide to tell me what is going on," she said through gritted teeth, turning around and marching away.

I closed my eyes and counted to five, knowing that I needed to keep my mouthy Dexter out of this. Within minutes she was out of the door, slamming it loudly. I was trying to do the right thing, and now I had really pissed off my girlfriend. Sex tonight was definitely out of the question.

How was I supposed to know that she would get suspicious? This plan seemed perfect at first and now I wasn't so sure. I marched around the kitchen, wondering how to fix this. When I started unpacking the shopping, I wanted to smash the bottle of champagne that I bought for both of us. Somehow I managed to calm myself down and sit and think. I had to give her an hour to cool down, to gather her thoughts.

After a few minutes, I opened the champagne and poured myself a glass, thinking that I had only one shot with this, but I had no idea if she was going to say yes after all.

Forty-Two

Sasha

I hurled my favourite coffee mug on the floor in frustration. Dexter had lied to my face. I thought that he would come clean and tell me about his trip to the strip club. I didn't want to cry, but when my stomach revolted I ran to the bathroom to throw up again, probably because I was so angry at him. Maybe I should have waited until we had dinner. The minute he came home I started interrogating him. This wasn't wise, so it was no surprise that he kicked off.

Dexter had seen that stripper for a reason, but he refused to say anything. Maybe he was taking drugs again and feeding me lies, thinking that sex could solve all our problems.

I stripped off, locked the door and had a long and relaxing bath. It was difficult to take my mind off the man that I had fallen for. I waited for him to tell me about the phone calls, the small box, the strip club, but he just stood there trying to pretend that everything was all right. The fridge in this apartment was empty, and I was starving. I left my purse in his apartment and I didn't want to go back there. We both had said enough. I never thought that this would happen to me again—for the fourth time? Deep down I think I knew that he wasn't cheating, but his lies had hurt me.

An hour later, while switching channels on the TV, I heard a loud knock and Dexter's voice behind the door.

"Sasha, I'm sorry, baby."

I was on my feet, marching towards the entrance. I unlocked the door ready to tell him to get lost.

"Go back to your own apartment. I don't want to see you," I said, realising that he was completely drunk. He took a step towards me, but he lost his balance and landed on the floor. He normally drank when he felt guilty or when he had a very stressful day. Maybe he did care after all. It didn't take him long to finish that champagne that he bought for both of us.

"Barbie, I love you so much. Please don't be upset," he mumbled, tangling his fingers through his hair. Dexter had changed his habits with whiskey and weed; now he drank in moderation. I had never seen him out of control over the last three years. This wasn't how I wanted to tell him about our baby.

"Come on, you can't stay here. We need to get you to bed," I said, keeping my serious tone, helping him back on his feet. Our argument was silly. I only wanted to know the truth.

"There isn't any other pussy, Sash. It's just you … my special—"

He didn't finish his thought before barging through the door and burping loudly. I helped him to get down on the sofa. My anger faded. Now it was just the disappointment and sadness of being lied to. Whatever was going on with him, it wasn't good.

"Dexter, I meant to tell you this before. I'm pregnant with your child," I said loudly, after about five minutes. When I glanced back at him, he was out, snoring next to me, mumbling words that didn't make much sense at all. I covered my lower belly with my palms, thinking about the life that was ahead of me. Maybe Dex wasn't ready to be a father. From what I remembered, Kirk was excited when I told him. I couldn't compare a scumbag like Kirk to Dex. They were very different and Dexter had changed for me.

I picked myself up and went to bed leaving him on the sofa. All of a sudden I felt exhausted, drained and wanted to push the last twenty-four hours out of my mind.

I was out within minutes and dreams took over. My baby was beautiful and it was a girl. Tears were streaming down my cheeks with joy and happiness. Dexter was with me and he couldn't wait to see this precious creature, to take her into his arms.

When I woke up there were arms around me, and I felt a little disorientated for a moment. Then everything came back: last night, our argument and storming away to the other apartment. Dexter had gotten drunk, because he felt guilty. This was easy to fix—he should have told me the truth. We could have avoided all these problems.

He was cuddled into me and he was fully erect. I felt his cock pressed over my ass.

"We aren't okay, so you might as well get up and leave me alone," I said, aware that he wasn't asleep anymore.

"I'm sorry, baby. I don't want us to fight and I have a killer hangover," he growled, kissing my neck. Why did I have to turn into a pile of mush when he was all nice and back to the usual Dexter? "This afternoon I'll explain everything, promise. I'll pick you up from work, all right?"

I turned around abruptly staring at his handsome face, still pretty pissed off. I couldn't tell him that I played a stalker and followed him to the strip club. That was a low blow. He obviously didn't remember my confession about the baby, and now it was time to tell him.

Come on, Sasha, do it.

"What for? You won't tell me the truth," I whispered back, fighting with myself about what was right and wrong.

"I will. Just trust me, please. Maybe this doesn't make sense now, but it will."

He kissed me again and then jumped out of bed, disappearing into the bathroom. I couldn't talk about the baby right now. I had to know what he was up to first. Ten minutes later, he nagged and nagged until I agreed to whatever he was planning to do. My gut feeling told me that there was never going to be a right time for this kind of talk.

Dexter

My head was absolutely banging. Last night I behaved like a complete asshole. Sasha was smart. I didn't realise that she would listen in on my conversation. We argued and then she slammed the door, telling me to stay away. I was angry, so I drank our champagne and some beer that I found in the cupboard.

She thought that I was fucking another woman. Shit, I should have known that it would have been difficult to keep this kind of secret from her.

This morning I left with a hard on, thinking about her gorgeous body. I had to bide my time and wait until later. Getting drunk was one thing, but executing my carefully prepared plan after messing things up was another. Sasha needed to be shown that sometimes I had a heart too.

She was still upset when I left for work and it took a bit of convincing for her to agree to go out this afternoon. The most difficult task was ahead of me.

The situation at work was complicated. We had a few large projects going on and I had to be focused. Rob was coordinating the work while I tried to act like I wasn't nervous about later. Many people wanted to hire me. I had gained a reputation in the market, and with meds my life was better now.

The hours dragged, but everything was ready. Harry was also involved; he suggested bringing her friends and my brothers. I agreed, and now my nerves were slowly eating me away.

I called her up to check if she was willing to give me a special performance tonight, but she didn't pick up. Maybe Lorraine, the stripper, was right. Women were insecure and I was crossing the line with using another stripper. On the other hand, Sasha had always been very comfortable in her body. She was bloody stunning.

At two o'clock it started raining. This wasn't a good sign. Instead of waiting around and risking leaving her a voicemail, I told Rob that I had personal matter to take care of. I had to surprise her, not anger her even more. There was no point involving another dancer. How could I be so stupid to think that she would like that sort of thing?

I headed straight to the strip club and managed to rearrange the setting. Lorraine wasn't too happy when I revealed that she wasn't needed anymore. The engagement ring was back in my jacket pocket. Harry looked relieved when I mentioned that I'd changed my mind. He suggested calling my brothers and Sasha's friends. After everything was sorted in the strip club, I headed straight to the hospital. My shirt was sticking to my back, and I was twiddling my thumbs waiting outside.

I knew one thing, Sasha was still pissed off with me, and I had to make this right. When I showed up on the ward, the nurses were glad to assist me. Sasha looked amazing in her white uniform that sparked up my dick's attention instantly.

"What are you doing here?" she asked, folding her arms over her chest. "You were supposed to call first, not show up while I'm still working."

"I left you a load of messages, Barbie, and you know that I'm not a very patient person."

She rolled her eyes at me.

"I have been busy, Dex. I only had ten minutes for lunch and I haven't even looked at my phone."

"Okay, I get it, but we need to go, now."

She shook her head, looking at me like I had lost my mind.

"Dexter, this doesn't quite work like that. My shift doesn't finish for another hour."

"This is important for me, Sash. Let me talk to your boss. I'm sure that I can convince her to let you go early," I said.

She opened her mouth, probably to argue with me, but I kissed her. This always worked, the distraction.

"You're truly the most annoying person that I have ever known," she said after I pulled away, hiding a smile. "Stay here. I'll be back in a minute."

Her ass looked awesome in the uniform. I had to bloody calm down. This wasn't the place or the time to get hard. She made me wait a while and by the time she came back I was struggling to keep myself in line.

"Okay, Dexter, I'm free to go, but I want you to explain to me what is going on."

"Not now, Barbie," I said, grabbing her hand. She was relentless, so I had to come up with something fast.

"Dex, I'm—"

"Everything will be clear to you in about half an hour. Please, Barbie, just trust me," I leaned over and whispered in her ear.

She gave up until we got into the car. Then she told me off about drinking last night, asking, probably hoping, that I would tell her where we were going. I kept quiet, telling myself to keep calm.

When we parked outside the club, I could see anger beginning to form in her soft features, my pulse started speeding and my palms were damp with sweat. It amazed me what I had to do in order to get laid again.

Jesus.

"Strip club? You can't be serious," she said, drilling me down with her green eyes.

"It's been so long since I've seen you performing. I thought that you could dance for me today," I said, grabbing her hands and leaning over, inhaling her alluring perfume. For a split second, I thought that she was going to hit me. Instead she pressed her lips in a hard line, glaring at me in frustration.

"So let me make this clear," she said, drowning a breath. "You want me to dance for you, after you got hammered and put yourself at risk?"

"Baby, I want to spice things up a little. I fucked up. Please just one dance. You haven't danced for me for so long," I pleaded, knowing that she was ready to break.

"And then you'll tell me what is going on with you?"

"Yes ... of course. I'm getting hard thinking about your stunning body."

"Fine, one dance, but don't get your hopes up. This won't solve all our problems," she scoffed, getting out of the car. My breaths were shallow and my heart was jackhammering in my chest, reminding me why we were really here. I couldn't wait to see how this whole afternoon would pan out.

"Welcome, Mr. Tyndall, everything is ready for you," said Larry, greeting us with a smile at the entrance. The club wasn't busy, so the timing was perfect. We walked through two sets of doors until we were in a private part of the club. The central part of the club had its own large stage and a large bar at the back. We didn't stop there but carried on walking further down the long dark corridor.

Larry opened the black door and vanished, silently wishing me good luck. I didn't need it. I was confident but nervous as fuck. Four walls were painted in red and there was a comfortable black leather sofa in the centre. I smelled vanilla in the air. The place had just been cleaned up. The decor was elegant and minimalistic. I was already imaging Sasha sitting on my face.

Shit. Stop it, Tyndall.

I had to pull myself together. This wasn't the reason that I brought her here tonight.

"Come on, baby, show me your best moves," I whispered, kissing her along her jaw line.

"Dex, I'm in my uniform."

"That's even better. You have no idea how long I have been meaning to ask you to wear it during sex," I said, sitting down comfortably on the sofa. She hesitated, looking around with open curiosity, but then our song began playing, and that was it. Her eyes shimmered with excitement. She recognised it.

It was the same song that Harry played during her first performance at the mixer party. "Sexy Can I" by Ray J and Yung Berg. I loved that tune.

Sasha dropped her bag on the floor and moved back.

"I can't believe that you remembered that song, Dex." She laughed, tossing her hair behind her. I shifted on the sofa, thinking that I was already losing control, and she hadn't even done anything yet.

Her eyes shifted, revealing burning desire and arousal. Blood rushed down to my groin as she began swaying her hips in the rhythm of the song, slowly at first.

I tensed up, swallowing hard. The air around me vibrated, thickening with crackling lust and the scent of vanilla. I had to concentrate and just be patient. She was such a turn-on moving around me. She licked her lips and began unhooking her uniform, slowly.

I didn't think that I could wait until the end. This woman controlled my desire, provoking me, drowning me of the last bits of control and resistance.

She brought her hands to her hair and bent down, keeping her eyes on me, biting her lip. I was melting down in my seat; my heart shuddered between my ribs. My cock was rock hard, ready, throbbing in my pants.

Sasha turned around, revealing an arm with a giggle, then bent down unexpectedly, showing me her magnificent ass.

That was the moment that I had been waiting for, the moment that I had craved. I reached out to my jacket pocket and went down on my knees, quickly opening the box that I retrieved earlier on from Lorraine.

The diamond was shining brightly, reminding me of the colour of her eyes. It suited her perfectly.

When she turned around, ready to drop her uniform, she stopped moving, finally noticing my position.

I was shitting myself, but this was it. There was no turning back now.

"God, Sash, you're so unbelievably sexy. I can't take it any longer. Will you fucking marry me?"

Forty-Three

Sasha

The ground had opened up and was slowly sucking me in, draining me of all my emotions. Time had stopped and the sudden realisation of what was happening hit me like a ton of bricks. Dexter was messing with me; he didn't really just ask me to marry him. The music stopped playing, and the lights came on as I stood in the middle of the room staring at him, bewildered. My heart pounded in my chest uncontrollably. He was on his knees showing me one of the most beautiful engagement rings that I had ever laid my eyes on.

Finally, everything clicked, the secret phone calls, the package and his trip to the strip club.

"Baby, say something. You're making me very nervous," he said.

My heart was beating so hard and fast that I couldn't catch my breath. The tension was palpable, vibrating through me, like an unexpected thunderstorm. I already had my answer, but the baby came first. I had to get over the fear and just tell him that there was a tiny life inside my womb. I swallowed back my tears, trying to shut off the explosion of emotions that I was experiencing. The anger and frustration that I had been feeling in the past few days finally faded.

"I already have my answer, Dex, but I need to tell you something first," I managed to choke out. Dexter frowned and inhaled sharply.

"Tell me what?"

I counted to five, slowing down my breathing. I needed to forget about the sudden panic and anxiety. His dark eyes were drilling through me. He wanted my answer, probably thinking that I was hesitating.

"I'm pregnant, Dexter. I've known for a week, but I was scared to tell you because I had no idea how you were going to react," I said, smiling through tears. "And yes, I'll marry you."

Dexter paled, widening his eyes and dropping back on the sofa, hiding his face in his palms. The silence was slowly killing me, dragging this moment on forever. I knew that the news would shock him, but his eyes were enormous, and I had no idea how he felt about it.

"A baby, Sash. Please tell me that you're not fucking with me?" he asked quietly, entwining his fingers into mine.

"No, I had forgotten my hormonal shot and I started feeling unwell after we came back from Spain. I've done the test and it came out positive. I'm pregnant, Dex. You're going to be a father," I explained. His breath was shallow and I had no idea what that meant. Was he happy? Angry with me that I kept this kind of secret for so long?

"Shit, Sasha, this is big. I can't believe it. I'm so happy, baby, so fucking happy," he said. "Come on, let's go outside to the bar. I need a drink."

I was so confused, but I picked up my bag and followed him out. When he opened the door to the bar, I heard gasps and snickers. Then I noticed familiar faces and my heart shuddered in my chest. Dexter's brothers, Gina, Harry and a few of my friends from the hospital stood by the bar, watching us with uncertainty.

"She said yes," Dexter shouted. "And I'm going to be a father. Sasha is pregnant!" Dexter lifted me up and pressed his lips down to mine. I heard screams and cheers. Everyone surrounded us, congratulating us and talking all at once. I was telling Dex to put me down, choking on my own tears.

He'd planned all this, and I couldn't comprehend how I didn't see it coming.

"You called them all?" I asked

"Harry suggested to bring them down here," he said, grinning. "I don't like sharing you, but I made an exception this time around."

"So you guys are now engaged and with a baby on the way? Wow, that's fantastic news, Dexter. Congratulations! You're a lucky bastard," Harry shouted, clapping Dexter on the back, beaming with happiness.

Dexter had me in his arms again, kissing me greedily and sensually. When he pulled away I was breathless and dizzy.

"There is a little human inside your stomach, Barbie. I can't believe that we made life. It feels surreal," he said, his voice vibrating. We were both emotional and I tried to stop crying, but tears kept pouring down my cheeks.

"Are you sure about this? Do you really want to get married?" I asked.

"Are you fucking kidding me? I want you to become my wife. The sooner the better, and all you guys are invited by the way," he said, when he finally let go of me.

"Bro, Mum will be ecstatic, but she will kill you when she finds out how you proposed." Jake laughed.

"Congratulations, guys. I'm pleased that you didn't freak out, Dex," Gina muttered, hiding a smile. Harry, who stood next to her, was staring at her with an interested smile and obvious curiosity. She pretended that she hadn't noticed.

"I need a few days to properly absorb it and come to terms with the idea of becoming a dad," Dexter said, smiling. "Drinks for everyone. The best champagne you have on offer, barman. It's time to fucking celebrate."

Everyone cheered when he kissed me for a really long time, grabbing my ass at the same time. I felt overwhelmed but truly happy. All the worries and anguish had gone away. Dexter handed me the ring and slid it on my finger. It fit perfectly.

I couldn't believe it—I was going to marry Dexter Tyndall. The biggest womaniser of all time. Life couldn't get any better.

Nine months later

Dexter

The screams of that small creature that came out of Sasha's womb echoed around the room. I was pacing back and forth, unable to gather my thoughts, panicking that something was wrong. This was happening so fast. Sasha was rushed to the ER after her water broke and I was freaking out. I couldn't breathe, forcing my contracted muscles to relax.

When she went into labour, I had no idea what to do. At first I was trying to keep her calm, then I was advising her how to breathe, but she was screaming her head off, telling me that I had no idea what I was talking about. I had gone outside to gather my thoughts for a minute, suddenly realising that everyone was already there. My mother, Jake, Connor, then Sasha's parents.

I panicked when they all started talking to me, telling me that everything would be all right, that this was the best moment of my life. I couldn't take the pressure, so I stayed with Barbie. She looked so exhausted but glad to see me again. I nearly passed out when the doctor said that it would take hours before anything would happen.

It didn't.

An hour later, the nurse handed me that small screaming bundle, after Sasha made sure that the baby had all ten fingers and toes.

As soon as this tiny creature was in my arms, it stopped crying and the time shifted into oblivion. I was slowly choking, unable to catch my breath, unable to stop looking at something so small, so precious, so perfectly beautiful.

"This is our baby, Dex, our little girl," Sasha whispered, touching her hand whilst the baby's fist clasped her finger.

I stared into my daughter's eyes, feeling like I was levitating. I couldn't compare these sudden striking waves of happiness to anything else in my life. My daughter had wide, large blue eyes and was looking straight through me, seeing the real me. In that moment, I knew that I had to keep being a good person, just for her, and staying healthy was a priority. She was so small, helpless, and I needed to keep my demons at bay, for this creature that my wife and I had brought into this world.

After a moment I looked at Sasha, who looked exhausted but radiant with joy.

"Thank you, Sasha. She's perfect and beautiful," I said, gazing at the love of my life. My Barbie.

"You're right, Dex. She is our pride and joy. I want to name her Rose. I know it's not the name that we discussed, but I think it fits. Josie can be her second name, you know, after Joey."

"Rose, yes, you're right. I like it. What do you think, Rose Josie Tyndall?"

Our daughter gurgled with approval and we both laughed, admiring the damn beautiful baby that we both made.

I imagined being able to stop time and cherish this moment forever and ever. I was in love and truly happy.

The end

Author's note

I would like to especially thank Lexy Dodd and Tash Starkey for their absolutely amazing beta reading skills and loving Dexter from the very first page.
You guys rock!

Book 2 is available to download now.
Scan the bar below to find out more!

CPSIA information can be obtained
at www.ICGtesting.com
Printed in the USA
BVHW030355080221
599613BV00011B/82

9 781393 352914